SECOND IN THE IMMORTALS OF INDRIELL SERIES

JUDGMENT

MELISSA A. CRAVEN

PRAISE FOR IMMORTALS OF INDRIELL

2016 RONE Award Winner – Best Book Cover
2016 YA Books Central Finalist for Best Indie
2015 Dante Rossetti YA Awards Finalist
2015 International Book Awards Finalist
2015 USA Best Book Awards Finalist

"I loved that Emerge wasn't the usual vampires, shape shifters and werewolves but an entirely new concept." Amazon reviewer ★★★★★

"Just when you think Allie's journey is coming to an end... Craven shows you just how wrong you were. You should NOT miss the end of this book." Amazon reviewer ★★★★★

"Craven has skillfully developed an Urban Fantasy set in a real life, believable context. I can almost believe this ancient race of Immortals actually lives among us." Hub Pages Reviewer ★★★★★

"Emerge is a story that begins as a single snowflake and ends in an avalanche. Craven has put together a story that unfolds again and again, revealing characters of unusual depth." Amazon Reviewer ★★★★★

"Craven has a talent for keeping her reader's attention as she reveals Allie's story, layer by interesting layer. And when you get to the last page, you're left wanting more!" Amazon Reviewer ★★★★★

"The immortal characters in "Emerge" all have a special gift, but so does the author. Craven's is a superpower that we can all benefit from: storytelling." Amazon Reviewer ★★★★★

JUDGMENT: Immortals of Indriell Book 2

By: Melissa A. Craven
Midnight Hour Studio INC
Atlanta, Georgia

For more information contact: **Hello@Melissaacraven.com** or visit the author's website at Melissaacraven.com

*Previously published as Emerge: The Judgment (Immortals of Indriell Book 2) © December 15, 2016

Cover design by: Zoe Shtorm and Daqri Combs

Edited by: Chase Night and Robin O

Interior design by: BooklyStyle

ASIN: eBook

ISBN: 9798675785414 Paperback

ISBN: Hardcover

First edition for print September 3, 2020

Printed in the United States of America

Also by Melissa A. Craven

Immortals of Indriell Series:

Emerge (Book 1)
Catalyst (An Immortals of Indriell Short Story)
Edge (Book 0)
Judgment (Book 2)
Scholar (Illustrated Character Journal)
Volunteer (An Immortals of Indriell Short Story)
Captive (Book 3)
Assignment: An Immortals of Indriell Novella
Heir (Book 4)
Betrayal (Book 5)
Runaway (Book 6)
Proving (Book 7)

Queens of the Fae Series

Fae's Deception (Book 1)
Fae's Defiance (Book 2)
Fae's Destruction (Book 3)

Crimes of the Fae Series

Fae's Prisoner (Book 1)
Fae's Power (Book 2)
Fae's Promise (Book 3)

A FREE OFFER

In Judgment, find out what happens when Allie finally shares her secrets with Aidan. And then download your FREE copy of SCHOLAR and discover everything there is to know about the Immortals of Indriell.

Visit **bit.ly/ScholarOffer** to download now

For Jenny
Some friendships are fleeting
Others last a lifetime
Happy Friend-iversary!

(Also, Get out of my brain!)

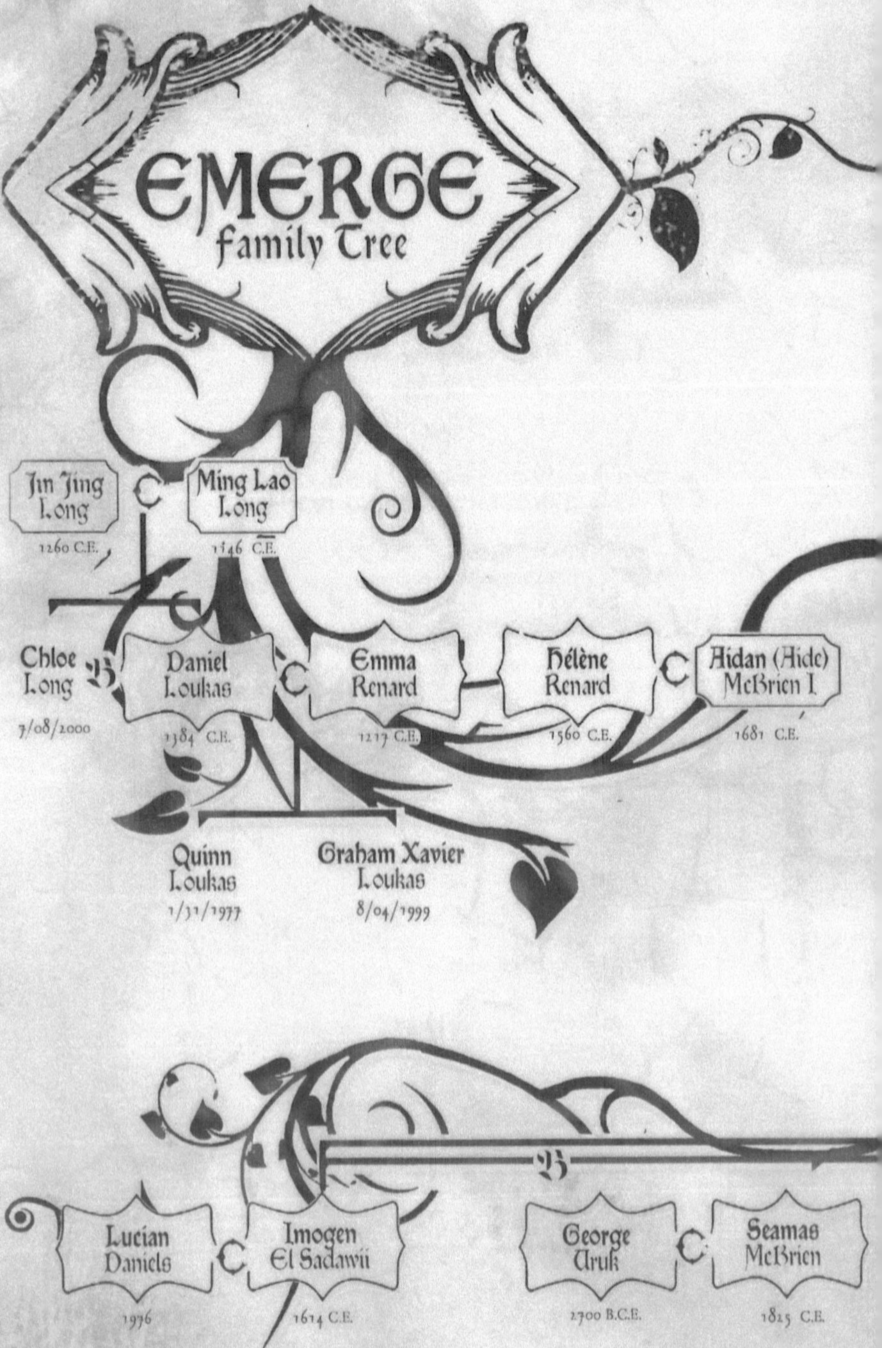

EMERGE
Family Tree
Jin Jing Long
1260 C.E.
C
Ming Lao Long
1146 C.E.
Chloe Long
7/08/2000
B
Daniel Loukas
1384 C.E.
C
Emma Renard
1217 C.E.
Hélène Renard
1560 C.E.
C
Aidan (Aide) McBrien I.
1681 C.E.
Quinn Loukas
1/31/1977
Graham Xavier Loukas
8/04/1999
B
Lucian Daniels
1976
C
Imogen El Sadawii
1614 C.E.
George Uruk
2700 B.C.E.
C
Seamas McBrien
1825 C.E.

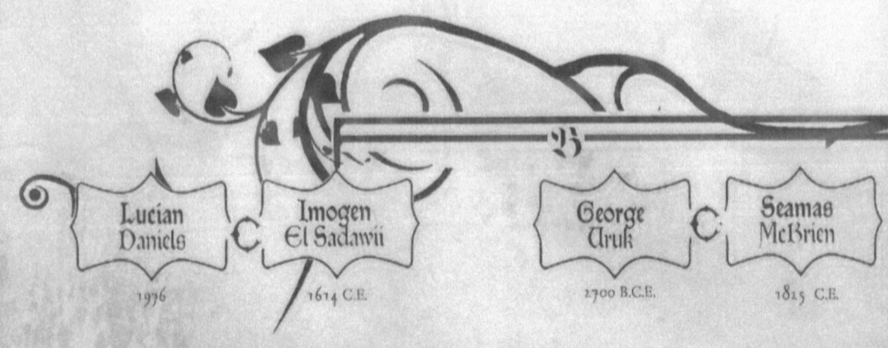

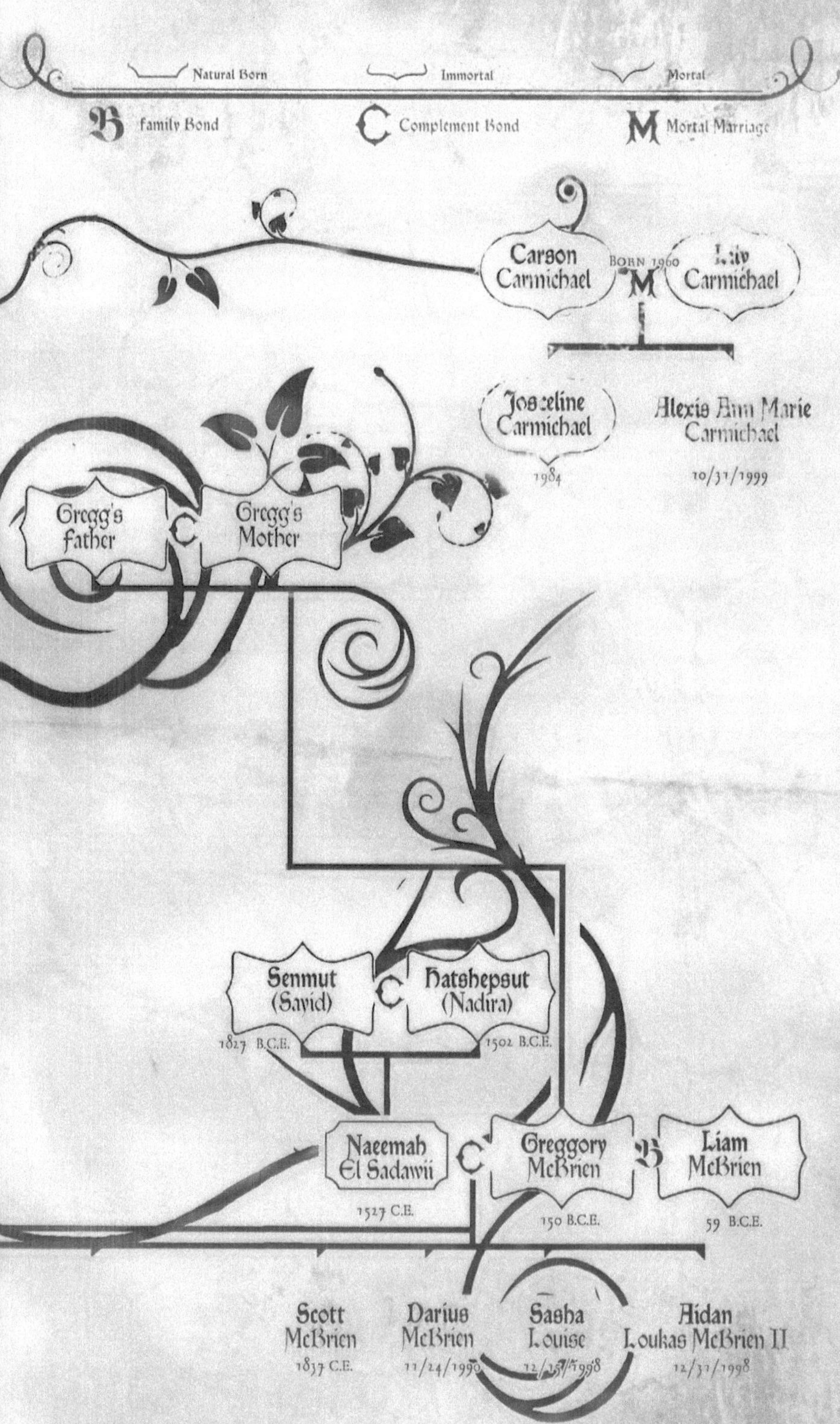

Natural Born
Immortal
Mortal
B family Bond
C Complement Bond
M Mortal Marriage
Carson Carmichael
Born 1960
M
Liv Carmichael
Josceline Carmichael
1984
Alexis Ann Marie Carmichael
10/31/1999
Gregg's Father
C
Gregg's Mother
Senmut (Sayid)
1827 B.C.E.
C
Hatshepsut (Nadira)
1502 B.C.E.
Naeemah El Sadawii
1527 C.E.
C
Greggory McBrien
150 B.C.E.
B
Liam McBrien
59 B.C.E.
Scott McBrien
1837 C.E.
Darius McBrien
11/24/1990
Sasha Louise
Aidan Loukas McBrien II
12/31/1998

Plato, Symposium

"—If there were only some way of contriving that a state or an army should be made up of lovers and their beloved, they would be the very best governors of their own city, abstaining from all dishonor, and emulating one another in honor; and when fighting at each other's side, although a mere handful, they would overcome the world. For what lover would not choose rather to be seen by all mankind than by his beloved, either when abandoning his post or throwing away his arms? He would be ready to die a thousand deaths rather than endure this. Or who would desert his beloved or fail him in the hour of danger. The veriest coward would become an inspired hero, equal to the bravest, at such a time; Love would inspire him."

—Plato, Symposium

Chapter 1

The Prophecy's about you, Red....

Those words had haunted Allie all summer. For four long months, they'd echoed through her mind, setting her heart racing and her blood boiling. Everything she thought she knew about herself was a lie ... again.

"You two do know there's a cozy little inside shelter on this tugboat?" Aidan called across the ferryboat deck.

Allie watched the choppy waves of Lake Erie bobbing up and down along the horizon. She hadn't noticed the thunder or the rain. Neither had Sasha. Allie glanced at her friend on the bench beside her, lost in her own thoughts. They hadn't seen much of each other in the last few months. Sasha had a rough summer working for the Senate and refused to talk about it since her return.

Neither girl felt quite like themselves after the horrible events the night of the Springtime Ball. Allie had to live with the gravity of her mistakes—her hesitations that led to Quinn's capture by the Coalition and so many months on the move. She'd almost cost her and her friends the home they loved. And Sasha ... just wasn't Sasha without Quinn.

"Come on, you two." Aidan stood over them, his blue-black hair growing darker in the rain. "You're looking a little crazy out here in this drizzle. Let's get inside where it's dry. We're almost home." He grabbed Allie's hand, urging her to release her clenched fist. "Stop doing that."

Allie relaxed her hands and winced at the sight of blood on her palms. The tiny crescent-moon cuts were already healing and the rain washed away the blood. She stood, smoothing her palms over her jeans.

"Sasha? You coming?" Aidan asked.

"Leave her alone." Allie turned and left them to their thoughts.

She caught a glimpse of Kelleys Island looming on the horizon and her spirits lifted. After so much time abroad, hiding out in Agra first and then later among the remote Portuguese islands of the Azores, she was eager to get home, now that Gregg finally deemed it safe enough to return.

Home. A strange concept for Allie. After a lifetime of moving from one place to the next with her mortal family, Kelleys Island was part of her now, and she was happy to be back. And she felt guilty for being happy when it looked as though Quinn might never come home.

"Don't feel bad because you're happy to be back, Lex," Aidan said, sitting beside her inside the covered shelter.

"I have to work on my facial expressions if I'm that easy to read." She still had him blocked. It took a monumental effort to achieve it, but there were things she just wasn't ready to share with Aidan. When you had a telepathic connection with your best friend, privacy and secrets were a luxury.

"I don't like the way you've shut me out. But I can still get a sense of what's going through your mind, even if I don't know exactly what you're thinking."

"I was beginning to think we'd never see this place again," Allie said. She couldn't wait to get to her tower bedroom for some much-needed peace and quiet. She'd spent the summer surrounded by people nearly every minute of every day. And now she was returning to an empty house, while her parents lingered for a few more days in Bali with her older sister, Joss, and her new fiancé.

"Beach date tonight? Or sleep?" She was looking forward to relaxing in her own bed for a change, but the dreams—she could do without the dreams.

"Sleep. Definitely sleep." Aidan rubbed his bleary eyes.

Allie nodded. He'd spent the last few days in the Azores soaking up as much *fun* with Naomi as he possibly could and it had left Allie just as exhausted.

"Yours or mine?" She knew she couldn't last another night without sleeping and when she gave in, the dreams would come. She needed Aidan to keep her sleep restful. When they were together, the dreams no longer tormented them. It was like putting a Band-Aid on an open wound, but it was the only thing that worked.

"Meet me in the underground later. We'll spend the night in my studio," Aidan said.

"I'm allowed to enter your most sacred domain?" She arched her brow in surprise. Aidan shared just about everything with her, but his music studio and his private room in the underground were off-limits.

"We share a brain and a bed, so why not?"

"I'll meet you there around one." She was anxious to see Vince. Her mortal boyfriend had spent several weeks with her in the Azores and it was just the distraction she needed. Like always, it was easy being with him in their no-pressure relationship. But just before Chloe's Awakening, Naeemah sent him home. After a hot and heavy summer together, Allie hadn't seen her boyfriend in nearly a month.

After Vince leaves?

"Stop doing that!"

I can't help it. I hear what I hear. Remember, I'm not the one trying to block you. What the hell happened in that room, Allie?

Allie threw up her strongest mental walls against Aidan, visualizing everything she didn't want him to know sealed up in a big box with chains around it and a sign that said, "Don't open till Christmas—especially if your name is Aidan."

"I hate that damned box, Allie. It's like I'm haunted by some perversion of my very own Pandora's box. It's always there, but we never talk about it."

"Then do us both a favor and ignore it." She would tell him when she was ready, but for now, she couldn't face it. Not until she got some answers. But Aidan's father had disappeared months ago, right after his startling revelations about her biological parents. When she saw him next.... Greggory McBrien had never *seen* anger in all of his two-thousand-plus years, but he was about to. He had to come home eventually.

"Lex, you're so angry. All the time. You try to stuff it all in that box, but you can't hide it from me. Not for long, anyway. That box is going to explode, and when it does, it's going to be messy. But I'm here whenever you're ready to crack that baby open."

"Aidan, please. Change the subject." She was dangerously close to losing her temper and that made it even more difficult to control the power swarming inside her.

"Come find me in the underground when Vince leaves. We both need a good sleep tonight."

Allie nodded as she leaned back against the bench. The cool lake breeze smelled like home. She absently smoothed her hair over her right shoulder to hide the scar that ran along her jawline to her throat and down her shoulder. The scar was a side effect of her gunshot wound—a memento of the night she escaped her captors. Immortals didn't react well to the magnetic poisoning from Coalition bullets, but the scar was a massive improvement from just a few months ago. It faded as her wound slowly healed, but the thin rope of tissue still throbbed and ached. It was just one more thing she'd struggled with over the last months.

"Don't let it define you, Lex," Aidan said softly. "It's just a scar."

"I know."

"Mortals can't see it and to us, these scars are a badge of honor," he reminded her.

She'd spent the summer learning to influence the way the mortal world saw her—an ability most Immortals her age didn't need to learn yet. But it was important that she blend in, only allowing them to see what she wanted them to see. Even so, it didn't matter who could see the scars and who couldn't. She knew they were there.

Chapter 2

The Prophecy's about you, Red. Gregg's earth-shattering declaration echoed through Allie's mind like a song stuck on repeat. She couldn't escape it.

She leaped from the Adirondack chair to pace the length of her rooftop deck, as if she could somehow outrun her thoughts. Frustrated, she leaned against the parapet overlooking the lake, but she didn't see the last rays of the beautiful sunset. Her thoughts were in turmoil, crashing from one thing to another. Her biological parents and that stupid prophecy.

She'd always known her father, Ashar, as Navid. He'd been part of her life since before she could remember, but only as a family friend. He was a telepath, like her, but she couldn't seem to reach him now. The last she'd heard from him was a warning to keep his existence a secret since their world believed he and her mother were dead.

"What am I supposed to do with that?" She shouted into the wind, her voice dying on the breeze. How was she supposed to deal with such a revelation? Gregg and Navid had completely abandoned her after that horrible night and she had no one to confide in. She knew she could trust Aidan with the knowledge, but she was afraid he would look at her differently when he knew who she really was. How would he react when he knew she was technically ... royalty?

Allie turned and fled down the steps to the beach just below her tower. This was the point when she usually threw herself into some sort of distraction to avoid that ridiculous word. It didn't mean anything anymore. Maybe ten thousand years ago when her ancestors ruled Indriell she would have been seen as royal, but not now. Surely people wouldn't think of her as First Princess of Indriell millennia after the kingdom collapsed?

She waded into the shallow waters of Lake Erie and let the waves lap at her knees. The water was always cool here, even in summer. The air still smelled odd to her with the absence of the salty ocean breeze she missed, but this place was home now and she loved it.

She heard the footsteps echoing behind her and her anger flashed hot and sudden as memories of that night came back to haunt her. Strong arms captured her from behind and she reacted instantly with an elbow to her assailant's ribs.

"Jeez, Allie! What was that?" Vince groaned as he backed away.

She whirled around, stumbling out of the shallow water to his side. "Crap—Vin, are you okay?" Her words came out in a tumble. She could have broken bones if she'd given it all she had.

"I'm good." He laughed, rubbing his tender ribs. "I should know better than to sneak up on someone who was recently mugged and completely traumatized by it. Not my smartest move."

Allie winced at the reminder that his memories of that night were gone and replaced with false ones that simplified everything to a run-of-the-mill mugging.

"How about this move?" He smiled as he took her in his arms. "Hey, you."

"Hi." She gave him a shy smile, enjoying the way his mere presence chased all thoughts of the prophecy far from her mind. She sensed his resistance to her touch, more than she had in a long time. The distance over the last month had sent them back to square one. He was aware of the strength of her power, like most mortals, but he never let it affect their relationship.

"I missed the crap out of you." He squeezed her tight, shrugging off the last of his hesitation in the way that made her fall for him nearly a year ago.

"Let's go swimming like we did in Ponta Delgada." Allie tugged him toward the water's edge.

He shrugged as he lifted his shirt over his head. Their clothes littered the beach and he grabbed her hand as they ran into the chilly lake together. They swam into the deeper waters, until the shore began to slope down into a rocky ledge and Allie could feel the tug of the strong current just beyond them.

"That's far enough." Vince pulled her back against his bare chest. "Don't want you to get swept away."

"I missed you." She turned in his arms. His smile and the ease of their relationship was like a balm to her tormented mind. And then her eyes drifted to the scar on his chest.

"How're you doing lately?" She frowned, remembering how close she had come to losing him. It was her fault he was shot and he didn't even know it. Having Allie for a girlfriend came with a price, and if he really understood what that price was, she didn't think he would be willing to pay it.

"Almost back to normal. I've hit physical therapy pretty hard since I got home, and I should be cleared for football by the time the season starts. You need to stop worrying, Allie. I'm fine. 'Gunshot wound to the chest' sounds way worse than it actually was. I was lucky the bullet didn't do much damage and I'm a super-fast healer." He splashed her and gave her a cocky grin as he swam circles around her.

They had Aidan to thank for his quick recovery. He'd worked his butt off to get Vince on the mend so his doctors would clear him for travel.

Vince brushed the damp curls from Allie's face and leaned in for a kiss, his lips warm against hers. She responded to his slow, confident kiss, pressing her body against him as his hands wandered over her curves in a familiar way.

"It seems like forever since we've been alone like this," he murmured, trailing kisses of fire down the column of her throat.

"It's been way too long." Her hands moved like they had a mind of their own, tracing the lines of his shoulders with her fingertips.

"Allie?" Vince eyed her as her hands slid lower. "Not here." His voice came out in a rasp.

"Then let's go to my room."

He hesitated, taking a deep breath. "Are you sure?"

"Positive." She pulled him close, the heat rising between them.

He was always so careful not to let it go too far, but she was ready and confident in her decision. He was the right guy. They loved each other and they'd waited nearly a year. Vince ticked all the right boxes.

He held her as they drifted with the gentle current back toward the shore. She was nervous, but excited ... everything she should feel, and Vince was definitely the right guy.

I totally won the boyfriend lottery. Her heart thudded in her chest as her power stirred hot within her core.

"I love you, Allie," he whispered against her ear, his voice a rasp of desire.

"I love you too." She gasped as he draped her legs around

his hips, heading closer to shore. His lips covered her mouth and she trembled at the feel of his body against hers, his hands sliding down her back.

She felt the warmth rising within her, unable to resist the urge to let her power flood her body. Her fingertips danced across the scar on his chest and a pang of regret shot through her for the pain she'd caused him.

"You are so beautiful," he whispered. "You sure about this, Allie? I want you to be certain." He laced his fingers through hers, brushing a kiss across her fingertips. "We can stop."

"I'm ready."

"No you aren't. Not here, anyway." He kissed down to her collarbone, his breath hot against her chilled skin. "Let's get out of this water."

"Vin." She gasped at the foreign sensation as his kisses trailed lower. Her hands slid through his damp hair. She arched into him, heat radiating from her core, her power surging in response to her desire. She moaned, her control slipping away from her for a brief moment.

The sandy lake bottom brushed against her back as they washed up on the beach. Vince pulled away and she ran her hands up his chest, eager to continue exploring such new territory with him, but she was trembling, fighting against the power that wanted to flame hot within her.

With a soft moan, Vince slumped over, clutching his chest.

"Vin?"

He wasn't breathing.

"No! Vince. Please, no!" She rolled him onto his back and dragged him out of the water onto the dry grass along the beach.

AIDAN!

Allie, what the hell? What's wrong?

She flooded him with the details in an instant, begging him

to come help. She stared down at Vince, unsure what to do. His lips were turning blue and she cursed herself for never learning CPR.

"Please, Vince. Just breathe." She scrambled to pull her shirt back on just before Aidan came charging up the beach from the grotto.

"Help him, please!" she sobbed. "He's not breathing."

"What happened?"

"I think it's his heart. One minute he was fine. We were swimming. And then he just collapsed."

Aidan placed his hands over Vince's chest, his jaw clenched in frustration, his eyes bright with hurt. She knew seeing them half-dressed like this was killing him.

"What did you do, Allie?" His voice low and filled with frustration.

"N-nothing."

"Did you lose control?"

"Maybe for a second. Please. Just help him," she whispered, hanging her head in shame. Not for what had passed between her and her boyfriend, but for the pain she caused Aidan. She knew what it felt like when the situation was reversed.

She watched as Aidan's eyes flashed golden, focusing his healing gift on Vince's still form. Aidan was young and some things were beyond his ability, but she knew he wouldn't let him die. Not like this. Not if he could help it.

"He'll be fine." Aidan finally let out a breath, swiping at the trickle of blood oozing from his nose.

Vince's chest lifted and fell, but he didn't open his eyes.

"He's breathing now, Lex. I just had to get his heart rhythm back to normal."

"I wasn't thinking. I-I didn't know. I-I wasn't prepared."

"Well, rein it in. Your eyes are blazing like green fire. Get it under control before you give the poor sap a heart attack."

"Aidan, how did this happen?"

"I don't know. At most, it should have just weakened him, but if you unleashed your full power on him ... that could have unpredictable consequences. You and I have to be more careful in these situations."

"I could have killed him."

"I'm sorry, it just never occurred to me to warn you." He ran his hands through his hair, the way he did when he was really frustrated. "I didn't actually think you'd have sex with him, Allie."

"We were just kissing."

"Should we take him to the hospital? He's not waking up." Allie chewed her lip, worrying there was something wrong with him that Aidan might not be strong enough to fix.

"He's just resting. Let's get him inside."

Allie grabbed the rest of their clothes and helped Aidan move Vince up the lawn and into the house. She fussed with the pillows, making sure he was comfortable on the couch, grateful her parents weren't home yet.

"Allie?" Vince groaned, his eyelids fluttering.

"I'm here, Vin. It's okay."

"What happened?" His eyes snapped open, glaring at Aidan. "Why's he here?"

"It's okay, you just passed out for a minute." Allie eased him back on the couch as the lie came to her far too easily. She was so sick of the lies.

Call Daniel, she whispered miserably.

Already texted him.

"I just keep hurting him." She paced anxiously across the living room.

"I'm fine, Allie," Vince said, but his color didn't look good. "Your eyes? What happened? We were swimming ... right?"

Allie's glance fell to the floor. Could he really see the power in her eyes?

"It'll be all right. He'll forget, Allie. Just let him ramble till Daniel gets here," Aidan said.

"I can't believe I let this happen." Allie brushed her hand across Vince's cheek. He flinched and she could see the accusation and fear in his eyes. He may not have understood what happened, but he could sense it was her fault. She had to end this. She wasn't mortal and it was time she stopped pretending with Vince. She loved him, but she was using him. *Time to face reality, Allie.* She gave herself a mental pep talk.

"What's going on here?" Daniel called from the kitchen garden.

"In here," Aidan said. "Allie lost control. Vince had a little episode with his heart and passed out. I revived him, but he needs to not remember any of this happened. And if you could do the same for me, that'd be great."

"His heart? That's, er ... extreme." Daniel avoided looking anywhere but at Allie in her half-dressed state.

"Make him forget?" Allie begged. "Please, Daniel, make him forget everything."

"Of course, sweetheart. It'll be okay. He won't remember any of this."

"No," she whispered. "Make him forget me."

Chapter 3

"You want me to what?" Daniel stared at her.

"Make him forget we were ever together," Allie said.

"Allie, wait! What are you saying?" Vince protested, confusion written all over his face.

"Shhh, Vin. It'll be over soon." She held his hand as she crouched beside him.

"Allie, you're upset. There's no need to do anything so rash as that. Go get dressed and I'll take care of this," Daniel said.

Allie turned and stumbled to the bathroom, grabbing her shorts and shoes as she went.

She slammed the powder room door behind her and collapsed on the vanity bench, resting her head on the cool concrete countertop. Daniel didn't get it. She'd never thought more clearly than she did right then. She'd known it all summer. The guilt she felt for Vince's injury was with her every day. She'd tried to compensate for that guilt by convincing herself that they were happy and she wasn't using him. But she was—and not in a bad way, because she knew she loved him, but she was using him as an escape and it was selfish of her to keep putting him at risk simply because she didn't want to face the reality of her life as an Immortal. She had to stop keeping one foot stubbornly rooted in the mortal world. It wasn't worth risking her boyfriend's life.

"Aidan, can you give us a minute? I'd like to speak to Daniel privately," she asked when she returned, fully clothed and her eyes dry. Vince lay sleeping where she'd left him. He looked so peaceful.

"Gladly." Aidan practically ran for the door. She could feel just how much this whole situation tormented him and it ripped her apart. She was constantly stuck between staying true to what she knew was right for her, and hurting the most important person in her life.

It didn't happen, Aidan. It never went that far. I-I think I was trying to talk myself into taking the next logical step with him. Like I could force this relationship to work just because I wanted it to.

His only response was a feeling of relief.

Am I still welcome in your sanctuary?

Always.

I'll meet you there soon.

"It is not safe for him to be with me anymore, Daniel." Allie squared her shoulders, firm in her resolve. "I've hurt him enough and the next time could be worse. I can't keep doing this."

"I won't do it, Allie. Especially not like this. Vince won't remember what happened tonight. I'll take him home and he'll sleep it off. He will remember your reunion up to a certain point and then he will remember going home. There's no harm done here. You can move on from this and be happy with the boy you love—but you must be more careful. You cannot lose control like that again. Not with anyone."

"There won't be a next time. I don't feel right about this anymore. It's done, we're done. Whether you help me make it easier for him or not." She sat on the edge of the armchair near the wall of glass overlooking the garden and stared at the late-blooming flowers. "After the summer we've had—it's been better than ever between us—he's never going to understand."

"I will not remove his memories of your entire relationship. That crosses a line I will not breach," Daniel said. "It wouldn't hurt him, but it wouldn't be fair to either of you to deny you both the experience of a difficult breakup, simply to spare his feelings. You must find a way to do this on your own."

"Can't you make him think we're just friends? That we broke up months ago for some stupid reason? Anything to make this easier? I just ... can't break his heart."

"I won't do that either, sweetheart. My gift is a tool, meant to help preserve the secrecy of our world. It is not to be used to ease a wounded heart. We just got back. Let things settle down first. And think about it long and hard before you make any decisions."

"I don't need to think about it. I should have done this months ago."

"Then take some time to find a way to end your relationship amicably. This is a good experience for you, Allie. Next time you will carefully consider what it means to date a mortal. It's not something you should feel you cannot do, but it never seems to end well for us or the mortals we love. We will discuss this further during our training session next week. Until then, don't make any rash decisions."

Allie nodded, but she knew she wouldn't change her mind. She was done with Vince. She would not interfere in his life any longer.

Allie slipped out of the house and across the garden to the small shed. She fumbled with the hidden latch in the floorboards that concealed the much more sophisticated entrance to the tunnels below. Punching in her code on the digital pad, she climbed down the long ladder, closing the entrance behind her. She hated this part. She could see in the darkness, but Allie didn't like the confines of the deep shaft that allowed her access to the natural caves and tunnels that sprawled out like a maze below the island.

The underground was like home to her now. As she ran along the tunnel leading to the common room, Allie wished she could run fast enough to escape what she'd done.

I almost killed him. She opened her thoughts to Aidan. This time it wouldn't have been an errant bullet to the chest—it would have been by her own hand.

It's not your fault, Lex.

She pushed him away again, unable to bear the unerring confidence of his thoughts. The way he saw her never ceased to make her feel inadequate, but right now she wanted nothing more than to forget this whole night ever happened and just get back to her normal routine.

Allie tugged on the enormous carved door that led to the common room across the great stone hall where all the Kelley's Island tunnels converged. The fan-vaulted ceilings, once so impressive, barely registered with her now, even after all the months away. Allie made her way on autopilot through the tangle of hallways to Aidan's office.

"You have got to chill, babe," Aidan said in amusement. "You're making me tense."

"Sorry," she muttered.

"It was an accident. Put it behind you. Now, how about a drink? It's been a long night and I raided Dare's stash."

Allie smiled to herself, grateful that she could trust him to know she did not want to talk about what happened. "Cheers to that." She flopped into the armchair by the cold fireplace.

She watched as he crossed the span of his office to pour her a glass of wine and himself a tumbler of Scotch he'd pilfered from somewhere when his brother wasn't looking. He looked tired and his dark, shaggy hair was a mess. In that moment, she knew they both felt a thousand years old.

Her thoughts drifted back to Vince. They weren't right for each other. She'd done everything she could to convince herself they were. She just hadn't been ready to let him go ... until now.

So ten months, then, not one. Aidan's dry humor echoed in her mind and she couldn't help but laugh. He'd expected her to come to this realization months ago. He'd pushed in his impatience for her to accept this life and move on with him at her side. Of course it blew up in his face, culminating in the worst argument they'd ever had and weeks of not talking to each other. She hadn't been ready—still wasn't ready for what he was offering.

You will be, someday.

She could feel his hopes rising and the thought of dashing them again filled her with anxiety. He meant the world to her, and the last thing she ever wanted was to cause him pain, but it seemed that was all she ever did.

Aidan, I ... don't know if I'll ever be the girl you want me to be. She was doing marginally better as she approached her first full year after her Awakening, but she still wasn't there yet. And she knew she could never be the vision of sheer perfection Aidan saw when he looked at her.

I've been an impatient asshat. Call it a personal fault I'm working on.

Aidan, the way you see me....

I see you, Lex. I'm not seeing anything more than what you are.

You forget I've got a front-row seat in your mind. I can literally see how you look at me and what you feel for me. I don't know if I can ever measure up to that. It would be so easy to let this happen between us, but I ... don't want to wake up one day and not know who I am without you. I need to know who I am on my own, and that's not something I'm going to figure out in a few months or even a few years. I can't imagine that's something you could really know about yourself either.

"You have a fair point, Lex. But there is one fatal flaw in your logic." He stared down at her as he handed her a chilled glass of white wine, courtesy of his temperature gift.

"And what's that?"

"You think I'm incapable of entering into an easy, no-pressure relationship with you. You think it's all or nothing with me, which tells me that you're the one who can't handle the depth of your feelings for me." His eyes twinkled as his cocky smile tugged at the corners of his mouth. She knew he also had a fair point.

"I'm ending it with Vince, but that doesn't mean I will jump into another relationship anytime soon. You know I don't want to be that girl." She took a grateful sip of her wine, ignoring his last comment because she didn't have an answer either of them would like.

"I know, Allie." He crouched in front of her, grasping her free hand. "Whatever hope you feel coming from me, it's something I can't help feeling, knowing you're finally going to end it with him." He shifted closer, resting his hands on the arms of her chair until his face was just inches from hers. "But I love you and I'm not going to apologize for that. Especially when I know you're head over heels for me, but you're just too scared and stubborn to admit it to yourself."

He tipped his glass back and drained it in one gulp.

"Patience is not one of my strongest virtues, as you so often point out, but I'm learning. I won't pressure you, Lex. Not on this. Take all the time you need. We have more important things standing between us than your relationship with Vince. Until you're ready to talk about that—about what happened in that room before we left for Agra—your dating life is the least of our worries. Whatever my father told you shook you to your core and that's what has me worried."

"Aidan, I—"

"I know, you aren't ready to talk about it. And I know that when you are, you'll let me know. We're both exhausted, so let's just go to bed." He held his hand out for hers.

She stared at it for a moment, wondering how she could be the kind of girl who would literally go from choosing to take her relationship with Vince to the next level, to sharing a bed with Aidan in the span of a few hours.

"Stop it." His laughter caught her by surprise. "It's just sleep, Lex. Vince got much further tonight than I will anytime soon."

"I hate you." She drained her glass and took his hand.

"It's a thin line between love and hate, babe. Come check out my music room. It's my favorite place in the world."

Allie had often heard Aidan talk about his music room, but he'd never offered to show her and she'd never pushed. It was his domain and she was pretty sure it was the place where he did his best brooding.

"Wow, this is incredible." Allie stepped through the doorway and wandered over to the glossy, black piano resting in a place of honor at the center of the dark room. The walls were upholstered in a rich plum color, with sidelights illuminating the dim interior. The plush gray carpet absorbed even the slightest sound of her footsteps, and a glass booth at the front of the room housed all the sound equipment for recording. Three guitars were mounted on the wall and a red violin rested on a stand in the corner. The studio was a part-gift, part-bribe from Gregg last year—an incentive for the office and teaching duties

Aidan really didn't want. But music was Aidan's ally and this place was a temptation he couldn't resist.

"I'll play for you tomorrow." He turned toward the sliding double doors to his bedroom at the back of the studio.

Allie let her hands wander over the piano keys, hearing a distant echo of Navid's words: *Allie, you should learn to play an instrument while you're young. Music is a part of who you are. Don't listen to others making music. Make your own.* She saw a flash of a distant future where she and Aidan played here together. The visions came to her like that now. It started over the summer with brief bursts of insight that she usually didn't understand. What she saw was only a possibility right now, depending on the choices they each made. She was used to seeing things that might or might not happen, but this was the first time she saw something she really wanted. They seemed so peaceful and at ease, it made her want to learn to play.

"You have me blocked so hard I can't fathom what you're thinking," Aidan whispered behind her.

She let her fingers tap the keys, lost in the possibilities of that future.

"I can teach you," he said.

"We don't have time for that."

"Allie, we sleep three nights in ten when our friends still sleep twice that. We can find the time if you really want to learn to play."

"I'd love to, someday."

"You have an ear for music, Lex, and this is something I would love to share with you. But right now, Aidan needs sleep. Come to bed." He pulled her through the double doors behind him into a room that was wall-to-wall bed. The entry was a small foyer with a chest and mirror. Three wide steps led down to a mattress covered in a thin sheet to keep the dust away while he traveled for the summer.

Aidan lifted the sheet and she saw the mattress was covered in soft gray suede. Pillows and books lay scattered around, like he was just there only last night.

"Grab a T-shirt and get comfortable. I'll get us a blanket." He ducked back out to give her some privacy. She grabbed one of his longest T-shirts from the chest and settled back on the bed. *It's like a cloud.* She rested her head on a suede-covered pillow.

Amazing, right? Aidan returned, bare chested in his boxers, and flung a blanket over her. As he settled beside her, she accepted the comforting embrace he offered, eager for the peaceful oblivion they experienced when sleeping together. With the lights off, the ceiling began to glow like the night sky dotted here and there with stars.

It's beautiful.

But something about it bothered her.

"Wait."

"Crap. I forgot, Lex."

You've never let me in here, but you let her? She wanted to take the errant thought back immediately. She hated how ridiculous she sounded when she had no right to be jealous of the time Aidan spent with Naomi.

"She did this for me months ago."

Naomi had a gift for creating illusions. She could make a place feel like an oasis of comfort and peace. Allie recently discovered that was why she loved hanging out in the grotto so much—and had since decided that knowledge had ruined it for her.

"When was she here?" Allie could hear herself talking but couldn't seem to stop the stupid from flowing out of her mouth. If it was anyone other than Naomi, she wouldn't have said a word. The two girls had taken an immediate dislike to each other over the summer and neither had gone out of their way to be civil.

"After spring break last year but before the ball. She was only in town a few days."

"I know you like her. Forget I said anything. You know I didn't mean it."

"Hey." He looked down at her in the dim light of the twinkling stars and she could see the tiniest flicker of power in his eyes. "I brought her here because I couldn't bear to take her anywhere you and I have slept. Until tonight, this was an Allie-free zone. You know how I feel about you. If you want me, I'm yours. But I'm not going to sit around forever waiting for you to get over your fear of us. Naomi is a great friend and we have fun together. I won't apologize for that. But she will never have my heart."

"What about Kayla?" She hadn't heard him talk about his mortal girlfriend in months.

"Allie, we were never anything more than friends. People thought we were dating so we let them believe it. We both have a thing for someone else and we bonded over that shared misery. That's it. We're just friends."

"You broke up?"

"There was never anything to break up from."

"Aidan, I'm so sorry if I've made you feel like—like I'm using you or leading you on. Our friendship is everything to me and I would never intentionally hurt you."

"You're just scared, babe. I get that. I'm a lot to handle." The cocky arrogance crept into his voice and she knew she was forgiven. "I can see how overwhelming I could be." He stretched back with a big yawn and wrapped his arms around her. "I can talk a big game about not waiting around forever, but you know I'll be here when you've gotten over yourself. You'll be ready for us one day, Lex. I can wait. But the hormonal seventeen-year-old douchebag inside me is an impatient little bastard. He just wants someone to throttle some sense into you."

"Bring it on, douche-boy. You know I can wipe the floor with you."

"Only when I let you win." He gave her a sleepy grin.

"That's total BS."

"Yeah, it is." He laughed. "You've been a beast in training lately."

"Well, I'm not letting anything like that night happen again. Ever." She balled her fists at the memory of how much of a failure she'd been when it really mattered.

"Go to sleep, Lex." He reached for her hand, prying her fist open. "This is our last weekend of summer and I intend to enjoy it."

"Night, Aidan," she murmured into his chest.

She drifted off to a peaceful sleep, confident he would keep the dreams away for one more night. Eventually she would have to deal with the dreams on her own. She could feel them swirling inside of her, begging to get out.

The longer she put it off, the worse it was going to be.

Chapter 4

"Get ready for fake Aidan," Aidan said as Allie and their friends headed across the courtyard of Cliffton Academy.

"I hate that guy." Allie shuddered, fidgeting with her blue and gray uniform. She'd had to talk herself into putting it on. Only one more year of plaid and she'd never have to look at it again.

"It's my armor, Lex. It's my way of coping with all the crap I feel in a huge group of mortals. If I harden myself to it, it doesn't affect me as much."

Allie understood he needed to do whatever he could to brace himself from the onslaught of every emotional and physical pain around him. She just wished everyone could know the real Aidan.

"I don't think any of us are ready for this year. I know I'm not looking forward to it." Allie slowed as they reached the Greco-Roman admin hall to pick up their new schedules. "I know Quinn wouldn't be with us anyway, but I feel the weight of his absence today. I miss him." A fresh wave of guilt had her clenching her fists again. If she'd handled things differently, it was likely her friend would be heading off to college now instead of rotting in some Coalition prison somewhere.

"Allie, my brother would be the first one to tell you not to blame yourself," Graham said. "And he'd be the first one to tell you to get over it."

"We have to get him back, Graham. I just don't know how we can help."

"I'm working on something. There may be a way for us to actually *do* something."

"How?" Aidan asked. "Dad keeps running into dead ends and he refuses to tell me anything."

"And Emma just keeps telling me how important it is to get back to my regular routine," Allie added.

"I'm looking for the kind of leads the governor's people would never be able to find," Graham said. "With my tech gift, it's really the only thing I can do." He shrugged as he grabbed his schedule and headed off to the junior hall.

Allie watched him retreat with shoulders slumped and his head down. Graham had lost so much of himself. He was no longer the spirited, happy kid he'd always been.

"We can't get sucked back into high school life and just forget about Quinn. I refuse to let that happen," she said. If she could trade places with him, she'd do it in a second.

"Agreed, but we have medieval history first period. Let's go get seats so we aren't stuck in the front row all year."

Allie followed Aidan and Sasha into the senior hall, feeling the culture shock more than she'd expected. Returning to their normal routine among so many mortals, and after such a long absence, made her feel like a fish out of water.

The auditorium classroom teemed with students. Aidan and Sasha were with her, but when Vince joined them, Allie felt a surge of guilt. His smile and eager greeting tore at her heart, but the feel of his hand encircling hers was so familiar and comforting. If she was going to end this, she needed to do it soon. The temptation to let everything go back to the way it was before was too much of a risk.

As Allie pulled her hand from his, she sensed a familiar presence—more than just one.

"Liam?" she cried. She hadn't seen him in months. The sight of her newly bonded brother brought an instant smile to her face as she launched across the room.

"Little sis!" He beamed, catching her up in a bear hug. He whispered cautiously in her ear, "I'm Liam Carmichael, your older brother and your new teacher. Try to take the enthusiasm down a notch—but God, it is good to see you, little one."

"You're teaching? Why didn't Dad tell me?" She grinned, going along with the cover story. He really was her brother now, but he was also a McBrien and Aidan's uncle.

"I wanted to surprise you. But until school's out, I'm your teacher, so take a seat, Red. And try to behave yourself."

Allie turned to scan the crowded lecture hall for her friends when her eyes landed on Aidan's older brother, Darius. Her heart leapt at the sight of him leaning against a desk, talking to Sasha and Aidan. Dressed in Cliffton attire, he seemed different, younger—much younger. She saw a flicker of how he must appear to the other students. He blended with the crowd. When his boyish smile turned on her, he winked.

"Darius!" She rushed up the steps to hug him tightly.

"Ahh, it's good to see you, killer."

"What's your story?" she asked softly.

"I'm Sasha and Aidan's 'cousin', a fellow senior, and your new bodyguard. I'm in all your classes, even the college courses you and Sash are starting next month."

"So what's this all about? Why all the babysitting?" Allie asked.

"Too much has happened. Gregg won't rest easy anytime soon, so that means—"

"Round-the-clock babysitters," Aidan interjected.

"Can't be too cautious, little cos." Darius slapped his back.

When the bell rang, Allie sat between Vince and Aidan with Darius and Sasha right behind them. She didn't care if they were there just to babysit; seeing her favorite McBrien boys all together was a good surprise.

"Allie, I didn't know you had a brother." One of Aidan's perpetual shadows leaned over her shoulder. The Cliffton girls were always trying to get closer to Aidan through her, but none of them ever lingered long. To them, he was an intimidating enigma.

"Sure, she talks about him all the time," Vince said. "Your dad really didn't tell you he was coming?"

"No, but they like their little secrets." It was painful lying to Vince when clearly Daniel had been busy making him and everyone else think she had an older brother she never mentioned. It still seemed odd to her that she felt the strong pull to Liam, considering she didn't really know him despite the family bond they now shared.

Plenty of time for that. Especially now that he's babysitting.

It won't be that bad, will it?

If I know Dad, Liam and Darius are just the tip of the iceberg.

"Everyone take a seat." Liam called the class to attention. "I'm Mr. Carmichael and this is Advanced Medieval History. This year, we'll be learning all about life in the Dark Ages." He paced around the room, passing out enormous textbooks. "One of the most fascinating aspects of medieval history is the art and architecture of the period. For that reason, I've asked my assistant to spend a portion of our time devoted to Romanesque and Gothic art history. She'll be along shortly."

"Oh, crap." Aidan fidgeted in his seat beside her.

"What's wrong with you?" Allie asked.

"Someone's in trouble," Darius said in a singsong voice only they could hear.

"You're not helping." Aidan glared over his shoulder at his brother.

"Ah, here she is," Liam said. "Please welcome Ms. Naomi Hauser, everyone."

"What the—?" Allie choked, shooting a hateful glare at Aidan.

"Don't look at me like that, Lex, I didn't know she was coming."

"Ms. Carmichael? Is there a problem?" Naomi handed her another large textbook, her perfectly shaped brow arched in mock surprise.

"Er ... no, ma'am," Allie muttered, grateful Aidan was distracting Vince with football talk. "Just surprised to see you ... teaching," she added in a tone the mortals around her would never be able to hear.

"Well, we thought about having me come back as a student but Liam and I decided I would be more believable as a teacher." Her low whisper and the fleeting sneer she gave Allie escaped everyone's notice. It had Allie clenching her fists, nails digging into her tender palms.

"Well, you always do like to play the adult, don't you?" Allie shot back. Naomi was twenty-seven going on three thousand. She refused to admit that she was just another one of the Unproven kids.

"Be nice, Naomi," Darius said. "You too, killer."

"Aidan, it's good to see you again," Naomi said in a whisper. "I've missed you since I left the Azores last month. We'll have to ... reconnect while I'm in town keeping watch over your little friend."

"This is not happening." Aidan shrank back in his seat but he couldn't seem to keep the grin off his face.

"What are you grinning about?" Allie huffed as Naomi drifted away, passing out her art history books to the other students.

"You're not just jealous, your head is about to explode." Aidan laughed. "You have nothing to worry about, babe. I was with you last night when I could have been with her." *But she was the last thing on my mind,* he added silently. He gave Allie his most arrogant wink, thoroughly enjoying her reaction.

"Dude, worst thing you could possibly say." Darius smacked him on the back of the head. "Don't anger the redhead."

"That's not it at all," Allie insisted. "She has no business teaching. She should be a student like Darius."

"Think about that, Lex. Would you rather have her as a teacher in one class or as a student in every class? You know Mom was the one who decided this, no matter what Naomi says. Maybe Mom just didn't want you two to kill each other?"

"Or Mom didn't want Naomi anywhere near baby McBrien," Darius added.

"Shut up, Dare."

"Hi." Liam crouched down in the aisle beside them. "Is my lecture bothering you guys?"

"Sorry, Liam. Er ... Mr. Carmichael." Allie flushed.

"Let's all just remember that I can hear everything you say, even if your classmates can't. That's my baby sister you're talking to, Aidan. If I hear anything more about you 'being with her,' you'll be taking your next few meals through a straw. Keep it in your pants if you want to keep it."

"Liam!" Allie shrank back in her seat, mortified. In some ways, it was nice having a scary two-thousand-year-old

Immortal Viking for an overprotective big brother. In other ways, not so much.

Aidan was right: Liam, Darius, and Naomi were just the tip of the iceberg. Allie was happy to see the familiar faces—most of them. But she wondered how tedious it would be under this constant supervision. It seemed Naeemah was serious about security. She wasn't taking any chances that the Coalition wouldn't come back for them all.

Aidan's older sister, Imogen, was the new head of security, and his cousin Erin was her assistant. Allie saw them patrolling the grounds during her morning break. Aidan's older brother Seamas was the new assistant art teacher and she was eager to learn from the man who had learned from the Impressionists themselves. His Complement, George, was the new assistant coach of the girls' basketball team as well as the varsity football team. And Aidan's other older brother Scott was teaching a special American literature class. Aidan's uncle Aide was teaching Allie's social sciences class and his Complement, Hélène, was teaching Allie's trig class. The extra funding for all the new teachers and new subjects had been donated by a "private organization." Allie felt sufficiently guarded and wondered if the others realized she was under more scrutiny than anyone else.

Really? You think I didn't notice that? Why the hell is Mom so freaked about your safety? What happened in that room, Allie?

She knew it was driving Aidan nuts, but she just wasn't ready to deal with it yet.

I'm trying really hard not to push, but I'm worried. Why do you need to be guarded so closely? What don't I know?

I promise, you'll be the one I confide in when I'm ready. "I don't understand why Naeemah would have us all guarded so closely at school, but not at home or anywhere else we go?"

"You've only noticed the guards you know," Aidan said. "I saw several familiar faces on the ferry this morning. But I don't know them all. Mom has her minions everywhere and they're good at what they do. We'll never even notice them."

CHAPTER 5

"Crap! They're home already," Allie muttered, pulling into the driveway. She rushed in through the back door, eager to see her parents just returning from their side trip to Bali.

"Hi honey!" Lily called from the kitchen.

The scent of pot roast hit her the second she walked in the door, making her mouth water. She was starving and it would be hours before that delicious roast was ready.

"Sorry about the mess, Ma. I wasn't expecting you till later." Allie dumped her books on the kitchen counter and grabbed a towel to dry the dishes her mother insisted on washing by hand because she was a total weirdo and enjoyed it.

"We caught an earlier flight. And I wouldn't have expected a clean kitchen anyway. You're just like your dad. Carson used to throw the dirty dishes away when I was gone for more than a day or two. I'd always come home to a new set of dishes."

"You should have introduced him to paper plates."

"Nah, it was more fun that way."

"Missed you, Ma." Allie gave her adoptive mother a hug. The more she grew to understand her own Immortality, the more significant her parents' mortality became to her. She had such precious few years left with them. She'd understood that before. Her parents were in their fifties, although they didn't look a day over forty. Before her Awakening, Allie accepted death as a part of life. It was natural for a child to outlive her parents. But the thousands of years stretched out before her, without her family—that scared Allie more than anything. It was better now that she had Liam as a brother. The fear wasn't as palpable anymore. She intended to absorb as much time with her parents as she possibly could while she had the opportunity, but there was so much about her life she couldn't share with them.

"How was your first day back?" Lily asked, placing the last dish in the cabinet.

"Good." Allie heaved a sigh, searching for something she could tell her mother. She wanted so badly to tell her everything, ask her advice, and have a good cry on her shoulder, but that couldn't happen.

"We have a bunch of new teachers," she finally offered so they might have something to talk about.

"I know, I'm on the parent board this year. We've been so busy this summer I haven't had the chance to tell you we have a couple of ... guests for the school year." Lily was struggling to remain nonchalant—struggling and failing. "Oh, screw subtlety." She turned to face her daughter. "It's Liam and his daughter. He'll be renting the guesthouse. You have ... a special *bond* with him, don't you?"

Lily dropped all pretenses so quickly Allie wasn't sure how to react. She simply nodded.

"I'm happy you'll have family. You always wanted a big brother," she whispered. "When he approached us about needing a place to stay, we offered him the guesthouse. We thought it would be a good chance for you two to get to know each other. And we like the idea of having someone close—someone to keep you safe.

He and the baby will join us for dinner tonight. I'll get started on the salad while you eat a sandwich, and then you can help me set the table before you go over to Aidan's for homework."

"I love you, Ma." Allie hugged her mother again. Her parents knew more than they let on, but Lily knew enough to keep her mouth shut and pick her moments. Maybe one day they could talk more openly, but until then, Allie needed to choose her words carefully. "I know you aren't my birth mother, but I don't think she could have handpicked a better mom for me."

"Oh, Allie-girl." Her eyes were bright with tears. She leaned in closely to whisper, "Your mother was an incredible woman."

"She did handpick you," Allie whispered.

"You know—what she was?" Lily asked. "What she was capable of?"

"Yes." Allie exhaled softly. Kassandre was the most powerful clairvoyant who ever lived.

"Then I'm sure you can imagine how hard she worked to make sure you were well taken care of."

Of course Kassandre would have seen things about her daughter's future and made preparations for her safety. She would have searched the world to find parents capable of caring for her Immortal daughter. But what Allie didn't understand was *why* Kassandre and Navid had given her up and placed her among mortals. And she couldn't reach Navid to ask. Her birth father was alive. Allie knew him well, and if he was alive, then her mother had to be too. Immortal couples could only be killed together in a violent ritual. So where was she? Was she a captive somewhere?

"Mom?" Allie frowned, picking at a bag of potato chips. "I, I really miss Navid. I could sure use a good talk with him." Her voice came out in a strangled whisper—not the casual tone she intended. "D-do you have his number?"

"I'm so sorry, honey." She stepped closer, keeping her voice low. "It's not safe for him. He ... um ... he always seemed to think you'd have your own way of reaching out to him when you really needed him."

"I do. But let's just say he isn't answering."

"Be patient with him. He has certain limitations. Just remember, you are always his top priority."

Allie nodded, feeling somewhat better after her talk with her mother.

"Hey, little one!" Liam called when he came whistling through the garden doors with baby Kahlynn on his hip.

"Shall I take the baby for a bit?" Lily offered. "I'm happy to babysit while you two catch up."

"Thanks, Lily." Liam smiled, passing Kahlynn off for a short while.

Allie wrapped her arms around Liam's waist, burying her face in his shirt. She'd missed him so much.

"I missed you too, sister." He held her for a while, silently stroking her hair.

"You know they have phones now, right?" She finally frowned up at him. "Tiny ones that fit in your pocket."

"Where I've been, making a phone call hasn't really been an option. But I'll do better next time."

"There better not be a 'next time' for a while. I'd like the chance to get to know my brother."

"That's exactly why I'm here now. You should know, you are the *only* one who could ever get me to teach high school. It's been one day and I've been tempted to make a few of my students disappear already."

"You know you can get fired for that, right?"

"Eh, some of the parents might thank me. So how's my

class?" Liam took a seat beside her, reaching for a chip. Her automatic reaction was to smack his hand away.

"Well, it was kinda boring, to be honest."

"*Boring?*"

"Liam, you witnessed a good bit of that history. You think maybe you could sound like you haven't swallowed the textbook? Spice it up, make it interesting."

"The textbooks are mostly fiction. I had to memorize the damn thing so I could teach it right."

"I'm really glad to see you." She reached to squeeze his hand.

"I'm sorry about the Vince situation. You doing okay, sweetheart?"

"Ugh! Does *everyone* know?" Allie clapped her hands over her face.

"I of all people should have warned you that could happen during sex," Liam said.

"There was no 'during.' No sex was had."

"I do not want to know the details, little one."

"I have to break up with him. I just don't know how to do it."

"You don't have to break up with him if you don't want to. I understand why you feel like you should, but I'm going to work with you on your control."

"Let's make that a top priority. I can't lose it like that again."

"Stay out of your boyfriends' beds for a good long while and you'll be fine," he said dryly.

"I do not have multiple boyfriends."

"That's not what I saw in Agra." Liam scowled down at her.

"What you saw in Agra was not what you thought you saw." Allie's ears turned bright red and she wanted the floor to open up and swallow her. That night was the most embarrassing thing. *Ever.*

"You have far too many admirers."

"Poor Kahlynn." Allie shook her head. "You're going to ship my niece off to a nunnery, aren't you."

"I already have pamphlets." His toothy grin was only a little bit terrifying.

"I've got training. See you at dinner?" Allie darted to the pantry for a handful of cookies to tide her over.

"You might want to double-fist those cookies, little one. Naeemah has a new regimen planned for you and you aren't going to like it. I'm going on record now saying I had nothing to do with it."

Is she serious? Allie asked.

'Fraid so, Lex.

"A diet? You want to put me on a *diet* when I'm half-starved already?" Allie glared at Naeemah through her ankles as she grasped her feet.

"It's not that kind of diet, Allie. You'll have plenty to eat, as always," Naeemah said.

Is she crazy?

Certifiable. She's been starving me with this diet crap half my life. Run, Lex. Run while you can.

"Don't listen to whatever garbage my son is telling you. I've never starved him a day in his life."

Oh, she's such a liar!

Go on, momma's boy. I can handle this. I don't live with her. She can't monitor every bite.

Ha! Just wait—and I'm a McBrien; we're all momma's boys.

"It's not about limiting what you eat or reducing your

calorie intake. You'll actually eat more. But you'll be eating lean proteins: chicken, turkey, and fish only; healthy carbs and lots of vegetables, with healthy fats, like avocados or coconut oil."

"It's not that bad, Allie," Sasha said from her Sirsa Padasana pose, where her feet nearly touched her head. "It just takes a little self-discipline and you'll get used to it."

Don't listen to her either. Her diet isn't nearly as strict.

"You can still have some of your favorite foods in moderation."

But say goodbye to butter, babe.

Like hell.

"You'll have lots of fruit and kale smoothies for breakfast with whole grains," Naeemah said.

Don't let her fool you. 'Smoothie' sounds good, right? It's not. I'd rather munch on the front lawn.

How does she get you to stick to this? Allie couldn't imagine Aidan giving up cheesecake or steak or going anywhere near anything with kale in it.

She's a dark witch. She's gonna get you, Lex. Just wait.

"But why?" Allie stopped Naeemah and Sasha before they could continue rambling on about all the merits of a gluten-free, fully organic diet. "What is the point of taking away the only clearly awesome thing about being Immortal? I can eat whatever I want. Why take such a strict approach to food?"

"You are a powerful girl," Naeemah said. "Your seventeenth birthday is just around the corner and you're going to be experiencing a lot of progress, quickly. I don't want you struggling to maintain control at such a crucial time. A clean diet will give you the added strength and stamina you will need in the coming months. Honestly, until you are Proven, a clean diet really should be an essential part of your training."

"Please, Naeemah." Allie clasped her hands together as she

moved into the Buddhist Stupa pose, begging. "Please don't take chocolate cake from me."

"You can have small treats here and there. Trust me, I know Aidan sneaks whatever he can at the first opportunity he has."

Damn straight.

"I promise, Allie, you'll feel better," Sasha said. She was never one to watch what she ate, but over the summer, she'd changed her tune. "You'll feel so much stronger and more focused."

Unfortunately, they have a point. I do feel better when my diet is clean. Just don't EVER tell Mom I said that or we're screwed for the next century.

"Naeemah." Allie sighed. "I don't think we can be friends anymore."

"You'll get used to it." She chuckled.

"Can I have the rest of the week to stuff my face?"

Naeemah tried unsuccessfully to hide her smile. "Try to do so with restraint. We'll start on Monday."

I'm going to eat my way through a mile of pizza and then I'm gettin' nachos.

Only if you share.

"All right, I'll concede to your crazy diet for the next few months," she finally agreed.

You do know she's not going to let you have coffee, right?

"What?" Allie lunged to her feet with clenched fists.

"Ah, I see Aidan's dropped the no-coffee bomb." Naeemah laughed as she rolled up their yoga mats for the day.

"Not happening, Naeemah." Allie drew the line at messing with her coffee.

"We'll wean you off with a little decaf-caf-soy-milk blend until you're only on decaffeinated coffee."

"Decaf tastes like feet and I'm not drinking soy milk."

"Then I'm cutting you to one cup a day—black. And I mean one eight-ounce serving." Naeemah crossed her arms.

She means business, Allie.

"One extra-large iced coffee with whole milk," Allie countered.

"One small coffee with almond milk. Take your pick."

"Fine." *I'll just sneak it on the way to school.*

Well, don't be surprised when the barista serves you something you didn't order. Naeemah's a sneaky ninja like that.

Allie shuffled through the common room early Saturday morning. The place was eerily quiet without the usual hustle and bustle, but her training sessions with Daniel were always early.

"How's it going, Red?" he asked as she entered his bright sunlit office. He was much too cheerful for such an ungodly hour.

"Coffee. Cranky. No-talkie." Allie flopped onto the well-worn sofa across from his desk, grateful for once that their sessions were usually more academic than physical.

"I'm way ahead of you." He handed her a steaming chai latte.

She took a careful sip and decided it wasn't so bad. "Et tu, brute?" She set the non-coffee on the table beside her and scowled at him.

"Trust me, the diet will help you, Allie. I eat a pristine diet myself. It's a challenge for any of us, so you have my sympathy."

She had dreaded this training session with Daniel. After her first week back at school, life was settling down to business as usual, but she still hadn't dealt with her relationship with Vince. She was tempted to let things continue in limbo, but she knew that wasn't fair.

"We've been back for over a week," Daniel began. "You've had some time to think about it now. How have you decided to handle the Vince situation?"

"I don't know," she said. "Now that we're home, maybe things will calm down and it'll be okay."

"That's what I thought you might say. I want to show you my only experience with loving a mortal. I'll be brief. I can't manage much more than a memory or two, but it's something you need to see."

She'd never visited Daniel's memories before. He'd shared stories of his past with her, but after nearly three centuries in a Coalition prison, cut off from his power, Daniel was practically an invalid.

"You know much of my past and the years before my imprisonment that I spent as an explorer," Daniel began.

Allie felt the familiar tug pulling her into his memories. She closed her eyes and gave in to it, not wanting to make this more difficult for him than it already was.

"I was a young fool out for adventure when the age of exploration was just beginning. It was an exciting time and I was so eager to set out on my own." Daniel's voice echoed around her as Allie fell into his memory. The world was a swirling mass of colors, land over sky that made Allie so nauseous, she thought she would vomit.

"Sorry about that. I have very little finesse when it comes to sharing memories," Daniel said, looking a little green himself.

She was startled to see him standing beside her, but she didn't say anything. Daniel's abilities were so limited, playing tour guide through his memories was probably the best he could manage.

Allie felt the sway of the rough wooden dock beneath her feet and when she gazed around, she found herself in the midst of a bustling Spanish port city.

"I came here about a year before I was taken," Daniel said.

"Where are we?" Allie asked.

"Palos de la Frontera, Spain," Daniel replied. "This way, I think." Daniel set off across the wharf and ducked into a sketchy-looking building on the corner.

The light inside was dim and Allie blinked. It was a bar, but a richly appointed one with sleek, dark wood polished to a shine. The place was empty, but she heard voices upstairs.

"I met here with the Spanish conquistadors," Daniel said as they slipped into a stifling hot room, filled with smoke and the stench of unwashed bodies.

Allie eyed the young Daniel at the center of the activity. He seemed so much stronger than the man who stood beside her now. She got a glimmer of what he might have been had he not been captured by the Coalition.

She listened as the men talked excitedly about the upcoming expedition, but she couldn't grasp much of what they said with her limited knowledge of Spanish. Her other teachers were always able to show their memories in English, but Daniel's limitations often held him back with the simplest of tasks.

"The expedition was an attempt to discover what lay beyond the Atlantic." Daniel pointed to the fourteenth-century map on the table before the group of men. "We would set sail as soon as the funding was approved, so I lingered here to await the launch of the *Niña*, the *Pinta*, and the *Santa Maria*," he said with a flourish.

"You helped discover the New World?" Allie gasped, but she knew that wasn't possible. He was taken captive before that expedition ever set sail.

The world churned again, but briefly this time. Allie stumbled like she'd just stepped off the Tilt-A-Whirl at an amusement park.

"Let's just watch here." Daniel took a step back into the shadows.

They were at a ball where the young Daniel danced with a lovely young mortal woman. Both clearly besotted with the other.

"Who is she?" Allie asked.

"She was Niña Pinzón. Her father was Captain Vicente of the *Niña*. He was visiting the Spanish court with Christopher Columbus, seeking royal permission and funding for the voyage. While they were away, Niña and I fell hopelessly in love. Of course, I sensed Emma from time to time, but Niña was far more real to me than some idea of a woman I'd meet in the distant future. We were young and in love and determined to marry as soon as her father returned. Only when Captain Vicente granted me an audience, I was in for the surprise of my life. Vicente was Coalition, and he would never allow his daughter to consort with an Immortal."

Allie watched the happy couple dance the night away, feeling a surge of fear for what their future held.

"He gave me a chance to leave and never come back," Daniel continued, "but I was stubborn and didn't fear him as I should, so I persuaded Niña to run away with me."

Allie felt the sway of the ship beneath her and her stomach roiled until she found her sea legs. With the wind in her hair and the images of the ball fading from her mind, she watched as Daniel's ship sailed at a fast clip, trying to outdistance the larger vessel quickly gaining on them.

The fight that ensued was a furious sea battle. Allie and Daniel watched in a world without sound as his crew was executed until only Niña and Daniel remained.

"He was more furious with Niña than with me. To him, I was nothing. A creature he would stomp under the heel of his boot. I did not know it at the time, but Niña knew what I was.

She had been taught to hate Immortals, but she loved me." He gestured at the scene before them.

Niña threw herself in front of Daniel, crouched in an attack stance with a sword clutched in her hand. She screamed at her father, but with a host of Coalition at his back, the lovers didn't stand a chance.

"I wasn't prepared for how my actions would affect Niña," Daniel said sadly. "I was taken prisoner but I assumed she would return home to her loving family. In our world, our children are precious and rare...."

Allie gasped as the Captain struck his daughter, turning her over to his men for punishment. Suddenly, Niña's screams echoed in the darkness of the void.

"I won't ask you to watch what happened next," Daniel said, back in the comfort of his office.

Allie felt dizzy and sick to think of what the Captain must have done to his own daughter.

"They tortured Niña as a traitor to their kind. I watched as they beat her—by her father's command—until she could no longer stand. Then they hung her for the simple crime of falling in love with the wrong man and then they threw her body to the sharks." Daniel's voice was flat and lifeless as if the memory still haunted him.

"They are pure evil." Allie shuddered at her own memories of the Coalition.

"I'm not suggesting that Vince's association with you could lead to such an end, but for some of us, when we love a mortal, it just never works out well for them."

"Thank you for sharing that with me," Allie said. Seeing Daniel's story was just the kick in the pants she needed to do this.

"You can get past this situation with Vince and he can be

safe with you, but you have to be sure your feelings for each other are strong enough to be worth the risk."

"Nothing's worth that," Allie insisted. "I never realized what being with me could do to him. I can't use him like that. I just need to get it behind us and hope we can still be friends."

"Believe it or not, Aidan has an idea that might work."

"Of course he does," Allie scoffed.

"That's why he asked me to help convince you. He's waiting for you in the yard."

"This ought to be good."

"He may have an ulterior motive here, but it's a good plan," Daniel said.

Allie made her way through the maze of hallways and stone corridors of the underground until she reached the huge cave opening that led into the yard. She and Aidan had been spending most of their sparring time here since they returned.

"So what's your brilliant plan for my big breakup?" She flopped onto the ground beside him. "It's so elaborate you needed Daniel's help?"

"No, I just needed Daniel to give me some credibility because something tells me you wouldn't believe me," Aidan said.

"So spill it."

"There's something about Vince you should know. Something that might make this breakup easier for both of you."

"Something you've neglected to tell me over the last year?" Allie felt her temper flare—an impulse she couldn't seem to control lately. She balled her fists and took a deep breath, stamping out the irrational anger.

"Exactly," Aidan said, nonplussed by the flickering in her eyes. "That's right, babe, you're not scary."

"Sorry. I'm listening."

"Dad has this gift with mortals. He can see their equivalent of the Complement bond. Your parents share a very strong Complement-like connection."

Allie nodded dumbly. It didn't surprise her to learn her parents were perfect for each other. She'd watched other married couples fall apart after years together, but her parents never had those troubles. They belonged together and she didn't need Gregg's gift to tell her that. But it was nice to hear the proof of it.

"So he sees Vince's match?" she asked, finally making the connection.

"It's Kayla."

"What?" But Aidan had always said Kayla was in love with someone else—with Vince.

"This whole time? She's just sat back and watched us together? And she's still been my friend?"

"She's an incredible person."

"Why didn't anyone tell me?"

"It's high school. I guess Dad didn't see any harm in letting you and Vince have your time together. Vince and Kayla will end up together eventually."

"But I've hurt him. I've put his life on the line. Twice! I've wasted the time they could have been together."

"They're young. They have plenty of time to be together—"

"No they don't! Can you people no longer comprehend what death means to them? How fleeting their lives are? What if Vince had died at the ball? What if he never got to be with Kayla? What if this last year was the only time they had and I took it from them?"

"None of that happened. And now you've come to the realization on your own that your relationship isn't good for him."

"I should have never been with him at all."

"As much as I hate to admit it, you two were good for each other. You've given Vince and Kayla some time apart—allowed them to experience other relationships, and that is a good thing."

"But now it's time to end it." Allie sighed, feeling a weight lift from her shoulders.

"And I have an idea how you can do it," Aidan said.

"Really?" The only plan she thought might work was to tell Vince she'd met someone else, and the only way he would believe that was if that someone else was Aidan.

We could run with that.

"How about you tell me your idea?" she said.

"About a year before you moved here, Kayla and Vince were headed toward a relationship, but the timing wasn't right. It was just after his mom died. He was a mess and Kayla was his closest friend."

"And then I came along and screwed it up?"

"No. Not for about nine months." Aidan let his words hang in the air between them and the revelation hit Allie like a ton of bricks.

"Oh, God! You're serious?" *They had a baby together?*

"No one knows. I don't think Vince even has a clue. She went away. Gave the baby up and then came home like it was nothing. I only know because my gift tells me she's given birth and it's torn her apart on the inside. I've tried to get her to talk about it, but she pretends like it never happened."

"So you want to drag it into the open?" Allie asked, horrified by the idea.

"He has a right to know. And if this comes out, it will give you a reason to end things with him amicably. You can tell him you feel like you have to bow out gracefully and give him and Kayla a chance to deal with their history and see if they have a future together. If we do it right, there's a small chance we could all remain friends."

"I don't want to do this, Aidan," she said miserably.

"You don't have to, Lex. It's just an idea."

"What other choice do I have?"

Allie couldn't focus on the computer screen in front of her. Her paper on *The Grapes of Wrath* was due soon and it definitely wasn't going to write itself. It was one of her favorite American classics, but her mind just wasn't on the struggles of the Joad family. She had her own struggles to worry about.

She absently rubbed her nose as her eyes glazed over and the computer screen went out of focus.

The overwhelming scent of ripe apples threatened to choke her. Her mind whirled with visions of forests and orchards, fire and smoke that burned her nose and made her eyes water. It was like taking a walk with Dante through his Inferno.

With a gasp, Allie grabbed the edge of her desk. Her vision cleared. She'd lost more than an hour to the visions and was left with a paper to write and the cloying scent of overripe apples clinging to everything.

Chapter 7

Allie sat, soaking up the sunshine on the grassy hill just above the beach by her house. She was waiting for Vince to arrive, hoping the strength she drew from the sun would bolster her for the coming evening.

An irrational rage swept through her, making her hands shake and her vision blur. In her mind, the late afternoon grew dim. Hot smoldering fires and churning black smoke threatened to suffocate her. Fury bloomed in her chest as blood boiled in her veins. She saw red. Everywhere. And then it was gone.

As the vision faded, Allie shook her head to clear her mind. Sweat beaded on her forehead and her hands lay fisted at her sides, her palms filled with blood. She cut her nails every night but they grew so fast, she was constantly hurting herself like this. She was used to the way these visions came over her now, but sometimes the intensity startled her.

She wiped her palms on the thick carpet of grass and watched the crescent-shaped cuts heal before her eyes. Her friends didn't heal quite as fast as she and Aidan did. It was still a novelty to see such a miracle with her own eyes.

"Hey, Allie," Vince called. "We studying out here tonight?"

She took a deep breath as she stood to greet him. "I don't

have much homework. Let's go for a walk while it's still light out."

"Let's just sit here for a minute." He settled down, lounging in the cool grass.

"What's up?" She knelt beside him, frowning. He looked so serious as he took her hand.

"You've been really distracted since you got back."

"I'm sorry, it's just—"

"It's okay ... I know this isn't really working anymore, Allie."

She stared at him, uncertain if she was really hearing him. *Is he breaking up with me? How did I not see this coming?*

"We had a perfect summer together traveling." He laced his fingers through hers. "It was incredible, but it was goodbye, and I think we both knew it."

"Did we?"

Allie squinted in the late afternoon sun. There was something weird about him—he looked almost ... green. *No, he is green. What the hell?* Allie gazed around her; the whole world had gone a funny color. Like the eerie light before a terrible storm. Her power churned hot inside her, a clear indication that something new was emerging. *Why now? I'm in the middle of getting dumped!*

"It's just ... I'm not the right guy for you," Vince continued, his tone forced and awkward.

Allie stood up to put some distance between them. She needed to focus on this conversation and she couldn't do that when Vince looked like Kermit the Frog.

"How about that walk now?" Vince asked.

She could feel his warmth behind her. Allie closed her eyes, dreading the thought of her life without this easygoing, wonderful guy who had done more than he could ever imagine to heal the hurt of so many lonely years. Aidan had done a lot for her in that regard too, but Vince was special. No matter how much her life changed, he was always there and he never made her feel like the pariah she once was.

"I so should have seen this coming." *I'm supposed to be clairvoyant.* She wrapped her arm around his waist as they walked along the beach. She'd planned to have the same conversation with him, but it caught her by surprise that he beat her to the punch. It was almost like he knew.

"I love you, Allie. That hasn't changed."

"Then where is this coming from?" *Shut up, Allie!* He'd given her the perfect out, and she was acting like this wasn't exactly what she wanted. *But why in the world is he green?* It was like her gift was telling her this was an important moment and she needed to pay attention.

"What's this?" He gestured at the two lounge chairs and remains of a driftwood fire.

"Oh, um ... Aidan and I hang out here sometimes."

"What have you been doing with me, Allie? I'm not the guy for you."

"Aidan is just a friend, you know that."

"He gets you. I can see the connection you two have."

"I know I've been distant, but I never wanted you to think it had anything to do with Aidan or my feelings for you. There's something you aren't telling me. I—"

"Screw it," he muttered. "Allie, I know we weren't mugged at the ball and I can still see that scar along your jaw every now and then."

"What?" she stumbled, not sure what to make of his confession.

"Sorry, that didn't sound so blunt in my mind. Let's sit down."

"I, I don't know what you mean." She sat on the edge of the lounge opposite him, completely at a loss for words.

"I think we both can agree I'm a terrible liar," Vince said.

"Yeah, but back to what you just said?" Allie was stunned. The moment he mentioned their supposed mugging after the ball last spring, the world flashed a vivid green and then the color faded to black and white, like an afterimage. She had to blink to get her bearings.

"I have holes in my memory," Vince said. "I know what that means, although I can't tell you how I know."

Allie instinctively reached for the knife tucked in her boot and stopped herself just in time. The only way he could possibly understand any of this was if he were Coalition. But she would have known. Surely Gregg would have known. They couldn't have missed something so vital right under their noses.

"What are you saying?" she demanded, resisting the urge to pull her knife.

"Let's just say my family has a long history." He placed his hand over hers. "A history my father broke away from before I was born. I was not raised ... the way he was. But I know things."

"What are you saying?"

"Listen to me, Allie." He held both of her hands in his. "If you hear nothing else, hear this. I did not know about you or your friends until recently. I was confused after the ball when my memories seemed so odd. But I dismissed it. Then it happened again the other night and the memories just don't feel natural. That's when I started putting it all together. I should have seen it long before now."

"Seen what exactly?" Allie managed in a whisper.

"I'm not the guy for you, Allie." He smiled. "But ... my kind has always been mesmerized by your kind. Some of us see a fascination and others see an abomination."

Her instincts told her to run. That she could never trust him again. She knew she needed Daniel to do some kind of super-deep memory wipe, but the part of her that grew up mortal, never knowing about this life, told her to trust him. Her gift was also clearly trying to tell her this was a critical moment in her life and she needed to pay attention.

"It's not exactly healthy for you to be saying any of this," she finally said.

"I know I'm probably breaking about five thousand years of sacred tradition and laws, but I know I can trust you to keep this to yourself."

"What do you remember? About the ball?"

"I remember what I'm supposed to. But I know it's not my memory. I feel something ... missing from that night. And I know I don't need or want to know what that was."

"You shouldn't be able to do that."

"Well, I'm not a hundred percent normal in that regard." He squeezed her hands.

"How?"

"That same ancient lineage that flows so strongly through you, still flows in me and those like me, but only the tiniest spark. We're just like everyone else, but we're more attuned to your kind. That's why ... my 'people,' so to speak, are so good at what they do."

"Stop." Allie shoved his hands away. "It's not safe for us to be having this conversation. It's not safe for you to be with me. That's why I've been so distant lately. We have to end this."

"I didn't grow up in that life, Allie. I'm not involved in it. I'd trust you with my life. I *am* trusting you with my life."

"So you can see this?" Allie touched her face.

"Only recently. It comes and goes, almost like a mirage. I know a very special kind of weapon did that. I'm so sorry that happened to you."

"I'm sorry this happened to you." She pressed her palm over his chest where he was shot. "This was my fault."

"I know you've only wanted to protect me."

Allie nodded. "I love you, Vince. You represent a life I thought I finally had, and I want to keep you so badly." Tears slipped down her face, but her voice stayed even. "But if you stay with me, you will get hurt and I can't do that to you. You're right; you're not the guy for me and I'm not the girl for you. If you'd died...."

"I didn't, Allie. Please don't blame yourself."

"Your life is precious and I won't risk it anymore. It's two times now. Did you know that? I've almost killed you twice."

"I know. And that wasn't your fault either, but that's when it all started coming together."

"Do you remember anything?"

"No, but I can guess. Did we...?"

"No, but we were headed there."

"It's probably best we didn't. I would never have let it go that far if I knew we were coming to an end."

"I'm going to miss you." Allie sniffed back her tears.

"Why? I'm not going anywhere." He smiled.

"Do you really think we can still be friends?"

"I hope so. I hope you know you can always count on me for anything. I will never ask questions, but I'll be there for you whenever you need me. Even if you just need to hang out with someone who makes you feel normal for a change."

"Thank you." Allie smiled. "I'll always be here for you. No matter what, no matter when."

"That means a lot." He stood to leave. "If you ever need to know anything about the world I come from, just say the word. I've got your back, and I'm not as helpless as I might seem. You cut me, I bleed, but I sure as hell fight back. I may not live that life, but there are a lot of people who would force me into it and I've had to learn to defend myself. I don't actually have an after-school job. I have training. Every damned day."

"Seriously?" Allie gaped at him.

"Seriously. But probably not as intense as yours. Take care of yourself, Allie." He pulled her up from the lounge where she sat and hugged her close, one last time.

"You too."

As he turned to go, Allie grabbed his hand to stop him. She saw him so clearly now. And his future. A new vision flashed in her mind, but this one made perfect sense. If he ended up with Kayla, he would live a long and happy life. If he resisted her, that path would lead him back to the Coalition, despite all his father's work to leave it behind.

"Don't keep running from her, Vince," she said in a voice she barely recognized.

"Who?"

"Kayla."

"She can do so much better than me."

"But she won't. Trust me. You're it for her. She's it for you. Don't let that scare you just because you're young."

"You should try listening to your own advice."

"Yeah, well, this isn't about me."

"I'm better on my own, Allie." He stared back at her in the growing darkness.

"That path will lead you to ruin. Your father fought hard to escape that life. Don't risk undoing it."

"I'm on a need-to-know basis, Allie. Don't tell me anything ... especially about the things you can do." Vince turned to leave again.

"She had a baby!" Allie blurted. She never intended to reveal Kayla's secret. It wasn't hers to tell. But she had to get through to him.

"What?" His shoulders went rigid, but he kept his back to her.

"She gave the baby up."

"Are you certain it's mine?"

"Positive."

"She doesn't know what that means...." He ran his hand through his hair. "You're sure?"

"The baby was conceived right around the time your mom died."

"I have to go."

"I'm sorry, Vince."

"Thank you for telling me." He reached for a last embrace, whispering softly in her ear. "You know ... there is precedence here, Allie." His voice wavered. "I'm not the first mortal to stand beside his Immortal friends. I'm here for you. I mean it."

Chapter 8

"Darius! Let's go already, we're going to be late!" Sasha called across the courtyard.

"Sorry, I got in trouble for sleeping in class again." He rushed to catch up with them. Darius was definitely enjoying his second round of high school, but the classes seemed to get in his way.

"Did you forget the whole 'you're here to protect us' part?" Sasha rolled her eyes. Darius was supposed to be their bodyguard when they left campus twice a week to attend classes at the Cleveland Institute of Art, but he tended to forget that minor detail.

"Come on, girls, we have to get you to class now. No time for goofing off," Naomi said, sounding like a soccer mom twice her age.

Allie's temper flared at the sound of her voice. The woman was obnoxious, the way she treated the girls like children and the boys like equals. And she seemed to get a special kick out of giving Allie a hard time. Naomi was acting as Aidan's bodyguard while he attended classes at the Cleveland Institute of Music. But Allie was pretty sure they spent the whole time flirting and very little time observing their surroundings.

With her eyes flashing like green fire and a death grip on

her steering wheel, Allie drove out of the student lot, waving at Imogen as they left the grounds. Her anger always simmered just below the surface and Naomi knew exactly how to push her buttons.

Today was their first official day of college. They'd all qualified to take a few courses during their senior year and Allie intended to take advantage of the opportunity to get a jump on her college education.

"Naomi, you sound like my mom." Darius elbowed her. "Give it a rest."

"Don't forget, we have a job to do," she said smugly. "The kids need us to be responsible adults."

"Say that when you haven't been sucking face with my little brother every chance you get."

"Darius, shut the hell up!" Aidan glowered at him in the rearview mirror. His ears turned red as he glanced over at Allie.

She gave him a grimace of a smile, an attempt to support his 'relationship' with Naomi.

"Sorry, bro. And forgive me, Naomi, for taking the opportunity to enjoy high school more than I did the first time. You should try it sometime."

Sasha shoved him playfully. "How in the world did you even manage to get this job?"

"No idea, but I'm not complaining." His dark blue eyes sparkled with mischief. "But maybe it has something to do with my uncanny ability to make my little sister smile?"

Sasha's grin was hard to miss; it was so rare these days. Darius was the only one who could pull her out of her funk. Sasha blamed herself for Quinn's capture, but ever since she came back from her summer job with the Senate, she hadn't been herself. Allie knew enough not to ask questions. Sasha would talk when Sasha was ready.

"Do you even have any artistic skills?" Allie asked, eyeing

Darius in the rearview mirror. He was posing as a student with them and she wondered how he intended to do the work.

"Not even a little bit, unless you count forgery as an art form. But Greyson has promised to look the other way and pretend I'm not there."

"Professor Greyson Hauser." Sasha sighed with a goofy smile.

"What's he like—besides gorgeous?" Allie giggled.

"Really? The long hair and accent does it for you, Red?" Darius rolled his eyes.

"What's not to like?"

"That is my father you girls are mooning over, Alexis." Naomi's voice dripped with venom.

"Oh, come on, Naomi, your dad is hot," Sasha said.

"He's had a hard life." Allie frowned, thinking of his past with Emma. Technically, she really hadn't met him yet, but she knew him from visiting Emma's memories, and they'd almost met in person last fall at the art museum.

"What do you know?" Sasha asked. "He had a thing with Emma, didn't he? Did she show you anything juicy?"

"It's not really my story to tell." Allie glanced back at Naomi.

"He was in deep with the Coalition for a long time, trying to earn his Complement's freedom. He never has," Naomi said sadly. "I guess she would have been my mother if we'd ever had the opportunity to bond. Dad's never stopped trying to find her. It consumes him."

"She's still a captive?" Allie frowned. "After all this time?"

"We've never been able to find out where she's been held."

"Poor guy," Darius said.

Greyson had a long time to come to terms with his wife's absence. But Allie watched Naomi in her rearview mirror. Her normally tough exterior grew even harder. Allie knew what it was like to have a mother she'd never met. But for Naomi, watching her father obsess over a woman she didn't even know probably accounted for her need to be the center of attention. *No wonder she's got issues.*

So maybe you could give her a break then? Aidan said. *Can you imagine what it's like to compete with a ghost for your father's love?*

They arrived early, as Greyson—Professor Hauser—had asked of them.

"Allie." Greyson beamed his beautiful smile at her when they entered the empty lecture hall. "I've been looking forward to officially meeting you. I've heard so much about you."

"It's nice finally meeting you too," Allie said breathlessly. He was so pretty it almost hurt her eyes.

"It's been a while since I've had the pleasure of teaching young Immortals." His accent was a fascinating blend of ancient and modern influences. She thought she could happily listen to him all day. No wonder he was such a popular teacher. Dressed in clay-dusted jeans and a faded Nirvana T-shirt under a well-worn corduroy jacket with the sleeves rolled up, Greyson looked more like a student than a tenured professor. He was about the same age as Gregg, but he appeared much younger, with only a slight touch of gray in the dirty-blond hair that hung down his back. He kept the hair at his temples swept back and braided with a leather thong—much as he had when she'd last seen him in Emma's memories from several hundred years ago.

"I called you here early to give you the courtesy of a warning." Grayson casually perched on the edge of his desk, giving them his undivided attention. "Sasha probably knows of my gift, but I wanted Allie to be equally aware. I think Emma must have hinted at it by now?"

Allie nodded.

"I can discern what your gifts are and how you can use them. For instance, that night at the museum when we almost met, I could sense your solar gift was emerging right at that moment. Since then, I see you've learned to use it as a weapon."

"Reluctantly so." She smiled shyly. "I'm not a fan of actually using it."

"I don't always show such transparency with Immortals I've just met, but I wanted you both to understand that I can see a great deal about each of you without much prying on my part. It's an instant recognition that I have little control over. I see what I see. So I probably already know more about each of you than you'd care for me to know. In fact, as young as you both are, I may know more about your power than you do. I've survived a very long time with such knowledge, so I can assure you, I know how to keep your secrets."

Allie felt a little surge of fear. She did not like the idea that Greyson might know more about her than he should.

"Rest easy, sweetheart. I'm a friend—not an enemy. Trust me, I would not want to get on your bad side."

Allie didn't have a chance to respond before the other students began arriving. It felt like Greyson was trying to tell her something, but she wasn't sure what it could be.

"Take your seats, ladies. Darius, just ... try to behave."

"Hey, I'm taking my bodyguard duties seriously."

"Let's hope so."

Allie was in her element once class began. Greyson sat on the edge of the desk, talking about the fantastic images on the screen behind him. He engaged the class, kept it interesting—fascinating, in her opinion. But at the same time, Allie was hyper-aware of Darius cramped in the seat beside her. There was something different about him. She didn't know if it was just the way she was seeing him as part of their group now, or if there was something more there—something that made her heart flip around in her chest just at the sight of him. Something she did *not* want in any way, shape or form.

As she sneaked a glance at him, he looked miserable.

"Bored?" She arched her brow. The classroom was huge and the seats were narrow, packed close together like movie theater seats. He was stuck between Allie and Sasha, looking like he'd rather be anywhere else.

"Out of my mind." He leaned back as far as the seat would allow.

"I can imagine your job would be much more interesting than an art history class." Although Allie was deeply engrossed in the lecture on prehistoric art, she knew it wasn't his thing at all.

"Well, my job is a little more exciting than this," he admitted. He was the youngest homicide detective for the Cleveland Police Department, recently promoted from narcotics. "But I couldn't pass up the opportunity to get to know you better."

"Real smooth, bro," Sasha quipped and Darius kicked her playfully.

Allie liked Darius more than she should, but he was nearly a decade older. Not a huge amount between Immortals—most would put Darius at the kids' table with the rest of them—but it was still too weird for her mortal brain to grasp.

"I hate to make you give up your work to follow me around. It's gotta be a huge inconvenience," she said.

"Don't worry, killer. I still have plenty of time for work after school. My teachers have been conditioned to *never* expect me to do actual homework. It's like a dream come true."

"So you work, you train, and now you're a full-time babysitter too. Busy guy. How do you have time for a life?"

"I don't, but that's nothing new. There's a serious lack of Immortal women my age ... so I'm stuck in a bad place. I'm either too old or too young. So I work, hang out with Scott, and train with George."

"Poor baby," Sasha interjected.

"Sasha, we are trying to focus on the lecture," Darius mocked. "I'm intrigued by this seriously hot Willendorfal statue thingy." He gestured at the figure on the screen.

"Venus of Willendorf," Allie corrected him.

"Why exactly is she holding her enormous breasts with her tiny hands? Is this supposed to be caveman porn?"

"She's a fertility statue. She represents the essence of motherhood—a phenomenon that was greatly revered nearly thirty thousand years ago when humans were still trying to propagate the species."

"Very good, Allie," Greyson said softly for their benefit. "But she dates back even further, possibly back to the heyday of the Queens of Indriell when fertility rates dropped just after the Great War. I've often wondered if an Immortal carved this statue. Its survival in this condition is borderline miraculous."

Allie flinched at the mention of her ancestors and quickly pushed thoughts of the prophecy to the back of her mind, stuffing it in that box with the rest of her problems she wasn't ready to face yet.

Allie wiped the sweat off her brow and adjusted her sai securely in her grip as she moved through the forms with Aidan at her side. She enjoyed their one-on-one training sessions in the yard. It was never about him teaching her or her teaching him. It was always about them working together as equals, pushing each other's boundaries and allowing the other to drop all the hesitations and walls they normally put up when sparring with others.

"You warmed up, Red? I'm in the mood to beat the snot out of something, and you're it." He gave a flourish of his blades and his most arrogant smirk. His favored weapon was a lot like her sai, but Gregg had modified the length to fit his enormous wingspan. He was a marvel with his dual blades. It didn't matter if he fought with them joined as a single weapon, like a quarterstaff, or if he separated them in mid-fight—those blades were an extension of his body, much as Allie's sai were for her.

"Bring it." She moved into the grassy clearing to take her stance opposite him. She twirled her sai over the back of her hand as she settled into a crouch and held her lead weapon up at the ready. Aidan was usually the one to strike first, but Allie was more comfortable fighting now and she was the first to make a move against him.

Gregg had done a great job choosing her weapon. She moved more naturally with the sai, like her resistance to fighting melted away when she held those blades. She wasn't sure it was the weapon so much as the fact that the sai once belonged to her mother and she could feel a connection with her when the blades sang. She ached to hear that sound. She drew strength from it, as if the sound came from all the women of her family urging her on.

After everything she'd experienced during her brief time as a captive, Allie's aversion to fighting had changed. She still hated the thought of hurting anyone, but with Aidan it was different.

As they fell into the rhythm of their fight, she let her power rise within, relishing the warmth as it flooded her body. She didn't feel the overwhelming instinct to hold back. This was Aidan and she was confident there was nothing she could dish out that he could not handle.

"Nice!" He scrambled to parry her thrust and almost managed to sweep her off her feet. She dodged his kick and returned with an uppercut to his jaw, tucking the sharp end of her sai along her forearm and using the blunted end to add some force behind her punch.

"Ow! That hurt, Allie!" He turned to spit blood, rubbing his jaw.

"I'm sorry!" She reached to see if he was okay and landed on her ass beside the brook. She rolled away just in time to miss the sharp end of his blade arcing down toward her shoulder.

"Asshat move!" she snarled as she scrambled back to her feet, dusting the dirt off herself.

"I know my opponent, babe, what can I say?" he mocked as he lunged.

She raised her lead blade and managed to connect with his longer one, but she wasn't quick enough. She felt the all-too-familiar slice of flesh meeting sharp metal and let out a startled gasp. She fell to her knees with a sob, tears blurring her vision.

"Lex! I'm so sorry!" Aidan dropped his weapons and rushed to her side. "Let me see. Is it deep?"

She hid her smile as she swept his feet out from under him. She had him pinned beneath her in a headlock before he could register what was happening. "And I know my opponent too, babe," she whispered in his ear.

"That was reprehensible, Alexis Ann." He broke her hold and flipped her onto her back. "You will pay for that, you little cheater." His grin was contagious and she couldn't help her laughter.

"Come on, tough guy, you know I won't break."

"Knowing you're capable and seeing you hurt are two totally different things." He stared down at her, the look in his eye making her feel all sorts of confused. She just broke up with Vince and already Aidan was looking at her differently.

Maybe it's because you're looking at me differently.

I'm not ready yet. The "yet" slipped out before she could even consider if she really meant it.

You said "yet." I can work with yet.

"You need to be able to handle seeing me hurt, Aidan." She brought their conversation back to training. "That's probably something we both need to work on." She stood to put some distance between them. "It could be a major weakness for us when it really matters." She knew she couldn't stomach seeing him hurt either.

"You might be right." He lunged at her again and she barely got her weapon up in time.

Allie threw herself into the fight, returning each strike with one of her own. Her muscles burned as she moved, her speed increasing with their game of attack and retreat. The smirk faded from Aidan's face as he concentrated on her movements, scrutinizing her every move, calculating what she would do next. He met her at every interval. They were both sweaty and out of breath, but it was the best sparring match she'd had in months.

"Nice one!" Allie laughed breathlessly as she ducked just in time to miss his blade. His only response was a grunt. His eyes were vacant, but the flicker of power there left her unsettled.

"Aidan?" she asked cautiously, lowering her lead weapon. But he didn't stop. He pressed on, his blades moving at lightning speed. Something was wrong. She blocked his advance, taking a step back.

Aidan? Are you okay? But his mind was a blank slate. He just kept coming at her, his brow set in determination.

"No more fake-outs." She parried his lead blade again, but his rear weapon caught her thigh and blood oozed from the shallow cut. Allie slowed her pace, but he was fighting so furiously. Methodically, like a machine.

"Aidan, stop!" she cried, backing up again. She flew into a low, sweeping kick, attempting to drop him to the ground to knock some sense into him, but his eyes blazed golden. He was in some kind of trance as his power raged inside of him.

He pursued her and she fought back, but she was soon covered in blood. None of his strikes cut her too deeply. She was a good fighter, and never let him get more than a graze in.

Aidan, stop. It's me! He looked right at her, but still didn't see her. *I have to disarm him.* But she couldn't touch him. She went in for an uppercut, hoping to knock him on his ass, but he moved aside as if her fist was just an annoying, buzzing fly.

Finally, she did the only thing she could think of. She threw her weapons down and ducked under his arm, slamming against his sweaty chest. She wrapped her arms around him and kissed him.

He faltered and dropped his weapons.

"Please, snap out of it. You're scaring me," she whispered as she held him. His arms slid around her and they staggered to the ground in a heap. His weapons lay forgotten beside them.

"Allie?" His guttural moan still didn't sound like him.

"What the hell was that, Aidan?" She looked down at him, his eyes still vacant and blazing with the full fury of his power. She ran her fingertips over his jaw, hoping her gentle touch would draw him back to her.

It worked, but not quite as she imagined. He slammed her back, rolling on top of her, his fingers sliding through her hair as his mouth crushed over hers in a searing hot kiss. She could feel his heart hammering against her palm.

Aidan.... Dammit, it was such a *good* kiss. But she couldn't keep letting this happen. *That night in Agra was a mistake....* That kiss had done something to them, and it was like they couldn't get past it.

"Lex," he murmured as she shifted beneath him.

She was reluctant to bring an end to it as she slid her fingers through his hair and pulled, flipping him onto his back with an extra pulse of her solar zap for good measure.

"Ow, what the...?" He gasped as the fire dimmed in his eyes. "Did you just *shock* me, Alexis Ann? Was that really necessary? Wait ... were we making out?"

"I pulled your hair too."

"You're bleeding!" He pulled her up and onto his lap before she could protest. Most of her bloodied cuts were already starting to heal, but some of them were deeper. Her sweaty hair hung limp in her face and her breath was ragged. She knew she looked worse than she felt and he was about to flip out.

I did this? He ran his hand along her arm. "I lost it, didn't I."

"I'm okay, but I don't understand what came over you. Are you all right, Aidan?" She reached to touch his face, not sure if he was really himself yet.

"I'm fine. Come, let me get you cleaned up." He helped her up, grabbing his shirt lying on the ground beside the cool, clear stream that ran through the yard. She came to sit beside him, her arms shaky and her head light from the intensity of their sparring match.

Or maybe it was the kiss.

Probably both; I'm a little lightheaded myself. He attempted a teasing tone, but he was still angry with himself. "I'm glad you shocked me. That wasn't cool. Kissing you like that when you didn't want it."

"Well, to be fair, I did kiss you first."

"Still not cool." He shook his head. "It's my gift." He wiped at the blood smearing her arms and legs. "I haven't lost control like that in ages."

"It's some kind of trance?"

"Yeah. I'm so sorry, Lex." He tossed his bloody shirt aside and pulled her back on his lap and held her close. She could feel his self-loathing rolling off him in waves. She had to shut it down now or this would send him spiraling.

"I know what that's like, Aidan. Losing control. Hurting someone you care about when that's the last thing you'd ever want." She pulled his face down close to hers. "Do not blame yourself, you broody son of a bitch. It's not worth it, so snap out of it."

"Yes ma'am." He laughed, grasping her hand and linking his fingers through hers. "I was in the zone." He shrugged. "I get super focused on whatever I'm doing and nothing else matters. I'm locked inside it and sometimes it's difficult to shake it off. I've never lost it so completely before. I'm actually glad it was with you and not Chloe or Graham. I'd have cut them to pieces."

"You've managed this around the others?"

"Yeah, I don't even think about it anymore. But when we're here ... like this ... I just drop all of my walls, you know?"

"Me too. It's nice to not have to focus so much attention on pretending like I do at school, or holding back when I'm working with Chloe and Graham, or even with Sasha. When we're here and I don't have to worry about any of that, it's a relief to just let go."

"Yeah. But not at this cost." He shook his head sadly. "We're equals and that means the world to me, but I can't ever forget that I'm slightly more powerful than you are."

"That's BS."

"It's true."

"I'm not a porcelain doll. You've never felt bad about kicking my butt before, so why start now?"

"There's ass-kicking and then there's the bastard who painted the ground with your blood. That will not happen again, Lex."

"Okay, so technically speaking, you may be a tiny bit more powerful than me, but it's not enough to matter." She stood and held out her hand for him. "This is just a thing we need to work on. You have perfect control with this gift with everyone else in your life. So we'll just work on it until you have perfect control with your equal too. Then this will never happen with anyone else."

He grabbed her hand and pulled himself up to stand next to her.

"Thank you, Allie." He pulled her close, tucking her head under his chin.

"For what?"

"For knowing how to pull me back." She could feel his

laughter vibrate in his chest. "The kissing I enjoyed. And I'm pretty sure you did too. But next time, go for the kiss before I turn you into a pincushion." He took her hand as they headed back to his office.

"Oh, next time there will be no kissing. Next time you might come up missing some parts." She dropped his hand and took a step away to put some distance between them, but she smiled, trying to take the sting out of her words.

"It doesn't have to mean anything, Allie." He pulled her back. "You put too much pressure on us." His eyes filled with amusement and she realized he was making a huge effort not to make anything out of this kiss.

"We can't let this happen again, Aidan. "

"I know, you just broke up with Vince."

"Technically, he broke up with me."

"What?" Aidan stopped walking.

"He beat me to the punch." Allie hadn't told Aidan the finer details of their breakup so she'd let him assume she'd done the actual breaking up.

He threw his head back and laughed. "Seriously? After all your indecision and *he* broke up with *you*?" His laughter echoed across the yard.

"It's so not that funny." Allie scowled down at him.

"I'm sorry, Allie. I don't mean to laugh." But he couldn't seem to stop.

"Har, har, funny guy. It still wasn't easy."

"I know. I'm sorry." He shook his head. "What was his reason?"

"He thought I was checking out of the relationship so he beat me to the punch and let me off the hook. It grew into kind of a mutual split from there."

"I'm sorry. I know the breakup wasn't easy for you no matter how it went."

"Come on. I need a snack." She turned toward the kitchen as they left the yard behind.

"Me too." He draped his arm around her, still chuckling. "I promise, I'm not going to push you into anything." His tone grew serious. "I know you still care about him, but nothing between us has to change just because you're single now.

"I think I'm over relationships," Allie said. "It was always easy with Vince. Even the breakup. I doubt I'll ever be that lucky again."

"There's a reason you two always had such an easy, no-pressure relationship. You're just alike. He's running scared from his feelings for Kayla just as hard as you're running from your feelings for a certain handsome Immortal."

"Yeah, Graham is pretty cute."

"Uh ... I don't think you're his type, Lex. Come on, I think you need a sandwich and maybe a few stitches. You still look like some asshole beat you up."

CHAPTER 10

Allie lingered in the bathtub, her aching muscles weary from a long week of training. The closer she came to her seventeenth birthday, the harder they worked her. She was covered in bruises from an afternoon of sparring with Aidan and Sasha, and she was pretty sure she had a few broken toes to show for it.

She closed her eyes and inhaled deeply. Her bedroom door creaked open and careful footsteps crossed her room.

"Ma?" she called, frowning at the swish of the door as her visitor left. She toweled off quickly and peeked into her room. Her gaze fell to the note on her nightstand. It was in Carson's neat script.

There is a reason for his silence. Go to sleep and think of the place where you meet Aidan, then ask him to leave. N will be waiting. Burn this (just try not to burn the house down with it).

Love Dad

The page heated under her fingertips as she released a trickle of her solar power into the paper. It smoldered to ash in her hands and fluttered into the empty wastebasket.

"Thanks, Dad," she whispered.

Dream date tonight? she asked Aidan.

You sleeping alone?

I need to give it a shot every once in a while.

See you there in a bit.

Allie lay in bed, staring at the ceiling. As she thought about the prospect of confronting her father, her hands balled into fists and her nails scraped her bruised palms. The anger surged within her so quickly, she wasn't sure she would be able to sleep at all. She didn't know how Navid would manage it, but if he could really meet her in the dreamworld, she had so many questions. She didn't even know if she was ready to see him—she was so angry. What if she lost control the moment she saw him?

Finally, she decided to meditate and focused on the deep breathing exercises that often helped her drift off to sleep.

"I thought you were going to stand me up." Aidan stood to greet her under the gnarled old laurel tree. This was where they always met when their dreams merged. It was an echo of the grassy hillside behind his house. Like an imperfect copy of the real thing, but this place held an otherworldly vibe she was only beginning to suspect was bigger and more powerful than they could imagine.

"Sorry, couldn't fall asleep."

"What's going on, Allie?"

"I needed to come here and this is the only way I know how. I've never been here alone, have you?"

"No, I tend to just drift until you get here."

"Me too. But I need you to leave now." She gave him an apologetic look.

"What? Why? I just got here."

"Please just trust me."

"I'm not sure I know how to leave. I usually just wake up or we drift into another dream."

"Wake up, Aidan. Please?"

It took several attempts, but as he finally faded away, Allie fought the urge to follow. The pull was strong and she had to force herself to stay behind. When he was gone, she paced around the old tree, anxious to see how Navid might appear.

Could she really do this? Talk to her father? She wanted to feel excited, but she felt nothing but that burning anger that was her constant companion lately.

"I'm so sorry, Allie." His voice echoed around her and she turned, spinning to scan the grassy slopes, but he wasn't there.

"NAVID!" His name ripped from her throat, the sound filled with all the anguish of the last months. The knowledge that he was her father and he was alive and well, but had left her to be raised by mortals, completely isolated from her kind. She wanted to hit something. She needed an outlet for her rage.

"Breathe, Allie. Find your center."

She screamed in frustration at the ghostly voice that was such a familiar part of her childhood. Her control was quickly slipping out of her grasp and she fought to rein it in. Allie fell to her knees, taking deep, shaky breaths. When she opened her eyes, her hands were tight fists, dripping blood all over the ground.

She looked up and he was there. Standing just feet from her.

Allie wondered how she never saw it before. In so many ways, she was the physical opposite of her father. He was tall, dark, and muscular, where she was petite, fair, and curvy. She had his eyes, his unruly curls, his quiet confidence she was just beginning to grow into. And his power. She had thought, from everything Gregg told her, that she got her power from her mother, but she realized now that she had much of her father's powerful nature within her.

"Why?" She choked on the word. Her seething anger was the only thing keeping her tears back.

Navid sank to the ground beside her. "Such a simple but difficult question to answer."

"How are you here? In this dream?"

"I am a dreamwalker. A telepathic gift very few know I possess. In the dreamworld, I am at my strongest, telepathically. In the waking world, I am hardly a telepath at all. It is very difficult for me to speak to another's mind. You have your mind locked up so tightly against Aidan, I've not been able to reach you. Carson said you were asking for me, and I'm so very glad to see you ... daughter." He struggled with that last word, his eyes bright and his hands shaking.

"I am angry, Navid. So angry I can hardly breathe." Her words were firm, but barely a whisper.

"You have every right to be."

"I love my parents."

"They are your parents; of course you love them. That will never change. I won't take your father's place in your heart, but I would like it if you could find a small corner for me too, someday."

"And what of Kassandre? Where is she in all of this?"

"If she could be here, she would."

"You gave me away! Who does that?"

"It was the hardest thing either of us has ever done in our many thousands of years."

"I remember you. You gave me away *before* you were supposedly assassinated."

"What do you remember?" His eyes grew wide. "We stopped visiting when we thought you were still too young to remember."

"I don't know if it's a memory or a vision, but I was three years old, running on the beach with Lily and Carson, but you and Kassandre were there too, walking in the distance. I ran after you, but you *left* me!"

"You think we wanted to? We lost one daughter we never knew. We could hardly face it, losing another. If we had raised you, Allie, you would have never had a chance to be the girl you are now. You know what your mother can do—she sees, Allie, she sees everything. We've seen your life a thousand different ways, but this was the only version that kept you safe and happy. This was the only version of your life that made sense. We gave you up to give you a better life—"

"To grow up completely ignorant of what I am? So many years? Thinking something was wrong with me! I wasn't happy. I just ... existed, going through the motions of life with little to look forward to and no one who understood me. And then going into an Awakening like that with no idea what was happening?" She took a deep, shuddering breath, forcing her anger back down.

"In this life you will know great sorrow and immeasurable joy. It is worth every sacrifice we've made to give you that chance. I cannot give you all the answers you deserve right now, but I promise you will have them in time. Just know that every decision that was made for you was meant to give you the strength and experience you need to face what you must."

"That damned prophecy?"

"Yes—but the recorded version is false. Your grandmother, Alísun, foretold that prophecy and she knew it would be her own granddaughter to fulfill it. She is the only one who knows the true prophecy. The women of your family have been protecting you for thousands of years, Allie.

"Enough." She stood to pace. "I don't want to hear any more—not now." She took a deep, calming breath. She was in control, but only just.

"It is not safe for me to linger here for long, even in this remote edge of the dreamworld," Navid said. "If my secret is discovered, I could lose this opportunity to see you and I will not risk your safety simply because it is my deepest desire for my daughter to know me as more than just a family friend. To see her beautiful face—so like her mother's. To watch her grow into her potential. To have the honor to teach her ... to hold her and comfort her when she is upset. I cannot give you the time you deserve, but if you want to see me—if you want to know and learn from me—then we can meet here briefly from time to time, but you must open your mind. Keeping yourself locked up so tightly is only contributing to that rage you feel burning in your core."

"How will I know when you'll be here? How can I come here on my own?"

"You wish to see me again?" His green eyes brightened.

"I am angry, Navid. I feel so much anger, directed at everyone and everything around me, but I want to know my father." She choked on the last word.

"Allie." He pulled her into his arms and she sobbed on his shoulder. "Deep breaths, sweetheart."

She'd never felt so close to the edge like this. She had to pull it together before she totally lost it.

"To come here alone, you must study the path that leads you here. As you fall into the world of dreams, focus and you will see. Come alone for now. But you must confide in Aidan. You need someone you trust. Share your secrets with him."

"I can tell him? About you?"

"Tell him everything, but you must do so in absolute privacy. You cannot risk letting anyone overhear you, but you can't shoulder the weight of this burden all on your own, either. Keep your mind open to him and I will hear you. I can speak to your mind, although it is difficult, and costs a great deal of strength to do so. When you have need of me, do not hesitate to reach out. I will hear you if you hold on to a thought with me in mind, but I may not always be able to answer. And when you enter the world of dreams, do not ever leave your own dreamscape. This is very important, Allie. This world is infinite and it is very easy to get lost here when you are not a dreamwalker. It could drive you mad if you found yourself trapped in someone else's dreamscape."

"How can I come here like this if I'm not a dreamwalker?" Allie asked.

"Because you are my daughter. This is your heritage from me. It doesn't make you a dreamwalker, but it makes you more susceptible to this world. It is part of you."

"Is it safe for Aidan to come here with me?"

"He has an affinity for telepathy, so he is able to travel here safely with another telepath, although I don't think he could manage it on his own. As long as you come here just as you always have, you both will be perfectly safe. But do not speak of this place to your teachers. Not yet. Emma Renard is your mentor, yes?"

Allie nodded.

"She is a formidable woman with a dark past, but you will learn a great deal from her. I could not find you a better example of a woman capable of great ruthlessness as well as great compassion. She may caution you about entering the dreamworld, but she won't know enough about it to teach you."

"When can I see you again?"

"We must be cautious, daughter. I will leave a sign for you here and we will see each other again soon. I am delighted you even want to see me."

"I can't say there won't be more screaming, but I need to know you. I need to understand everything happening around me. This is *my* life, Navid. I can't have other people deciding my fate for me. Not anymore."

"I will teach you everything you need to know about the

choices we've made for you. But you are doing remarkably well, sweetheart. I'm so proud of you."

She could feel him slipping away and was reluctant to let him go. No matter how angry she was, she still loved him, just as she always had when she knew him only as a family friend.

"Goodbye for now?"

"For now." Navid pulled her back into his embrace and she faded away from the world of dreams.

I love you, my beautiful daughter....

Her father's words echoed through her mind.

"Allie, wake up. Please." Aidan's warm hand clasped tightly around hers as her eyes fluttered open. Her cheeks were wet with tears. "I came as soon as felt you freaking out. What have you seen?"

"Your music room, in the underground—it's soundproofed, right?"

"Yes. Darius sealed it himself."

"Take me there? I'm ready to talk. My thoughts are a jumbled mess right now and I just ... I need to get it all out before I can really let you back in."

"Let's go."

CHAPTER 11

"What's going on, Allie? You're scaring me." Aidan closed the door to his studio behind them and Allie headed to the surround sound system, hoping some music would drown out their voices in case someone happened to overhear them.

"We're safe here, Lex. No one will hear us. Now, please—"

"I'm a natural born," she blurted.

"What? How?"

"The usual way, I suppose." She managed a wry smile. "That's what Gregg told me before we left for Agra this summer."

"How did he know?"

"It seems he suspected who my real parents were, but wasn't certain enough to say anything ... until I told him Livia was interested in me because of my necklace." She remembered the way Gregg had looked at her necklace—the one Lily had given her years ago. It was a family heirloom, only she hadn't realized Lily meant it was from her birth family.

"Who are they? How did he know them?" he asked, but Allie held up her hand to stall his questions.

"Your father and my mother lived as husband and wife for nearly a century before my mother recognized my father."

"Jeez, Da." Aidan winced. "It seems he's been friendly with

all my friends' moms. Come on, I have a feeling this is going to be a long night. We might as well get comfortable." He grabbed Allie's hand and towed her to the bedroom, the soft, soothing music still playing.

Allie made herself at home. The night sky twinkling down on them barely registered as a reminder that Naomi had been there.

"Now spill it," Aidan said as he draped his arm around her and she relaxed for the first time in hours. "How did you end up with Lily and Carson if you're a natural born?"

"My birth parents chose them to raise me. My mother knew they would die and she knew I wouldn't be safe, so she hid me in the mortal world." Allie propped up on her elbow and looked down at him, fearful of the thing she was about to divulge. "Can I trust you?"

"You know better than to even ask that question." He scowled.

"Can I trust you with my mortal family's lives?"

"Nothing you say will leave this room tonight. No matter what."

"Lily and Carson know far more about me than I've ever let on."

"What? How? It isn't safe for them."

In that moment, she loved Aidan for worrying about their safety before anything else.

"We've danced around the issue occasionally, but they know ... at least a little of what I am. There is so much about myself and my past that I don't understand, but I do know my intuition is something I trust and my intuition has always told me to keep them out of it—to keep them safe. So we ignore the giant, pink, tap-dancing elephant in the room and pretend everything is peachy."

"Allie—I'm so sorry." He reached up and brushed her hair aside, cupping her face in his palm.

"We make up trivial things to talk about so we'll have something to say to each other." She shrugged. "It's depressing."

"How did your birth parents die?"

"Our world thinks they were assassinated nearly fourteen years ago." She could see the reality of what she said dawning in his eyes.

"No." He turned toward her, propping up on his elbow to face her. "It's impossible, Lex. They had a natural daughter centuries ago."

"Yeah, and then they had me too." She stared into his dark, worry-filled eyes.

"A second natural daughter?" His worry turned to fear in the span of a heartbeat.

"My maternal grandmother was Queen Alísun." Her voice shook and she couldn't look at him, so she stared down at his chest instead. She absently ran her fingertips through the short tufts of chest hair he never bothered manscaping.

"The prophecy?"

"It seems she foretold of my birth and recorded a false version to keep me safe."

Aidan pulled her against his chest, murmuring words of comfort, but she could feel his anger and his fear—and his relief, too, that the prophecy wasn't about him.

"How could he keep this from you?" he finally said. "How could Dad let you continue thinking any of this was just chance?"

"Believe me, your dear ol' da is on my list. But I think he was in denial. Gregg loves me like a daughter; he thought he was protecting me—waiting until he was sure. The necklace was the final clue. It's hers." Allie lifted the teardrop pendant from the chain around her neck. The sparkling black stones caught the light from the stars above them and the worn serpentine loop snaked around the teardrop in a figure eight.

"Allie, you're like ... royalty."

"Screw that, Aidan Loukas," she snarled, shoving him back.

"Certainly not a well-mannered princess," he said dryly. "You would be the closest thing we have to true nobility. People would freak if they knew you were Kassandre and Ashar's natural daughter. They would flock to you like royalty for that alone. If they knew about your connection to the Indriell Queens ... you'd never have another moment's peace."

"I trust you won't treat me differently." The tone of reverence in Aidan's voice was not something she could take from him. "I swear, I will throat-punch you right here if you don't snap out of it!"

"You're still Allie and I'm still Aidan." He laughed. "You know I will never treat you differently where I can help it. But you are different. Your identity has to remain a secret. It isn't safe for you—and that will always worry me."

"People are protecting me, Aidan—have been protecting me and watching over me my whole life."

"Who?" He frowned.

"My birth parents," she whispered. "They're alive."

"What—how?" he gasped.

"I don't know how they faked their death ... but I-I've known my father most of my life. I always thought he was just a friend of the family. I-I'm not sure about my mother—I think she might not have made it through the assassination attempt unscathed. She must have been taken."

"You've met Ashar?"

"I know him as Navid. It was such a shock when Gregg showed me a picture of my parents. He did it to show me how much I look like my mother, but I couldn't take my eyes off my father. Gregg doesn't know. No one can know, but Navid told me I could confide in you—he said I needed to."

"When? Is he here? Have you seen him?"

"There's a reason I'm a telepath. I inherited it from him."

"Ashar was— is a telepath?"

"A dreamwalker, actually. He can only speak to me directly with a great deal of effort. He's spoken to me a few times. Once during my Awakening and then again when Quinn and I were taken. The last time he spoke to me was when Gregg dropped this bomb on me. Since then, I've kept my mind locked tight against you, but against him as well. Not on purpose. I was just ... licking my wounds, I suppose." Allie heaved a deep sigh. It felt so good to finally let it all out.

"These last few months, I've been so angry," she said softly, staring up at the twinkling sky above them. "My whole life has been a lie and there he was, all this time, with all the answers. But I need him—there's so much I have to know."

"He's a dreamwalker? So that's why you wanted me to leave. He came to you there? Ash—Navid?" Aidan's brow creased in frustration.

She nodded. "We didn't have long, but we talked. He didn't have a lot of answers, but I think he will in time."

"Are you sure you're okay, Allie?" He turned to face her with a look of concern. "That's a lot to take in."

They lay there quietly for a moment in the dim light of the twinkling stars.

"No ... but this helps." She smiled, but her smile wavered. She was so comfortable with him and there was no doubt their relationship was changing—had been changing since Agra. If the intimacy between them continued to escalate, she would either have to break his heart or take a leap of faith. But right now, she didn't want to put a label on whatever this was.

Aidan absently stoked her hair and kissed her forehead and

Allie shoved all of her conflicting emotions into that slightly smaller box in her mind. For the moment, an immense burden had lifted from her shoulders.

"My mother is clairvoyant."

"An understatement from what I know of her," Aidan said.

"Navid says they saw hundreds of different versions of my life and this is the one they chose for me."

"So they've manipulated every aspect of your life? That must be a tough pill to swallow."

"Knowing that my own parents gave me away and strategically planned every moment of my life.... I'm so angry, Aidan. I've never felt such rage. My anger scares me." She held up her hands so he could see the faded crescent-shaped scabs on her palms. "I feel like I'm losing control of everything—especially my power."

"That's not a good sign." He frowned, tracing the lines on her palm with his fingertip. "We need to work on that."

"Liam's been helping me—since the whole Vince thing."

"You've had a shitty few months, Lex."

She wasn't sure why she did it; she didn't even think about it. It felt so natural to tilt her head back, letting her lips find his.

She felt his surprise, but he quickly got over that as his hand slid down to her waist. His other tangled in her hair. The minty, earthy taste of his scent filled her senses. His lips were soft but demanding as they moved over hers.

For once, she refused to think about the consequences. Tonight, she needed his comfort.

Do not overthink this, Lex.

No strings?

It's just a kiss.

Promise?

Alexis Ann ... shut up and kiss me.

Chapter 12

She shouldn't have kissed him. She kept telling herself she shouldn't have kissed him. But over the last week, Allie couldn't think about anything but that kiss.

It can't happen again. But she was struggling to remember all of her perfectly reasonable arguments for why kissing Aidan was such a bad idea when it felt so damned right.

The night was late and the music was soothing as Allie attempted to read her book.

Aidan dozed, his bare chest warm and distracting against her back. His lips pressed against her shoulder and his hands began to wander ... again.

I am, without a doubt, the biggest dumbass ever. Hands, Aidan!

You have a lovely ass, baby, he murmured sleepily.

Aidan....

Sorry, my hands seem to have a mind of their own. He pulled away.

You are here in a keep-the-dreams-away capacity. If we are back at intimacy issues, then you might need to go find your own bed for a while. The thought of facing her dreams alone sent a shiver of fear through her.

"It's much more difficult now that you're single." He rolled over onto his back with a stretch. "But I will not shirk my dream duties."

"I might be single, but I'm trying really hard to give myself some time. I don't want to be the girl who jumps from one boyfriend to another. I'm sorry I let things go too far the other night. I don't know what I was thinking."

"You were hurting and you needed me. I shouldn't have taken advantage of that," Aidan said.

Allie snorted in amusement. "I promise, I was perfectly aware of what I was doing and at the time, it seemed like a really good idea."

"Eh, you've wanted me since Agra." He flashed his arrogant smile.

"We agreed to *never* talk about Agra." Just the thought of that night had her face flushed scarlet. She'd made such a fool of herself.

Allie's phone rattled on her nightstand and Aidan reached for it.

"Why is my brother calling you so late?" He scowled at her caller ID.

Allie rolled her eyes—it seemed the boy drama would never escape her.

"Hey, Dare," she answered, cringing when her voice came out all breathy and teenagery.

"Hey, good, you're still up. I have tickets to that concert in the flats this weekend."

"Fink?" She grinned. "I'm so jealous!"

"You're coming with me, killer. For your birthday."

"Uh ... like a date?" She really liked Darius, but she wasn't about to stir up boy drama between the brothers.

"Hell, no. Allie, you're like four."

"Exactly."

"Don't worry, this is definitely a non-date between friends. You can tell little brother he can stop fuming now; I'm not going to steal you away from him."

"Sure, man. You know she thinks you're a creepy old dude, right?" Aidan said.

"I do not." Allie gave Aidan a shove.

"Night, killer."

"Night."

It's not a date, Aidan. She put her phone back on the bedside table. The tension he felt had shot right through her the moment she answered the phone. "Your brother is my *friend* and that is it. I cannot wrap my mortal brain around the idea that he's technically our age. It's not exactly creepy, but it's definitely creepy-adjacent, so we're friends who like the same music—end of story. Now can we please go to sleep?" She was excited about her non-date with Darius, but she knew Aidan expected her to be with him if she was going to be with anyone.

"Did I utter one word in protest?" He pulled her back against his chest and curled around her.

"No, but I know you don't like it. I love hanging out with Darius. We're really good friends. I won't insult you and say there isn't some kind of weird flirty attraction there—but I would never act on it. I'm not going to be another Naomi, making her way through the McBrien boys, careless of their feelings."

"I know, Lex. But to be totally honest, I don't like the way you two look at each other. With Darius you're more like your old self. Like the weight of everything you've been dealing with isn't so heavy when he's around."

"I swear it's not like that," Allie insisted. It wasn't remotely like that. They were just friends, but it was true she did feel more like herself with him.

"It took me a while to realize Vince was the guy you

needed. And now he's gone and ... I don't know, maybe I'm afraid Darius is the guy you need now."

"That's just it, Aidan." She rolled over so she could see him, taking his face in her hands so she could make sure he really got it this time. She tried not to tremble when his arms snaked around her waist. "I don't want to *need* any guy. I don't want to be the girl who can't figure her own shit out so she uses her boyfriend as a crutch to lift herself up." She pressed her forehead against his. "I especially don't want to be that girl with you. Maybe I'm afraid to be with you because I feel like I'm just going to weigh you down."

"That's bullshit. The way you see me—it's not remotely accurate."

"Right back atcha," she whispered, her lips dangerously close to his as they breathed the same air, staring at each other. Her heart beat against his chest and she really wanted to throw all her fears aside and just kiss him.

"Nephew, if I have to throw you out of here one more time, it will be head first off this tower." Liam stood on Allie's balcony glaring at them both.

"Liam, I swear this isn't like Agra," Aidan said. Since that night, Liam had developed a habit of checking up on Allie and routinely kicked Aidan out of her room.

"You're half naked in my sister's bed and I'm pretty sure I've interrupted at just the right moment ... again. I'd stop talking while you're ahead." He shot an icy glare at Aidan.

"Liam, I promise this isn't—"

"Zip it, little one. Aidan, I'm certain you have a bed of your own to get to."

"Fine. Between my brothers and uncles, I'm never going to get any sleep tonight anyway. Sorry about the night terrors, Lex. Just remember I'll be suffering right along with you."

Aidan had clearly had enough; he was gone before she could protest.

"Night terrors?" Liam scowled.

"Yes, you big oaf! He sleeps here for a very good reason that has nothing to do with sex!" She threw her pillow at him.

"Trust me, that's all that's on his mind."

"Liam, when I dream, it's usually terrifying, whether I understand what I'm seeing or not. When I sleep with Aidan it's like our telepathic minds merge when we're in the same sleep cycle. I don't know if it's an extension of his healing gift or what, but this is the only way we can actually sleep. When I see, it's not restful sleep—for either of us. If it weren't for his help, I'm not sure I'd still be sane."

"Of course he wants to *help* you, Allie. He gets to sleep with you."

"It's not like that. It's not that simple."

"He is seventeen years old, little one. It is that simple." He folded his long arms across his chest.

"It doesn't even matter. It's sleep with Aidan or no sleep at all."

"I see." His scowl grew deeper. "That is not a permanent solution."

"We know. But it works. What else can we do?"

"Discuss this with your mentors like you both know you should. There must be a way for you to manage your dreams on your own."

"It's complicated, Liam. And it's late. And apparently I have some dreaming to do."

Her hands shook as she retrieved her pillow. She'd had dozens of disturbing dreams since they began months ago. They were always about fire and churning black smoke. A dark night filled with screams under a terrifying blood red moon.

But she never understood what it meant. Her only reprieve was Aidan.

"You really are scared to go to sleep, aren't you?" Liam's anger subsided, now that it seemed he finally grasped the severity of the situation. "You're shaking like a leaf."

"Dreaming's not fun. But I'm exhausted." Allie settled back into her bed and pulled the covers up to her chin.

"I can stay here with you and wake you if it gets to be too much," Liam offered.

"Sure. That'd be nice." She rolled over and prepared for the onslaught. She didn't have the heart to tell him he'd never be able to wake her.

Let him observe, Aidan said. *Maybe he can help. He's right; this has never been a permanent solution.*

Will you be okay? Allie hated her dreams, but she hated making him watch even more.

It's okay, Lex. Don't worry about me.

"Relax, little one. Take deep breaths and close your eyes." Liam's voice was soft and soothing. He drifted into an old Norse song. His tenor voice sent waves of intoxicating peace through her and within moments she fell into a deep sleep.

Blackness engulfed Allie like the oppressive void she fought during her Awakening. Her breath grew labored as the familiar panic overwhelmed her. She drifted. But not aimlessly as if she had no body. She could sense the world around her. The rough wood of the small boat beneath her was little more than a raft. The gentle rocking of the listless waves was much too peaceful for this ominous setting. The chill of the heavy mist spoke of something more sinister. The scrape of the marsh grass against her shoulders made her shiver.

Shapes began to emerge from the fog, and Allie realized she was adrift along the marshy bogs of Lake Erie, far away from the city. The world around her was an unnatural green, like the eerie light before a storm. The murky water was thick with the grass and muck that hid whatever creatures lurked in the bog below. The marshes stretched all around her in every direction. She couldn't even see the shoreline in the darkness.

Allie trembled in anticipation. Something churned in the water.

I have to get back to shore. She searched the small boat for an oar, anything she could use to paddle out of the bog and back home where the water was clear and nothing could harm her.

The boat was empty and the only way she could maneuver out of the swamp was to pull herself through the wet grass growing in thick patches along the surface of the water. She'd gone only a few feet when the lake erupted around her. Slithering bodies churned as far as she could see.

Snakes! She couldn't stand the sight of snakes and they were everywhere. Huge and black with shiny scales and empty, red eyes.

Pay attention to the important elements and discard everything else. The rest is just noise. This was the mantra she'd repeated to herself over and over since the cave dreams started months ago. It was just noise, but she had to decipher what her gift was trying to tell her amidst all the chaos.

Allie screamed as the huge snakes swarmed the boat, writhing around each other and sending her into the frigid water. All sense faded from her mind as she panicked. She felt their bites—their venomous fangs; the slither of their bodies as they pulled her under.

There are no poisonous snakes in Lake Erie. This is just a dream. But the water filling her lungs was real. The pain of the long fangs sinking into her flesh was real. The burn of the venom in her veins was like acid and the feel of their cold, scaly bodies constricting around her as they dragged her to the bottom of the lake was much too real.

Chapter 13

Allie woke gasping for air, fighting with the blankets and sheets wrapped around her.

"Calm down, little one. I am here." Liam's voice pulled her out of her nightmare.

Her heart raced and her vision blurred so everything she saw still had the stormy green tinge of her dream. She shook her head to clear her mind and thought she was going to be sick. She could still feel the snakes twisting around her.

"It's okay. Just breathe." Liam's fingers combed through her damp hair. He sat on the bed beside her, propped against the headboard. Her head rested on his lap and his arm draped protectively around her.

Snakes. Anything but snakes, Aidan whispered.

Cheers to that. Allie took another shaky breath. *You okay?*

I'm fine, baby.

Try to get some sleep.

"I see now why you prefer not to face your dreams," Liam said. "You did not sufficiently prepare me for that."

"You think?" She sat up, rubbing her eyes until everything returned to its normal color. "I'm guessing you couldn't wake me, then?" She reached for the bottled water beside her bed, feeling like something the dog threw up.

"I didn't try. And that was not an easy thing to do. Letting you scream with no sound, thrashing around like someone was trying to murder you. Damn near killed me just watching. But I won't coddle you the way Aidan does."

"He doesn't coddle me."

"I know he can't help but want to comfort you after seeing that, especially given his front-row seat in your mind." Liam tapped her forehead. "But you're letting a man take care of you, sweetheart. And no sister of mine is going to let a man protect her when she has the strength to protect herself. You have to learn to live with your dreams and function on your own so when he can't be here for you, you won't fall apart. I don't want to see you tethered to him like this, unable to last a week without Aidan by your side. Not that he isn't worthy or that he doesn't care for you."

"Oh my God. You're right. I never thought about it like that. Ugh!" The temptation to avoid her dreams was strong, but after she'd just told Aidan she didn't want to be *that* girl, especially with him, Liam held up the mirror and showed her that was exactly what she was.

"There's nothing wrong with seeking a peaceful night with him every now and then, as much as I hate to admit it. I just don't want you to *need* it. You're stagnant right now. You are not learning what your gift is trying to teach you. What you're doing ... it's just putting a Band-Aid on an open wound. I think you've spent so much time trying to avoid your dreams, that they're just piling up, like spam email in a junk folder. Then when you do dream, they are terrifying because they're trying to get your attention. I'm hoping if we give your dreams the focus they need, they will no longer be quite so frightening and we may actually be able to figure out what they mean."

"We?" Allie glanced up at him.

"Of course. I'm going to help you with this, little one."

"Any ideas how I could possibly handle this on my own?" A surge of hope filled her. This was something she had never felt comfortable talking about with Gregg or Emma, but with her brother, it didn't feel awkward at all.

"For starters, you are going to put your big-girl pants on and face your dreams. It may take a few more nights of observation, but I'm going to help you sort this out. Now, tell me what you saw, before you forget."

"I won't be forgetting that anytime soon. It was snakes. Every-freaking-where." She shivered.

"Well, that makes a lot more sense," he muttered. "Has Aidan ever told you how active you are when you dream?"

"Not really. He sees most of what I see so I think he's been focused on that. What did I do?"

"Well, you punched me." He rubbed his jaw and she could see a hint of a proud smile tugging at the corners of his mouth.

"Sorry."

"You move your hands a lot. It took me a while to figure out what you were trying to do." Liam reached for the sketchbook on the bedside table. "This is probably one of the most amazing things I've ever seen, and I've seen a lot."

He opened the book to a page filled with sketches of the same symbol. Several pages were filled with the drawings at different levels of completion. She didn't remember drawing them.

"I did this in my sleep?" She took the sketchbook from him and studied it carefully.

"It seemed like you were trying to write something so I gave you the sketchbook and a pencil. You immediately sat up and for the next few hours you drew these. You never spoke. You never opened your eyes. You continued to scream and thrash, but you never made an audible sound."

"What do you think it means?" Allie ran her hand across

the page of writhing snakes. Some were a figure eight, and some were circles, but they all clutched their tails in their mouths.

"It's an ancient symbol."

"I feel like I've seen this before," Allie said.

"These are two iterations of the ouroboros," Liam said. "Historically, the figure eight—or infinity—is exactly what it appears to be: a serpent devouring its own tail. It symbolizes the cycle of nature and the universe: creation from destruction, life from death. The snake eats its own tail to sustain its life in an eternal cycle of renewal. We are the only exception to that cycle. We can live forever, but we are still bound to nature because we are human. We may not die easily, but we still experience cycles of destruction and renewal just like all things of nature. This symbol began with us. It is one of the oldest symbols in the world—it is the crest of the Indriell Queens."

"What does that have to do with me?" She stood and paced to her closet for a sweater. She was cold, but more than anything she wanted to avoid any talk of Indriell.

"Everything."

"You know?" She whirled around to face him.

"Recently, yes. Gregg told me."

"It wasn't his secret to tell." Allie was furious. She should have been the one to tell her brother in her own time.

"Perhaps. But you are young and you need me. I am the only Immortal family you have and I needed to know. I also knew your parents. Your mother was an incredible woman, but I knew your father best. He mentored me a very long time ago. In a weird way, he was like a father to me too."

Allie closed her eyes. It took everything she had not to tell him her parents were alive. *Damn you, Navid. This secret is killing me.* She knew he wouldn't respond but it felt good saying it, knowing he would hear her. *I don't like secrets and lies. My whole life has been nothing but both and I'm sick of it!*

"So this symbol? What does it mean for me? Why am I drawing it in my sleep?"

"This is your family crest." He pointed to the large figure-eight symbol she'd drawn in intricate detail. "It represented the longevity of your line. During the days leading up to the Great War, many perversions of this symbol arose. Including the circular version. Its meaning has changed throughout the centuries. Some think the perfect 'O' ouroboros was a symbol of the Enlightened who brought about the war. Some see it as the 'undoing' of the Indriell line. Perhaps you are dreaming of it because you know who you are now and your gift is trying to show you how to learn more. Where to start."

"I don't want to learn more." Allie sat back on the bed beside him. "At least not yet. I haven't wrapped my brain around the idea that I'm a natural born, much less that my parents were so important."

"You take all the time you need, little one. And when you're ready to talk about it, I'm always here. Gregg will be home soon, but he's a bossy son of a bitch."

Allie laughed and felt the tension in her body slowly relax. "I love you, Liam." She rested her head against his shoulder. "I'm glad you're my big brother."

"Me too, little one. Go to sleep; we have a few more hours before school." He pulled the covers up over her.

"Hmmmm," Allie mumbled, her head nodding against him.

"I never realized I've been waiting my whole life for you, my little sister—my family. Not Gregg's or anyone else's. You and Kahlynn are my whole world now. Who knew I'd be such a softie for a couple of little girls."

Allie felt the rumble of his laughter as she fell into a peaceful sleep.

CHAPTER 14

"Hey, Allie. Come on in." Scott held the door open for her. She'd never been to the apartment Darius shared with Scott, aka Fitzie. It was a huge warehouse loft downtown, probably big enough for four or five roommates, but she imagined the top floor was probably outfitted for Darius's training.

"Hey, killer! Be down in a sec," Darius called from the upstairs.

"I'm pretty sure he was late for his own birth," Scott said as he led her into the gigantic living room.

"This place is gorgeous." Allie took in the view of the city from the floor-to-ceiling windows.

Aidan, this isn't a date. But can you—?

Make myself scarce? Yeah. I'm out with Naomi tonight anyway and I think she's going to break it off with me. I'd like to not have an audience for that. She's the 'dump them before they dump me' type and I haven't been around much lately. And she's—

He threw a brick wall up so fast, Allie had to shake her head from the impact.

Dude, what the hell was that?

Nothing.

What don't I know about Naomi?

You'll just get mad.

Tell me.

She's kinda into Liam now, he said in a rush.

What? No, not my brother. He can't possibly fall for that. You have to stop her.

How? I don't know if you've noticed, but Naomi does what Naomi wants. Nothing I say is going to change her mind.

Aidan....

Don't 'Aidan' me, Lex. I'm not getting involved. Liam's a big boy; he can do what he likes.

Sorry about the whole getting-dumped thing. I know you like her.

It's fine. We make better friends anyway. The chemistry's just off. She blames it on my feelings for you and she's probably right. She deserves better than that. So if Liam makes her happy, then I say she's long overdue for some happiness.

You're right. I just wish she'd find happiness somewhere else.

"Crap, Fitzie, I'm sorry." Allie shook off her spaced-out look and shot Scott an apologetic glance. "That was so rude." She and Aidan had gotten really bad about checking out of a conversation with those right in front of them.

"It's fascinating to watch you two communicate, but you have to be more careful. It's fine to drop all pretense with me, but you cannot do that in public."

"I know. We're working on it. We were so good at concealing it for so long, but once we didn't have to hide it anymore, we just developed some bad habits."

"You ready, Red?" Darius took the stairs two at a time on his way down.

"Yeah." Allie turned to greet him. Her heart doing that weird flippy thing it did when Darius was around.

"Try to remember to be alert, both of you?" Scott warned.

"I'll be in the area if you need me. And don't forget, Darius, if you run into anyone you know—"

"I know. I'm not Darius the cop, I'm his little brother, Dan, who looks an awful lot like him."

"Let's go, Dannie boy," Allie said playfully. She forgot the world would see him as an eighteen-year-old boy, and that helped her mindset tremendously. She was used to him blending in with the kids at school, but his age was a sensitive issue for her.

"Wait! Darius, show me how to do the thing with the map again?" Fitzie held out his iPhone like it was a bomb.

"Seriously, you haven't mastered this yet?" Darius took the phone from him and went through a painstakingly awkward lesson in navigating Google Maps.

"I just got used to texting and Darius decided it was time I upgraded to this century and get a smartphone. I think it was too soon," Scott said irritably. "I hate technology."

"You gotta get over that, bro. It's only going to get worse."

"I know, I know. That's what I get for keeping my head down for too long. The world doesn't stop turning and we can't stop moving with it. Night, kids. Have fun."

As they walked down the hill to the flats, Allie decided not to let the age thing be an issue tonight. They were just friends, and she intended to enjoy the evening.

Darius slipped his hand around hers and pulled her to a stop. His eyes seemed troubled.

"What's up, Dare?" her voice came out all weird and trembly and she had to resist the urge to roll her eyes at herself. Her reactions to his attention never seemed to match her emotions.

"I'd like to have a good time tonight and not let the age thing feel awkward."

"You sure you aren't a mind reader?" She grinned.

"What's little brother up to tonight?" He tapped her forehead and she knew that was what bothered him. She realized, possibly for the first time, how strange it must be to look into her eyes and know Aidan was present in there to a certain degree, like a third wheel.

"Getting dumped, actually. He's not here, Darius. We mutually decided on total privacy tonight."

"Can you do that now?" His eyes widened in surprise.

"It's not always easy, but we're getting better. I still feel him there, skating on the edge of my thoughts. I'd have to stop and focus on what he is thinking or doing. That's as private as it gets these days."

"Dumped, huh?" He grinned. "Bummer." He draped his arm around her and they ducked into the club.

It was a small dive bar that had a reputation for hosting some of the best indie bands. The lights were dim and a mellow bass beat filled the air.

"Grab a table, killer, I'll get drinks."

Allie slipped into a booth and Darius joined her, sliding in beside her. He set a cold beer in front of her. Underage drinking wasn't something the Immortal world frowned on. It would only affect her for a few minutes before her buzz would fade. Not like that night in Agra.... She'd never been so completely out of it like that.

"Definitely not a cop tonight?" She smiled.

"I made your ID; it's totally legal." He turned toward her and rested his arm on the booth behind her.

"Really? Like, legal, legal?"

"I have a gift with forgery. I make all our documents. When your identification becomes outdated, like your Social Security number, I'll create a new one for you."

"I've never asked—I didn't want to be rude, but I really have no idea what you can do."

"Well, I'm a homicide detective for a reason. My defining gifts actually teeter on the edge of clairvoyance. Nothing like you, of course. It only works with crimes. I can sense them happening all around me. And when I'm surveying a crime scene after something terrible has happened, I can just see it. My gift allows me to recreate what happened."

"Like a vision?" It would be really nice to talk to someone who could see the way she did.

"No, it's not that evolved. When I'm assessing a murder scene, and there's a blood spatter, for instance, I can see sort of a reanimation of that spatter—like a ghost image, which helps me replay the events in my mind. Most any forensic tech can do the same thing; I just get there faster and more accurately. I can also see what's missing, almost instantly. Where most investigators would study what is present in a crime scene, I see what isn't there, which is usually very important information."

"Like the murder weapon?" she asked.

"You don't find this gruesome?"

"Yeah, but it's fascinating too."

"Sometimes I can see the absence of the murder weapon as soon as I walk onto the scene. And if I'm really on fire, I can get a sense of where the murderer tossed it—even if it's nowhere near the scene. I call it my CSI sense."

"That's kinda awesome, Dare."

"Yeah, well ... taking a page out of Greyson's book, I owe you some long overdue transparency." He sighed, reaching for his beer.

"What's up?" She frowned.

"I'm very observant. I read people. Really, really well."

"You want to read me?" She sipped her warm beer and Darius signaled the waiter for another round.

"No way, Allie. Let's just say I can see things about people that they don't often see about themselves. It makes me a killer profiler, but not a very good friend."

"So you just know things about me just by looking at me?" She picked at her beer label, feeling a little uncomfortable.

"It's kinda like Greyson's gift, except I don't see anything about your power. But like him, I can't control what I see. I learned a long time ago it's best to keep it to myself. But I like my friends to be fully aware of what I can do."

"Thanks for the transparency." She drained the last of her drink and signaled for another.

"Listen, I'm always here if you need someone to talk to—but I know Aidan is that guy for you. Let me be the *friend* who reminds you to have fun and not take things too seriously. And right now, we have a concert to enjoy." He offered her a fist-bump. And just like that, the serious mood dissolved and they cheered with the crowd when the band took the stage.

The music was cool and bluesy and the indie band was one of her favorites. The vibrato of the bass guitar seemed richer and the vocals more mellow than she remembered from listening to them on her iPhone. Allie was drawn into the excitement of the crowd as the band played a full set of her favorite songs.

The slow, sultry beat of the music made her want to get up and dance. This was the first time in ages that she'd actually had fun. She'd needed this night out so badly, and now that she knew how strongly Darius could see, she had a whole new respect for him. If he could look at her and see the worst things about her—and still count her as a friend—then she could trust him with whatever knowledge his gift gave him. There was a weird flirty vibe between them, but at the same time there was an equal desire not to act on it. The result was a feeling of complete trust and a level of intimacy with zero expectations.

"You're a million miles away, Allie. What's up?" Darius asked after the last encore.

"Sorry, I guess I was just really into the music," she said breathlessly. Her eyes were bright and she felt energized as they pushed their way through the crowd to the exit.

The cool evening breeze lifted her hair and she danced a few steps ahead. "The acoustics were fantastic; it was like I couldn't even hear the crowd."

"Oh, that was me. I have this thing with sound too. There isn't much I can't hear, but I can also enhance sound or reduce it—make something soundproof. Screech like a siren. That sort of thing."

"Like my very own, smart-mouthed, blue-eyed surround sound system?"

"Come on, killer. We've got some time before the last ferry; let's go dancing."

"You sure you can handle it?"

"Aidan is not the only good dancer in this family."

"Bring it on, old man."

Rage consumed her ... unlike anything Allie had ever felt before.

The world was bathed in blood. Red, with smoldering fires and churning black smoke billowing in the distance, but Allie could only see the flames dancing before her eyes. She could only feel fury as her blood boiled in her veins.

An anguished shriek echoed in the darkness. She wasn't sure if the sound came from an injured animal or if it came from her.

"Allie!" Darius grabbed her arm and pulled her back onto

the sidewalk. "I generally prefer it when my friends stay in one piece."

"What?" Allie gave him a blank look.

"You just walked out into traffic, sweetheart. What's going on?" They stepped into the shadows of the parking garage near his building. "Your eyes are practically smoldering. What has you so angry?"

"Nothing. It was nothing. Just a vision."

"What did you see?"

"Fire. Smoke." She shrugged. "Nothing that makes any sense."

"You're working with Liam and Emma on your dreams and visions, right?"

"Every day. But the things I see, it's just junk. It doesn't mean anything."

"That anger you feel. That means something, killer. You need to deal with it before it eats you alive."

"Are you serious? You want to risk Gregg's wrath—not to mention Naeemah's—and our eternal freedom to sneak off to some kind of Immortal nightclub?" Allie flopped onto the sofa beside Aidan, casting a wary glance at the others. They were gathered in his office after training. It was one of those rare nights when they were all up late together.

"When you put it like that it sounds stupid," Aidan said. "It is stupid." *Especially for us*, he added, "but we have to go."

"When you have a big brother who can track you like a tagged seal, sneaking out loses its appeal."

"We need to do this, Allie," Sasha said, surprising her.

"You're on board with this?" She didn't buy it. Sasha wasn't interested in much of anything anymore. Allie wanted to agree, just because it was so good to see her friend interested in something—anything.

"What aren't you guys telling me?"

"It's not exactly ... safe," Graham said as he straddled the sofa arm beside her. "But there is a small chance we could find a new lead on Quinn at this place."

"You should have led with that. Let's do it." She was on board with anything that might help him, even if it was a long shot. "What do we need to know about this place? Why is it dangerous?"

"The Senate doesn't approve," Aidan said. "So the club owners keep the location constantly moving, like a rave, but it's more than just a party. But the Senate can never seem to catch them before they move on. And for the first time ever, it will be right here in Cleveland. Dad knows about it, but the adults can't get in."

"And why do we think we could get a lead on Quinn there?"

Graham whipped out a black notebook from his back pocket. She recognized it as the journal he kept for all his techie ideas and sketches. As he flipped through the pages covered in notes about his brother's situation, Allie realized how much this had affected him. Graham was lost without his big brother, but he wasn't just sitting around doing nothing about it.

"So we know he's with a faction of the Coalition based in Atlanta," he continued. "But I overheard Dad saying they are pretty sure the same people also run the club. I've done some research on them but it's been one dead end after another. They hide everything behind some fake company called Soma so they appear to be completely above board, but they're shady as shit. They only hire the best young Immortals they can find and then it's like they brainwash them, pulling them away from their families until they have nothing left but Soma. We need to get into this club and we need to dig until we find something. We have to do it. The adults would never get past the front door."

"And why is that? Why couldn't Imogen and Lucien go?"

"No one Proven can get in. It's only open to the youngest generations," Aidan said.

"Then we have to go," Allie said. "Just to see what we happen to see, right? But what about Chloe?"

"Chloe will be fine." Chloe rolled her eyes. "My gift sucks big, fat—"

"Chloe!" Aidan laughed at the look of disgust on her face.

"Well, it sucks." She scowled. "But it only sucks around mortals. It's not so bad with everyone else."

Chloe's defining gift had manifested quickly after her Awakening. She could see the path of least resistance—meaning she could see the choices those around her struggled to make, and she could sometimes tell which choice would result in the best outcome, but she'd suffered some minor setbacks recently.

"It's still not any better?" Allie asked, feeling bad about how out of touch she was with what her friends were going through.

"Well, imagine if you were telepathic with *everyone*." Chloe shrugged. "I can't hear distinct voices or anything, but everywhere I turn, I'm faced with someone struggling with a decision. I can hear the whispers of their indecision—it's like really loud white noise. I can't turn it off or ignore it. So the quick fix has been using my headphones to block the constant noise with music. That helps give me a reprieve between classes so I can get through a few hours of school. But I don't need the headphones when I'm with you guys. I promise, I will not be a liability. We all need this opportunity to contribute. Quinn is my nephew and I *hate* sitting around doing nothing when he's out there suffering somewhere. We're doing this and I am going to be there. Are we all clear on that?" She gave them all a glare.

"She's right. Auntie Chloe can handle herself just fine." Graham gave her a wink.

"So what are we going to do when we get caught?" Allie asked. "You know it's going to happen. Gregg and Naeemah are the freaking governor and you know as well as I do, they're going to expect us to do exactly what we're talking about. So if we're doing this, we have to make it worth the trouble. We need a plan."

"We have to be very careful not to draw too much attention to ourselves," Aidan said. "Amrita is a huge draw for our generation so we need to blend in with the crowd as best we can."

"Amrita? What is that, something clever and ancient?" Allie tried to place the language.

"It means Immortality in Sanskrit," Chloe said, ever the walking encyclopedia.

"What's the draw? It can't be just a party. What makes it worth the risk? I mean, even for people who want to go for fun ... it still has to be dangerous for a bunch of Immortal kids to come together like that."

"It's nothing, really. It's just an excuse to have a good time." Aidan gave her a funny look and she knew he was lying. Or at least not telling her the whole truth.

"What aren't you telling me?" She shot him a glare. *You're blocking me. You never block me.*

"It's not a party, Allie." Graham said. "Well, it's not *just* a party."

"What did I say?" Aidan punched Graham's shoulder.

"Whatever, your plan to spring it on her in the car on the way there was a terrible idea. We're trying to fool a clairvoyant, dude. It's clearly not working."

"What am I missing?" Allie frowned. "Why does this club have you all freaked out?" She directed her questions at Sasha. She understood why Sasha was so eager to go, but she had a really bad feeling about this place.

"It's totally stupid of us to even consider it," Sasha said. "It's a dangerous place with sketchy connections. There will be tons of kids there, just looking to have fun, but it's the kind of place where anonymity is crucial and information can be discovered if you pay attention."

"I'm fine with all of that," Allie said. "I'm in, but let's get back to the 'springing it on Allie' part."

"I knew you would be down with anything to help Quinn," Graham said. "But—"

"Wait for it," Aidan said.

"It's not just a party ... it's a freakin' fight, isn't it?" Allie said. "A stupid, let's-try-to-kill-each-other-for-entertainment-fight?"

"There it is," Aidan said dryly. "Yes, Lex, Amrita isn't just a dance club. There will be games too, which is why I wanted to wait to tell you because I knew you would handle it better if you didn't have time to overthink it."

"Games? Like on the island?"

"Not really," Graham said. "At Amrita, it's more about fun —of the dangerous, stupid sort—and less about learning. Think paintball or laser tag, but our version is a little more—"

"Violent? Scary? Inappropriate?" Allie supplied.

"Exactly."

"Gregg's going to kill us. And then he's going to enjoy watching us slowly heal as he lectures us, knowing we can't escape."

"Probably," Sasha said. "But these people have Quinn. I don't care what happens to me."

"You're right." Allie nodded. "Tell me about the fights."

"Right. The fights will start at sundown and last through the night. They're super-competitive, arena-style fights," Graham began. "There will be three rounds and everyone there has to compete at least once. Anything goes—hand-to-hand combat, weapons, and gifts are all allowed. Then the final competition will be a melee-style fight among the best competitors, which none of us need to aspire to. The last one standing is declared the winner. And then there's a big party after."

"All right." Allie gave a determined nod. She didn't mind the fighting part so much anymore. She'd finally learned to enjoy the sport of it, but she still had issues with the hurting-people-on-purpose part.

We have to try, Lex.

I know. And I'm all in. I just don't have the warm fuzzies about this place.

"We just need to figure out how to pull this off without getting caught until after. When is this thing?" Allie asked.

"We don't know the dates yet, but it will be soon."

"And about the not-getting-caught part?" Allie asked. "They'll be expecting us to go."

"I don't think they even realize we know about it," Graham said.

"How *do* we know about it?"

"Amrita has ways of getting the word out to the Unproven crowd. As long as we can get in before the parents figure out what we're up to, then we're good. Once we're in, they can't crash the party. Once we're in, we're there for the duration. You don't get to leave Amrita early."

"So we'll deal with the consequences after, but by then, hopefully we'll have some news that can help Quinn."

"Exactly," Sasha said.

"All right. I guess we're doing this, then," Allie said nervously.

"Not a word of this to Darius." Aidan shot Allie a glare.

"Not a word about what to whom?"

They all jumped at the sound of Darius's voice echoing down the hall. Allie turned to see him at the door a moment later.

"Sorry, there isn't much I can't hear, guys. Now what's this ridiculous idea about sneaking off to Amrita?" He waggled his eyebrows devilishly as he flopped onto the sofa beside Allie.

"How do you know about it?" she asked.

"You forget, I'm Unproven too, killer. I get the emails."

"Darius," Aidan said. "Just forget whatever you heard."

"You taking a page out of my book, little bro? Naomi and I took Erin and Dean there when it first came to the U.S.—but think again. Gregg will flip his biscuits if he finds out you guys even know about Amrita."

"Come on, Darius!" Chloe begged. "You know we're the only ones who can get in without causing suspicion."

"You guys might feel confident risking the wrath of Gregg and Naeemah, but that situation looks a lot different this side of eighteen. Dad will just kill me if he finds out I let you go, but mom will give me the 'I'm-so-disappointed-in-you-Darius' look. She's too good at making her momma's boys feel like total a-holes when we've screwed up. Sorry, guys. It's not happening."

"Dare?" Allie said. "It's not just about Amrita. Please, just look the other way."

"Oh no, put those green eyes away. I can't let you do this. I know you think you're going to get a lead on Quinn. But that's why I'm going. Alone."

"Well ... what if you come with us? You know, like for protection. A chaperone."

"Lex, be serious," Aidan said. "He's not coming."

"I *am* going," Darius said. "Alone. And if I see you guys there, I'm bringing you right back home and then no one will get the chance to do any digging."

"I'm totally serious. Darius, six pairs of eyes and ears will be so much better," Allie said.

"And with your cop stink, you aren't going to find out anything, anyway," Aidan added.

"Please, Darius?" Sasha said softly. "I need to do this. I

need to do *something* before I lose my mind. Once we're in, Dad can't come barreling in after us. We'll deal with the consequences after, but it'll be worth it if we can find a new lead on these Soma people."

"Oh, blue eyes. Not you too?" Darius sighed.

"Please, Darius?" Chloe added softly.

"Fine. I'm a sucker for the begging. I'll go with you on one very important condition."

"Sure," Allie agreed.

"You all have to listen to me. That includes you too, little brother." He glared at Aidan. "We are going there to listen and observe. None of you will be getting in over your heads. If you see anything suspicious, you come to me and I will handle it. Are we clear?"

"Yes, yes. Thank you!" Sasha readily agreed.

"Are we clear, Aidan?" Darius asked again. "If I'm going to be the pseudo-adult in this situation, I need to know you will listen to me. I'm not trying to take over, but I've been to Amrita before and I know how crazy it can get. You think it's just all about fun and goofing off, but people take this seriously and a lot of shady shit goes on there. You gotta work with me on this, bro."

"Fine."

"Guys, don't make me live to regret this."

Allie tossed and turned in a fitful sleep. Her nose burned from the acrid smell of smoke, and the heat of the fires had her face flushed hot and her pulse racing. Ever since Liam had started working with her on her dreams, she dreamed often of fire and rage—of a bloody world filled with darkness and fear, and so much anger. But it never coalesced into anything she could understand. The terror continued to plague her with no end in sight. But this dream was different. She could hear screams echoing in the forest, but she couldn't seem to find the source.

"Mom!" The terrified shriek filled the night.

"Chloe?" Allie ran through the hazy forest until she stumbled onto an empty path. Her heart nearly beat out of her chest with the intensity of her fear. She couldn't see anything that truly frightened her, but she could sense the chaos happening all around her.

"Chloe, you shouldn't be here," Jin cried, his voice anguished. "Go now; we cannot stay with you." The voices came from a great distance, but Allie could hear their distress. Ming Lao's wails chilled her to the bone. Something was wrong. Something unnatural.

Everywhere she turned, raging fire blocked her path and Allie grew angrier and more frightened with every step—not for herself, but for Chloe's family.

"Chloe!" Ming Lao screamed.

Allie could sense their struggle, but she couldn't see it. She could hear Chloe's tortured cries and the clash of weapons as Jin and Ming fought to protect themselves and their daughter. From what, Allie couldn't see.

"Allie? Please help them," Chloe sobbed, appearing just ahead of her along the dark path. Her face was streaked with soot and tears, but it was as if Chloe was trapped in some other world where she could see the things Allie couldn't. Just as quickly as she'd appeared, she vanished.

Allie wandered along the forest path until she caught the scent of apples and found herself alone in an orchard. She searched through the rows of trees until she found Chloe again, standing at the edge of the forest. Allie took a step closer, but Chloe pointed behind her and she whirled to see the fires bearing down upon them.

"We have to save them, Allie. Both of them."

The fire blazed hot, blistering Allie's skin, and the smoke suffocated her. But the rage filled her, overwhelming her fear. With an otherworldly shriek, Allie threw her head back and her screams echoed in the darkness as she lost her battle with the rage boiling inside of her.

She blacked out when the chaos won and her dreams pulled her in another direction. Soon she bobbed among the lazy waves of the lake marshes, drifting in the small boat as the snakes teemed in the waters around her. This time she didn't panic. She had no idea what she was supposed to discern from the things she saw, but she refused to be pulled under again. She would not be undone.

She concentrated and a paddle appeared in the boat. Allie made her way toward the shore. The snakes continued to writhe, twisting around each other and biting themselves. She ignored them, setting her sights on the horizon in the distance as she paddled into the deeper waters.

"The snakes are just a symbol. They can't hurt me now."

Allie choked on the smoke filling her lungs. Arms and legs flailing, she landed with a thud on her bedroom floor, a tangled mass of hair and sheets and ... blood.

"You do that a lot," Liam said.

"What, fall out of bed?" Allie grimaced as she wiped her bloody hands on the sheets. They had only been working together for a short time, but she'd made little to no progress, still struggling with the bizarre nightmares that didn't make any sense.

"You clench your fists till your nails puncture your skin. I've tried to make you stop, but you're damned strong. I'm going to start making you sleep with stress balls taped to your hands if you don't stop it."

"Har, har, mister funny man." Her legs shook beneath her as she stood and she dropped to the bed with a groan. Nothing was worse than waking up feeling like you hadn't slept in a month.

"You overslept. I tried to wake you. Better get moving if you don't want to be late for school."

"Maybe I'll skip."

"Maybe I'll give you detention."

"Maybe I'll be late?" She gave him her most pitiful look.

"Maybe I'll look the other way." Liam winked. "See you in class, little one." He turned to go and halted at the door. "It may not seem like it now, but you are making progress."

Chapter 16

"Hey, sweetheart, what can I help you with?"

Allie smiled at the gruff old police officer as she entered the precinct. She was looking for Darius. After a few days of dealing with a new gift that was driving her crazy, she realized Darius could probably help her. And if he couldn't, it was going to officially drive her over the edge.

"I'm looking for, er ... Detective McBrien?" She'd just finished training for the day and since Emma hadn't been much help, she came looking for Darius. Emma's advice was to suck it up and deal with it as part of her clairvoyance, but there had to be something more she could do.

"Sure thing. You his kid sister or something?"

"Er ... something like that."

"Straight back to the left. You should find him at his desk—if he hasn't eaten it," he added dryly.

Allie made her way to the back of the office, watching Darius as she approached. He was yelling at someone on the phone. He'd sensed her, but was preoccupied with his work.

"Allie." He sighed, running his hands through his hair in frustration. "You okay, sweetheart?"

"Just hoping to talk. I suppose I should have called first."

He was different here. This was not Dare. This was Detective McBrien, the youngest on homicide in the whole CPD.

"Give me five minutes? I was just going out to find some decent coffee and dinner."

"Sure."

She watched him make a few more phone calls and bark out orders to the sergeant at the front desk.

"Let's go, killer." He was gruff and distant as he hung up the phone. She couldn't tell if he was annoyed with her for just showing up.

"Are you sure? It can wait."

"Get me out of here, Red. I'm seriously cranky, in need of some food and caffeine. And despite my bad manners, I'm very happy to see you." He gave her a smile.

"Sergeant, be back in an hour; taking my little cousin out for dinner." Darius shrugged into his jacket and motioned for her to follow.

She'd never felt like such a kid before in her life.

"You coming?" He winked and she got a glimpse of the Darius she knew.

"Right behind you, Dare." She followed him out of the precinct.

As they walked along the busy sidewalk she saw him relax. The transformation was extremely odd. One minute he was like a stranger. Detective McBrien, someone his colleagues respected and probably feared more than just a little. Then he was her good buddy, Dare, completely at ease with her as he always was. Giving her the smile that made her heart do those annoying somersaults in her chest.

"Sorry about the 'little cousin' thing. I had to come up with something to make me not look like a total perv. I'm two very different people and it's not often my two lives collide."

"I should have called."

"You can come visit me anytime you like. I just worry that seeing me like that might confuse you ... and my coworkers."

"There's not much about you that isn't confusing, Dare."

"I could say the same for you," he muttered. "But I love my job. It's the only place I get to be an adult, where people actually take me seriously. But I also love going back to school with you guys. It gives me a chance to really be myself in a way I haven't been able to do in a really long time."

"Let's get you some food. And then I'm going to need your help."

"Bad pizza okay?"

"I love bad pizza—just don't tell Naeemah I'm about to eat my weight in cheese."

"What diet? I don't know anything about a diet." He led her around the street corner to a dive pizzeria he claimed had the best bad pizza in the city.

Allie slid into the thread-worn booth, her stomach growling in anticipation of something delicious for a change.

"What can I get you?" the waitress asked.

"White pizza with extra cheese, a side of chicken wings, and a giant Coke," Allie said.

"We're out of the Caesar salad, but I can get you the antipasto; it's really good if you're in the mood for salad. We have bottled water and hot tea to drink." The girl gave her a blank stare.

"No, I want *pizza.*" Allie nearly cried. Naeemah had hit just about every restaurant in the city. Every time she ordered a burger and fries, she got broth soup and a club sandwich on wheat with no mayo and turkey bacon. If she ordered pizza, she got salad. Allie banged her head on the table in frustration. "If she brings me salad, I refuse to eat it."

"I'll have a white pizza and a double-pepperoni pizza,

breadsticks, a basket of wings, and two large Cokes," Darius ordered for them.

"Thank you," Allie muttered.

"So how do you need my help?" Darius asked.

"I've got something emerging, some sort of extension of my clairvoyance. And it's driving me insane."

"Not that I'm disappointed, but why did you come to me?"

"It reminds me of your gift. The way you said you can just see what you see about people with little control."

"How's it manifesting for you?"

"It's like I can see a person's true nature. Like I can ... weigh their character."

"So you can tell the good guys from the bad guys?"

"It's just there. All of a sudden. Like our waitress, she's an absolute angel—besides the fact that she wants to bring me rabbit food. She's kindhearted, would give a total stranger her last dollar. But that guy over there—he's selfish, greedy, and lazy. And I just see it, plain as day. Like he has a neon sign flashing 'douche-nugget' over his head."

"Want a job? I could park you in front of the precinct and you could just arrest all the bad guys. Make my job easier. I could sit at my desk, play a video game. Take a nap."

"How do you do it, Dare? You observe people so easily. You see and you know so much about the people you interact with. How do you ignore it when it's there *all* the time? Can you turn it off?"

"Nope. It's one reason why I do what I do. I meet someone like Mr. Black Soul over there—which BTWs, I agree with your assessment. He's a criminal just waiting for his next golden opportunity. So I'll keep my eye on him and those like him, and when I can catch them in the act, I do."

"Here we are," the waitress said, placing all the real food in front of Darius and a sad little salad and a cup of water in front of Allie.

"Um, thanks," Allie muttered, resisting the urge to throw a full-on hissy fit.

"Can I get you anything else?"

"I think we're good," Darius said, sliding one of his Cokes toward Allie.

As soon as the waitress turned her back, Allie went for the white pizza.

"Cheese, where have you been, my friend?" She nearly wept at the delicious tangy taste of garlic and parmesan.

"Make sure you save room for that salad," Darius said.

"Shut it. Wait, can I try your wings?"

"Go for it."

Allie managed to get back to the conversation after her second slice.

"So what do I do with this?" She took a giant gulp of her Coke.

"You want the honest truth?"

"That's why I came to you."

"Nothing. You do nothing."

"How can that be the best use of this ... horrible 'gift'?"

"Because you are seventeen years old with about a million lifetimes ahead of you. Don't stress about this gift, Allie. You can be the adult who polices the world someday, but right now, you do nothing. You've got responsibilities to yourself. We don't get much of a childhood. Enjoy what little normal life you've got while you can. Take stock of what you see, learn how to use it in every possible way, don't suppress it, and maybe someday you can put it to good use, but not now. It's not your responsibility."

"Not quite what I expected from you." She smiled.

"I can be responsible from time to time. I could just see it.

Our very own little redheaded vigilante roaming the streets. Something tells me I'd have to arrest you."

"Thanks, Darius. I can always count on you to make me laugh."

"I'm not going to lie, I'm totally going to use you. I just have to figure out how to get you a badge. You could just come along with me, tell me who's got the guilty soul."

"Well, something tells me you're pretty good at figuring that out all by yourself." Allie picked at the last piece of pepperoni, feeling only a little queasy from all the greasy food. She'd probably pay for it later, but it was worth it.

"Come on." She slid out of the booth with a groan. "We need to find you some decent coffee. I need to send you back to adulting in a better mood. Your poor coworkers will thank me for it later."

"Ahh, they know how to put up with me."

"You should remember they're mortal and can't keep up the pace you set."

"I do suck at remembering that." He frowned.

"Most of you do." It was weird how much she still identified as a mortal, but she was completely in this life now. The Immortal world was Allie's domain, but she still felt trapped in the middle somewhere.

As she walked back to her car, Allie's heart raced. She could feel her face flush as visions whirled through her mind. She could hear the clack of her boot heels on the asphalt as she crossed the parking lot, but in her mind, she wandered through the orchard again.

A warm, familiar hand encircled hers, grounding her in the

midst of uncertainty. She was drawn to him in such a strange way.

Focus on the important details and discard the rest....

The world went green all around them. A warning for her to pay attention. But this was so different from anything she'd ever experienced before. This wasn't a nightmare. It wasn't confusing. It was a simple happy moment with a guy she cared for deeply. This felt so much like her clairvoyant dreams, but she was too happy. She rarely saw happy things in her visions. It made her suspicious.

She couldn't see his face, but she knew he was one of the most important people in her life.

The sparkle of his midnight blue eyes sent her heart hammering in her chest as he turned to face her.

"Darius?" That couldn't be right.

CHAPTER 17

"All right, Red! Let's get started!" Gregg sauntered into his office like it was any other day. Like it hadn't been months since she'd last seen or spoken to him.

"Really? That's how you want to play this?" She scowled up at him from her perch on the couch.

"Probably not." He took a seat opposite her and gave her a rueful smile. It was good to see him again but she couldn't decide if she wanted to throat-punch him or hug him.

"You drop a bomb like *that* and then you leave? For months?" She tried to keep the venom out of her voice, but his leaving had hurt.

"I'm sorry for that. My attention was needed elsewhere, but you've never been far from my thoughts these last months, sweetheart. I just figured you could use a little time to yourself."

"We need to work on your definition of 'a little time.'" She picked at a paint stain on her jeans. "A little time is a week or two. It's been five months, Gregg. Five months with that information rolling around in my head and no one to talk to about it."

"I assumed you would have confided in Aidan by now."

"I did ... recently."

"I know you're angry—"

"Angry? Anger doesn't even begin to describe what I'm feeling."

"Aye. You're so much like your mother. I should have known this would eat you alive."

"Kassandre was a stranger who gave me away. Her lineage means nothing to me." Allie furiously scraped at the paint on her jeans, refusing to look at Gregg for fear of bursting into tears. She'd missed him more than she realized.

"She gave you up to protect you, Allie."

"Hooking up with my birth mom a thousand years ago doesn't make you an expert on why she made the choices she did." Allie shot to her feet to pace the office. She felt like throwing things. She was so angry. The constant churning rage, boiling just below the surface—it wasn't her. Or it wasn't the person she used to be. She could feel how closely linked her anger was with her power and she feared that if she didn't conquer her anger issues, she would lose control of her power.

Gregg's jaw clenched irritably at her accusation. "Kassandre and Ashar meant the world to me. You have no idea how deeply I mourned them when they died. A piece of me died with them, Allie. They may be gone, but I am the closest link you will ever have to them. Do not disrespect their memory or their sacrifices. Not in my presence."

Allie heard the anger in his voice, the regret and sorrow. But she saw something else in his eyes. He had secrets. He probably knew more than he was willing to tell her right now. She wondered briefly if he knew they were alive. She was sick of all the lying and secrets. *Can't anyone in my life just tell me the truth? Does it always have to be a game of who knows what?*

"When did they bond as Complements?" She didn't know anything about her parents but she didn't want to talk about

Indriell, the prophecy, or anything about the future her parents saw for her.

"I don't know when Kassandre finally recognized Ashar as her Complement. It wasn't a blinding epiphany for her. It came upon her slowly, as the Complement bond often does." Gregg eased back into his leather chair as if he sensed Allie's need to understand who her parents were before she could face any of the other stuff.

"I guess I still thought it was an instant recognition. Like once she laid eyes on Ashar, at a time when she was open to the possibility of the bond, it just happened?"

"You are confusing it with the family bond. You've experienced that with Liam. But the Complement bond is different because it requires a choice to solidify the connection, and that takes time."

"A choice? I never realized that."

"I don't think you are ready to see my memories of your parents, but I'd like to show you how Naeemah and I finally found each other."

"I'd like that." Allie was relieved for the chance to talk about something else.

"Sit back and relax and let's see what we see," Gregg said.

Allie settled in for a trip through Gregg's memories.

"I lived without Naeemah for one thousand nine hundred and thirty-seven years," he began softly. "Much of my early life was spent as a soldier fighting in one campaign or another, but later when the world began to change, I found myself adapting with it. So many Immortals failed to keep up with the rapid progress mortals began to make in the sixteenth and seventeenth centuries. I embraced the Industrial Revolution when many of my kind clung to the past. For a long time I lived the life of a lonely nobleman. I educated myself, looked to the future, and made a fortune that has kept this family worry-free for generations. But I longed for Naeemah like I never had before. I obsessed about her day and night and drifted away from my family."

Listening to the soothing sound of his voice, Allie closed her eyes and waited for the sensation of falling into his memories.

The cool mist tickled her skin first and then she saw the dense fog of London in the late eighteenth century. She stood before a gated mansion on a busy street and realized this was the wealthy Londoner's version of a townhouse. Allie's head was full of her idealistic view of Victorian London so she wasn't prepared for the filth and the stench of the reality. London was a city that had seen rapid growth during the early years of the Industrial Revolution, but there was still a hint of the ancient past. She watched as Gregg ventured out the front door of his townhouse and down the walkway to the street where she waited. He was dressed to perfection and his wealth was apparent, but the poverty of the London streets lurked in every corner.

By the look on his face and the manner of his dress, Allie assumed Gregg was on his way to a funeral. She was quite surprised to arrive with him at an elaborate mansion with a party in full swing.

"You are late, sir." Allie turned at the accusation to find a beautiful woman waiting for Gregg to join the festivities in the ballroom.

"My apologies, Georgina," Gregg said graciously. "I was unexpectedly delayed."

Allie sensed the lie. Gregg wanted to be anywhere but at the mansion of Georgiana Cavendish, Duchess of Devonshire. She was the most fashionable woman of London and if Naeemah were a member of the *ton*, it was likely she would be drawn to Georgina's balls. That was the only reason Gregg was in attendance tonight. He had no intention of staying long—only long enough to pay a visit to the Immortal ladies to see if any of them were the one he sought. More than a century had passed since he'd last seen Naeemah in Nepal, just before she disappeared. He was getting desperate in his attempts to find her, but he knew she was a regal woman of great fortune. He needed only to search the cream of the crop and he would find her ... eventually.

"You owe me a card game, Greggory McBrien," Georgina said in her flirtatious manner.

"You've lost enough of your husband's money to me, Your Grace; give the poor man a respite from your expensive pastimes."

"Nonsense. I always win."

Gregg left the duchess to her admirers and made his way around the room, nodding at those he recognized. After taking a champagne flute from a passing waiter, he sat sulking in a corner, giving surly looks to any mortal woman who might have it in her head to dance with him.

Allie saw her first as she entered the ballroom behind him. Naeemah was breathtaking in her simple gown among all the overdressed women trying to outdo each other. The peach silk made her copper skin glow. Her hair was styled fashionably, but not ostentatiously. She was regal without even trying. She greeted Georgina warmly and followed her into the salon to greet the rest of the *ton*.

Allie watched Gregg, waiting for him to sense her. The look on his face went from blank and bored to complete awe in the span of a heartbeat. He stood, scanning the room for her, prepared to cause a scene if she should evade him again as she had in Nepal. He caught a glimpse of her as she slipped away, heading for the ladies' parlor upstairs.

Gregg crossed the room, keeping his distance as he

followed her down a long corridor. Allie saw the way he was shaking, completely terrified and uncertain how to proceed—completely un-Gregg-like.

Naeemah finally sensed him and halted on the stairs. She felt the intensity of his lifeline and her shoulders tensed as she reached for the weapon concealed at her hip. As she turned and laid eyes on her Complement for the first time, she swayed on her feet as the realization came to her.

The light in Naeemah's blue eyes glowed golden and the hall blazed with heat and light.

"My God, is it really you?" she whispered uncertainly.

Gregg opened his mouth to speak, but the ancient Scott couldn't form any words. He took a step forward and the two were in each other's arms.

Allie glanced away; she didn't want to spy on their special moment. She'd seen enough to know that they'd recognized each other and they were thrilled to finally meet, but they had not yet bonded.

The hall whirled around her like a kaleidoscope of colors and Allie watched the days and months following as the couple took the time to get to know each other. It was good to see them so happy and content.

"I'm so sorry, Naeemah," Gregg said.

Allie found herself in a walled garden, watching the two sitting on a bench, enjoying a private moment together.

"It is not your fault, Greggory McBrien," Naeemah said as she squished his cheeks together playfully. "You're just a stubborn old man, that's all."

"Aye, I'm old, love." He smiled as he took her hands in his. "I want to do this. I want to solidify our bond right now, but there is something in me that can't seem to let go."

"Don't you dare do it now! I want our dear friends to stand

as witnesses and protect us when we are vulnerable. Ming Lao and Jin Jing will be here soon enough."

"To think of all the years we've each known them, and neither one of them ever thought to introduce us?" Gregg's face was serious and grim but Allie could see he enjoyed teasing the woman who would be his wife. "It's not that I'm afraid to die with you, Nae—"

"Death is a foreign enough concept to me and I'm one thousand six hundred and seventy-seven years *younger* than you."

"You didn't have to do the math. I know I'm old. I'll get there; I guess I just need more time than I want to take."

"We have the rest of our lives together, Greggory. I know your hesitation has nothing to do with how you feel for me. The possibility of death is nothing to take lightly—and you aren't the only one struggling with it. We've each lived our lives as an 'I.' To become a 'we' is not easily done on a whim. Our power is the only protection we've ever had. It is no small thing to relinquish control, after all we have been through."

Allie's vision grew dark until tiny pinpricks of light shone overhead. It was night and the moon was bright. She was still in the garden, but others were present. Ming Lao stood behind Naeemah and Jin Jing behind Gregg. They were fully armed and ready to protect the vulnerable couple.

"We will be here as long as it takes, my friend." Jin nodded to Gregg.

"Join hands and breathe deeply to relax your hold on your power," Ming said. "It takes as long as it takes, so just let it happen and do not worry about us. We have been where you now stand. We understand the task before you is not an easy one."

Allie watched for hours as Naeemah and Gregg joined hands and waited—for what she wasn't certain. The moon gave way to the sun and the sun took its slow journey across the sky until the moon rose high again. Still they stood, together, staring into each other's eyes.

Finally, she saw a glimmer of their power, stirring within their eyes. Gregg pressed Naeemah's hand against his chest and whispered, "My power is yours for as long as we walk this earth together."

Naeemah pressed his hand over her heart and murmured the same oath.

A light as bright as the moon radiated around them, caging them in, with Ming and Jin standing guard outside.

Allie saw why it took them so long to perform this ritual. They were each surrendering the control of their power to the other. The level of trust that would take was astounding. Allie couldn't imagine the effort it would take to accomplish such a thing after a lifetime of maintaining iron control.

The force of Gregg's power filled Naeemah and she clutched his hand tightly in her free hand. The circle was complete when Naeemah's power filled Gregg and they released control to the other, allowing their Complement to safeguard their power during the ritual. They stood inside the cage of light created by their mutual power, completely separate from the world around them. They were more vulnerable at this moment than they had ever been or ever would be. Ming and Jin's protection wasn't just a traditional part of the ceremony. It was necessary.

As their power mingled, it burst from the circle around them and arced high up into the sky. As the light dissipated, Naeemah and Gregg clung to each other, completely spent. But they were bonded now. Together they were a single entity. Neither was the same person who had entered the garden before the ritual.

Allie blinked at the lights overhead, and a sadness washed over her to leave such a beautiful sight behind.

"That was nothing like I thought," Allie finally said. "That was an intensely personal thing you just shared with me."

"Aye. I've never shown that memory to anyone."

"Why did you share it with me?"

"You've struggled so hard to understand the bond and you're not fond of talking about it. You haven't grown up in our world. Unless you happened to stand witness to a ritual in the near future, you would continue struggling to understand it. You needed to see it and I'm happy to be the one to show you."

"Thank you, Gregg. You know I love you both so much, right?"

"Aye, we know, sweetheart. And we love you too—as much as any daughter we could have."

"I'm sorry for snarling at you earlier."

"You have your mother's she-devil tongue. It's like music to my ears."

Allie sat in her armchair by the balcony later that night reading a book on the history of the Immortal Senate. As she read, her mind wandered. She felt the spiraling plunge of despair she was learning to associate with her worst nightmares and an overwhelming sadness filled her heart. The vision caught her by surprise as her foot fell against the soft, grass-covered path she traveled almost every night she slept now. She was back in the forest, near the orchard. She heard the rustle of light footsteps and turned to see Sasha along the path ahead of her. Sasha turned and beckoned her to follow.

"This is new," she murmured into the early morning fog. Her waking visions were never this clear. This was more like her dreams. Yet she was still aware of the armchair beneath her and the heavy book in her lap. Lately she dreamed of this place a lot, but she was always alone. Or she followed the random shadows and ran from the fires, haunted by screams of terror as she choked on the billowing black smoke. It was her constant companion now. But every time, the dream got a little less scary and a little more boring as the fires grew farther away.

"We have to find him, Allie," Sasha whispered, waving her forward.

"That's definitely new." Allie followed her friend, once again, not at all sure what her gift was trying to tell her.

"Hurry," Sasha demanded. "Before we're too late."

Allie picked up her pace to catch up. She matched her two strides against Sasha's one.

"Er ... what are we doing, Sash?"

"We have to find him," Sasha replied. Allie didn't think her friend was even aware of her presence at all.

"Okay, where should we look?" Allie asked, not sure if she wanted this creepy ghost-Sasha to answer her.

"Along the hillside just before dawn. We have to hurry."

"What hillside?"

"Near the gates. Come, we don't have much time."

"Gates? I don't remember any gates and I've been all over this place."

Sasha whirled on her, marching toward her with fire in her eyes. "Explore everything. Do you hear me? Everything!"

"Yes ma'am." Allie took a step back in alarm.

"There is much more to this place. You have to study it, Allie. Now hurry."

Allie crept along the winding path behind Sasha. They traveled farther than she ever had before until they stepped onto a paved driveway, sweeping across the rolling grassy hills. She could feel Sasha's urgency. The two walked quickly through the damp grass to the base of a nearby hill where tall iron gates stood at the crest of the driveway.

Sasha stopped, crouching low among the dense laurel trees.

"See? Just there." She pointed across the hill. "No, not there by the gate; ignore the gates. Just there on the opposite side of the lawn near the low-hanging tree limbs. You see him?"

"Quinn?" Allie shot up from her crouched position. "He's here? What does it mean?" Allie watched the shadowed figure in the darkness. She couldn't make out if it really was Quinn.

"It's him. You see him?"

"Yeah, Sash, I see him. What does it mean?"

"He has to see me. He has to know he can come back."

Allie felt the heartbreak then. The torment Sasha felt every single day that Quinn was gone. Every single day that she blamed herself for all that had happened to him. The enormity of her friend's pain hit her like it was her own.

"I'm so sorry, Sasha. I don't know what any of this means. …"

"She will never forgive us if we don't get this right." Sasha turned to watch Quinn in the eerie pre-dawn light.

"She? She who?" Allie frowned.

"Sasha," Sasha said.

"Wait—what?" Allie took a step back and watched the ghost-Sasha. But it wasn't really Sasha.

"Holy balls, I'm talking to my gift."

The ghost-Sasha wasn't Sasha at all; she was just wearing Sasha's face. It was Allie. The part of Allie that understood her gift.

"You understand now, yes?" Ghost-Sasha turned to her with dead eyes.

"That even my subconscious thinks I'm rather dim when it comes to how my gift works? Yeah. Thanks, I got it." Allie gave her a thumbs-up.

"He has to see her."

Focus on the important details and discard the rest....

"At some point are you going to tell me what all this is about?"

"As soon as I know, you'll know," Ghost-Sasha said. "We're still trying to figure it out."

"We? Who's we?"

"Me. You. We." She looked at Allie blankly.

Allie watched Quinn move in the shadows across the lawn. Darkness swarmed all around him like a barrier she wouldn't be able to breach in this vision.

The book slipped off her lap and crashed to the floor, jarring her from the waking vision. All this time, she'd seen the forest and the orchard in her dreams and she'd just dismissed it as nothing of importance. But this was different. Allie's clairvoyance was trying to warn her. Her dreams weren't just junk anymore.

CHAPTER 18

On Friday, Allie rushed home to change after her training session with Emma. Graham had texted everyone an update that Amrita was happening tonight. The club seemed to take great pains to keep everyone on pins and needles about when and where this thing would happen. Allie felt sick after leaving her mentor for the day. Emma knew something was up, but Allie hoped she wouldn't catch on to what they were up to.

"You're not wearing that." Sasha rolled her eyes. The trip to Amrita seemed to be doing wonders for her. The possibility of doing some small thing to help Quinn had brought her back to life.

"What's wrong with my outfit?" Allie glanced down at her jeans and hoodie. "We're going to fight."

"We're going to fight, but we're going to look good doing it." Sasha marched into Allie's closet and started pulling clothes from hangers.

"Sasha, I can't fight in heels!"

"Wear the boots with the chunky heel, then, but you are not wearing sneakers. Put these on." She shoved a pair of slim-cut dark jeans in her hands. "And this—it'll look good with your hair."

Allie pulled on the jeans and the silvery boat-neck sweater that brought out the silver strands of her hair. She always thought the silver made her look like she was going prematurely gray, but in the Immortal world it seemed to be some kind of mark of status that linked her to the Indriell royal line—most would freak if they knew how short that line was. Sasha's hair was threaded with gold, which some said linked her with one of the noble houses as well.

"And this." Sasha threw a black leather jacket at her. "At least you'll be presentable for the party. If we're doing this, we're doing it right. Amrita's a big deal and people will be dressed to kill."

"For a fight? That's crazy." Allie shrugged into the fitted jacket.

"I guess you'll do," Sasha finally relented. "Don't forget to arm up. This isn't exactly smart, what we're doing. Amrita is known for erupting into chaos—I've heard that's when it's the best, actually." She ducked into the bathroom to change.

Allie shoved her newest set of sai into her boots—her mother's ancient weapons would be too conspicuous tonight, especially if the blades started to sing. She grabbed her new bracelet, which concealed a set of throwing blades, and slipped it over her wrist. With a heavy ring on each finger, her fist would pack quite a punch. And if it turned into a really bad night, she'd bring out the short, sharp blades with a twist of each ring. She looped a long necklace over her head; a sharp dagger rested inside the huge blue pendant. At the last moment she caught a glimpse of herself in the mirror and the world went green. The strange color was becoming a beacon she recognized now. Something needed her attention. She stared at her reflection, examining each detail. Something was off. Her gaze landed on the teardrop pendant she wore. It belonged to Kassandre. "Right, best leave this at home." She tucked the necklace into her jewelry box. The last thing she needed tonight was for someone to recognize it.

"Who are you talking to?" Sasha called from the bathroom.

"Myself," Allie said. She supposed since she was talking to her gift, that was the same thing.

Allie shoved her weapons belt into her bag with her collapsible quarterstaff and her growing collection of daggers and throwing blades—her aim had improved considerably since the games last year thanks to Emma's target practice over the summer.

"Ready?" Sasha frowned in her direction as she stepped out wearing dark leggings, red boots with a ridiculous heel, and a loose black sweater that fell off her shoulder. Her interest seemed to have evaporated in the short time it took her to dress. Sasha looked absent, as she did almost constantly these days.

"He would want you to live your life, Sasha," Allie said quietly.

"How?" Her voice was hollow and distant. "How can I possibly move on when I have no idea where he is or if he's even okay? How is it remotely acceptable for me to even think about fun? I know we're doing this for him, but I shouldn't be worried about clothes and looking forward to the fights and the party."

"Take it one day at a time, Sash. And when it seems like that isn't working, remind yourself that Quinn is a powerful guy. He will take care of himself. And he will come home."

"But what if he doesn't?"

"Then we never stop trying."

As they drove across the Veterans Memorial Bridge into the city, Allie felt both nervous and excited for the evening ahead.

The fights would last all evening and then the party would end at dawn. She couldn't imagine where something like that could take place within the city that wouldn't attract unwanted mortal attention.

Allie pulled into the parking garage at Darius's apartment building and found him waiting for them near the entrance. He was dressed in black from head to toe, and Allie had a hard time not staring.

"Your brother's looking hot tonight," Allie muttered.

"Ew." Sasha laughed.

"What? I'm single, I can look." She was attracted to Darius in a weird way, but the thought of actually being with him was laughable. Her feelings for him were at such opposite sides of the spectrum, it just didn't make any sense.

"Thanks, Red." Darius winked and she turned bright red.

"Damn his ears."

"We gotta go to the West Bank," he said as he hopped in the back seat. "We're meeting the others over by Nautica Pavilion, then we'll get an update on where to go from there."

"We still don't know where this place is yet?" Allie asked.

"Graham should know soon," Sasha said as they headed back across the bridge to the West Bank of the Cuyahoga River.

The parking lots around Nautica were full and the sidewalks were packed with people heading off to dinner and a night out at the clubs. Dressed as they were, Allie and her friends blended with the crowd.

"Arm up," Darius said before they exited the car.

Allie strapped on her weapons belt and tugged her sweater down over it. She tucked her sai into her boots and slipped her quarterstaff into the loop at her hip.

"This way, guys." Graham waved them over to where he and the others waited. "We have to head down to the old bridge on Center Street," Graham said. "It's going to be a challenge to get into this place." His grin sent a wave of dread through her. If Graham thought it was fun, she was sure to find it terrifying.

The walk down to Center Street was a short one, but they were in the industrial part of the city now. The crowds thinned as they approached the old rail bridge.

"Well? Where is it?" Aidan asked.

"We're going up there." Graham pointed to the Veterans Memorial Bridge towering high above them.

"What do you mean, up there? We were just there," Allie said.

"Keep your hair on, Red. We're climbing," Graham announced to the group.

"Of course, the old subway tunnel," Darius said. "The bridge has two levels and not many people know the lower level used to be a subway. It's been closed since the early fifties. It's perfect for Amrita. The noise of traffic will mask the sound of the fights, but it's right here in the midst of everything."

"How're we getting up there?" Allie asked. She knew there would be risks involved in the fights, but she hadn't expected getting into the club would be such a challenge.

"We're supposed to head under the big bridge. It's a ghost town down there so we won't be seen."

"And the party? It's up there too?" Sasha asked.

"It's in the lobby entrance to the tunnel. It's supposed to be some huge Art Deco relic of the twenties," Graham said.

"All right, I'll climb a bridge to see that," Allie said.

"Really?" Aidan gave her a wary look. "I expected lots of whining."

"I do not whine. Besides, you had me at Art Deco. Oddly, I'm okay with the climbing part. I'm more worried about the getting-caught part if some mortal sees us hanging off the side of a bridge."

"I'm sure it's hidden," Graham said. "Someone with a gift

like Imogen's or Quinn's will probably mask us while we climb."

Just the mention of Quinn's name was enough to chase any worries from her mind. That was why they were here tonight. "Let's do this, guys," Allie said. They headed across the old rail bridge that was completely eclipsed by the massive Memorial Bridge that towered over the industrial part of the city. Allie glanced back to see if anyone followed. Surely other young Immortals were making their way to Amrita tonight.

"Wouldn't it be easier to go up top and climb down?" Chloe asked.

"We have to perform the challenge to get in. There are several entrances to the old subways, but we have to go the way we're told," Graham said, checking his phone again.

"How are you getting this information?" Allie asked.

"I'm not the only techie out there. We have websites with encryption mortals couldn't even dream about."

"Immortal net? Really—?"

"She's about to make a Harry Potter analogy," Aidan said.

"—It's like wizard radio."

"And there it is."

"What are you babbling about?" Darius looked at Allie like she'd lost her mind.

"She's been re-reading Harry Potter lately and she's been making comparisons ever since."

"Such a weird little mortal girl." Darius shook his head. "Come on, killer. Let's do this. And you owe me a dance before this is all over."

"Lead the way." She followed him into the shadows of the bridge.

Allie gazed up at the enormous structure towering above them and wondered how she would manage to get up there without freaking out. When she looked back down, she halted when she saw five strange men waiting for them ahead. It startled her when she realized they were Immortal.

"It's just the guards," Darius whispered.

They aren't very powerful, Lex. That's why you didn't notice.

I should be more aware!

Well, we're all used to being around some of the most powerful of our kind.

That could be dangerous, Aidan. Getting too complacent.

They couldn't touch you. You'd have them on their asses before one of them managed to lay a finger on you—if they even dared to try.

Still, I don't like getting startled like that. Not after last year. Look at them. They're all shifty and nervous.

Because the six of us together are not exactly a comforting sight.

Oh, right.

Yeah, remember, our friends are pretty scary too.

What does that make us? To them, I mean.

Legendary.

"Ix-nay on the elepathy-tay." Darius elbowed her hard in the ribs.

"Ouch."

"No names, no phones, kids," the first guard called in a shaky voice. "Show us your weapons."

"Stay here. I'll go first." Darius stepped forward, drawing his Italian sword from its sheath at his back and his dagger from his hip. A double-bladed Bo staff followed, and then brass knuckles and a dozen throwing blades.

"I'll just need to touch each of you briefly on the shoulder to mark you," the man said hesitantly.

"Explain," Darius said flatly, crossing his arms over his broad chest.

"It's like a wristband or a stamp you would receive at any nightclub. The Amrita staff will see my mark like a beacon that tells them which opponents have been selected for each match. We will watch over you carefully until you leave the vicinity of the club, and then my mark will fade and you're on your own."

"Will it fade?" Darius was not pulling any punches and he sounded exactly like a cop. He wouldn't get very far tonight if he kept that up.

"Yes sir, you will see it fade. I am not strong enough to sustain the mark for more than a short radius. And I am no longer drawn to the mark after a few hours."

Is that like a weaker version of Liam's gift?

Exactly, Aidan said.

"Fair enough," Darius finally relented.

"All right, weapons out, kids," the man called, waving them all forward.

It was comical, really, how many weapons Sasha managed to pull off her person. Even the burly guard eyeing her cracked a smile. "Going to war, sweetheart?"

"You never know." She shrugged.

"This one looks like she's seen her fair share of battle." The guy in charge nodded at Allie. Her hand drifted to her throat in a self-conscious gesture. The comment caught her by surprise. She was used to most people in her life not seeing it or acknowledging it.

"Battle scars are a matter of pride, girlie," he said in a gruff tone. "I trust you made the Coalition bastard who gave it to you live to regret it?"

"Yes sir. My brother and I did," she whispered, remembering clearly just how much her captor deserved what he got. First from her and then finally from Liam. If she had been quicker to retaliate, Quinn would be here with them now and they might be attending Amrita completely for the fun of it.

Allie watched as the man in charge touched them each briefly on the shoulder. He shuddered when he touched Aidan and again when he marked Allie with his gift.

Is this a good idea, Aidan? Letting so many people see how powerful we are?

Definitely not, but Amrita has a strict 'don't ask, don't tell' policy when it comes to that.

That may have been so, but Allie had a bad feeling about the way the guards were looking at them.

"Who's paying?" one of the guards asked gruffly.

"Here," Darius pulled an envelope from his pocket.

"Twelve grand. You'll forgive me if I count it?"

"Twelve—" Allie gasped. That was two thousand dollars each!

Did you think it was free? Aidan rolled his eyes.

"Through the arch and into the shadows. You'll find another patrol waiting for you. When you reach the subway tunnel, head back toward the East Bank and you'll find the arena. The lists will be announced once everyone has arrived."

Allie took her weapons back, tucking her collapsible quarterstaff at her hip and her sai into her boots. The late afternoon light was tinged with that eerie green light she associated with her clairvoyance.

Anything in particular I should know? Aidan eyed her carefully.

No, but we're definitely on the right track. Be careful tonight, Aidan. I'm not sure what this is going to cost us.

Chapter 19

"Up here, kids." The Amrita patrol instructed them to follow as they passed under the shadow of the massive arch. This side of the bridge was completely deserted. Allie looked over her shoulder to the salt distribution plant several blocks away.

It's just over there. Aidan gestured down the hill to the hat factory where she was held captive just six months ago.

Seems like a lifetime since then.

Full circle, I guess. We're back here now, still looking for the one we lost that night.

Right. Let's do this. That was all the resolve she needed. Allie gazed up at the mountainous bridge. It would be a long climb, but she knew she could do it. A year ago she would have been quaking in her boots, but she had a lot more confidence in herself now.

"Careful, kids. No one falls. You fall, I lose my bonus, so don't make me have to catch you." The guard gestured them forward. "One at a time till you get halfway and then the next goes. Plenty of foot and handholds, so up you go, and be quick about it."

Aidan went first and he didn't hold back as he scrambled up the massive stone pillar between two arches. He moved confidently. As soon as one foot found purchase, he reached for the next handhold.

"How high is this thing?" Allie watched him shrink in the distance.

"Oh, about twenty stories," Graham said.

"Wish I hadn't asked."

"Who's next?" the guard barked.

"I'll go," Allie muttered, wanting to get this part done. As she looked up, Aidan was nearing the halfway point and seemed to be slowing down. *You all right?*

It's really windy up here. Be careful, Lex.

"Sasha, next time we talk about footwear, I'm not listening to you." Allie placed her foot on the first foothold she could reach and carefully made her way up, one step at a time, until she found her groove. She kept her eyes on the wall in front of her and refused to look down as she began to move faster.

You behind me? Aidan asked.

Yeah, how much farther?

You might be nearing halfway by now. I'm not looking down to check. It turns out I'm not crazy about heights and lake-effect wind.

Oh, so I have a case of mortal brain when I don't like tight spaces, but you get to be scared of heights?

Apparently I have a case of mortal brain. I'm not exactly afraid of getting hurt, although I'd like to avoid the long recovery. It's the whole falling part with the sudden stop at the end that has me totally freaked out.

But you jump off my tower all the time!

That's like twenty feet, max. This is ten times higher, windier, and scarier.

This was an odd twist for them. Aidan was never afraid of anything. Hearing and feeling how vulnerable he was caught her completely off-guard. He was always such a rock.

Let me introduce you to that pedestal you put me on ... it seems I'm about to fall off it. Literally.

Just keep moving, Aidan. I'm right behind you. We'll do this together. Allie moved faster, closing the gap between them until she was right beside him.

"Hey, so this is high as shit, isn't it?" She looked down nervously.

"Funny." His face was white as he reached for the next handhold. He wasn't exactly frozen with fear, but he clearly wasn't enjoying this either.

"Don't look down, Aidan. Just look at me. If we fall, it'll suck, but maybe it'll be a fun ride down and they might even manage to catch us."

"Don't you dare fall, Allie." He moved up a few more feet with the next step.

"Then let's get off this bitch, okay?"

"Yes, let's."

"You're right, you know," she said, grasping for anything to distract him from the height and his embarrassment. "I see it now."

"See what?" He inched up slowly with her.

"I had no idea I put you up on a pedestal too, but I totally do."

"Nice to see my failure is doing some good here."

"It's not a failure to struggle, Aidan. It's human. I don't care if you're mortal or Immortal. It's a failure to give up and go home. But it's never even crossed your mind to not conquer this wall."

"The alternative is falling."

"I'm just saying, it is *really* nice to see you aren't perfect," she said in a teasing tone.

"Never said I was."

"You're an intimidating guy, Aidan. On the surface you

seem to have it all together. Everything's figured out and the world is at your feet, just waiting for you to come into your own. I have a front-row seat in your mind, and you're so damned confident. And you're only seventeen! I can't fathom what you'll be like once you're Proven."

"Look at me, Lex."

She glanced over to see him clutching the ledge with white knuckles. She reached out to stroke his hand. He needed to relax his grip or he would crush the handhold.

"Whenever you look at me and you think you see perfection, you remember this guy right here. Remember how you had to talk me up this wall."

"You aren't moving. Aidan."

"I can see that, but I can't seem to make my hand move."

"Here, give me your hand." She tried to help him release his grip. "Let go. I won't let you fall." She pried his hand off the ledge and laced her fingers over his, placing his hand on the next ledge.

"Let's just do this, okay?" He moved forward.

"Look, we're almost there!" She pointed up. They were nearly at the top.

"Come on, babe, get me off this wall." His tone was full of relief.

"See, we're not really moving slow; it just feels like it. We did that last fifty feet quick." She babbled, looking for anything to keep him talking.

"I can't believe you're doing this in those ridiculous shoes."

"I blame your sister for that."

"Almost there, kids!"

Allie looked up at the strange voice to see another Amrita guard waiting to pull them up.

Just a few more feet, babe. You got this.

Ha! You totally just called me, babe. Aidan grinned.

Did not.

Did too.

Oh, just go already. She watched as he grabbed the guard's hand, grateful the man was there to pull them up over the edge.

Allie collapsed on the cool stone floor, leaning against the wall beside Aidan. They were perched on the outer ledge of the subway level now, with Chloe and Graham not too far behind.

"Oh my God." Aidan peered over the edge. "Tell me we don't have to climb down to get out of here? If we do, I live here now."

The guard chuckled. "No, son, the climb's just part of the price for admission. I can't decide if you kids are all stupid or brave."

"Stupid. Definitely stupid." Aidan laughed.

Even in his embarrassment and fear, he owned it and didn't try to hide it to save his male pride.

I'm back on the pedestal, really? After that?

It has that dusty, lived-in look now. Besides, we're equals, remember? When one of us falters, the other stands up and takes point. Allie held out her hand for him. *And that doesn't always have to be you.* She pulled him to his feet.

His arm slid around her waist and he pulled her close. "That is an incredibly comforting thought. Thank you," he whispered.

She shivered at the feel of his warm breath against her ear. It was getting harder and harder to resist the pull of Aidan. Sometimes she couldn't quite remember all the good reasons why it was such a bad idea for them to be together.

"Everyone here now?" the Amrita guard asked.

"Yeah, I'm the last," Darius said.

"Follow the tunnel toward the East Bank and you'll find the arena. And remember the rules, kids. No names, no phones, no cameras. Don't ask about powers, and for God's sake, don't tell. 'Specially you two." He gestured at Allie and Aidan.

"Got it," Aidan said.

They headed down the gloomy tracks through the darkness.

"I don't think I care for rock climbing," Graham announced. "I prefer the indoor recreational walls without all the wind."

"Me too, little dude," Aidan said.

"Allie, Aidan, walk with me." Darius gestured them to fall back with him. "I know this goes without saying, but you two don't need to play all your cards tonight."

"We know. Best not to talk about it."

"What?" Allie asked.

"I trust you'll fill her in?" Darius asked. "And be cautious."

"Got it."

What's he talking about? Allie frowned.

Watch your facial expressions when we talk like this. The guards are really weirded out by us—all of us. But as you might imagine, you and I completely freaked out a couple of them.

Did you expect them to knit us sweaters?

No. He tried not to laugh. *But we need to do as much as we can to appear less threatening.*

How?

Well, for starters, no one here needs to know we can do this.

That's a given.

Stick to your basics tonight, Lex. Keep it simple. You fight well, but neither of us should win this thing.

And you?

Help me stay out of the zone? If I look like I'm getting too into it, can you pull me back?

I'll pay close attention. But what if they pair us together?

Then I'll let you win. He winked.

Maybe I'll let you win—

"Are you kidding me?" A familiar voice echoed down the long tunnel behind them.

"Really? Who invited her?" Allie groaned.

"Lovely to see you too, little one." Naomi gave her a perfect sneer.

"Don't you ever call me that again," Allie said.

"You have clearly lost your mind," Naomi said, turning to Darius. "Bringing the young ones with you."

"Shut it, slim," another familiar voice said. "They aren't much younger than us. And I think we were even younger when *you* brought *us* here the first time."

Allie turned to see Aidan's cousins Erin and Dean with Naomi.

"Let's go, guys," Sasha said.

"Just a second." Aidan motioned Allie and the others to come in closer. "Let's remember why we're here. Be careful, but if something happens and we get separated, get to me or Red."

"Right. We all know they're our best chance of sticking together," Darius added. "And everyone please keep an eye on our little newbie."

"I'll be fine!" Chloe rolled her eyes. "Let's just do this, guys."

Allie and Darius moved ahead of the group. As they stepped away from the series of open arches where they'd climbed through, they entered the enclosed subway tunnel, black as night with the dim glow of torchlight far in the distance. Four lanes of track stretched out before them: two sets on either side of a wide center aisle, with a narrow aisle on the outer sides of the tracks.

Allie was in awe of the classic twenties American architecture. The Roman arches flanking each aisle held that idealistic Roman look that was indicative of the Art Deco and revival architecture of the period. The brick path was rough and cracked and some of the pillars crumbled with neglect. She could hear others ahead of them on the left aisle of the tracks and others behind them on the right. They seemed to be the only ones arriving along the center path.

The rough concrete walls gave way to white tiled walls, cracked and dull with age. The torchlight glowed brighter and she could see the paint peeling from the once-white arches. Orange graffiti-covered pillars sent a pang of regret through her. The artist in her saw this place as a work of art and she hated to see it left to crumble in the dust.

The path widened ahead and the sound of a crowd reached them.

"Nearly there now," Darius mumbled.

The rough brick path became smoothly packed dirt. Torchlight glowed from the brackets where gaslights once burned. The sound of contemporary music filled the silence. Between the music and the graffiti, there was an air of danger—a taboo element to the atmosphere. It was perfect.

Dozens of people milled about the open arena. Some looked uncertain. Others looked like they'd been there before. A cool breeze blew in from the open arches nearby. Allie gazed out at the city that was completely unaware of what was about to take place right under their noses.

Wooden benches stood around the perimeter of the makeshift arena. The ceiling was higher there and the span between the arches was wider. In some ways it was seedy and sparse, but one glance across the river and the city skyline became the backdrop of the arena. The noises of the highway right above them filled her ears and reminded her that the mortal world was but a stone's throw away.

It was all very well planned. A perfect place for an illegal Immortal gathering of her peers. Everyone here looked to be in high school or college at most. Several groups had formed, and some of the more adventurous were busy socializing, waiting for the fights to start.

"It's actually a pretty clever location," Darius said. "We're secluded enough not to be seen, but close enough to be dancing on the edge of discovery. That's one of the many reasons some people would like to see Amrita shut down."

People continued to arrive, but Allie and her friends stayed together. They would venture out at some point, but for now they had an unspoken agreement to stay put until the events began.

"I didn't expect to see so many people here," Allie whispered, staring at the crowd building up around them as more and more people arrived.

"Hey, you guys going to skulk in the shadows all night or are you here to play?" Erin's voice rose above the din of the music and conversation as she and Dean crossed the pit. Erin was so much like her father, Aide, it was uncanny, while Dean was more like their mother, Hélène.

"No skulking here." Aidan grinned as he and Dean did that stupid jock-boy handshake-back-slap thing.

"Everyone gather round!" The booming call sent the crowd into silence. "Welcome to Amrita! I'm Bob, your commentator for the events." He was clearly of Persian decent and probably the oldest one in the room by a few thousand years. If "Bob" was his name, it was short for something much more complicated to pronounce.

"Here we go." Erin beamed eagerly, cheering with the

crowd. "Ooh, how 'bout a rematch, Red?" She poked Allie playfully.

"You're so on," Allie giggled. "But don't expect to win this time."

"I bet I'd get my ass handed to me." She grinned like she couldn't wait.

"All right, everyone take a seat till you're tagged for round one. My man Joe here has been busy making the lists." Joe was the guard from the gates. "Some of you met him on the way in, but sit tight and he'll be quick about it while I tell you the rules."

Allie watched as Joe walked the perimeter of the arena, tagging everyone with his special marks he would use to reveal each match.

"My rules are law," Bob continued. "You break them, you're out! Everyone will have a chance to fight because we don't tolerate spectators. If you're here, you fight. We will pit you against a fair opponent. He or she might be more or less powerful, but we've chosen each pair to ensure a good, fair fight."

"We'll go three rounds. Hand-to-hand, weapons or gifts, I don't care. Anything goes. The best of each round will compete in the final melee. The last one standing then will be our winner. And then we party."

The crowd roared their approval, all eager to make it to the melee. Allie had no intention of moving on that far.

"'Scuse me, princess." Joe tapped her shoulder as he made his way through the crowd, pairing up the matches.

"No names, no phones or cameras," Bob continued. "Once you leave here, no gossiping about talent or lack of—you think I won't find you, but I will. No hospitals and absolutely no stealing. You break my rules, you will regret it. I reserve the right to kick you out of my club at any given moment if I feel you are even thinking about breaking my rules. If you're caught stealing power that does not belong to you, I'll hand you over to the Senate. If you're an ass about it, I'll hand you over to the Coalition. Do not test me on that. I've done it before and I'll do it again."

Allie was pretty sure no one was stupid enough to test this guy on his rules.

"Round one starts now. Do we have our first match, Joe?"

"We do." With a nod, Joe revealed the first match up. The handprint on Dean's shoulder glowed in the torchlight.

"First up." Erin grinned. "Do us proud!" She shoved him forward.

Allie watched nervously as he stepped confidently into the pit, shrugging out of his shirt and stretching like he did this every day.

It's called training, Lex. We all do this every day.

Oh, right.

He'll be fine. Look.

Allie watched as Dean's opponent met him at the line drawn in the dirt. She was strong and powerful. A good match for Dean, but Allie was certain he would do well.

"At the sound of the bell, fight's on, kids," Bob shouted. "Get us off to a good start!"

CHAPTER 20

Allie watched nervously as Dean took his place in the dirt arena. His opponent was a tall, slim girl with henna tattoos along both arms. She looked like he could break her in half, but Allie could sense her power. The girl would give him a fair fight, and from the look on her face, she meant to win it.

"Don't look so nervous, princess. It's all in good fun."

Allie turned at the unfamiliar voice to find a handsome, stocky young guy at her elbow.

"Can I help you?" He was at eye level, something she didn't experience often, especially with boys. She could see it instantly in his smile. He made up for his short stature with a cocky attitude. And he was fairly powerful too.

"Come on, princess, relax."

"Lost cause," Aidan said in a friendly tone.

"Why's everyone calling me princess?" Allie gave New Guy her best glare, but there was something about him she liked. His cocky act was a lot like Aidan's, but her judgy gift told her he was a decent guy—with a little more than his fair share of arrogance.

"It's the hair," he said. "You can call me ... Jim." He gave her a wink that said, "That's so not my real name."

"All right, Jim, you can call me Red."

"Sure thing, princess."

"I have more nick names than a thesaurus," she muttered under her breath.

"Defense!" Aidan clapped and cheered Dean on. "Watch your back!"

Allie watched as Dean and his opponent circled each other, each making a lunge here and there. They were moving so fast, they were almost a blur.

"I can't keep up." Chloe sighed beside her. "They're too fast."

"Pay attention to the individual movements as a whole," Allie said. "Don't watch the way you always have before. Use the power of your new sight to slow it down and look at the big picture. You'll start to see it all more clearly when you concentrate. Eventually, it'll click and it will get easier. It's just a new way of using your eyes and the information they give you. It takes a while."

"Look at you, being all teachy," Chloe said in a teasing tone.

"Who knew, right?" Allie elbowed her friend as they turned back to the fight.

Dean grappled with the girl, who gave just as good as she got. In a flash, she had him flat on his back in the dirt with her knee to his throat. But with a grin that was so reminiscent of Quinn's, Dean was back on his feet with his chest to her back and her head in a chokehold.

Quinn. That's why we're here. She glanced at Aidan.

Right. Let's just ease in and talk to some people and see what we see. But don't forget to watch the fights. That's why everyone is here, so it will be suspicious if you don't pay attention. Aidan drifted away from her just far enough to chat with some other spectators, leaving her alone with Jim. The rest of her friends were within sight, but everyone was busy doing what they came here to do.

"You might not want to drift too far away from your friends tonight, princess," Jim said. "This place can be misleading."

"Uh ... thanks." She resigned herself to the new nickname for the evening, hoping no one would actually make the connection to her true identity.

"Big stretch over there your boyfriend?" He gestured at Aidan.

"Nope." She turned toward Jim with a smile. It was time to do some digging, and it wouldn't hurt to start with the one who approached her first.

"Nice to meet you." Allie smiled, reaching to shake his hand. Touch would give her a better sense of his character, but she had to be careful not to make it too obvious.

As he took her hand she noticed a mark on his neck, half obscured by the collar of his shirt. It wasn't a tattoo. It looked more like a brand—but what kind of brand didn't heal on an Immortal?

Probably the same way Erin's tattoos don't heal and fade because it's part of her gift. But a brand would be strange. Get a closer look.

Working on it.

"Your friend seems to be flirting rather than fighting." Jim gestured at Dean in the ring with the beautiful but ferocious young woman. They were clearly having a good time.

"D doesn't get to hang with many Immortal girls who aren't his sisters."

"Story of every straight guy's life around here."

Allie took a step closer, trying to get a peek at the mark on his neck. She was certain she'd seen something like it before.

The crowd roared as the fight in the ring escalated and Allie finally had a chance to see the brand clearly. It was a snake in the shape of a circle. The snake held its tail in its mouth—the ouroboros from her dream.

She caught herself before she said anything. She was dying to ask him what it meant, but this was not the right time and definitely not the right place.

Allie forced her attention back on the match and cheered for Dean. What started as a flirtatious sparring match had turned into an all-out battle. She almost missed the winning strike. The girl took a running leap for Dean; her intent was a fly kick to his face, but he intercepted. With a whirling roundhouse kick of his own, he knocked her to the ground where she landed with a loud thud.

The sound of a whistle ended the fight and Dean was declared the winner. He graciously helped his opponent up and the two left the ring together, smiling and laughing like they were having the time of their lives. Allie wondered what it would be like to attend Amrita just for fun, without the worry of getting caught somewhere she wasn't supposed to be, or worrying about how powerful she was compared to everyone else.

"Let's hit the buffet, killer." Darius slipped up behind her, nodding to Jim.

"Ohh, there's food? Yes, let's. You coming, Jim?" Allie invited him. She wanted Darius to see the brand.

The three made their way around the arena and through the crowd, nodding at Sasha to follow them. Allie wasn't going anywhere without several friendly faces nearby.

As they passed through a huge set of arches into another section of the subway tunnel, the atmosphere changed. People milled about with drinks in hand and plates of appetizers like it was some kind of garden party. But Allie was on edge. She was missing something. The familiar green aura danced in her peripheral vision—her gift's way of telling her to pay attention; that she was on the right track. There was much more going on here than any of them realized. She just couldn't put her finger on it yet. The fights, all the young Immortals ... none of that was the point of Amrita. It was the draw, but it was also a smokescreen for what was really going on. She just had to find out what that was.

"You ever come to Amrita before?" Allie asked Jim as they waited in line for the buffet. The sounds of the fights echoed behind them in a bizarre mixture of the barbaric and civilized activities. She wondered if this was what it was like back in the gladiatorial age—at least for the wealthy Roman spectators. Watch some fights, drink some wine, eat some food. She'd have to ask Gregg about it since he had a first-hand account of the Roman arenas—from the crappier side of that situation.

"Yeah, a few times. It's a fun distraction."

She didn't quite buy his story. She got the sense that he had a lot of experience with Amrita.

Sasha trailed behind them, piling her plate high with appetizers, listening and watching everyone around her.

As Jim leaned over the buffet to reach for a slice of roast from the carving station, Allie gestured for Sasha and Darius to look at the brand. When Sasha saw it her eyes widened.

"Hey, we're going to go get a drink. See you in a bit," she called over her shoulder gesturing for Allie to follow.

As Allie stepped away to join her friends at the bar, a hand wrapped around her wrist like a band of iron.

"Hey." She glared back at Jim.

"Sorry. I have a message for you." He chanced a look around, and Allie realized he was afraid.

She narrowed her eyes at him, her heart beating wildly in her chest. She didn't like this.

"He doesn't blame you."

"Who?" Her voice came out in a whisper. But she knew he meant Quinn.

"He wants you all to forget about him and stop trying to

find him. But I'm adding my own message. He doesn't belong where he is. It's not too late for him, but he won't leave without trying to save everyone."

"Who? Who's everyone?"

"Not important right now."

"How can we help?" Allie asked.

"You see that room up there?" He nodded toward a section back in the recesses of the tunnel. Beyond the arches where the fights were taking place, there was a raised section for spectators. It had a VIP feel to it. Tucked safely beyond the tracks and behind the aged, golden Art Deco railing, a small crowd of well-dressed men and women stood watching the fights. She saw money changing hands and the whole scene started to come into perspective. Illegal gambling.

"You need to get back there and see what you see. Don't let anyone suspect you're anything more than a clueless kid out for a good time. Watch, and then tell his parents. He doesn't have much time left."

"Why are you helping him?"

"Because I'm not an asshole. And he's a friend." Jim turned to walk away. "Oh, and he's going to need all of you to be there when it happens."

"What?"

"I have no idea. It's just a feeling I get every now and then." He shrugged. "That feeling and the scent of apples. It's driving me crazy."

Before Allie could respond, Jim had slipped into the crowd and disappeared.

Did you hear that? Allie asked.

"Every word," Aidan said and she turned to find him right behind her. *Don't tell Sasha. She'll lose it.*

What should we do?

I don't know yet. You think we can trust him?

Yes. My judgy gift likes him.

That's good enough for me. Go find the others and stick together. I'll grab Naomi and Erin and we'll make our way around to the VIP section and meet you there.

Allie nodded and left to find Sasha and Darius.

"What do you make of the brand?" Allie asked as they filled their glasses at the champagne fountain.

"I've seen that mark," Sasha said.

"Me too." Allie gave her a wary look, wondering what her friend knew about the symbol.

"I've seen it before. Just like that guy. A brand."

"Where did you see it, Sash?" Darius asked.

"While I was working for the Senate this summer."

It was the first time she'd ever mentioned her brief job with the Senate.

"Do you know what it means?"

"No, but if we can figure that out, it might explain a lot," she murmured, her thoughts a million miles away. "I'm going to go put some feelers out. See if anyone else has that mark." Sasha left to wander through the crowd.

"You think we could talk our way back there?" Allie nodded toward the lounge.

"Maybe, but it looks like you're up next."

Allie glanced down at her shoulder to see a glowing handprint signaling it was her turn to fight. Nerves threatened to overwhelm her. Allie really didn't like anything that put her at the center of attention. All those years alone had left her feeling self-conscious in an unfamiliar crowd, but when she saw her opponent step forward, her nerves vanished.

Naomi.

Oh shit. Aidan groaned. *This is going to be bad. Please don't kill her.*

Of course not, babe. I'll hand her back in one piece.

"This ought to be interesting," Naomi said as she took her place in the ring.

"Entertaining for sure," Darius added.

"Bring it," Allie said.

"Don't you worry, little one. I'll bring it."

I don't think I can watch this. Aidan tried looking away, but he couldn't seem to manage it. *There is no good outcome here.*

It'll be fine. We're a good match and it's better like this than in the classroom when she's being an overbearing witch.

You know, you two might be friends if you'd stop with all the bitter jealousy.

I don't see that happening anytime soon. Not as long as she's trying to worm her way into my brother's life when she's clearly still sleeping with you.

We broke up—

Not now. I'm a little busy.

"All right girls, I sense a good catfight brewing," Bob said as he went over the rules with them again. "Let's see a good show, ladies."

At the sound of the bell, Allie reached for her sai blades. She wouldn't actually hurt Naomi, but she wasn't about to take a beating either.

Naomi fought with a pair of long serrated blades. They reminded Allie of Aidan's weapon of choice and she was confident stepping up to this challenge. She'd faced Aidan's blades often enough in training. She knew how to win this fight. This would be the only one she'd win, though. She didn't need everyone here to see what she could do. Especially those watching and placing bets.

Allie and Naomi circled each other, but Naomi was the first to strike. Allie never fought on the offensive. She'd always fought defensively, except when sparring with Aidan. But tonight that was going change. With her left blade tucked against her forearm, she took Naomi's first blow with the blunt end. Before Naomi could strike again, Allie sent a zap of her solar energy into her weapon and gave her a nice little shock to keep her on her toes.

"That was childish," Naomi said in her most patronizing tone.

"What can I say, I am a child. But at least I own it." She circled her opponent.

Naomi was relentless, but Allie refused to give her an opening.

Some might think the animosity between the girls was about Aidan or Darius ... or Liam ... and to some extent, Allie had to admit that was part of it. But for her it wasn't completely about jealousy over Naomi's obvious connection with Aidan or her past relationship with Darius or her current relationship with Liam. It was about the way she made her way through the McBrien boys according to whatever whim struck her. One moment she seemed to have her sights set on Aidan and the next she was playing house with Liam and his daughter or flirting with Scott or Darius. Deep down, Allie knew that hurt Aidan more than he would ever admit and that was the real source of the friction between the girls.

Aidan had enough heartache in his life without Naomi stirring up more. If she truly wanted to be with him, Allie wouldn't stand in the way of their happiness, but to watch her toy with him, that she would not tolerate.

But isn't that what you're doing to him, Allie? she asked herself. A huge part of her wanted to just be with him and damn the consequences. But her same old fears kept her from letting that happen. She couldn't—wouldn't—risk losing him. But when she wavered, when her resolve slipped, she knew she was no better than Naomi.

Could you please keep your mind on the fight? I can't handle much more of this, Lex.

What? Ew. Aidan, really?

I'm sorry, it's hot, so make it stop, please?

You can't be serious? You're actually enjoying this?

Immensely, but my brain is going to explode. You know how I feel about you. And I do have a soft spot for Naomi, but I'm not in love with her and she knows it. I'm a big boy and I can see the difference between the way she feels about me and the way you feel about me. It's not even close. I know you're just afraid of losing me. But Naomi's always wanted to be part of the McBrien family and one day she might settle on one of us, but she isn't malicious about it. She doesn't mean to hurt anyone. Now please finish kicking her ass so I can breathe again.

I'm working on it. Allie advanced on Naomi. Tucking her right blade in her belt, she rushed forward, gripping Naomi's left arm to force her to drop her weapon.

In one quick motion, Naomi caught her with an elbow strike to her face and Allie went down, her blade clattering across the dirt floor.

Naomi reeled back, and the victorious sneer on her face was too much for Allie. She grasped the blue pendant around her neck, unsheathing the hidden dagger. She thrust her weapon up, just as she stood, catching Naomi's lead strike.

Allie took advantage of her opponent's shock, grabbing her remaining sai blade tucked in her belt. She managed to disarm Naomi of her left blade, leaving her with just one weapon. Allie retreated, only to come at her again with a running leap. She landed a flying knee strike to Naomi's chin, taking her down long enough to relieve her other weapon, bringing an end to the fight.

"Looks like the little princess is our winner!" Bob announced, raising Allie's arm up in triumph.

Allie took a step toward Naomi, offering her a hand up, but Naomi refused.

Hey, I tried.

Give her a break. She's not used to losing.

Allie watched as Naomi went to Aidan's side.

"Is my face broken?" Allie turned to Darius.

"No, killer, just a black eye and a fat lip. But you've got a few nasty cuts. Come here, I'll play healer." He checked her injuries, using butterfly bandages to stop the bleeding long enough for them to begin healing on their own.

"Allie, you broke a few fingers." Darius taped three fingers of her right hand together to stabilize them while they healed. They would be fine in a day or two.

"Is that why it feels like an iron-hot poker is ripping through my arm?"

"That'd be it."

"Great."

I'll fix it later

No, we shouldn't risk it.

Well, as soon as we leave here, I'll take care of it.

Thanks, Aidan.

I know your emotions are all caught up in some kind of twisted jealousy and need to protect me, but it would be really nice if you two could get along.

I'll try to be nicer.

I guess that's something.

Chapter 21

Allie and Darius wandered through the crowd, making a good show of watching the fights and socializing with the other young Immortals. Some congratulated her on her win, but most kept their distance, speaking only to Darius. It was a disturbing reminder of Allie's life before she came to Kelleys Island, back when she didn't know it was her power that made everyone uneasy around her.

"We need to get back there, Dare," Allie whispered. "I can see it, you know. When my gift is telling me something's important, everything goes all green in my peripheral vision, forcing me to pay attention. It'd be nice if it would just light up like a Saint Patrick's Day parade with arrows pointing to the important clue. But I'm pretty sure that VIP room is where we need to be."

"I see a way we can talk our way in."

"How?" Allie followed his gaze to a sketchy-looking Immortal standing guard at the entrance to the VIP section.

"That guy works for Mom."

"For real?" Allie couldn't imagine Naeemah working with such a thuggish-looking dude. He was grungy with short dreads and a scraggly beard.

"Believe it or not, she has spies all over the world."

"Will he let us in?"

"Let's go see. But once we're back there, you stick to me like glue. Do not let go of my hand, you got it?"

"I'm the honey on your biscuit. Let's go."

They walked casually, hand in hand, up to the lounge room, guarded by the scary-looking bouncer.

"Oh, no. What are you doing here?" The bouncer's eyes widened at the sight of Darius.

"Same as you, but it seems like I might have more range. Seeing as how I fit the Amrita profile better."

"She will murder me. Or worse ... make me murder myself."

"She won't ever know. Let us back there and we'll just hang out."

"Make it quick." The big guy stepped aside and let them pass. "If anyone asks, you got in on the other side. If *she* asks, I never saw you."

"Will do."

Allie and Darius skirted the edge of the room set up like a swanky, high-end club with gray leather sofas and white lacquer chairs scattered about. The loud music faded and a low murmur of voices hummed as everyone focused on the fights. Some were placing bets. Everyone was drinking and not paying them any attention.

"I don't know about you, killer, but my Spidey sense is in overdrive right now. All kinds of crime happening here—or thinking about happening."

"I'm definitely getting some sinister vibes. Not the nicest people here," Allie agreed.

"Let's just act like we belong. Watch the fights and see what we see."

"Look who's up." Allie nodded to the arena where Aidan

faced a much larger opponent. Aidan was tall and muscular, but next to this guy, he just looked lanky.

Good luck.

Where are you?

VIP room with Dare.

What? Allie! I told you to wait for me!

We had an opportunity and took it. Don't worry about us. Just concentrate on that big wall of a guy in front of you. We'll be fine.

Allie looked around the room at everyone placing bets—some in Aidan's favor due to the strength of his power, and some in the other guy's favor due to his size.

"Do we know who the small one's parents are?" asked a woman sitting nearby in a leather armchair. She sipped a cocktail and discussed the fighters like she was trying to pick the best horse to bet on. Preferably the one with the right pedigree.

"That is exactly the kind of thing that's *guaranteed* not to be discussed here," Darius murmured.

"We aren't certain on that one yet." The Amrita executive spoke in a low voice. He was dressed in a sleek black bespoke suit and held an iPad in his lap as he took his client's bet. He divulged precious information to his client about the fighters who were told they would be protected from this very thing.

"We've not encountered him before. He is young, and clearly powerful, but we will collect what information we can for next time. The other young man is the better bet. He is Jeremy Lang, the eldest natural-born son of Richard and Amelia Lang, the first lieutenant governor of the southeastern region. He attends Ohio University where he is a pre-med student. A good choice for this match. His strengths lie in his swordsmanship and brawn. He is powerful, although not particularly gifted."

"Five thousand on the brawny one, then." The woman

looked bored and not at all concerned that she was doing anything illegal.

"Not cool." Darius looked pale in the dim light of the bar. "So much for complete anonymity." He stepped up behind Allie as they leaned against the railing, his arms on either side of her so they could talk quietly and not look suspicious. They were just a couple getting close as far as anyone could see.

"What, you think they're using Amrita to gather information on people?" Allie asked.

"Let's not have that conversation here. Let's just watch."

Aidan was making a good show of struggling against his opponent, but Allie knew how much he was holding back.

"He's powerful enough to kick that kid's ass. Why isn't he even trying?" The complaints came from more than one person who'd bet on Aidan.

Give them a little something for their money. A little fire maybe?

I'm trying not to call attention to myself.

It's having the opposite effect.

Let's try a little flashy, then, but pull me back if I get in the zone, okay?

I'm here. I'll call you back. Allie watched as Aidan circled the ring with his opponent. His weapons flashed in the torchlight and she knew what would come next.

The crowd roared their approval when it looked as if the fight would end with Aidan's defeat. But just as their swords clashed and Aidan barely managed to avoid losing his head, fire rained down from every torch circling the arena.

Aidan, that's mean! Allie laughed as she watched a stream of fire chase Jeremy Lang around the ring like some kind of fire-breathing dragon, hot on his tail. The crowd laughed and applauded the show of power, but Jeremy was furious and came after Aidan with renewed vigor.

She could see it in his eyes, even from here. As Aidan retaliated, his movements grew more fluid and graceful and he began to take the upper hand.

Aidan, snap out of it. But she didn't get a response. He was battling Jeremy like an Immortal five times his age and he was showing way too much to far too many prying eyes.

Come on, Aidan. You can control this!

"What is he doing?" Darius said. "Is he trying to win this?"

Aidan? Remember that night in Agra? I was so mortified the next day but you were such a gentleman about it. I've never been so wasted in my life. I told you I didn't remember anything ... but I lied. I remembered everything. I—

You stinking little liar! Aidan gasped. *You know how bad I felt about that!*

Allie breathed a sigh of relief, happy her confession had brought him out of the zone. *And you warned me about how intoxicating that would be, right? Mr. Liar-liar-pants-on-fire.*

I guess we're even. Glad you remember it. That was one of the top most frustrating nights of my life.

Agreed.

Thanks for pulling me back, Lex. You think I can officially lose this thing now?

Allie watched the spectators. Some were cheering him on and others were booing his sudden advantage.

Go for it. Yay losing!

You are such a dork.

Thank you.

"I don't know what you two just did, but I'm glad no one is watching you right now," Darius mumbled.

With a loud groan from the crowd, the bell rang and Jeremy was proclaimed the winner.

"Wait! No! He should have won!"

"You bet on the wrong horse, mate."

"One more fight and I'll pay what I owe." Allie heard the desperate voice behind her. She and Darius drew back into the shadows, pretending to have their own quiet conversation.

"That was your last chance. You either settle for cash now, or we take the payment the hard way."

"Uh-oh," Darius whispered. His eyes lit with the golden light of his power and she knew he was seeing something with his gift.

"What's happening?"

"The Immortal equivalent of busting some kneecaps."

"What do you mean?" Allie turned to see two men escorting a third from the bar. They ducked through a curtain and Allie got a glimpse of another room, her vision tainted with green. Without thinking she ducked through the curtain to follow.

"Allie, no!" Darius tried to pull her back. Before anyone could see them, they hid behind a large crate of champagne bottles. The corner was curtained off like a makeshift stockroom behind the bar, but they had a good vantage point from their hiding place. The room beyond the storage area was huge, with dozens of important-looking people milling about. They were in the lobby entrance to the subway. The Amrita staff was busy setting up for the party that would happen there later.

"Will anyone sense us back here?" Allie asked.

"Too many Immortals around. With the sensations coming from every angle it's impossible to pinpoint the direction."

"No! Just give me a few more days and I'll come up with the cash." The guy who'd lost the bet on Aidan was desperately trying to talk his way out of a bad situation. The poor guy cowered with his back up against the wall as the two brutes towered over him.

"You've fed us that same line of bullshit for the last month.

If you could get your hands on that kind of cash, you would have paid by now. Now it's time for a visit with Selena."

"No! Please, I—" But the man's protests were cut off. He still talked and rambled, but no sound came from his throat.

"Thank you, Linus. What a useful gift you have. You know how I hate to hear them beg." The striking Spanish woman joined the two men restraining the third. "How much does he owe?" Selena asked.

"About three hundred grand."

"So much? His gifts must be useful to accumulate so much credit for one so young."

"Just the one ability. It's about all he has that's worth anything."

Allie and Darius watched in horrified silence as the woman gripped the young man's head between her palms and his mute screams tore from his mouth without a sound.

Allie had never seen anyone lose a gift like this before. A vaporous glow floated around the unfortunate man and Allie had to look away. There was something revolting about the act. Seeing the man's gift laid bare like that was an abomination.

She flinched when they left him crumpled in a heap on the storeroom floor.

"You will learn from this, yes?" She nudged him with the toe of her shoe. "I don't like doing this to people. Don't make me do it again. Your debt is paid in full and it is within my power to give your gift to someone who can sustain it—and afford it. You would do well to seek another path for your fortune. Gambling obviously isn't within your skill set. Now get him out of here."

The woman turned to cross the wide room. No one showed the slightest concern over what just happened.

"Must be a common occurrence," Darius muttered as the two men dragged the younger man from the club.

"I don't understand what just happened, Dare. Why would that guy risk his power on a bet?"

"Why would a mortal risk his kneecaps on a bet? No one ever thinks it's going to happen to them. Then you get in too deep and owe too much and there's no way out."

"Such a risk for money?"

"Living forever is expensive, Allie. And working a nine-to-five for a couple of hundred years with a week or two of vacation here and there, with no retirement in sight, living from paycheck to paycheck, struggling to pay the bills ... it's exhausting. We're lucky we have family who are more established. Dad, Liam, Emma, George, they all lived through that same struggle over a thousand years ago. It was different then, but still a long road to get to the point where they no longer had to worry about money. But imagine a child born into a younger family without such wealth? Imagine how difficult and exhausting it would be to see your future stretched out before you with nothing but a long life of hard labor ahead of you? Now imagine a place like this where you can open a line of credit, putting your gift up for collateral. You make a few successful bets to set you up with enough money to invest and start earning a substantial passive income. The relief that kind of income could give a family would be an enormous weight off their shoulders. I can see the draw, but the price isn't worth it if it goes badly."

"I can't imagine risking it." Allie shook her head.

"Let's get out of here before we get caught." Darius grabbed her hand and they stood at a crouch, waiting for a chance to slip back into the VIP room unseen. Something tugged at Allie, though. Her peripheral vision was still green. They hadn't seen the worst of it yet.

She glanced back into the lobby where people were beginning to settle down. A familiar face drew Allie's attention—a face she never wanted to see again. It frightened her to her wit's end that she would see him again in a place like this.

"What's wrong, Allie? You're white as a ghost."

"It's Jon ... and Ella." She scrambled back, pulling Darius down with her until they were back on the floor.

"Who?"

"The assholes who kidnapped me."

"Why the hell is the Coalition here?" He rose up to peek over the crates into the open room beyond. "They're just over there mingling with ... damn."

Allie knelt beside him and watched as even more people spilled into the lobby, like a meeting was about to start. Some were just workers setting up for the party, but others were preparing to watch something on a large screen.

"This is bad," Darius said.

"What is it?"

"That is a group of Coalition *and* Senate members together."

"What? Why?"

"No idea."

"So Amrita's working both sides? They're luring in the youngest generations on the pretense of a fun night out and a chance to show off in a safe environment—and they're using it as an opportunity to collect information on us?"

"Yeah, they're looking for the ones to watch," Darius said. "The best of our generation."

"But why?"

"I think we're about to find out."

Allie watched as the large screen came to life, flickering with a vague image of a logo for the company Graham had told them about: Soma. The indistinct image of a serpentine figure around a challis caught her attention. It was eerily like the brand she'd seen on Jim's neck.

The waiting audience fell silent as Ella approached a podium at the far end of the room. She looked different from the girl who had kidnapped Allie and Quinn just a few months ago. Her hair was still partially shaved on one side, but she was more polished and refined, like she'd suddenly come into an influx of cash. Apparently Ella had done well for herself after the fiasco the night of the ball.

"Thank you for joining us this evening, ladies and gentlemen," she began. "Please have a seat and the auction will begin soon. Bidding will begin at five million and will increase as the quality of the product increases. Once your payments have been wired, your purchases will be delivered when they are ready."

Murmurs of anticipation filled the room as the audience shifted anxiously.

"I don't like this, Allie. We need to get out of here before we're caught."

"In a minute. We have to see what they're up to."

"Sweetheart, this is a slave auction. We can't be anywhere near this place."

"We have to see what's on that screen, Dare."

"First up we have cadet number 00857." Ella began her presentation of the "product" and the screen filled with the image of a beautiful young girl with a vacant expression on her face. "She will be fully trained and broken, but she is still very young, only thirteen. Already, this cadet will acclimate to any situation with little effort from her trainer. She will adjust to her new owners with ease since 00857 has trained with us nearly all of her life. She is extremely cooperative and will be quite gifted. Her training will be complete shortly after her Awakening. You can find further details in the dossiers you received last month. Bidding will begin at five million."

Allie watched in horrified silence as the girl was sold to a

Senate governor for seven million dollars. Neither Darius nor Allie could break away as they watched dozens of faces fill the screen, each with the brand she'd seen earlier on Jim. Allie was horrified, but she couldn't make herself stop watching and waiting to see the one face she hoped she wouldn't see.

"This is way bigger than anything going on in the VIP room," Darius finally said. "That's just a smokescreen to fool anyone snooping around."

"It's him." Allie's voice shook. He looked older. Harder. Stronger.

"Cadet 01015 is not fully trained yet," Ella announced. "We will accept early bidding on this powerful young man. His training is expected to be complete sometime next year. Bidding will begin at twenty million."

"Let's go, killer. We've got what we need. Dad will know what to do."

"Grab another three cases of champagne for the fountain; it needs refilling again." The voice came from the bar behind them.

"Shit, what do we do?" Allie hissed as the bar-back stepped through the curtain.

"I'm so sorry about this, Allie," Darius said and then he was kissing her. His arms snaked around her waist and she resisted before she realized what he was trying to do. She relaxed and kissed him back, putting on a good show for the guy who was about to catch them. But she felt ... nothing.

"Damn kids, get out of here!"

"What? Oh, sorry." Darius grinned, reaching to pull Allie up. "We'll ... uh, get out of your way, sir."

"Sorry." Allie giggled and followed Darius through the curtains and back into the VIP room. She did her best to act like a silly teenager, but she was reeling inside, fighting to keep control of the rage that swelled within her and the tears that threatened to flow.

"It's okay. He'll be okay, Allie," Darius assured her, sounding more like he was trying to convince himself.

"It's not okay. We have to get him out of there."

"We will. We still have time. They don't plan to sell him for a year."

"And what do you think they're going to do to him in that time?" Allie snapped.

"Try to break him. But I know Quinn. He won't make it easy for them."

"You're right." Allie heaved a big sigh. She had to calm down.

"I'm so sorry about the ... kiss."

She knew he didn't have a choice and it was the best way to get them out of there and dismissed as nothing more than a couple of stupid kids, but she hadn't been prepared for his kiss. It wasn't at all what she would have expected. They had such a great connection that she'd expected it to be ... hot. Maybe it was just the situation, but something was off. Like the chemistry just wasn't there despite their obvious fascination with each other.

"It's okay. It was a good plan."

They made their way quietly back to the arena in an awkward silence.

"I feel like a dirty old man," Darius said.

"You shouldn't. I've been around you long enough to know you're the least mature of us all."

"True." He laughed. "But that is not something that needs to happen again. At least not till you're in college."

"It's fine." She elbowed him playfully, hoping he would snap out of it. "It just caught me by surprise, that's all. And the little passenger in my brain is probably not too happy with me right now for a number of reasons."

He didn't have much of a choice, Lex. I'd have done the same thing. But you know I can feel what you feel. It was bad enough with Vince, but please don't make a habit of kissing my brother. I'm nauseous right now.

Actually, I'm a little nauseous too.

Enough with the risk-taking tonight, please? You almost gave me a heart attack.

We've got what we came for, Aidan. She wanted to let herself have a good freak out, but they couldn't risk letting the shock of what they just discovered overwhelm them. *We're going to get him out of there.*

Damn straight we are. Dad will know what to do. Hell, he'll buy him if that's the only way.

"Knock it off, Allie," Darius said. "You're going all glassy-eyed again and it's kinda obvious you aren't talking to me."

"Sorry."

"Is he freaking?"

"Not really, just trying to keep his lunch down."

"Come on, us making out is not *that* disgusting."

"He can feel what I'm feeling. So just then it was kinda like he was the one making out with you."

"No. No. No. Unsay it, Red. Please unsay it."

"Next time give me a little warning and I'll block him."

"There is not going to be a next time, killer. That was weird."

"It was weird, wasn't it? I thought it was just the situation."

"Maybe. But let's leave it a mystery."

"Let's."

Allie glanced down at the glowing hand-print on his shoulder. "Looks like you're up next, Dare."

Darius fought well in the first round of his fight against a much smaller guy. But when his opponent trotted out his gift, landing every single punch with the strength of a man three times his size, Darius was quick to take a dive and bring an end to the fight. They had much more important things to focus their attention on anyway.

Allie was eager to leave, but it would draw far too much attention if they attempted to slip out. She stayed close to her friends and prayed for a quick and painless end to the night.

It'll be over soon and then we can get to work on getting Quinn out of that place.

But what do we really know now that we didn't know before? Other than the slavery thing?

We know for sure now that Amrita is connected with Soma and they are the ones taking kids like Quinn. We know they are affiliated with the Coalition and the Senate, but they seem to be working independently of either group. We know a lot more, Lex. We're getting him back.

Allie thought about Jim's cryptic warning and wasn't sure what to make of it. Clearly he was indicating something about her dreams, but she still wasn't sure what she was seeing or how she should react to the visions that didn't make any sense.

Her gaze drifted around the arena. Everyone was having a good time and the atmosphere grew more celebratory the closer they came to the melee.

Aidan groaned when the mark on Chloe's shoulder lit up and it was her turn. "I don't think I can watch this," he said.

"She's a great fighter, Aidan. She kicked my ass for months. She'll do fine." She watched as Chloe took her place in the arena, looking so small, but fierce at the same time. Armed with her bo staff and her subtle gift, Chloe launched against her opponent, fading to the right at the last second when he attempted to strike her from the left.

Remember, she can see the decisions he's faced with so she knows what his best move is before he makes it.

Right, her path of least resistance. Aidan grinned. *She's definitely making him work for it.*

Allie thought Chloe would run the poor guy till he fell from exhaustion, but eventually, she started giving him the upper hand. Inch by inch, she made small mistakes that allowed her opponent to land a strike.

"She's doing a better job at throwing her fight than the rest of us combined," Sasha muttered.

"She's a lot stronger than we give her credit," Allie agreed.

"And she's a hell of a lot smarter than we are," Aidan said.

"Speak for yourself." Graham gave him a playful punch.

"Are we all done with this part now?" Allie asked hopefully. "We've all fought and lost, right?" She had technically won her fight against Naomi, but they got such low marks for a sloppy fight, they didn't qualify to move on.

"Yup," Graham said.

"So none of us will be in the melee?"

"Too bad. Any other time and I would have won this shit," Aidan said wistfully.

"Maybe next time you can beat the hell out of everyone." Allie patted his arm in mock sympathy.

"Let's get seats. This could take a while," Sasha said.

Allie followed her friends to the benches set up around the arena. The last fights were wrapping up and the twelve best winners of the night were chosen to compete in the final. The last one standing would win.

"What do they get?" Allie asked absently. "A trophy?"

"Fifty thousand dollars," Aidan said.

"I'm glad I didn't know that," she said. She would have

been tempted to go for it. That was college tuition. Darius had really made her think about the future and the finances she didn't have. Her parents would only be around for so long. After that, she was on her own forever.

I'm pretty sure between your bio dad and your Viking brother there are probably already a couple of substantial trust funds sitting around earmarked for your future.

I have issues taking money I haven't earned.

That's an argument for another day, Lex. Aidan nodded at the center arena.

The twelve best of the night stood ready for the final round and Allie wasn't sure she wanted to watch. Within the first two minutes of the melee, she was positive she didn't want to watch, but like a train wreck, she couldn't look away.

"It's like Shark Week. They're just tearing at each other."

"I'll admit, I'm kinda glad I'm not down there," Aidan said, wincing with the crowd as one guy with a gift for causing confusion among the others took out two at a time when they collided against each other with their weapons drawn.

"It's so bloody." Allie cringed. "What happened to the 'don't put anyone in the hospital' rule?"

"They're fine. It's all superficial," Darius said. "But that girl in the middle is going to win it."

"She seems so little." Allie shook her head.

"Size doesn't matter here. She's drawing strength from the fight. The more they fight, the stronger she gets."

Allie watched, mesmerized as the petite blond stayed in it until it was just her and the giant wall of Jeremy Lang that Aidan had faced.

"She's got him," Aidan said. "He's all about intimidation and size, but she's quick and she's got all of the strength of the other ten fighters pumping her up."

It was bizarre, seeing the barely five-foot teen bring down

the huge brawn of her opponent, but he landed with a thud, his energy and stamina completely spent.

"He passed out?" Aidan stood up, craning his neck to see.

"Did she drain the big guy?" Darius laughed.

"She waited until she had only one opponent left and she sucked up all his stamina." Allie laughed. It was a brilliant strategy. "I like her style." She was happy to see the girl win and she hoped she'd actually get the money and not have any repercussions for it later. But at the last second, Allie saw the small brand on the girl's ankle. Like Jim, she seemed to be a slave working the Amrita crowd. Of course they would have planted one of their own as the winner so they'd never actually have to pay the money.

"Can we get out of here now? This place is giving me the skeevies."

"We still have the party, Lex."

Can't we just sneak out?

We need to play by their rules. Pretend like we're having the time of our lives and then we can go home.

As everyone drifted into the lobby—the place that had just held a slave auction for kids just like all of them—the atmosphere really began to change. The thump of music grabbed Allie's attention and the lights dimmed. She could feel the pull of the party; even her blood seemed to respond to the atmosphere, like a drug.

Someone is trying to make sure we enjoy this, Aidan muttered.

Should we resist it?

I don't think that's a good idea. Aidan cast furtive glances at the others. It seemed like they didn't have much choice but to give in to the mysterious influence. *Let's give in about forty-five percent. Maybe they won't notice if we're not as into it as everyone else.*

Allie wasn't in the mood for a party and she was having trouble going with the flow.

"Come on, Red, let's dance. I bet I can get you to relax." Aidan pulled her onto the dance floor.

The music was loud and the revelry was at an all-time high.

"All right, why not." The last of her resolve cracked and she yielded to the night. Fifty-five percent of her was ashamed of herself for daring to have fun when Quinn was in such a precarious position. But forty-five percent of her was on cloud nine.

Chapter 22

"You think they'll be waiting on us at the marina or at home?" Allie asked as she slipped into the backseat of the nondescript car Aidan had left parked at Tower City mall earlier in the week. They needed to be very careful after leaving Amrita. To make sure they weren't followed, they walked around the city, stopping for breakfast at a local cafe before they circled back to the car at Tower City. Allie was with Darius, Sasha, and Aidan; the others were with Naomi and Erin. They were going to meet back at the marina and head home together.

"They might not realize what we we've been up to," Sasha said.

"They know," Allie said. "It's just a matter of how mad they are at this point."

"Once we tell them what we discovered, they'll have other matters on their mind. Dad's probably not going to be in a listening mood, though." Sasha looked worried. Now that it was over and they accomplished what they'd set out to do, it was time to face the music, and none of them were looking forward to it.

"I'll probably take the brunt of it," Darius said as he drove toward the marina at Edgewater Park. "I'm supposed to know better."

When they arrived, Naomi and the others were already there. And so were Gregg, Daniel, Liam, and Greyson, Naomi's father. None of them looked too pleased with their children—or in Allie's case, it was her brother glaring daggers at her.

"Liam looks bigger when he's mad," Allie said nervously. "How does he do that?"

"Let's just get this part done, guys," Aidan said. "I'll take as much responsibility for it as I can."

They all stepped out of the car and into the silent morning. Naomi stood by her father with her head hanging low and her ears bright red in embarrassment. The others seemed to be on the boat already.

"Sasha, Darius, go with the others," Gregg said softly.

"Naomi and I will be leaving now," Greyson said. "I just wanted to make sure you all got here in one piece. I'll sweep the area, Gregg. Make sure they weren't followed."

"We weren't followed," Naomi said.

"None of you are experienced enough to know what the hell you're doing in a place like that, which is why I told you not to go! You want to be an adult, Naomi, then act like one. Make better decisions."

For once, Allie identified with Naomi. She was just a kid like the others. She'd messed up and had to pay the consequences like the rest of them. Allie tried giving her a sympathetic look, but Naomi was as abrasive as ever, ignoring Allie's gesture.

"Gregg, Daniel. I apologize for my daughter's part in all of this. She is hot-headed, and far too spoiled. We will rethink her position at the school. If she can't be trusted, then maybe she needs more training and less freedom. Like when she was the sixteen-year-old."

Allie actually felt sorry for her. To be embarrassed like that in front of everyone was probably more than the high-spirited girl could take.

"To be fair, Greyson, she only came with Erin and Dean. I'm the one who brought the others and she tore me a new one for it," Darius offered.

"Thanks, Dare," Naomi mumbled before she darted to the car and slammed the door behind her.

"I will speak with you later," Gregg said, pointing to the boat with a glare. Darius cast a glance at Allie and Aidan and joined Daniel and the others. Allie was surprised when the boat pulled away from the dock. Apparently, she and Aidan were in the most trouble.

Allie trembled nervously as she watched Gregg's jaw tighten and flex. He was barely in control of his anger.

"Da, I'm sorry—" Aidan barely managed to get the words out before Gregg whirled around and slammed him up against the boathouse. His head made a crunching noise against the wall as the stucco cracked and fell to the ground.

"I don't want to hear it, Aidan. Not this time." Gregg gripped him by the collar, his face red with rage. "Do you have any idea what you've done?"

Aidan's eyes blazed with fury and hurt. He'd never seen his father this angry.

"Not here, Gregg," Liam said. "Let's go."

"Liam?" Allie whispered uncertainly.

"Do not speak to me yet, little one. I am too angry. Let's just go." No one spoke as Liam guided the small racing boat out of the boathouse and headed for open water. The quarters were cramped inside and the tension was palpable. The yelling started once they were away from shore.

"How could you be stupid enough to risk going there?" Gregg finally asked.

"It's supposed to be discreet," Aidan said. "That's supposed to be the main draw."

"But it's not, is it. You found that out, didn't you?"

"Yeah." Allie nodded reluctantly. She wouldn't let Aidan take all the blame for this. "It's not his fault, Gregg. I have a mind of my own. I could have said no."

"And why didn't you?" Liam asked, not looking at her.

"We didn't go there for fun," she muttered.

"Aye, you went to stick your noses in things you've no business sticking your noses in. I know you kids want to help Quinn, but you have to trust us to take care of it. You think we weren't capable of having people there tonight?"

"The bouncer, Da? You know as well as I do he had no hope of finding anything. The Amrita people are affiliated with that Livia woman. We know that for sure now," Aidan said. "She has him. He's not in some Coalition prison. If there was ever a chance to find out something you couldn't possibly find out on your own, it was at Amrita last night. And none of your people could get in there like we did."

Allie admired the way he stood up to his father, but she wasn't so sure now was the right time.

"It wasn't worth the risk, son."

"Quinn's not worth it? How can you say that?" Aidan gave his father a look of disgust.

"Our world is not ready for you two," Gregg growled. "They might not ever be ready. You have the kind of power the rest of us can only dream of. And you've put that power on display to the wrong people."

"We didn't show all our cards, Gregg. We're not that stupid," Allie said.

The boat began to slow, but they were still miles away from Kelleys Island. She glanced at Liam and saw he was gripping the steering wheel so hard she was certain it would disintegrate at any moment.

Finally he turned toward her and was suddenly in her face, his icy blue eyes sparking with anger. "You are too important to risk, Allie." He towered over her, trapping her between his long arms. Allie backed up, but there was no escaping his anger.

"I'm sorry, Liam," she whispered, feeling the threat of tears choking her throat.

"There is nothing about you that wouldn't attract attention, Allie. With that hair, your power, and with all of you there as a group, you call attention to yourselves. You all are so sheltered ... you don't know how intimidating and impressive you all are as a group. Don't think for a moment that people won't be talking about all of you. Especially the redheaded spitfire they saw tonight. Do you have any idea what that could mean? I don't know how to protect you from that kind of attention, short of shaving your head so you're not so recognizable. And don't think I won't do it."

"We were careful Liam," Aidan said. "I promise. People may talk about us, but no one will know who we are or where we live or—"

"You're both unknowns," Gregg said softly. "Or at least you were until tonight. That place was full of the most corrupt members of our government."

"What do you mean we're *both* unknowns?" Aidan asked, looking stunned.

"We felt it was best to give Allie some time to adjust to this world before we registered her with the Senate. We didn't want to risk them taking her away from her family. And when we adopted you ... your mother and I decided to shield you for as long as we could. As far as the Senate knows, we do not have a son named Aidan. It's one of the reasons I named you after my brother. Partly because you reminded me of him so much and partly because anyone hearing the name Aidan McBrien would think of Aide and not wonder about it."

"Why did you never tell me?" Aidan whispered. "The accident last year. I should have been punished. But you said the Senate let me off with a warning."

Aidan had made a huge mess of things when he decided to race a train one night simply because he was bored. Technically he died in the accident, long enough for the paramedics on the scene to take him to the morgue. Gregg had to move heaven and earth to get him out of that mess. He'd always wondered how he had been so lucky not to be called before the Senate. Now he knew.

"You're so young, Aidan." Gregg sighed.

"I'm not an infant, Da. I know you can't see me as anything but a little boy, but I had a right to know!"

"What does this mean?" Allie dared to ask.

"Neither of you are registered with the Senate. To them, you do not exist. It's a daring move, especially for Aidan, since we are so well known among the Senate. Even as a baby we knew he would be the strongest of his generation. By giving you obscurity, we bought you time, son. Time to grow up and become the man you're destined to be—and I don't mean the prophecy." Gregg waved off Aidan's rebuttal. "I wanted you to have the freedom to become the man you are in here." Gregg thumped Aidan's chest. "Not the man they would make you. If the Senate knew of your power, they would interfere in your training. They might even take you away from us on some pretense that you deserved the best training they could offer. I wouldn't allow that, under any circumstance. So we kept you a secret. And we let you have the most normal life we could possibly give you."

"Am I meant to live my whole life in secret?" Aidan asked

softly, his eyes blazing with some combination of fury and love for his parents who took such a dangerous risk, just for him.

"No, we intended to deal with it after you reached your Proving."

"Da, that could be a hundred years from now!"

"Not with you. You'll reach your potential early. Both of you will. And once Proven you'll have the strength and power to protect yourselves. To not be manipulated or used. Once Proven, you'll both be able to fight for the right to live the lives you want to live. But now, if the wrong people saw you last night.... If word gets out about you two, people will talk and it's only a matter of time before you're found out. I know a few decades seems like a long time to hide, but it's nothing compared to the rest of your lives."

"If you trusted me. If you realized I'm capable of making good decisions, you would have told me long before now." Aidan shook his head. "I never would have risked what we did last night if I'd known we were *both* unknowns. It never occurred to me that you wouldn't have registered Allie by now, much less me."

"Aye, I should have told you. I just didn't think you'd be stupid enough to pull something like this."

"Well, if we're all done yelling now," Allie said, "would you like to hear about how Quinn is up for sale like some trussed-up prized pig in an Immortal slave market?"

Chapter 23

Once Allie and Aidan finished telling Gregg and Liam all they had discovered at Amrita, the adults ran with the intel and the kids were back in the dark, with a warning to *never* do anything like that again or they would all be grounded to the crypt for a decade. Allie didn't know what the crypt was, but she was pretty sure she didn't want to know.

Allie absently flipped through her art history notes spread across Aidan's bed, prepping for her next exam. Aidan sat at his desk, studying for his music theory class. Sasha was holed up in her room, supposedly studying as well. The brief return of the old Sasha faded quickly after Amrita and she was back to isolating herself again. Aidan worried about her even more now, but Allie knew she would come to them when she was ready to talk.

"What do you want to do for your birthday, Lex?" Aidan sprang the question on her at least once a day now. She would be seventeen in a few days and she'd made it clear she did not want the traditional Immortal seventeenth birthday party. It was meant to be a unique celebration and a time to reflect on the past year and how far she had come since her Awakening a year ago, but Allie didn't want to have a party her parents couldn't attend. She really didn't want a party at all. Really, she just wanted to ignore it as if it were any other day.

"I don't want a party."

"I didn't say anything about a party. I asked you what you wanted to do."

There was one thing she really wanted, but she wasn't sure he'd go for it.

"I want a tattoo."

Aidan nodded. "Okay, we can go see Erin. What did you have in mind?"

Allie pulled out her sketchbook, not sure if she should show him the full design or not.

"I'm going to see it eventually, Lex. Show me."

Allie flipped through the pages and turned the book toward him.

"Allie, no." He shook his head. "You don't need to cover up your scar with this."

"Read it."

"Read what." He frowned down at the intricate drawing of vines and flowers. He changed his attitude when he saw the lines of poetry she'd worked into the black and purple vines that would follow the path of her scars. It all spoke of positive body image and accepting her perceived imperfections as part of the unique and beautiful person she was, inside and out. It was a message to herself. She didn't want to let the ugly scar affect her anymore, she was ready to embrace it as the badge of honor it was.

"Let's go." He shut his textbooks and shoved them into his bag.

"What, now?"

"Yes, now. If you're going to get a tattoo, it needs to be spontaneous. Are you sure this is all you want for your birthday?"

"Yes." She was actually really excited. Aidan's cousin Erin

had a way with her creative gifts. Allie couldn't go into just any tattoo studio. They would wonder why she kept healing so fast. But Erin could create the most amazing tattoos for Immortals. And she could change them or remove them at any time.

Erin's school was only a short drive from the ferry dock at Edgewater Park. When they arrived at the row of townhouses, Erin was waiting out front for them.

"Will this hurt?" Allie asked. "I forgot to ask if it hurts."

"Of course it hurts," Erin said as if the suggestion that it might not would make her less of a tattoo artist.

"Great."

"Now let me see your sketches for this mega-birthday tattoo."

Allie followed her into the townhouse she shared with her brother, Dean, and decided to just let Erin do her thing. She was a pro at this and Allie trusted her to translate her designs just like she'd planned.

After much deliberation over the sketches, Erin was ready to roll.

"This is going to be fantastic. Boys, out." She shooed Aidan and Dean from her small studio space on the first floor.

"What? I want to watch," Aidan protested. "This is for her birthday. I thought I might get something new too."

"You want him here when I tell you to take your clothes off?" Erin asked.

"Nope." Allie laughed at Aidan's look of disappointment.

"Seriously? How big is this thing? I though it was just along your scar."

"And you haven't seen my whole scar." Allie gave him a shove in the direction of the door.

"Yeah, there's going to be some side boobage involved in this design. Now get out of my studio," Erin said.

Aidan's eyes widened as he took another look at the swirly vines.

"I don't think 'boobage' is a word, Erin." He gave them a wink and went to play some sort of loud video game with Dean. *Have fun, Lex. And happy birthday.*

Thanks. But I'm blocking you, so no peeking.

I'm not that big of a tool, Lex. I can control the urge to peek. Most of the time.

What do you mean most of the time?

"This won't take long." Erin helped her get situated on the padded table and Allie shifted to her side. "You want me to make it visible to mortals? Like a regular tat?"

"You can make it visible to Immortals only?"

"That's my usual. Aidan's are mostly only visible to us. Those are easier for me to change. How about we make the vines along your bicep visible to everyone and everything else will be hidden with my gift? That way your snooty school won't flip their pedigrees when they see you. "

"I like the way you think." Allie gave her the go-ahead. She took a deep breath and relaxed as she listened to the humming of the needle. She winced at the first prick of her skin, but eventually the sensation dulled and her mind drifted.

She was well aware of the needle tracing the lines of the vines on her body. And she was equally aware of Erin's lively chatter. But Allie was in the orchard ... again.

"I'm getting sick of this place," she called loudly into the pre-dawn light. She came here almost every night she slept now and none of it made any sense. She'd walked every inch of the forest, from the orchard near the red barn, to the path through the woods, to the long driveway that led to the mansion on the hill, and then down to the beach below the cliffs to the little lake-side cottage and back up again to hike the hillside up to the orchard. Over and over and over.

"But for what reason?" she screamed, knowing no one would hear her.

"Why so screechy, killer?" Darius stepped from the barn, his hands in his pockets, the corner of his mouth turning up in that half-grin she knew so well.

"Please, I can't handle my weird-ass, un-funny gift-person wearing your face."

"Meh, I'm just a dream." He shrugged. "Nothing special, just your run-of-the-mill daydream about your handsome cop friend." He stepped beside her, tucking a loose curl behind her ear. "And you know why I'm here."

"No, I don't, actually. But I'm sure you're about to tell me something that makes no sense."

"You know why I'm here; you just haven't figured it out yet. Honestly, neither have I, but we'll both see it soon. Right here."

"Don't be cryptic. Just be my good buddy, Dare, and tell it to me straight."

He stepped closer, looking into her eyes, his half-smile tugging at her heart in that confusing way it always did. The warmth of his hands around hers calmed her frustration with these reoccurring visions.

"You and I have something special. We're linked—"

"What are you saying, Darius McBrien?" She stepped away from the comfort of his embrace. She didn't want this. Not with him.

"No, this isn't *that*. I don't think so, anyway. You and I, we're complicated and confusing."

"Why do I feel such a strange vibe with you? What is it? It's not like I'm falling for you, although sometimes in a weird way it does feel like that and it creeps me out."

"Yup, me too. But we're connected. We just don't know it yet. It's going to happen right here in this orchard. Right when we need it most."

"What's going to happen, Dare? It's not like you to be so evasive." She gave his arm a playful punch.

"I don't know exactly, Allie. I just know it will happen soon, and when it does, this thing between us will make more sense. Until then ... all I can tell you is that I'll always be the guy you need me to be. I'll always tell it to you straight. When I can."

"You okay, Allie?" Erin asked, pulling her back into the moment.

"Yeah." But she wasn't. Nothing about that vision was okay. Whatever that was needed to stay far in the distant, nondescript future. She couldn't deal with boy drama right now. "How's it going?" She peered down at her arm to see Erin's handiwork so far.

"We're done."

"Seriously? The whole thing?"

"Yeah, come see it."

Allie stood before the mirror with a sheet draped around her. The thin black and purple vines snaked across her skin in a subtle pattern that followed the ridge of her scar. Rather than mask the scar, the vines highlighted it. Before, when she looked in the mirror, she thought the scar made her look weak. With the tattoo, she looked strong.

"That's a big smile." Erin nudged her playfully. "You like?"

"I love it. Erin, you did an amazing job." She turned, following the vines along her bicep where they curled and flowed down her side to her hip with small purple flowers dotted here and there. The part that was visible to mortals shimmered in the light. It was perfect. The whole tattoo was subtle and simple, but it meant something special to Allie.

She dressed carefully in her jeans and tank, leaving her hoodie off so the boys could see most of the final design.

"Thank you, Erin." Allie tried to pay her for her hard work, but she wouldn't hear of it.

"A hug will do just fine."

Allie gave the petite girl a hug and saw a flash of dark clouds in an ominous sky. Something terrible lay in Erin's future—something that could not be avoided, but it was just a brief impression and then it was gone.

"So, what do you think?" Allie turned to see Aidan's eyes tracing the path of the vines filled with poetry.

Oh, I'm just wondering exactly where that thing ends.

The main part is showing, Aidan. Focus on that. What do you think?

"You look strong. Confident. You look more like you than you have in a long time."

She felt like it too.

"Thanks for helping me study, Allie," Kayla said as they pored over her college art history notes Thursday evening. Kayla was attending Kent State University and was struggling with this one class.

"Glad to help. Your course looks a lot like my intro to art history at CIA so it's useful study time for me too. Anytime you want to catch up and do some studying, I can talk about art for days."

"It sounded like an easy class, but I'm totally bombing it. I don't get this assignment at all."

Allie poured them each a cup of hot coffee, gagging when she realized it was decaf, and went to hunt for snacks. She was happy when Kayla called her. Things had been weird with them since Allie and Vince broke up and he and Kayla started dealing with their past. She was pretty sure they were already dating.

With her head in the fridge, she rummaged for something edible that wasn't on Naeemah's stupid diet. She wanted something with gooey chocolate, but there was nothing in the fridge but veggies and hummus.

Naeemah is an evil dark witch. Somehow she'd managed to get Lily in on this diet thing and there was nothing truly edible in the house. Lily was a steadfast carb-and-cheese-ivore—how did Naeemah manage to get her mom to buy tofu?

"What's the assignment?" Allie settled on celery sticks and peanut butter.

"We have to do compare-and-contrast essays every week on a different period of art history. So we talk about something old and then we show how it's still applicable today. I just don't get it. How are caveman paintings used anywhere in today's world?"

"I kinda want to do this assignment." Allie pulled the textbook over to see the examples of cave art Kayla was struggling with.

"I knew I came to the right art dork."

"Yes, you did. Okay, so the cave art at Lascaux would be the ancient example of how man wanted to leave a record of his time there, right?"

"Sure. Looks like useless stick figures to me, though."

"Think of it like a 'Joe was here' kind of thing."

"Like graffiti?"

"Exactly. So find some seriously cool street art to compare it with and talk about how even today we have a pathological need to doodle in public places to prove to the world we were here and we were important."

"I knew you would be useful. What about the pyramids? Luxor in Vegas?"

"Too obvious; everyone will use that. You could do the Louvre in Paris, the Rock and Roll Hall of Fame here, or the Transamerica Pyramid building in San Francisco."

"Okay, I think I get it now."

"Whenever the art part starts to get confusing, just remember it's like any other history class. Most of what we know of history comes from the art and artifacts of the different periods so it all connects."

"Thanks, Allie. I wasn't sure if it was a good idea to call you. With the whole Vince thing. I know you know there were a lot of ... extenuating circumstances."

"We're fine, Kayla. I want us all to still be friends. Especially since I think I might transfer to Kent State next year. CIA is an awesome school, but it's really expensive and the KSU art program is just as good and Sasha is probably going there too."

"What about Aidan? Where's he going?"

"He says he's going to Oberlin Conservatory just outside the city, but I know he's always planned to go to the Musical Conservatory in Germany and I don't want him to give that up."

"Well, if you come to KSU, maybe we could be roommates? Or we could all get a place together?"

"Yes, absolutely." Allie grinned. She had been afraid she and Kayla would drift apart since she and Vince were getting closer now, but Allie knew they belonged together so it didn't hurt as much.

Kinda like the way it's supposed to work with Complements, Aidan interjected. *You're with someone and then they find their Complement. You aren't angry or hurt, you're just happy for them.*

Right. I guess I never thought of it that way. It does kind of take the sting out of it.

"Allie!" Liam called from the garden just before he rushed into the living room with a sticky Kahlynn wiggling in his arms.

"Hey, Liam, what's up?"

"Oh, sorry, I didn't know you had company. I'm so sorry to interrupt, but can you babysit? I have to run out for a little while."

"Sure, I'll take her off your hands if you can clean the sticky goop off her first."

"She had Rice Krispies Treats for a snack and she's wearing most of it. It won't kill you to clean her up, Allie. I gotta run." Liam passed his daughter off to her and with a quick kiss to both their foreheads, he was gone before she could protest.

"I need a raise, Liam!"

"I don't pay you," he called from the foyer.

"Exactly my point!" The slam of the front door was not the answer she was hoping for.

"Come on, little girl, let's get you cleaned up and then you're going to show Auntie Allie where the Rice Krispies Treats are." Allie sat her niece on the counter and reached for the paper towels to clean Kahlynn's hands and face.

"Sorry about that. He's a single dad so I get babysitting duty sometimes." Allie glanced up at Kayla and saw she was white as a ghost and her hands trembled. She shook her head like she couldn't make sense of what she was seeing. Allie's eyes clouded over and a green aura washed everything in a weird light. Allie looked down at Kahlynn, grinning at her, her blue eyes sparkling with mischief. She looked up at Kayla again, her blue eyes wary and uncertain. Then Allie did the math.

"Her name's Kahlynn?" Kayla asked.

"Yeah. D-do you want to hold her?"

Kayla nodded. Her long blond hair fell over her shoulder as she reached for Kahlynn. Their hair was the same color.

Kahlynn didn't care for strangers too much, but she reached for Kayla with a smile.

Without thinking, Allie blocked Aidan from seeing this. She didn't understand what—or even how—this was happening, but she knew this wasn't something anyone else needed to see.

"So what can you tell me about the Etruscans?" Kayla asked in a calm voice. She sat with the baby in her lap, smiling down at her like Kahlynn had hung the moon.

"Lots of figure art and sculpture come from that period." Allie pulled the textbook toward her and followed Kayla's lead.

Chapter 24

"Oh good, you're here," Allie said the moment her brother stepped foot in her bedroom. "I was afraid you forgot about dream babysitting."

"No, I didn't forget," Liam said. For the past several weeks, he had watched over her as she slept. He let her dream while he watched and observed. Sometimes, when the dreams were bad, he was able to sing her through them. Liam's voice could be intoxicating as well as calming. He also made sure she had pencils and paper ready on those nights when she sketched what she saw. She had nearly filled an entire sketchbook with flames and smoke and trees with skies filled with a blood red moon. It was all useless because she still had no idea what her gift was trying to tell her and she felt an overwhelming fear that she was running out of time.

"I will help you get to sleep, but I will be leaving you to your own devices tonight. I want to see how you do on your own."

"Am I ready for that?" Allie felt her throat closing up as the fear coiled tight in her chest.

"We won't know until we try. There is nothing to be afraid of, little one. You can do this."

Just no more snakes, Aidan said.

Allie shuddered at the memory of their writhing bodies and sharp fangs.

But he's right, Lex. You can do this.

I know. I just need to toughen up.

Dream date first?

Yes, please.

See you in our usual spot. Night, babe.

Night.

With the soothing sound of Liam's voice, Allie managed to slip into a tranquil sleep when she might otherwise have tossed and turned half the night away. Every time she went to the dreamworld, she thought about Navid. Maybe this would be the night she would see him again.

In a whirl of darkness, she fell into her dreams. She recognized the signs now and was getting better at traveling there on her own. She opened her eyes to the hazy light of the dreamworld. Tonight the sky was purple, somewhere between night and day with no visible sun or moon in the sky. It was cool and crisp like the first fall evening. As she hiked up the hillside that was a replica of the one near Aidan's home, Allie mentally adjusted her clothing for the cooler weather. In an instant, she wore her favorite hoodie and jeans with her warmest boots. The tall grass bobbed in the breeze. Green in the real world, here the grass was a brilliant shade of yellow, a perfect complement to the purple sky.

Aidan hadn't managed to fall asleep yet so she wandered around the hillside toward the cliffs. Heeding Navid's warning not to go wandering off into the dreamworld without him, she was always careful that they stayed in her dreamscape.

Navid? Can you come for a visit tonight? She let the wind take her words to her father. He would hear her and if he could, he would come.

She stared down at the crystal waves below as they crashed over the jagged rocks. Much of this world reminded her of her drawings. Sometimes the edges were blurred in shadow and sometimes things were crisp and clear. She could focus on an object and eventually it would become more defined, but it always held a carbon-copy drawing quality to it.

She turned when she heard Aidan's approach, but it wasn't Aidan. Allie couldn't believe her eyes as she took an unsteady step forward.

"Quinn?" she whispered. "Is that really you?"

He walked slowly toward her, gazing through her at the cliffside with sadness in his eyes. How he must miss the only home he'd ever known.

"Quinn? Can you hear me?" She wondered if he was really there or if he was just a figment of her imagination that her subconscious mind had created because she wanted so badly to know he was okay after everything they'd just learned. But he wasn't okay. Not judging by his appearance. He looked like the Quinn she saw on the screen at Amrita.

He couldn't hear her, but Allie followed him, afraid to touch him. She feared he might disappear the instant she did.

He looked terrible. His dark skin was haggard and the lines around his eyes made him look older than his nineteen years. He was thinner in some ways. In others, he looked stronger. Harder. Meaner. Less like the quiet boy she knew. His hair was shaved close and his clothes hung loose around his narrow waist.

He spoke, but she couldn't hear him. He eased his long frame back into the tall grass, sitting with arms resting on his knees, gazing into the distance at the indistinct skyline of the city across the bay.

Allie sat opposite him and stared at his gaunt face. Wherever Quinn was in the waking world, he was not doing well.

"Allie?" Aidan called from their usual spot near the old laurel tree.

"Over here!" She stood, but kept her eyes trained on Quinn.

"Who is that?" He ran toward her. She could hear the anxiety in his voice. It was always just the two of them here. The sight of someone else startled him. "Quinn?" Aidan fell to his knees beside him.

Allie stopped him just as he reached for his friend.

"Don't," she whispered.

"What's happening, Lex? Where did he come from? Are you doing this?"

"He can't see or hear us, but he's here. Right? You can see him too?"

"Yes. He looks like hell. But what does this mean? Is it just ... something we want to see?"

"I don't know. We need to ask Navid. I asked him to come but I don't know if he heard me."

They both stared at Quinn, aching to help him in some way, but too scared they might do something wrong.

"He's really here. It's not just an illusion of what I want to see. If I conjured him somehow, it would be the version of him I remember. I don't know this guy."

Navid, please hurry. I need you, she whispered urgently, knowing he would hear the desperation in her voice.

With a silent sigh, Quinn rose to his feet and turned away from the cliffside to make his way back down the hill. He moved quickly, as if he couldn't stand the sight of home for another moment.

"Stay where you are!" Navid's voice echoed like a boom all around them. Even Quinn faltered, gazing up at the sky with a look of confusion.

Navid rushed across the hillside. "Do not leave this place, Allie. You must let him go." Navid reached to hold her back.

"But we have to follow him. We have to help him," Aidan protested, taking another step toward the edge of the forest.

"You are not a dreamwalker. Neither of you can navigate this world beyond this place. If you wander too far from here, you could get so lost in the world of dreams, it would drive you mad. You will cause more harm than good. Let him go."

"Why can't he see us?" Allie asked as they watched Quinn shuffle along the path ahead, his hands shoved deep in his pockets and his shoulders hunched as if to protect himself.

"He doesn't understand where he is yet. He just thinks he's dreaming of home."

"But he could get lost," Allie said tearfully, watching his sad retreat. "You said it could drive him mad."

"Quinn *is* a dreamwalker. He has been here before, although I've never seen him. There have been rumors of a new, untrained walker, wreaking havoc in this world. I will help him if I can."

"Go now. Go help him," Allie urged. "Find out where he is. Please, Navid."

"I will do what I can. I will try to come back soon."

"Thank you, Navid," Aidan said.

Navid gave Allie a quick hug and pressed a kiss to her forehead, and then he was gone. Quinn's footsteps faded in the darkness of the forest.

"Don't tell anyone what you have seen here." Navid's faint voice carried with the breeze.

"This is incredible," Aidan said. "I don't want to get my hopes up, but if Navid can talk to him, this might bring us one step closer to bringing Quinn home."

"Let's not get ahead of ourselves." Allie cautioned his excitement. "We don't know if Navid will be able to talk to him, or even if he can find him."

"You look more like your dad that I realized," Aidan said.

"It's the curly hair." She nodded.

"And the freckles." He smiled. "But you seem to have the same temperament too."

"I feel like I should have seen it before, you know." Allie crossed her arms over her chest. She wasn't sure if she'd ever get used to thinking of Navid as her father.

"Navid might be a while, and I believe you have some dreaming to do," Aidan said.

"Right. I hope I can stay focused enough so I don't disturb you."

"Don't worry about me. I'll be fine. Just aim for anything other than snakes. Literally anything."

"What about clowns?" She smiled.

"No clowns either." He shuddered at the thought. "How about turtles? Or bunnies?"

"Try to get some sleep, Aidan. We'll do everything we can to help Quinn."

"I know. Sweet dreams."

"Har har, funny guy."

Allie found herself wandering along the path through the woods again. Her dreams were becoming more consistent and a lot less scary. The longer she worked with Liam, the less frightening they became. She still dreamed of fire and smoke, but it didn't consume her now. The fires stayed in the distance and the forest was always the same.

A shadowed figure ran past her in a whirl.

"Quinn?" She raced along the familiar path after him. She sensed there were others, but they were shrouded in shadows. Allie stood alone near the orchard, calling his name, but he still couldn't hear her.

He moved like a lynx through the trees. Dressed in dark clothes and a black leather jacket, he blended with the night.

As the blood red moon peeked through the branches, Allie noticed the absence of the green otherworldly tinge that normally colored her dreams. This vision was more realistic. Sharper and more focused.

Focus on the important details and discard the rest. Her mantra was her lifeline.

She was here to observe. That was the difficult thing to remember when she was caught up in the throes of her most terrifying dreams. Nothing could truly hurt her here. She knew that now.

Allie followed Quinn through the forest. There were others hiding among the shadows but she couldn't tell how many.

"They are in the house," Quinn said. "They don't suspect anything." His voice was vacant and held no emotion.

Allie couldn't see the person he spoke with. The shadows thickened, creating an impenetrable barrier.

"There are only six of them." His voice was flat, as if the Quinn she knew was long gone. "They are powerful so we'll have to overwhelm them with our numbers. They won't go quietly."

He seemed so hollow, so ... empty. She wondered if he would even recognize her. They needed to do something—anything. Quinn was running out of time.

"We have to get him out of this. Whatever this is," Allie murmured.

"Allie!" Navid's voice echoed all around, pulling her abruptly from her dream. She felt an unfamiliar tug forcing her back to the dreamscape she shared with Aidan.

"Allie," Navid called as she wandered through the tall yellow grass again.

"Did you find him?" Her heart leapt in her throat at the thought her father might be able to bring Quinn home.

"I did. He is not well. He doesn't trust me."

"Where is he in the waking world? Atlanta?"

"He refused to say."

"Can you help him? Please?"

"Of course, sweetheart. I will help him as much as I can. But I may not be able to help you find him in the waking world. He seems to not want to be found. Right now my priority will be to teach him to navigate this world safely."

"Can I come with you next time?" Allie asked.

"I need you to stay away from this dreamscape for a while."

"Why?"

"He can sometimes hear you and Aidan, but he can't see you. It upsets him. Quinn is not in his right mind and he desperately needs my help."

"You'll teach him, won't you?"

"Of course. But I'm afraid that means I cannot visit you. I am a powerful dreamwalker, but I am limited by how much time I can spend here. The longer I stay, the more difficult it is to leave."

"Oh. So if you help him, you won't have enough time left over to visit me?"

"I'm afraid not."

"Go. Help Quinn. We will see each other again soon."

"I may not be able to speak to you at all, Allie. This could be the last time we speak for a while."

"I'm okay, Navid. I'm doing well. I'm safe and making good progress with my dreams. Quinn needs you more than I do right now ... not that I won't miss you."

"I will call you back to this place as soon as I'm able. I do not think it's wise to tell his parents about this. I will help him in this world, but he may refuse help in the waking world. I believe he fears his family will suffer if they keep trying to find him."

"Please, try to let me know what you find out?"

"I will, daughter. It is good to see you doing so well."

Allie waved as he faded away. She would miss him, but she hoped it wouldn't be long before she would see him again in the real world.

Chapter 25

The yard. Midnight. BYOKS
—Graham

"Did you just get this text from Graham?" Allie asked. She was curled up on the sofa in Aidan's office, studying for her AP English class.

"Yeah, we haven't done this in forever." He grinned down at his phone.

"What the crap does BYOKS mean?"

"Bring your own kitchen sink." He laughed. "That's Graham for bring food and lots of it."

"Party in the yard? Junk food? Please say there will be buckets of junk food."

"Looks like it. Let's go raid the kitchen. We'll grab a couple of bottles from Dad's bar on the way."

As Allie pilfered the kitchen for anything that didn't look like it belonged on the list of Naeemah-approved foods, she saw a glimmer of Graham pacing nervously across the yard, waiting for them to arrive.

"Wait." Allie handed Aidan a bag of cookies. "Um ... I think this might be an important thing for Graham tonight."

"What do you mean?" Aidan asked as they headed down

the hall toward the yard, arms loaded down with everything they could carry.

"Let's just say if Graham were to make an ... announcement, would you be prepared for that?"

"What kind of announcement? Could you be more vague—oh!" Aidan stopped and looked at her. "Well, it's about time."

When they arrived at the yard, Chloe and Graham were busy putting drinks in an ice chest while Sasha set up chairs around the bonfire blazing bright under the growing darkness.

"Great, you're all here." Graham had all the food they could steal spread out on a table with pizzas and cold beers for everyone.

"We should do this more often," Aidan said, digging into his pizza.

"Hello, food. How I've missed you. Would anyone judge me too harshly if I dipped my cheese pizza in the nacho cheese sauce?" Allie asked, eyeing the bubbling cheesy goo perched on a hot stone by the fire.

"Ew. That's gross, Allie." Chloe laughed.

"I don't care, it sounds delicious. I'm doin' it."

As Allie reached for the cheese dip, Graham cleared his throat and shifted nervously.

Allie gave him her best "you-can-do-it" smile and sat back, letting him take his time to get to the reason they were all there.

"How about a toast?" Graham said.

"Go for it, little dude." Aidan gave him a pat on the shoulder.

"I know we've all been preoccupied with our own shit lately. We're all dealing with issues. We all miss Quinn and everything is just messed up these days. But I love you guys and I miss this." He raised his beer for a toast.

"Here, here," Aidan said.

"And I'm gay, by the way. But I'm pretty sure none of you

have a problem with that, so ... let's drink to that." Graham smiled and tapped his beer bottle with Aidan's.

"Cheers to that." Allie beamed at him, knowing it was a huge relief to have that behind him now.

"He would be proud of you," Sasha said softly.

"I miss my brother." Graham nodded, staring at the label on his bottle. "I feel like ... making it official like that means I'm moving on without him."

"He wouldn't want any of us to stop living," Allie said. "No matter what happens, no matter where he is, Quinn wants us to go on living. To be happy. We can do that and not feel guilty because we are doing everything we can to bring him home."

"Well said." Aidan lifted his bottle and took a drink.

Allie's mind swirled with colors and images as she fell into a vision. The night was dark and moonless. She couldn't see her own feet as she stumbled along the steep path leading down to the beach. The only sound that reached her ears was the crunching of the fall leaves beneath her feet and the occasional hoot of an owl in the trees. She felt a complete absence of fear this time. Nothing here could hurt her. Nothing could scare her because it was just Allie and the darkness.

It was boring. She could smell the fires, but saw no flames. It was like the cold blackness of the void she experienced in the final moments of her Awakening. But this time all her other senses were alive.

Focus on the important details and discard the rest....

"Clearly sight isn't important tonight," she whispered softly into the darkness. "Why can't there ever be a flashing neon sign that just says, 'Allie, your vision means you'll eat chocolate chip pancakes for breakfast.'"

As she trudged ahead, she tried to focus on each sense individually. The night air was crisp and cold—like the night before the first snowfall. If she could see, she knew her breath would come out in a steady puff of white fog. She listened to the waves lapping at the shore, but something was off. "I'm nowhere near Kelleys Island."

She turned toward the lake with a frown. Her sense of direction was completely skewed. Allie gazed up at the distant stars, looking for the familiar constellations and the North star, hoping to get a better sense of where she was. With her head tilted to the sky, Allie turned until the world righted, and she faced north.

She was somewhere just to the south of Niagara or Buffalo. Wherever she was, it was in the middle of freaking nowhere. Allie stepped onto a well-worn path along the beach—the faint light of the stars illuminating the way. She followed the path behind the little cottage where it turned sharply to rise along the sloped dunes to the apple orchard secreted away in the middle of the huge forest. A big red barn sat nestled among the apple trees. The cloying scent of the fruit threatened to make her nauseous. She'd spent so much time in the orchard lately she wasn't sure she could ever stomach the sight of an apple again.

She could sense the fires and chaos just out of reach beyond the shadows. She wasn't bothered by the horrors of being right in the thick of it anymore. Without the fear, she could focus and examine the mundane details carefully. This vision was important. She didn't know how. She still didn't know what any of it meant, but it was time she figured out what her gift was trying to tell her.

As she continued along the path across the orchard and through the woods again, Allie made her way back into the clearing, near the gates. The blood red moon burst from behind the clouds and flooded the sloping lawn with light. A rambling old mansion rested atop a distant hill with miles of green lawns and gardens surrounding it. Allie could feel the heat of the fires drawing in closer. She couldn't see the flames, but she could smell the smoke. As she approached the house, her vision blurred and she saw red. Everything was red. The green lawn was bathed in blood and her vision blurred and cleared until she was back among her friends beside the bonfire.

You okay? What was that? Aidan asked.

A vision. I've never had a waking one quite that long before. It's usually over pretty quickly and it never makes much sense.

Something terrible would happen at that house. She just didn't know what it could possibly be.

Any idea what this one means?

No idea.

You've never actually been there, have you?

Where? You recognized the place?

Yeah, that was Imogen and Lucien's house up near Buffalo.

Her visions had officially struck way too close to home now.

Chapter 26

"Allie, I just don't think there's enough to go on," Liam said.

"I know. I'm sorry. I just wish this all wasn't so hard to decipher." Allie paced the length of her room. All she could really tell him was that she had a bad feeling something terrible was going to happen at Imogen and Lucien's house at some point in the nondescript future. He was right. There was nothing she could do to prepare for such a vague possibility from the visions and dreams she didn't fully understand yet. There was something she was missing. Some small piece of the puzzle she hadn't figured out yet.

"Allie, don't apologize. You are young and you're human. We are not perfect, nor infallible. All you can do is to keep doing what you've been doing. You're making so much progress, little one. I'm proud of you. You're handling your dreams all on your own now."

"Thanks, Liam." But Allie had an overwhelming sense of urgency about these dreams. She didn't figure it out soon enough last year when she first started dreaming of the caves. She never wanted to make that mistake again. The next time she dreamed of the orchard, she *had* to look for the details she was missing.

The stench of overripe apples made Allie gag.

God I hate apples. She could feel the cool breeze wash across her face and the grass tickling her cheek where she lay in the orchard. After what felt like hours of searching, she'd come up with nothing.

"Wake up, we have work to do," a familiar voice said. "You need my help this time."

"No, that can't be right," Allie muttered.

"Up!"

"So much nope. I'm going to lay here, pretending I haven't lost my mind."

"Get. Up."

Allie cracked her eyes opened and closed them again quickly. "Jeez. I'm talking to myself now. Literally, talking to myself."

"Come on, I figured it out and there isn't much time left now. You have to put your face on the game, sister."

"I think you mean 'put my game face on.'" Allie groaned as she reluctantly got to her feet.

"That's what I said."

"How can my subconscious gift be such a dork?" Allie stared at the identical version of herself looking blankly back at her. "Please tell me my hair doesn't look like that?"

"Shut up and let's do this," gift-Allie said. Her face was so serious and pale, the real Allie knew this was not going to be good. After weeks of dreaming about this place, something significant might finally happen now.

"Show me."

"Come on. And pay attention. We only get to do this once."

"I can't be that bossy," Allie muttered as she followed

herself through the orchard and along the well-worn path to the big house on the hill.

"Come on, keep up."

"I'm coming." Allie hurried to match her gift's faster stride. Clearly this was important.

Or clearly, I have finally cracked and I'm on my way to the loony bin.

"No jokes, funny girl. This is serious. Pay attention."

"What are you, a mind reader?" Allie snapped.

The withering glare she gave herself could have cut glass.

"Right, that was totally dumb. Don't tell anyone I said that. So what are we looking for?"

"We're eavesdropping." Gift-Allie sank into a crouch as they approached the back of the house. She slipped up to the patio door and crept inside.

Allie heard familiar voices coming from the living room.

"Can they actually see us? Couldn't we just walk in and take a seat and see what's up?"

"Oh, right." The shock on gift-Allie's face was rather insulting.

"Oh come on, let's just do this." Allie stood and walked across the empty kitchen to the living room at the front of the house where Gregg and Naeemah sat in conference with Imogen, Lucien, Aide, and Hélène. Allie and her gift sat on the couch beside Naeemah and watched.

"Pay attention."

"I will if you'll shut up," Allie hissed.

"What can we do, Gregg?" Aide sighed in frustration. "It's been eight months."

"We know exactly where he is now, and we know what they intend to do with him. But we can't get close enough to make a move." Gregg's frustration was evident in his tone.

"Oooh, this is about Quinn," Allie said. "It's about time they come up with a plan."

"Shhh!" Gift-Allie elbowed her.

"Why can't we just set up a Senate raid on Soma?" Hélène asked. "We have all the right connections and I can't stomach the thought of my little brother with that vile woman for one more second."

"Livia?" Allie asked. "Have the found her?"

"Shhh!"

"Right, quiet."

"The Senate is in Soma's pocket," Gregg said. "We'd never get approval for a raid."

"So we are at an impasse?" Aide asked. "Is there nothing we can do to get Quinn out of there?"

"We aren't asking the right questions." Gregg frowned into his tumbler of bourbon.

"Can't we just offer to buy him back?" Naeemah asked. "I know they probably won't agree, but it's worth a shot."

"That's what I said." Allie thought it was a good idea, but Naeemah was probably right—they'd never go for it. Soma wouldn't want an eyewitness out of their control and the Senate wouldn't want someone who could corroborate the existence of the slave market, nor their involvement in it.

"Soma will not accept a bid from anyone they haven't vetted first," Aide said. "What do we know of Livia's recent activity?" Aide pulled his notes in front of him. "Let's go over it all again."

Allie jumped up to hang over his shoulder to see the dossier on Livia. It wasn't much. Just a few grainy pictures of her speaking with a young Hispanic girl at a coffee cart on a busy city street corner. And Aide's handwritten notes.

"She isn't registered with the Senate," Imogen said. "No one's ever heard of her outside of Soma. She heads the company but she is an enigma, rarely showing her face publicly. She has executives who handle everything for her. I just can't imagine how she's made it over two centuries as an unknown."

"She is in deep with the Coalition," Lucien added. "She sits high among the Margrave as a trusted servant to the current Marches, but others on the Margrave's council don't seem to know of her. She spends much of her time in Atlanta at Soma's headquarters in Sterling Tower. Her movements suggest she comes and goes as she pleases, but she is impossible to track. We can't seem to get close no matter what we do."

"And until we find her, we have no hope of rescuing Quinn," Imogen said.

"We must draw her out." Gregg drained the last of the bourbon from his glass.

"How?" Naeemah asked.

"Give her what she wants—or make her think she can take what she wants by force."

"Me. He's talking about me," Allie realized.

"Shhh!"

"What? It's a great plan. I'm awesome bait."

"If we knew what she wanted, that might work," Aide said.

"Aye, but I do know what she wants."

"How do you know?" Hélène asked. "We've been digging for months and found nothing."

"She wants the same thing she wanted last summer. It's what drew her out the first time. We'll just make it seem as if we've gotten sloppy and give her the opportunity again."

"No," Naeemah snarled.

"Nae, I wouldn't even consider it if we had another prospect, but we're running out of time."

"What are we missing?" Lucien frowned at their heated exchange.

"What she wants more than anything is Allie," Gregg said.

"Allie?" Imogen gasped. "But why?"

"There is more to Allie's past than we first assumed. But it's up to her to tell everyone when she is ready," Gregg said. "Livia risked her cover when she came to inspect Allie and Quinn—and for someone of such high rank, it was more than a cursory interest that brought her out. We just need to give her another opportunity to do the same—while keeping our Allie perfectly safe," he added before Naeemah could protest. "It has to happen, Nae. It's the best option we have to reach Quinn—before it's too late. It is worth the risk now while we have the time to carefully plan and act. To wait any longer, we run the risk of acting desperately."

"We will not use her as bait, Greggory McBrien!"

"I'm afraid we have to, love."

"I'm cool with that," Allie said. "If it helps bring Quinn home."

"This isn't why we're here, Allie," her gift said. "Keep watching."

"We've got company, Gregg." Aide stood to peek through the blinds into the darkness.

"What? How? The gate is impossible to breach without a code." Lucien leapt to his feet.

"How many?" Naeemah asked, rising to join the others.

"Mortals. Six of them. Immortals too. They're swarming the lawn and their fires burn for us already," Aide said.

"Get to the barn!" Hélène ran to the hidden entrance that provided a means of escape through the man-made tunnels. But she wasn't fast enough. The front door splintered and a swarm of Coalition filled the room. They had a bullet through Hélène's chest before she could react, and a slim metal collar clasped around her throat.

"Count them!" gift-Allie demanded. "We need to know how many we're facing."

"I see a dozen here with eight more out on the lawn." Allie darted away from the window just as she saw a familiar mark. The ouroboros brand. Just like the one she saw at Amrita! This wasn't just the Coalition. This was Soma, which had to mean Livia was behind this.

"Go!" Hélène turned to her husband. "Now! Gen, please get him out of here!"

Imogen and Gregg pulled Aide away from his wife and retreated farther into the house to escape through the back.

Allie ran after them, watching as Naeemah and Gregg split up. Panic seized her chest.

"Stay calm. This isn't happening," her gift reminded her. "At least not yet."

"This is our chance to see everything and stop it," Allie said in determination. "Pick out the most important information and discard the rest."

"Exactly," gift-Allie agreed.

Allie headed for the beach. She knew from all her wandering around that they could escape down the cliffs to the beach and circle around and back up the steep path to the orchard and the barn where they would be better equipped to fight. They would regroup there to fight for Hélène, but they had little choice but to leave her behind for the moment.

"They need help," Allie said. "If they had more numbers, they could handle this."

"It's more than that," her gift said. "There is something we aren't seeing. Some detail has us blind. Keep watching. We don't make any decisions until we see everything."

"Right." Allie jogged beside herself and down the steps to the beach below.

The eerie silence descended and Allie couldn't even hear

the waves crashing along the rocky shore. Green shadows blurred her peripheral vision and she stumbled in the unnatural darkness.

"This is weird. What aren't we seeing?"

"I don't know, something has us blocked."

"What do we do?"

"Do what we can with what we've got and hope like hell it's enough," gift-Allie said.

Allie caught up to Gregg and Aide as they crouched along the path leading back up to the orchard.

"Where is Naeemah?" Allie searched but couldn't see her anywhere.

"They'll separate the Complements. That's the first line of defense," gift-Allie said.

"Right. You were paying more attention to Daniel's lessons than I was."

"I am you, you nitwit. You were listening."

"Aidan's right. I'm totally mean."

"Shhh!"

As they made their way up to the barn, more Coalition waited for them. Fires blazed out of control in the forests around the house, and black smoke filled the sky, just like it had in all her nightmares before. This time she was back in the thick of it. But this time she had the whole picture ... almost.

Gregg and Aide fought their way through the trees, with Imogen bringing up the rear, but they were completely unprepared for this attack. They weren't even armed.

"That's why we're here," gift-Allie said. "This is *not* going to happen."

"If we have anything to do with it, it certainly won't," Allie agreed with herself, reaching for a fist bump but got a blank stare in return.

Shadowed figures swarmed the orchard.

"How many here?" gift-Allie asked.

"Fifteen? Thirty? I don't know. It seems like the same group from the house, but I wouldn't bet my life on it," Allie said.

"It's their lives were betting on." Her gift pointed to the fight playing out before them.

Gregg wielded a knife from his boot, taking out several mortals before three Immortals took him down. He didn't leave them unscathed, unleashing the brunt of his electromagnetic power into them. The three men fell to the ground, twitching and jerking. But the collar that snapped around Gregg's neck was done so by mortal hands, not as affected by his magnetic pulse that could separate an Immortal from their power.

"No!" Allie gasped at the sight of the strongest man she'd ever known, down on his knees in the dirt. Unarmed and helpless with that damned collar around his throat. "This will *not* happen!"

"Focus on the important details and discard the rest," gift-Allie said. "Do not let your emotions cloud what you see. Watch without fear so we can stop this."

"Naeemah!" Gregg cried at the sound of gunfire.

Allie stared as Naeemah fell from the trees, her body riddled with bullets. She'd tried to travel through the trees to reach Hélène, but they were watching for her.

"They know what their abilities are." Allie gasped as the realization struck her. "They're prepared. They know exactly who they're facing and they know exactly how to use their power against them."

"But the question remains, how did they get past the gates?" gift-Allie asked.

"Lucien's an architect. He designed this place like a fortress. He would have made it impossible for anyone to break in," Allie said.

"And yet, it seems they've managed to just walk right in."

"We've been betrayed," Allie said. "But who? How?"

"That's what we need to find out."

Allie took a step back and stumbled to her knees, watching in horror as Gregg, Naeemah, Aide, and Hélène were all collared and forced to their knees beside a raging fire.

"No," Allie choked as she caught sight of two bodies lying on the ground behind them. "Gen? No, please no...." Allie's tears streaked down her face, mixing with soot and sweat. Her heart broke for Aidan. He adored his sister. But Lucien and Gen lay dead beside the fire. "How can they do this? Imogen was so talented and Lucien was so young. It's just wrong. We have to stop this!"

"Focus." Gift-Allie forced her to turn away from the awful sight of Aidan's dead sister and her Complement—Complements no longer.

Green shadows danced in her peripheral vision, and distant voices spoke. Allie reeled from seeing so much happen in such a short time. But she had to focus. She needed to watch objectively if she was going to gather the information she needed to stop this.

"You will bend knee to the Coalition or this ends here, for all of you." The Immortal man was dressed all in black and he spoke with authority, but he was not the one in charge here. He was just a mouthpiece.

"You will have to kill us too," Gregg spat. He was not afraid to die if he must. He grasped Naeemah's hands and they turned to face their enemy, resolved to meet their death together.

Eerie, unnatural silence filled the night. Muted voices sounded just out of reach, and dark shadows whirled around them, like a movie with the sound turned down.

"What aren't we seeing?" Allie cried, fearing what would

come next. It was bad enough seeing Imogen and Lucien dead, but she couldn't handle watching an execution.

"Drain them, then end them." The Immortal's voice returned, loud after his long muffled silence. "But keep the other two. Use the male to control the female. She might be useful."

"No!" Hélène screamed as they took Aide, binding him with magnetized cords, and dragged him away from the others.

Hélène succumbed to the same treatment, tears streaming down her face as they dragged her through the dirt. She met Naeemah's steely gaze one last time. "Be strong, sister," she whispered.

When they were gone, Gregg turned to Naeemah and her eyes filled with tears.

"Nae, love. Do not cry. Be strong. Where we go, we go together."

Allie sobbed. "I can't watch this." She turned her head, wishing she was anywhere but here.

"We have to." Gift-Allie pulled her hair back and made her watch. "This is the only chance we have. Everything we're seeing now—it's going to happen no matter what we do. But we can change it. This is not set in stone. It will happen, but it doesn't have to happen like this. And we have to be prepared to react. Every decision we make now will affect what happens here. It will affect how this plays out, so we need to have all the information."

Dark, gloved hands grasped their skulls as Naeemah and Gregg's shrieks echoed in Allie's mind. Shaking and trembling they held each other, completely drained of the gifts that made them who they were.

Blood oozed from Gregg's nose as he cried out in agony, his voice full of grief and regret. The knife—his own—pierced his heart.

Naeemah gasped when the same knife ripped through her chest a moment later. Their bond was broken by their mortal wounds, and all that was left of them began to slip away.

A bloody hand tossed their still-beating hearts into the fire and the night exploded in golden-amber light.

Naeemah slumped forward, collapsing onto Gregg, their vacant eyes blank and staring.

"No!" Allie sobbed, her shrieks ripping through her throat like broken glass. The world flashed a brilliant shade of chartreuse and then faded to black and white—the afterimage branded in her mind forever.

"That can't be it?" She struggled as she fell into the darkness of the void. She still didn't know one very important piece of the puzzle—the most important detail of all. She had no idea when this would happen.

Chapter 27

"Allie!" Aidan shook her. "Wake up, please wake up!"

"No!" she shrieked, her eyes flying open. She sat up in bed, tears drenching her face. "No, Aidan, no!" she sobbed. "I'm so sorry! I'm so sorry!" She held him tightly. "It hasn't happened yet. We won't let it happen ... not like that."

"Breathe, Lex. We have to pull it together. It was a dream, baby. Take a deep breath and tell me everything. Do you know what it means? Can we stop it? How much time do we have?"

"We can change it." She nodded. "But I don't know when it's going to happen." She shivered, still caught up in her nightmare. How could she miss such an important detail? "I don't know how ... I don't know what to do."

"We have to find out when this is happening. Think, Allie, please?" His eyes were wide with the horror of witnessing his parents' gruesome death.

The thought that it could happen at any moment—that they might have to sit back and helplessly do nothing while so many of their family were brutally murdered—left them both terrified.

"It doesn't have to be this bad, but we can't avoid it completely. I, I just need to think." Allie's hands trembled as her mind whirled with visions too fast for her to process.

"Shhhh, Lex. Pull it together. We need you."

She couldn't still her sobs. The horror of Naeemah and Gregg's murder was still too fresh in her mind.

"Aidan, what the hell is going on?" Liam growled. "I thought we agreed you would stay out and let her dream."

"This is bad, Liam." The tears in his eyes were enough to convince his uncle of the seriousness of the situation.

"Liam," Allie cried, scrambling into his arms. "I can't stop it. Please ... tell me what to do."

"Deep breaths, little one. We'll sort this out." He turned to Aidan. "What did she see?"

"Gen. Lucien ... and Mom and Dad's execution. It was awful. She doesn't know when, but she saw them drained and killed and Aide and Hélène were—are taken."

"Let's go. We'll call everyone to the common room and we'll figure this out together."

Allie fumbled with her clothes, dressing quickly, and then Liam gathered her in his arms. She was shaking so hard she could barely stand.

She needed to calm down. This was important and she didn't know how much time she had. Allie couldn't afford to fall apart now. This was a puzzle she needed to piece together.

Pick out the most important information and discard the rest as junk.

She had all the information she needed. She'd been dreaming about this for weeks and it was time to figure out how it all fit. One thing she knew for certain, she had some difficult decisions to make and it would be important to make the others listen to her when their instincts told them Allie's gift was too young to trust so blindly.

Allie needed to look at the big picture and distance herself from her emotions. Like it or not, it was up to her to decide who lived and who died.

When they arrived in the underground, Allie was feeling better, more confident and focused on the task ahead. They had time. She wasn't sure how much, but she imagined a few weeks at least. But she had a nagging feeling she was missing something huge. Why would her gift show her so much, but then not reveal when it would happen?

"Where are they?" she asked, combing her hands through her tangled hair. Everyone else was there, but Naeemah and Gregg were suspiciously absent.

"They left for Imogen's house early this evening," Ming said gently.

Allie nearly fainted. They were out of time already. This was happening *now*. Her mind whirled with green shadows, smoke and fire, making her dizzy. Her eyes glazed and she saw the sun blazing overhead followed by a blood red moon rising high over the lake.

"The moon." That was her clue all along and she missed it. "When is the next lunar eclipse?" She glanced around the room as everyone looked to Naomi for reasons Allie couldn't fathom.

"It will be a full harvest moon tomorrow night. The first true blood moon we've had in years," Naomi whispered. "I will be at my strongest on such a night. You draw your strength from the sun, I draw mine from the moon."

"Call them back. Get them out of there!" Allie nearly lost it again, dropping to her knees. She pressed her forehead to the cool stone floor and took deep breaths. She couldn't let her fear and her grief cloud her judgment. She had to put her big-girl pants on and do this. *Keep looking for the important information, Allie. We still have time.*

Her breath grew even and steady as she knelt on the floor.

Ming Lao crouched beside her, a comforting hand resting on her back. Allie cleared her mind and focused, using the breathing techniques Ming had taught her.

Gregg's words from her dream came back to her now. *What she wants more than anything is Allie ... We must draw her out ... Give her what she wants—or make her think she can take what she wants by force.*

Livia was behind all of this. For some reason she chose Imogen's home for this attack—and if Allie's hunch was right, they could thank Quinn for that. At least she wasn't coming here. Allie got to her feet and gazed at the ashen faces all around her. She knew what she had to do.

"No." She shook her head. "They need to stay where they are. We have to face this one way or another. Better there than here. Get them on the phone. I need to talk to Gregg. We have thirty-six hours to prepare for this." Allie's voice sounded cold to her own ears. But if she was going to do this, she had to be calculated in her decisions. If she let herself feel, she wouldn't make it through this.

"Allie, you've done well." Gregg's voice drifted from the speakerphone. "But we can handle this. We have time to prepare. You've given us more than a full day to gather our forces to fight this threat."

"It will not be enough." She could see it now. As they made decisions, the tenuous future changed and morphed. She didn't need to dream to know simply preparing wouldn't be enough. *Look for the important details and discard the rest.* Her mantra echoed in her mind. "I need to talk to you privately." Allie took the phone and headed for Aidan's soundproofed music room.

"I know why you're there, Gregg," she said carefully as she closed the door behind her.

"Tell me everything you've seen, and don't leave anything out."

"I know you want to draw Livia out and I know you want to use me as bait. So let's do it. She's coming for me, so let's make her think she can do it. There is a lot I can't see. I won't lie to you about that. I've not actually seen her there, but she's wrapped up in this, I just know it." Allie paced the length of the room. "You can't die, Gregg. We all need you, but ... I can't lose you. I love you ... Aidan loves you ... and you're the only connection I have to my mother."

"She always said she had to focus on the details that mattered and ignore the rest. You need to look at your visions objectively and don't be influenced by the terrible things you see. You know this can be altered? The future is never easy to read, Allie. It's always changing and things set in motion years ago can affect what will happen."

"We cannot escape this attack."

"But why does she think she can get to you here?" Gregg asked. "That's the part that doesn't make sense. How does she even know to come for you here?"

"I, I don't know. That's one thing I can't see yet. I just know it will happen there or it will happen somewhere else. And it will be soon."

"Best to let it happen here."

"But everything else—your death, Gen and Lucien's. Aide and Hélène's capture ... it doesn't have to happen, but I don't know if we can escape without some loss. We can always try to rescue anyone captured. They can always escape. But we can't undo death, so let's try to avoid that."

"We must focus on the big picture, sweetheart. I hate to see you make such difficult decisions, but I need you to tell me everything you're thinking. We need to be on the same page, Allie. I don't want you thinking you can sacrifice yourself to save us—"

"If it comes to that, I will. I won't let you die to protect me, but I won't be making any heroic gestures unless I have no other choice."

"Allie, I'm an old man. I've lived long enough to not fear death—"

"Well, I haven't, so I'll be fearing your death for you. We don't have time for arguing, old man. I need to know you'll trust me when I say something must happen. I know I'm young but I understand my gift now. I know what we need to do. It's just going to take a lot of manipulating the situation to reach a less sucky end."

"You are her daughter. You have my complete confidence and my trust. But hear me now, Alexis Carmichael. You are not infallible. You can only do the best you can do. No matter what happens, we all know that."

"I need you to stay where you are. Call in whatever help you can get, but I don't think increasing our numbers will be enough. You'll be fighting Immortals and mortals who know exactly what you can do, so your gifts aren't going to help you much. Get yourselves armed now. They will fight dirty—they know what you can do—"

"How?"

"I have a theory about that, but I'm not a hundred percent sure."

"Tell me, Allie. I need to know."

"It will only distract you. It's not important now. They already know and you need to prepare for that. They will expect you to use your electromagnetic weapon; they will expect Naeemah to take to the trees. They'll have Hélène before she can blink—don't even try to run for tunnel entrance. You won't have enough time. We have to be careful not to make any big moves at the beginning. Give them a false sense of confidence that it will all go as they have planned. Once it begins, then we make our move."

"The future is such a tricky thing," Gregg said. "All you can do is be confident in your decisions and trust your intuition."

"It's already changing. It's changing so fast I'm having trouble keeping up with it and answering questions."

"Work with Ming; she will help you relax so you can see."

"How will I get there?"

"Liam will bring you early tomorrow afternoon. We don't want everyone flooding in at the same time."

"We will need more numbers. But we have to split up the Complements. Send them back—"

"We don't have time, Allie. The Complements will have to fight. I'll fight with Emma, Nae will fight with Jin, Ming with Greyson, and George with Daniel to keep us all separate and the enemy confused. We have no other choice."

"I don't like this. We need more."

"Aye, we're going to need all hands on deck. We don't know their numbers, do we?"

"It seems like a few dozen, mostly mortal, but I can't see everything. It's like I can feel there are many more present, but I just can't see it."

"We'll call everyone who can get here in time."

"You're right, we do need all hands on deck, Gregg." Allie paused, hoping he wouldn't flip out at the mere suggestion that Allie and her friends should be there to help.

"No."

"It will make a difference if we're all there." Allie knew she would have to fight him on this. He wouldn't let the kids help, but she knew more than ever now that they would each play a key role in this. Quinn warned her through the cryptic message he sent to her at Amrita. And there was a reason her gift had worn so many faces throughout her recent dreams. It was vital to their success that each of her friends be present in this fight.

"Absolutely not. I don't even want you there, but if Livia is behind this, she needs to think she can get to you."

"She'll see right through it if I'm the only one there. We all need to be there."

"No."

"You said you would trust me."

"You're asking me to jeopardize my children. I'd rather die than see anything happen to them. I can't worry about six children during a fight for my life. Worrying about one child I love is nearly killing me. Allie, I have to refuse you on this. We will have enough numbers without them. We need to be able to focus on the fight."

She'd expected it would go this way. She hadn't really thought he would concede. Aidan would have to get them there some other way.

"Keep me updated—and thank you, Allie. She would be proud."

"Just don't die, Gregg. I can't bear the thought. I love you both so much—"

"Aye. And we love you too, sweetheart. I'll not let anything happen to you."

"I'm not worried about me, Gregg. Just ... please be safe."

"Relax Allie. This won't work if you are too keyed up to focus," Ming Lao said softly.

"This is a waste of time."

"No one expects perfection, sweetheart. You need to relax and take a minute to breathe and focus. We all trust you to do your best. Drink this tea. It will help." Ming was trying to help her relax to see if she could sleep again. Allie lay on the sofa in the dim light of Ming's office. If she could dream again, it could give them more of an advantage than they already had, but Allie was so restless, she doubted she would be able to sleep until this was over.

Allie's hand brushed Ming's and she stilled at the contact as hundreds of horrifying images flashed through her mind.

"No." Her hands trembled as she took the cup from Ming.

"Careful, this tea is very powerful." She took the cup and set it aside.

Allie's tears ran silently down her cheeks. She was lost in her visions, not heeding Ming's words.

"What have you seen?"

"I don't understand." Allie shook her head in confusion. Her eyes glazed as she sought her teacher's hand. She couldn't tell her. It would be too cruel. Something terrible would happen to Ming and Jin. Something that would change their lives forever, but she didn't understand what she'd seen. It would happen no matter what they did now. As the hours ticked down, the future began to solidify. But if they could survive, they could recover from anything.

"It's nothing." She gave Ming's hand a squeeze and reached for her tea.

"If you've seen something regarding our fate ... know that we have lived a long and full life. We do not fear death. My biggest fear is for my child. If something should happen to Jin and I, be there for Chloe? She loves you so much. She looks up to you like a sister."

"Just be careful, Ming." Allie didn't know what they faced. Whatever it was, it was an abomination and Chloe had to be there to help them. If she wasn't ... her parents wouldn't make it.

"Lie back and breathe, Allie. Clear all thought from your mind."

She was right; Allie needed to relax and then gather her

thoughts. She needed to go through everything she'd seen in her dreams these last weeks. She would study every detail. Only then could she carve out the path that would lead to the least amount of loss.

Chapter 28

We need to talk, privately, Allie said. She was supposed to be resting since it was the middle of the night and nothing could be done yet. But it was impossible and a total waste of time. Liam had been watching her every move and he was driving her nuts, fussing over her like a mama hen. He finally left her alone so she could rest, but Allie needed a moment with Aidan to figure out a plan. She had an idea, but it was crazy and she wasn't sure he trusted her quite *that* much.

Meet me in my office.

She could feel his anxiety through their connection and it killed her. She would do anything in her power to keep them all safe. She couldn't afford to make any mistakes and ignoring her instincts, and Quinn's warning that they all needed to be there, would be the biggest mistake she could possibly make right now. Aidan and the others had to be there. She didn't have the time or patience to convince Gregg, but she knew Aidan would trust her and this was a conversation that needed to take place in person.

"Have you lost your damn mind?" Aidan stood waiting at the doorway of his office when she approached.

"Just hear me out." She closed the door behind her. Apparently, Aidan had picked up on what she was considering.

"I'm listening, but I'm going to say no." He folded his arms across his chest, giving her that arrogant stubborn look he'd mastered so well.

"I need you to get yourself and the others to the orchard near Imogen and Lucien's house by sunset tomorrow."

"I don't have a problem with that. Even though Dad will literally lock me in the crypt until I'm eighty if we show up."

"You have to be there, Aidan. All of you."

"Chloe too? She's so young, Lex—"

"If she isn't there, her parents *will* die tomorrow."

Aidan paled. "We'll be there, I'll make sure of it. I just have to figure out how to give the babysitters the slip. And then get us all there in time. And your idea sucks." He pointed at her and paced across the room in frustration.

"I know, but just trust me, Aidan. You need to get there within the next twenty-four hours, and walking out the front door isn't an option. I know you don't like it, but we have to call Vince," Allie said.

"And you know we don't have time for arguing."

"I wouldn't even mention it if I wasn't one thousand percent sure it's safe. If you can get out of here, Vince will help you guys get to a car."

"Like hell he will."

"Trust me. We can rely on him for this. He won't ask questions. All I have to do is call him and tell him where to meet you."

"What if that's in the middle of the lake and we all come popping up through the ice? You think he'll overlook that?"

"Yes. He will not question it."

"You realize you're telling me he knows more than he should."

"I never told him anything." Allie took a step forward, closing the distance between them.

"Lex, I don't trust that guy—"

"Then trust me." She grabbed his hands. "Trust in my gift. I know he will not betray us. And we don't have time for this, Aidan, so how are you going to get out of here?" His grandparents, Nadira and Sayid were staying behind to keep an eye on the kids, so they would have to find a way to leave without their knowledge.

"The only way out that my grandparents probably won't think about is through the yard. Seamas and Fitzie will be guarding the main hall so they won't notice we're gone till it's too late. There's a tunnel that leads to the water and we can swim out that way, but it's going to be cold as a—"

"Can you warm the water as you go?"

"I can do something, but I don't want to zap all my energy before we get there."

"No. Definitely don't do that," Allie said. "Take care of yourself, Aidan. This is not the games and it's not Amrita. This is real."

"Just have Vince pick us up three miles northeast of the island late tomorrow morning. And tell him he's to ask no questions and he's to leave the second we get to the mainland."

"I'll handle that. You just get yourselves there and be safe."

"I don't like this, Allie. Are you sure we can trust him?"

"I know we can. Now go keep Liam off my tail long enough to make this call and then I need to go home at some point to gear up. I want my mother's sai with me tonight."

"I'll go with you whenever you're ready."

Allie watched as he slipped out of the office. She knew he hated this idea.

She blocked him as she scrolled through her phone book.

Vince answered on the third ring.

"Allie? What's up?" He sounded groggy.

"Sorry, I just realized it's the middle of the night."

"You sound worried. What's wrong?"

"You don't want to know the details, but I have an enormous favor."

"You know you can count on me not to ask questions. What do you need?"

"I need you to get to the island and steal Aidan's boat."

"I could do that. I have no problem screwing with him, but this sounds serious. Is it dangerous?"

"Not this part. I just need you to meet Aidan and the others about three miles northeast of the island in the morning. Pick them up and get them to the mainland where they can get a car. Aidan will give you directions. As soon as you drop them off, *leave*. Immediately."

"Does this have anything to do with some people I know?"

"Yes and no. Let's just say they're the super-sized version of the ones you know, and they are playing a much harder game."

"Shit, Allie, those Soma people are dangerous."

"You know about Soma?"

"I know they're batshit crazy. Text me the coordinates and the time and I'll be there."

"Will do."

"Be careful, Allie. I don't like this, but I'm not asking questions. I do not want to know what you guys have gotten yourselves into, but I've got your back whenever you need me."

"Thank you, Vin. I knew I could count on you."

Allie turned around and ran right into a hard chest.

"He's Coalition?" Aidan hissed.

"How did you—"

"You blocked me, but did you forget my ears still work?"

"Ahh, crap."

"Answer me, Alexis Ann."

"No. He's not Coalition."

"Allie—"

"We don't have time for this. I need you to trust me." She thumped his chest to get through to him. "This is our best option of getting you there. I promise he will not ask any questions or make any trouble."

"I don't like this."

"You think I do? I don't want to put him in danger again."

"Allie?" Liam stomped into the office. "You're supposed to be resting."

"Sorry, I was just … uh … saying goodbye."

"Come on, we are leaving in a few hours and it would help if you can manage some sleep first."

"I'll … see you soon." Allie stepped away, but Aidan pulled her back. Hard. He held her tight against his chest, but his lips barely brushed hers. "Be safe," he murmured in her ear before letting her go. *I'll meet you in the tunnels whenever you can slip away. We'll go get your stuff and check on your parents. I asked Dad to put a few guards near your house for the next day or two.*

Thank you for thinking of them, Aidan. He knew she would worry about their safety through all of this.

"Enough of that. Come on, little one, you've said your goodbyes."

Chapter 29

Finally, Aidan said when Allie stepped into the tunnel leading to her house.

Liam's in full-blown big brother mode. She shrugged. *It's kind of nice, but annoying at the same time. I had to convince him no one was going to attack me in the middle of the night in the tunnels.*

Allie ran swiftly beside Aidan. The closer they came to her house, the more she worried about the safety of her parents. What if something happened to them in the middle of all of this?

They'll be fine, Lex. Dad wouldn't leave them unprotected.

I know, I'll just feel better seeing it for myself.

They took the side entrance to her tower bedroom and slipped into the house quietly, trying not to wake her parents.

"Let's get your things, babe." Aidan grabbed her hand and led her upstairs to her room.

"I need my sai and my weapons belt." She headed to her closet to gather her weapons from their hiding place.

"Where's your gear?" Aidan asked.

"In the bathroom at the back of the linen closet."

She heard him rumbling around for her black armored fatigues. She hadn't worn them since the games last year. *Hope they still fit.* She fumbled through her closet for her bladed quarterstaff and the jewelry box containing her growing collection of concealed weapons. Her hands shook as she lifted the coiled bracelet—a whip in disguise. She hadn't worn it since the night of the ball.

"Got everything?" he asked.

"Almost." Allie lifted Kassandre's necklace over her head, feeling her mother's protection wrap around her like a comforting blanket. Just knowing it was there gave her strength.

Allie laid her things on the bed, taking stock of what she might need over the next twenty-four hours. She chewed her thumbnail, racking her brain for anything she might be missing.

"Relax, Lex," Aidan said as he stepped behind her, his breath stirring her hair.

"I don't think I can. Not till this is over and everyone is safe."

His hand slipped around hers, turning her to face him. His arms snaked around her waist as he pressed his forehead against hers. "Promise me you'll be careful, Alexis Ann. Don't you go trying anything heroic that will jeopardize yourself. No one expects you to fix this all on your own."

"I know. But I have to try, Aidan. I can't let our—your family die."

"They are just as much your family as mine and they all love you.... I love you. I love you for doing everything in your power to protect them." His breath was warm on her face and her heart thumped in her chest. She knew he could feel everything she felt in that moment, both through his gift and their connection.

"Aidan ... I—"

"You don't have to say it. I know you aren't ready. Your fear of us is your fatal flaw." His arrogant smirk chased her nerves away.

"Well ... maybe I'm not so scared anymore." She gazed up at him. She was so tired of resisting him when that was the last thing she wanted. With everything they faced, she could feel her walls crumbling and she just wanted to be near him. To feel his arms around her.

His irritable growl rumbled in his chest. "You have the worst timing ever." He crushed her against him.

"I can take it back." She pressed her face into the warmth of his sweater.

"Don't you dare." He laughed, holding her tighter.

"Take care of yourself, Aidan. I, I don't want this to change you—to change us," she whispered. The visions flashed through her mind so quickly she struggled to keep up with the important details. She saw so much looming before them, beyond the immediate threat—the one the thing she feared the most. If she failed him when he needed her, he might never forgive her. But if she saved him, he would never look at her the same again. It was a no-win situation.

"What have you seen? What do I need to know, Allie?" He tilted her chin up to meet his gaze. "You're blocking me again."

"Just promise me you'll take care of yourself and don't worry so much about me. I'll be with you, Darius, and Liam. I'll be fine."

"I'll never be able to stop worrying about you, but I'll stay focused on what's in front of me. And right now that's you." He leaned down and kissed her. His lips were soft and gentle—the kiss a promise of something more if she was ready, but it was over before she could really enjoy it.

She trembled, the moment completely overwhelming her.

"What do you need, Lex?" He frowned down at her. "I'm here, baby. What can I do?"

"Aidan, I'm so tired of being angry and scared all the time," she whispered. "I've been in such a rage for months—I'm sick of it. I want to feel something good. I need to forget. For a little while." She reached up to cup his face, her thumb scraping over the hint of stubble along his jaw. She was done resisting the pull of Aidan.

"Alexis Ann, you're killing me," he whispered as he held her close and brought his lips down to hers. They tumbled to the bed, scattering her battle gear as Allie moved to peel his shirt up over his head.

They'd slept together so many nights that feeling his bare skin against hers wasn't a foreign sensation anymore, but she'd missed it. Missed him.

"Allie, what is this?" Aidan leaned back, taking a slow deep breath. "If you want me to make you forget for a while, I can do that. If you want me to make you feel good, I'm *dying* to do that, baby." He kissed her throat, taking another deep breath, inhaling the scent of her hair. "But I do not want to risk our friendship on an impulsive decision. You know how much I love you. You have my heart." He pressed her palm over his bare chest. "I want *us* ... more than I've ever wanted anything. I'm in this, Allie. But I don't ever want your regret." He was asking her if she was all in, and this time she was ready.

She could feel the rhythmic thudding of his heart, beating as fast as hers. She slid her palm down his chest to his waist, taking a moment to really think about what was happening between them. She'd fought for so long, resisting him since the day she first met him. Her fear seemed like such a trivial thing now. She wasn't sure she could articulate in words what she was feeling. Allie opened her mind to Aidan's and let her thoughts speak for her.

No matter what happens between us, we will always be more than just friends. We will always be equals. It would break my heart to lose you, but you're part of me now. The best part of me. No matter where life takes us, we will always have that. "I love you, Aidan." She reached up to stroke his face, hovering over hers. "That is the only thing I'm certain of now. But you knew that long before I did." She pulled him closer, wrapping her arms around him.

I love you, Allie. Nothing will ever change that. But are you absolutely sure about this?

I have no doubts about us, Aidan. Don't overthink it. Just kiss me, now—please? Allie let go of all thought about the coming struggle. In this moment, only she and Aidan mattered. She gasped as he broke away from her, lifting her shirt over her head. He stroked the curve of her hips as she arched back to unclasp her bra. His hands, rough and calloused from years of training, trailed along her sides, making her shiver in anticipation.

He'd seen her naked before. It was kind of difficult to hide from their shared thoughts. They'd gotten over their shyness a long time ago, and he'd always been a gentleman about it. But now his eyes raked over her as he worked her jeans down over her hips.

I've been dying to see all of this. He traced the vines of her tattoo with his lips, his hands wandering over the curves of her body.

"Aidan?" Her voice trembled as she fumbled with his jeans.

"I got it, baby." He kissed her slow and deep, pushing her hands aside as he shed the rest of his clothes.

The feel of his lean, hard body nestled fully against hers was both frightening and exhilarating at the same time.

"We don't have much time, Allie," he murmured, nipping at her throat, just below her ear as he draped her legs around his hips. *I want to go slow and relish every moment of this with you ... every part of you.*

We don't have time. Aidan, I just ... I need to feel close to you. Her power churned in her chest as warmth flooded her body.

I don't want to hurt you, baby. He looked down at her, concern filling his dark eyes.

You won't. I'm your equal; your power won't hurt me.

"I wasn't talking about that part, silly." He chuckled as he moved over her, resting his weight on his elbows.

"Oh. Right. Um ... I think I can handle it." She arched up against him, her hands resting on his lower back. She wanted to explore every inch of him too, but they only had these few stolen moments.

He moved so slowly, so carefully, like she was made of glass. His lips were warm and firm against hers; her hands glided over his strong back, eager to bring him closer.

More. She wanted to forget the horrible images that continued to flicker through her mind. She wanted to feel anything but the boiling anger and fear in the pit of her stomach. She wanted to feel love. And in Aidan's arms was right where she knew she would find it.

You've always had me, Lex. He moaned, his breath hot against her fevered skin.

Sensation bloomed inside her as they began to move, fluid and sure, like they'd done this a thousand times. He knew what she wanted and he gave it to her and then some. Their minds completely open to each other with no secrets between them, she felt his pleasure as well as her own. Her breath came faster, his sexy growl a deep rumble in his chest, his hands all over her body. Allie had never felt so much all at once. For so long she'd resisted what he'd offered so freely. She'd held his love at bay, too scared to risk the heartbreak she knew would kill her if she ever lost him. But this—she would never get enough of this ... of him.

"Aidan...." She clutched him as her body responded to his.

"Allie." His voice came out in a strangled rasp. "I love you." He pressed his forehead against hers, his eyes like simmering gold in the darkness, staring into the green fire of hers. They breathed the same air, gazing at each other in complete awe of what passed between them.

Aidan pulled her against his chest, holding her close. "If I had a choice, I would never let you out of this bed." He kissed her softly. "If I had a choice, I would lay here all night, just holding you, making sure your first time was memorable."

"It was definitely memorable, Aidan." She traced the lines of his face, examining every detail—the curve of his lips and the golden sparkle of his black star sapphire eyes, so full of love she wasn't sure she would ever be able to fathom it.

"As memorable as Agra?"

"What a stupid night that was." She laughed.

"We could have saved ourselves a lot of drama if we'd just done it then," Aidan said. "Think of all the opportunities we've missed over the last six months."

"I had a boyfriend then—I'm just glad he wasn't there that night. I had no business throwing myself at you like that. And in front of everyone too." She was mortified all over again.

"I blame Liam. You're immune to his poison, but you definitely are *not* immune to his intoxicating song."

"I blame Liam too." She nodded. That night had been sort of a celebration. Sasha was about to leave for her job with the Senate and everyone wanted to have a going-away party to cheer her up. But when Liam sang, coupled with the hardcore shots she and Aidan had sneaked from the bar, Allie got sloshed.

"Drunk Allie is super cute, though." Aidan smiled at the memory.

"Drunk Allie apparently has *zero* inhibitions." She and

Aidan had danced with their friends, but she wasn't subtle in her hints that they should go make out somewhere.

"I wasn't sober either, but I didn't want to take advantage of the situation. I knew you would regret it and then you'd never forgive me." Aidan sighed.

"Well, I didn't make turning me down very easy." By the time Liam had come looking for them, the situation was intense and he'd interrupted at just the right time.

"I've never been so happy and so pissed to see Liam in my life." Aidan rolled over, tucking her under his arm.

"I think we scarred him for life."

The morning after, Allie hadn't been hung over, but she was mortified and demanded no one ever speak of it again.

"I'm sorry it took me so long to get here, Aidan," she whispered.

"I'm just glad you finally made it. Just promise me you're not going to freak out and take it all back once you've had time to think about it. I honestly don't think I can handle that."

"I'm all in, Aidan."

"Me too. But we have to go, Lex."

"I know."

"When this is all over. I'm taking you to bed and we're not coming up for air for an entire weekend." His arrogant smile lit his face and she laughed.

"Don't laugh, baby. I'm dead serious." He pinned her beneath him, kissing her so hard her toes curled and she gasped into his mouth, feeling the familiar warmth spread through her body.

"Damn," Aidan growled. "Shouldn't have done that."

"Come on, babe. We have to go." Allie wiggled out from under him, reluctant to leave their happy bubble. After this was all over, who knew how this would affect their relationship, but she had no regrets. Aidan was always the guy for her. She just hadn't been ready to stand beside him as an equal. She didn't want to be the baggage he had to hold up beside him. But she thought she was ready to stand on her own now and he was the one she wanted standing beside her.

She grabbed her clothes and darted for the bathroom.

"Need some help?" Aidan called behind her.

"Something tells me that would be counter-productive."

"You're probably right."

Allie rushed to get dressed, checking the time on her phone. They had to get back before Liam came looking for them.

"Besides..." She stepped back into the room with her protective gear on. "...I think my parents are up now, so we should behave ourselves." Allie paced across the room, stuffing her weapons belt into her bag.

"Those are from last year?" Aidan asked.

"What, my fatigues? Yeah."

"Were they that tight?" Aidan stepped behind her, running his hands over her hips.

"Are you saying I gained weight?"

"No, ma'am. I'm saying I think you got curvier in all the right places. You look hot. I'm a little tempted to shove a sweater over your head."

"Aidan. We don't have time for this, silly." Allie grabbed her hip-length leather jacket and zipped it up. "That better?"

"Slightly."

Allie grabbed her bag in one hand and Aidan's hand in the other. "Let's go check on my parents and make sure they'll be safe. Then we have some a-holes to deal with."

"What are you going to tell your mom?" Aidan met Allie at the kitchen door, like he'd just arrived for an early breakfast.

"The usual, I guess." Allie shrugged. She knew her mother wouldn't ask too many questions.

"Where are you kids off to so early this morning?" Carson asked when they joined her parents at the bar.

"Kayla's ... having a party tonight," Allie lied.

"Isn't it a little early for a party?" Carson looked at his watch.

"We're helping her with all the setup," Aidan offered, shooting Allie a "you-suck-at-lying" glance.

"Yeah, but ... her parents will be there. Um, I think we're just going to stay there tonight and then go shopping tomorrow. So I won't be home till Sunday night."

Wow, you really do suck at this.

"Aidan." Lilly smiled. "Your mom was going to tell me about her next advanced yoga class at her studio and I seem to have misplaced her number. Can you give it to me?"

Allie watched her mother's transparent attempt to distract Aidan and she turned to her dad with a question on her face.

"My office. Two seconds and I'll let you get to your 'party.'" Carson steered her toward his office across the living room.

Allie blocked Aidan, hoping he wouldn't push her for answers later.

"What's up, Dad?" She watched as he shut the door and turned on some background music to drown out their voices.

"I don't know what you're up against, but I'm pretty sure it's not a party." He crossed the room to his desk and pulled a gun from his top drawer. A Beretta.

"I'll assume you know how to use one of these by now?" Carson kept his voice low enough that Aidan wouldn't be able to hear.

Allie nodded. Guns weren't a typical weapon of choice for

most Immortals, but Emma had made sure she knew how to use one. Target practice was a huge part of her training over the summer and was the reason her aim had improved so much recently.

Carson crossed the room and quickly went through the instructions for loading the gun and removing the safety.

"I don't want a repeat of last spring. So whatever it is that had you so upset in the middle of the night last night, I'll feel better knowing you have this as an added precaution."

"This might not help where I'm going," she whispered. She hadn't even considered that her parents would have heard her screaming when she woke from the worst nightmare of her life, but of course they knew. They always seemed to be one step ahead of her.

"I'm not worried about your kind, sweetheart. I know you and your friends can take care of yourselves. I'm worried about my kind and whatever they did that gave you that scar." He traced the line of her jaw with his fingertips.

Allie gasped in surprise. Her parents shouldn't be able to see her scar.

"Relax, Allie. I just want you to be safe. Shoot first and ask questions later. Aim for the kneecaps and take care of yourself."

Allie nodded as she tucked the gun at her back.

"We love you, honey. Always know you can call us for help. You may find us more capable than you think."

"Thanks, Dad." Allie stepped back into the living room, her mind a whirl of possibilities. Her parents knew more than they should, but they also knew how to pick their moments. Maybe one day they wouldn't have to.

"Your parents really don't ask a lot of questions, do they?" Aidan asked as they pulled out of the driveway and back toward his house. They would slip back into the underground there, hoping they weren't missed. She would get back in time to meet Liam for the long ride up to Imogen's house. Her heart ached at the thought of leaving Aidan behind.

"They trust me," Allie said. "Which is why I hate lying to them so much."

"It's for their protection, Lex." Aidan nodded toward the two cars parked at the end of her driveway. She wasn't sure who was guarding her family, but she knew they were friends of Gregg's and that was good enough for her.

"I know." Allie thought about the gun that was now resting at the bottom of her bag. Somehow, knowing it was there made her feel a little better about everything she would face in the coming hours.

CHAPTER 30

Armed to the teeth and fidgeting in her protective gear, Allie sat in the backseat between Ming Lao and Daniel. Liam drove and Darius sat beside him. It was eerily similar to her frightening trip through the night nearly a year ago.

"Stop squirming," Ming said. "You've done well, Allie. We're sufficiently prepared. We'll all get through this, thanks to you."

"Don't thank me yet," Allie muttered. A thousand things had to go right for this to work and she was the only one who could orchestrate it all. If she missed even one minor detail, this intricate house of cards she was trying to build would come crashing down around her.

Where are you now? Allie asked.

Two feet farther than the last time you asked. You need to chill, babe, or you're going to drive us both crazy.

Let me know when you're in the water.

Oh, I'm pretty sure you'll know.

"How long until we're there, Liam?" Allie asked.

"It's nearly a three-hour drive, little one. We just left."

She trembled, feeling a chill creep into her bones.

"Are you cold?" Daniel asked.

"A little," she lied. She felt like she'd taken a dive into an ice bucket. Aidan and the others were in the lake now. It would be a quick swim in the frigid water before they would meet Vince.

You okay?

Freezing off some rather important parts, but I'll live.

How are the others?

They're doing okay. I've done what I can to give them a little extra warmth, but I don't want to overdo it.

Did anyone suspect you guys were sneaking out?

No. The yard has always been a last-resort escape route. It's been there so long, no one really thinks about it anymore. I just hope Vince is not waiting up there with a bunch of his buddies.

He won't be.

Almost there.

Allie could feel Aidan's relief when he broke through the thin layers of ice at the surface, but the chilly winter wind was almost worse than the swim.

She could see through their connection as Vince approached in Aidan's boat.

The bastard stole my boat?

Borrowed. With my permission.

When they were out of the water, shivering and near hypothermia despite Aidan's efforts to keep them all warm, they quickly shed their wet clothes and changed into the dry clothes they'd brought with them in a waterproof pack. Allie watched from Aidan's perspective as they donned their gear and weapons. She knew Vince would never ask questions. But Vince wasn't alone.

Why the hell would he bring Kayla? Aidan practically snarled. He still cared a great deal for Kayla and didn't want her anywhere near the danger they faced.

Allie should have anticipated that Kayla wouldn't want Vince doing this alone. She must have been there with him when she called.

Just let it be what it is. They're giving you a ride. That's all.
I don't like this.
I never expected you would.

Allie sat back, eyes closed, relieved Aidan and the others were on their way. She needed to go over every last detail in her mind now, but she had to fully block Aidan first. She couldn't chance letting him see what she saw. It would overwhelm him to see every possible scenario of what might happen to his family. And there were things about herself—about what she might have to do—that she never wanted him to see.

But she couldn't just block him this time. She had to go into the box in her mind where he'd never been. She'd never attempted it before, but when she felt confident that she was completely alone with her thoughts, Allie ran through everything again and again. Darius in the orchard. The barn. The beach. The house. Aidan on the lawn. Sasha by the gates with Quinn. Chloe with her parents. Graham keeping the enemy's communication confused. She couldn't mess this up now. Not when her gift had spent the last several weeks preparing her for this.

Why didn't I see it? She was young and her gift was new, but it was all right there in front of her face for weeks. It had taken her way too long to put the pieces together.

"Are we there yet?" She cringed at how obnoxious she sounded.

"Almost, little one."

"So what's the plan while we wait for tonight?" she asked.

"Darius and I will wait in the barn with you," Liam began. "Emma and Jin will wait in the tunnels near the house so they can help when the attack begins. Ming and Daniel will be hiding near the beach cottage so when they run from the house they'll have immediate backup waiting. George will wait up near the gates to alert us all when they arrive. Lucien, Erin, and Dean will wait for the attack and follow. We want to give them a false sense of security that their surprise attack is still a surprise. The goal will be to bring the fight to the orchard where we can contain them all and bring this thing to an end quickly."

"It won't work, but it's a good plan for starters," she said absently as the constant parade of images raced through her mind. One day she might be able to absorb it all, but right now she could only catch glimpses here and there.

"What do we need to do to make it work?" Daniel asked.

"I don't know yet. Just run with your plan until I tell you otherwise. Listen when I tell you something needs to happen and do it. And ... you know ... try not to let them capture you," Allie said dryly.

"Will do." Daniel gave her a half-hearted fist bump.

"I know it's killing every single one of you to put so much faith in such a young gift, but I promise, I'll do my best."

"We know, Allie," Ming said softly. "No one expects you to shoulder all the burden of this night. We will heed your instructions, pray for the best possible outcome, and no one will hold you accountable for any of this."

Allie nodded, but she wondered if they would really feel the same way after it was all over.

Chapter 31

"Stop pacing, Allie. You're making me nervous." Darius pressed Allie back to her seat on a bale of hay.

"Sorry," she muttered. They'd arrived at the barn just before sunset. It would be a long wait, but she was happy they'd had the time to prepare. Everyone involved was strategically moving into the area, taking their places to wait for the coming attack.

It was bizarre, seeing the orchard in the waking world. Everything, down to the finest detail, was exactly as she'd seen it in her dreams. That alone was enough to truly make her see just how powerful she was.

"This must be killing little bro, missing out on all the fun." His tone was light and typical Darius, but she knew he was just as tense as she was.

"Who's missing out?" Aidan asked as he and the others crept in through the back near the ancient-looking cider press.

"Why am I not surprised?" Darius groaned. "I knew you all agreed to stay behind way too easily."

"I'm sorry, I had to get them here, Dare," Allie said.

"You know Gregg's going to kill you, right?" He shot her a look of reproach.

"He doesn't even need to know they're here." Allie paced

back to the barn entrance. "At least not yet." She could smell the smoke in the hazy twilight. The Blood Moon hadn't made its appearance yet, but there was something strange about the evening light. Like the rose tinted light before a storm.

The shadowy figures would be swarming the front lawns by now. Their smoldering fires setting the forests ablaze. Ready for the inevitable—but she intended to change that. Allie's heart clenched in agony when she realized this was it. It was actually happening, here in the real world and not in the safety of her dreams. There would be no gift-Allie telling her what to do tonight. She was cut off from Navid and there would be no do-overs. It was up to her now. She'd done what she could to prepare everyone, but she wanted so badly for none of this to happen.

"Allie, seriously, sit down. You're going to wear a hole in the ground." Darius pulled her back down beside him on the hay bale. They needed to wait for the fight to come to them—but the waiting was killing her.

"I just want to ... make it stop." Her voice was full of frustration.

"Look at me, Allie. I can't imagine how hard this is for you, but we need to react intelligently, not emotionally."

"Of course." She squeezed his hand. "Thank you for being here with me."

"I trust you, killer. But Liam should never have left if you knew they were coming." He gestured at the others. Graham was busy fiddling with one of his contraptions and Chloe paced quietly on her own. She had her own limited way of seeing what they faced tonight. Every decision that needed to be made would plague Chloe, and Allie wondered how her little friend was coping with the stress.

"Liam's just on the other side of the orchard, standing

watch. He'll be here when we need him, but right now, I need to talk to them and I didn't need him flipping out."

"All right, let's do this. Tell us how this is going to go down."

It was time to tell them everything, but she wasn't sure she was ready to set things in motion.

The time is now, Lex. We all trust you.

She looked up to catch his unwavering gaze across the dusty barn floor. *What if I make the wrong decisions?*

You'll make mistakes. Anyone in this situation would. We all understand there are limitations to what we can do. We are human, not heroes in a comic book. Even the strongest of us have failed. But we pick ourselves up and we try to do better next time.

Thanks, Aidan. She nodded. Taking a deep breath, she turned to face her friends.

"Chloe, I want you to stay away from the fight. I need you to watch. Keep an eye on your parents and don't think about anything else. Don't get distracted by all of the decisions people are making around you. I need you to try to focus on my decisions and help me make the right ones. You'll see Ming coming up from the beach below. And Jin will be with Emma in the tunnels so they'll come out through the barn. When you see your parents ... acting strangely, get between them," Allie said. "Let them see you. It will help."

"What do you see for them, Allie?" she asked fearfully. "I sense something, but I don't understand it."

"I don't either, Chlo. Just keep an eye on them. I can't see everything; there are holes. Stuff I don't understand. I just know they will fare better if they are focused on keeping you safe."

"Graham, stay with Chloe. She'll need someone watching

her back. Is there anything you can do to keep us in communication with each other?"

"I'm on it," Graham said, passing tiny Bluetooth headsets to everyone. He picked up three small drones the size of Frisbees and flung them in the air where they hovered, as if waiting for his instruction. With a flick of his wrist, the drones flew off in three separate directions.

"That. Was badass," Aidan said.

"Sweet, that's what I was going for." Graham gave him a cocky smile. "The drones are connected to my phone so I can watch everything play out from above. I'll try to keep you all informed. The headsets are linked so we can all talk to each other. Just remember to turn them on before things get crazy."

"Genius," Allie said. "I knew there was a huge reason for you to be here. But I need you to stay hidden, Graham." She continued. "When you see ... Quinn, you cannot react. Do not let him see you."

"He's here?" Graham whirled around to face her.

"Yes, but he won't be himself. If he sees you it will just upset him. He'll get confused. And if your parents see you both, it won't go well. Emma and Daniel cannot worry about both of you or it will end badly for all of you. We're going to try like hell to get him back tonight."

She turned to Sasha, looking her in the eye. "Sasha, Quinn needs to see you. He *has* to see you. But don't get too close. You need to go now. Go find Liam and tell him to take you up to the gates to wait. He'll be mad you're here, but explain what I've told you and he'll do as you say. Wait until you see Quinn on his own on the opposite side of the gates. Let him see you and then turn around and come back here. He'll follow you but Liam needs to stay where he is. Naeemah will need him more than I will in the beginning. But when you see Quinn with Emma, get his attention. I can't see what happens after that. All I know is Quinn will snap out of it when he hears your voice. But you can't go to him. I need you to stay with Chloe. She's going to need your protection. Otherwise, stay back. Keep your bow with you and take your shots from the cover of the barn. Take out anyone you see around me. I can't fight tonight. I need to watch events unfold."

Allie couldn't stop now. She had to get it all out so they would know what to do. "Dare, I need to know you and Aidan are covering me, but we have to keep moving so I can see everything."

"We've got this, Lex," Aidan said softly. "We'll do everything you say, when you say it."

"Everyone, please be careful," Allie begged.

"Will we ... get him back?" Sasha's face was even and controlled but her voice wavered. Allie knew she was dying inside.

"We'll try."

"There is no trying, Allie. This is the only chance we're going to get."

Allie nodded, thinking of the way her gift had come to her wearing Sasha's face. She was right; Sasha would never forgive her if she screwed this up.

"You three, *please* be careful tonight," Darius said. He was struggling with his role here. He didn't want to be responsible for his youngest family members, but Allie knew he trusted her and she was grateful he was willing to follow her blindly. He just didn't know how blind Allie really was. She knew they were doing everything they could, but there was so much she wasn't seeing. So many dark spots. So much she didn't understand.

"Aidan, keep me in your sight—at all costs," she said. "Do not get distracted and fall behind."

"Lex, I know you see something and I know you think

you're protecting me by keeping it from me, but if you have something to tell me, tell me now."

"I cannot lose sight of you, Aidan. Stay nearby. Stay alert and we'll be fine."

"Are you sure about that, killer?" Darius asked. "What's your role in all of this?"

"I'm doing it right now. I just have to hope it's enough and that I haven't missed anything important."

"And what do I need to know?" Darius turned his piercing midnight gaze on her.

"Give us a minute?" Allie asked the others. She needed a quiet moment with Darius. Whatever this was between them, it was about to be resolved right now and she didn't want Aidan to have a front-row seat for it.

You too, she added as they all drifted farther back into the barn and out of sight.

Are you going to lock me out tonight?

It's for the best. You cannot be distracted by my thoughts and what I see. You need to go help the others get organized. We have some time before the fighting comes this way. Come find me when you hear the first signs of battle.

She reluctantly watched him go as Aidan left to join the others. She shifted the block against him, sealing her mind off to him again. She turned back to Darius, dreading what was coming because she still didn't know what it meant. They stepped away from the barn, into the last row of trees at the edge of the orchard—the same spot where the dream version of Darius had come to her.

"Are we alone now?" he asked, tapping her forehead.

"Yes."

"Then answer my question, Red. What do I need to know about tonight?"

"You ... can't save Erin ... or Dean. I've seen it a hundred different ways and it always happens and you always try but you never get there in time." Her eyes bright with tears. "I won't tell you not to try, Darius ... but they drain you. Every single time. You have to let them go. We can always try to rescue them later. That is the best chance they have. Stick to Aidan like glue. He will need you to pull him back. Erin has a chance, but only if we leave it up to her to save herself."

"And Dean? Is there nothing I can do to help them?" His eyes held deep anguish for the two friends who were more like siblings. Erin was to him what Chloe was to Allie and her friends. The little sister. And he and Dean were as close as brothers.

"Let Erin help herself. But Dean.... I'm sorry. Don't ask me how—I just know when fate will have her way no matter how I might try to stop her. I've seen it so many times, Dare. I'm sorry. There's just not enough time. They'll take him no matter what we do."

Darius leaned against one of the largest apple trees as if he needed the support. "I will try to heed your warning." He nodded, his face gray with the severity of what she'd just told him. "But they are my family. I don't know if I can stand back and not help them."

"You have to, Darius. Please. It will be so much worse if they take all three of you. Do nothing and you and Erin have a chance to walk away to fight for Dean another day."

"I will ... if you give me an honest answer to my next question."

Allie nodded. She knew what he would ask and she owed him the truth.

"Will you make it through unscathed, or do I need to worry that you plan to sacrifice yourself to save everyone else? I'd like to know I can trust you to look after yourself. You're more than capable."

"I'll be fine, Dare. I see something. I'll do ... something. But I just don't understand it yet." It was one of those things she wouldn't understand until it happened. All she saw was blood and all she felt was rage. "I just know the fewer witnesses, the better. So if you can cause a distraction at the right time, that would help. There's so much I don't understand yet, but I know even you will look at me differently after tonight. They are here for me. I've brought this down on us. I just don't know why this Livia woman is so hell-bent on capturing me. But I will do whatever I can to keep that from happening, and not just for my own safety and freedom. If they capture me, they will use me for my power and it will be bad. They have ways to force me, but I can't see how. So I have a lot of motivation to keep myself safe. I just want everyone to have the information they need to get through this with the least amount of loss. I need everyone to trust me when every instinct they have tells them I'm too young to know so certainly. There is a lot I don't know, but everything I do see is crystal clear now. I know what is within my power to change and what isn't."

"I trust you. I'll leave Erin and Dean to their fates if there is truly no other way."

She felt that now-familiar tug in her chest. The feelings she had for him were so confusing but she knew she couldn't stop this from happening. Her warring emotions were at an all-time high where he was concerned and it left her breathless.

"Darius?" She wanted so badly to cross whatever line they were about to cross, but she just didn't understand it—she was terrified of where it would take them if she gave in to the pull of Darius. She couldn't—wouldn't—do that to Aidan. Especially now. Especially with Darius. But she wasn't sure she had a choice anymore. She could feel her free will slipping from her grasp. This was happening whether she wanted it or not.

"I know, sweetheart." He hugged her close. "I don't know

what this is between us. I'm insanely attracted to you, but I know I don't want to be with you like that."

Allie's heart nearly beat out of her chest as she stared up at Darius. He was the one person who always made her laugh and never let her take life too seriously. She loved him, but she wasn't in love with him. She was attracted to him in a thousand ways, but at the same time she knew he wasn't for her. She wanted him to be part of her life, but she didn't want him to be her whole life. She knew he was part of her—a missing piece that she'd always felt the absence of, but never truly realized until this moment.

"What's happening?" Darius whispered, clutching her hand.

"I don't know." Allie's heartbeat slowed until it grew sluggish. She could barely breathe. She couldn't take her eyes off Darius. This couldn't be ... *that.*

"Wait. No. We're ... bonding." He fell to his knees, pulling Allie down beside him. "It makes sense now." His breath grew shallow, matching her own.

Allie was finally beginning to see Darius clearly. As if the strangeness of their feelings for each other was finally sliding into place. As her heart stilled in her chest and she gasped for breath, a green aura blazed around them.

"Of course." She was elated by the new understanding dawning in her mind. Darius was the most important person in her life now. Her heart began beating again, but she felt another beat there now—like she had twin hearts, one an echo of his heartbeat in sync with hers.

"What is this?" Darius asked. "I can feel your heart beating in my chest. I love you so much it hurts."

"It's so real. So pure," Allie whispered. "What *is* this?"

"I have no idea. We'll have to ask Dad later. We don't have time to figure it out right now."

"Don't leave my side tonight, Dare."

"I can't be away from you. Not now." He grasped her hands tightly.

"We fight together." Allie nodded.

"Be safe, Allie," he whispered. "I don't want to lose ... whatever this is." He pulled her into his arms and all the uncertainty and all the stress threatening to suffocate her just evaporated.

She turned her attention away reluctantly. She would have to marvel over this new bond later, when she had time to grasp the enormity of what just happened. If she thought about it right now, she would totally freak, and nobody had time for that.

"What the hell was that?" Aidan asked, his face white as a sheet as they returned to the barn, only to realize he'd been watching the whole time. Allie glanced down at their entwined hands.

"It's not what you think," Darius said. "It can't be. There was no choice involved."

"Then what is this? I can feel your bond and I don't like it." Aidan's voice was like acid and his eyes blazed with hurt and fury—like the two people who meant the most to him had betrayed him.

"We have no idea what this is, Aidan, but *please* do not let this distract you. Not tonight. I need you focused," Allie pleaded with him. She was shaking with the aftershock of her bond with Darius and the hurt she could see in Aidan's eyes. The hurt she felt at the mere thought that he might not understand. That he would think she could ever willingly betray him.

"Lex?" Aidan stepped forward as her eyes filled with tears.

She felt like her heart was breaking, like she didn't have enough of herself for both Aidan and Darius.

"Deep breaths." Aidan pulled her close. "Get control, baby. It's okay. I can see this is not something any of us has ever seen before. It's just bad timing. We'll ask Dad about it when all of this is over. Look at me." He tilted her chin up to meet his gaze. "We're okay."

Allie nodded. Taking a deep breath, the ache in her chest began to subside.

Just don't ever make me choose. It will destroy me. She let the thought pass between them and then she closed her mind off and knew she couldn't risk it again. Not until this was all over.

Aidan pressed his lips against hers, holding her close.

A fist came out of nowhere and Aidan was on the ground in the next instant.

"What the hell, Darius?" Aidan growled, reaching for his bloody lip.

"Shit, I'm sorry!" Darius scrambled to help Aidan up. "Apparently I do not like you kissing her." He flexed his hand and continued to profusely apologize. "I have no idea what this is, bro. I'm so sorry."

"Is this some kind of sibling bond?" Aidan asked, spitting blood on the ground.

"No," Allie and Darius said at once.

"It's not—"

"No," they both replied just as vehemently.

"I seriously can't describe it, Aidan. It's not a family bond, but it's definitely not the other-not-to-be-named bond either," Allie said. "At least I hope not. No offense, Dare."

"None taken."

"Can you give us a minute, Darius?" Aidan asked. "Go tell everyone to take their positions and get ready."

"I'd rather not."

"Darius, please." Allie sighed, taking his hands in hers. She took a step closer, into the circle of his arms and felt the unsteady thump of his heart in her chest. "We're running out of time and I just need a minute with Aidan."

"Just make it quick, sweetheart." He tucked a loose curl behind her ear. "I'm not comfortable leaving your side with what's about to go down."

"Son of a bitch!" Aidan spat, kicking a rock into the forest in his frustration. "Do you have to look at her like that?"

"Sorry ... I'll just be in the barn." Darius reluctantly left them alone.

She sensed Aidan step up behind her, his arms wrapping around her. The empty echo in her mind was a reminder that it was up to her to keep him safe—even if it meant revealing the darkest part of herself to everyone here.

"I don't like this. Any of it." His breath brushed the top of her head. "I don't like whatever this is with you and my brother and I don't like you blocking me."

"Me either." She turned toward him, wrapping her arms around him tightly. "I don't like the separation from you, but I need to focus tonight." She could feel Darius in her blood, the thump of his heart beside hers—the sense of calm and reassurance it gave her.

"Be safe, Alexis Ann. I can't bear the thought of anything happening to you."

"I will be fine. Aidan Loukas." She gripped his jacket in her fists. "You have to promise me you won't do anything stupid. I can't lose you now."

"We've got this, babe." He took her hand as they moved closer to the trees nearest the path down to the beach.

Allie reached to turn her headset on. "Everyone with me?" She heard the echoing replies of all her friends. "Good luck."

Allie would gladly give up her immortality to see this thing not happen, but she didn't have that luxury. Her peripheral vision went green and she took it to mean she was choosing the right path.

"How are we doing Chlo?" Allie asked over the headset.

"As good as can be expected."

"Should we try to get closer to the beach or stay here?"

"Stay where you are. You're in the best spot for reacting quickly when this thing reaches us."

Gregg and the others were lying in wait up at the house. Everyone was as prepared as they could be, given the fact that Allie still saw so many dark spots. But at least they had numbers this time. She'd never forget the dreams. The slaughter was branded into her mind forever, but this time, they would all have a chance.

God, please let this work.

She could sense Darius approach, crouching just behind her. It was like she could feel his every move without looking. He was part of her now.

"I see movement toward the orchard in all directions," Graham's voice echoed in her ear. "Everyone get ready for this."

Allie heard the first sounds of battle in the growing darkness. The enemy wasn't prepared for their quick reaction and mobilization.

"There are more than I anticipated." Allie chewed her bottom lip. Dark figures swarmed the sandy dunes below. Allie watched as the people she loved made their way to the beach. Several shadowy figures followed in hot pursuit. But they weren't prepared to find Emma and Jin waiting there as backup.

"Do not let me out of your sight, Lex," Aidan said softly. "We're doing this together."

"You too," she managed in a strangled whisper as they stood.

"I've got your back, killer," Darius said. "You just tell us what needs to happen and when."

Allie nodded, gripping her mother's sai, aching to hear them sing. The sound felt like her mother's presence and she needed all the inner strength she could muster tonight.

As their family came up the steep path, Allie, Aidan, and Darius crouched among the bushes, waiting to join the battle. Gregg and Emma streaked past them, unaware, while Naeemah and Jin followed. Their quick reaction seamlessly split Naeemah from her Complement in such a subtle way that Allie doubted those following even realized.

"Where are Aide and Hélène?" Allie asked desperately. "They were supposed to be with them!"

"Looks like Aide and Gen are coming down the path from the gates with ... shit! My great-grandparents are with them." Graham said.

Ju Long and Lu Li were Ming Lao's ancient parents. Allie had never seen any version of her visions with them in it. She felt like it was a bad omen that they were here now.

"And Lucien and Hélène just came up through the tunnels," Chloe added. "I think everyone is accounted for so far."

At the top of the path, Gregg and the others turned to meet their attackers. Allie lunged after the last figure, taking him by surprise. She fought to fully incapacitate her Immortal opponents and to only maim the mortals she faced. Now wasn't the time to be squeamish, and Allie had come a long way these last months.

One of Sasha's lodestone arrows zipped past her to fell an oncoming assault. Allie moved with speed, scanning the small clearing, looking for the dark spots, the information she was missing.

She heard Gregg's growl of irritation when he realized

Aidan and Sasha were there, but there was no time for that now.

Hélène and Lucien burst through the barn with Ming and Daniel behind them. Imogen and Aide were coming down the path through the woods that led to the gates with Liam and George right behind them. Everyone was present now—almost everyone. She still hadn't seen Quinn yet. Just as she planned, the fight was coming to them in the orchard. The first step was a success. The orchard swarmed with Coalition and Immortals she didn't recognize—more than she ever saw in her dreams. But she spotted familiar faces, too. Dean and Erin were with Greyson, and Naomi fought with an Immortal man Allie didn't recognize. They had friends here. Their numbers were good.

"We can do this," Allie murmured.

"Allie, you need to decide now. Move or stay where you are, but do it now," Chloe said.

"Come on." Allie darted along the rocky path back to the orchard. Aidan and Darius followed, fighting furiously at her side, keeping her free to observe. She saw familiar sights; events were unfolding in their favor, but she needed to know—needed to understand the cause of her blind spot.

"Go right, Allie, back toward the barn and across the orchard," Chloe's voice crackled over their connection. "She won't see you."

Allie followed Chloe's advice, and then she saw her, standing at the end of the orchard. "It *is* Livia." She exhaled in a rush as the missing information began to fill in. Allie understood more of what she'd witnessed in her dreams and visions now. Livia had been blocking her all this time.

Livia was caught up in a battle with Ming Lao and Daniel. She was outmatched. Ming was ruthless, but Allie knew it wouldn't go well for her. Somehow, what was about to happen would affect Jin, who was across the battlefield fighting beside Naeemah.

To her utter horror, Allie saw Quinn, fighting alongside Livia, oblivious of his family's presence. He didn't seem to realize he fought against his own father—he was too far gone.

"He's broken," Allie realized. Had he seen Sasha yet?

When Livia disappeared, slithering away to appear again just out of Ming's reach, Allie understood. She was using Quinn's gift. She'd latched onto him like a parasite. That was how she'd escaped with him last spring.

"What do you see?" Aidan panted as he regrouped at her side. Sasha's arrow sailed right through the eye of an approaching enemy. He hit the ground hard, buying them time to get away.

"Sasha, go!" Allie cried as they scrambled through the rows of apple trees.

"It's Livia. She's my blind spot. She's blocking me somehow. That's why I could never see who Quinn was talking to in my dreams—she's using him, using his gifts. I don't think he's even aware any of this is happening."

"Erin!" Darius shouted.

"I'm so sorry, Darius." Allie turned away. She didn't want to watch him try to save Erin, but she had to leave the decision up to him. If he did, he was lost—better off dead, some would say. She wasn't sure she would survive losing him like that so soon after their bond.

She heard Erin's screech and couldn't hold back her sobs, but she needed to keep moving. She didn't want Livia's attention just yet.

Sasha's arrows stopped. Allie turned to find Quinn standing with his sword drawn against Ming, his own grandmother, a grimace of confusion on his face as Daniel tried to talk him down.

"Quinnton Greggory Loukas!" Sasha screamed his name. She stood at the center of the orchard, hair crazy, eyes blazing. "Snap the hell out of it!" She pointed her dagger at him, glaring so fiercely, Allie thought she would stare a hole right through his chest. Something unspoken passed between them. But it worked. It was enough to bring Quinn back to himself. He dropped his sword to his side and stumbled away from Livia.

Livia, still battling Ming Lao, hissed in fury at Sasha's interference.

Jin Jing's sudden roar of agony cut right through Allie. "It's happened!" She searched frantically for Chloe. Her parents needed her *now*.

"Go Chloe!" Graham called through the headset.

Ming was failing in her attack. Livia had done something to rend her nearly catatonic. She fell to her knees as Jin streaked across the orchard to her side.

With an anguished cry, Daniel took up the fight against Livia, shoving Quinn behind him and toward Ju Long and Lu Li.

"Ming?" Jin sobbed. The two regarded each other, completely heartbroken.

"She ... broke their bond." Aidan gasped, shaking his head in utter disbelief.

Allie could see it too. Their Complement bond was destroyed, like something that lay shattered at their feet. Their heartache was palpable. Ming dropped her sword, clutching her chest like she'd lost the will to live.

"Where is Chloe? They need her. They need something to hold them together until we can figure this out."

"Mom!" Chloe burst out of the barn and through the trees, flinging herself between her parents, boldly standing between them and Livia. It was enough to snap them out of their torment. The reminder of the blood family they shared was enough for now.

"Chloe?" Daniel roared in surprise to see his little sister there.

With a sickening thud, Livia's sword came crashing down, sending Daniel's hand and his sword to the dusty ground. He stumbled, holding the bloody stump of his arm, trying to stay on his feet. He would heal, but it would be slow and agonizing. The injury was enough to incapacitate him. Livia shoved him down with the toe of her boot.

Her laughter rang out across the bloody grove. "You send their child to distract them? Very clever, girl. Where are you hiding?"

Livia's cold gaze sought Allie. Ming and Jin eased away from Livia, clutching their daughter between them. Allie shook with relief.

"It worked!" Allie called across the distance separating them.

"Oh, but I can do much worse, my dear Alexis," she taunted. "You've done them an unkindness. How can they live knowing they are no longer Complements?"

"Liv, don't do this," Quinn begged. "Please. We'll come back with you." He struggled against his great-grandfather's grip, but Ju Long held him steady.

Rage swelled within her core as Allie took a step forward.

"No!" Chloe shrieked when Livia lunged toward Jin.

Allie watched as Jin shoved his daughter behind him. Livia's sword flashed silver and Allie's scream caught in her throat. *No longer Complements?* What did that even mean? Their Immortality lay within the Complement bond. If that bond no longer existed....

"Stop her!" Allie darted along the path between the trees.

But Livia's sword arched toward Jin's chest. She was going to kill him and Allie wouldn't get there in time.

Allie scrambled for the gun she had tucked in her belt, grateful for Carson's insistence that she bring it. She fired off a shot, striking Livia in the chest, but it was too late. She watched helplessly as Ming Lao slumped to the ground. She'd jumped in front of her husband, taking the strike that would end her Immortal life.

"Momma!" Chloe shrieked, dropping to the ground beside her.

"It is best that one of them not survive this, child," Livia said, ruffling Chloe's hair before she turned, gripping her shoulder where Allie's shot found purchase, and set off across the orchard. Her minions swarmed up around their injured leader, taking anyone they could get their hands on.

"We have to go, Lex." Aidan pulled her away as Chloe's mournful shrieks cut right through her. The fury Allie had struggled to keep at bay for so long was about to overwhelm her. She needed to get out of there. Allie turned, the rage burned, scorching hot inside her now. She fled Livia's pursuit, just as Dean, George, and Emma moved in to intercept Livia. Everyone would do their part to get through this. Some would make it, some wouldn't. She felt a pang of regret when both Aidan and Darius let Dean pass, leaving the boy's fate to play out.

"Ming," Allie choked. She couldn't seem to wrap her mind around her death—actual for-real death. They ran along the path that led to the gates, but Allie had trouble focusing and that would spell disaster for them all. She would have to mourn for Ming later.

"She's dead?" Aidan struggled to get the question out.

Allie nodded. "But Jin will survive." She felt bile rise in her throat.

"He'll wish he hadn't," Darius said.

What have I done? In her desire to see them all survive, she never anticipated this outcome. But she didn't have time to dwell on her mistakes. It was time to make sure Gregg and Naeemah made it out alive. Saving them had cost Ming Lao her life and Allie was more determined than ever not to fail. But that meant risking Aidan's future. She knew he would never forgive her if she didn't try. She would never forgive herself if her actions cost even more lives.

They scrambled along the path through the woods, the battle growing distant behind them, smoke drifting along the path in front of them.

"What's next?" Aidan asked.

"We have to find your mom."

"Naeemah is up by the gates with Gregg and Liam," Graham said, his voice lifeless and flat after witnessing his grandmother's murder.

Allie needed Gregg and Liam; they would react quickly when they saw. But first, Naeemah needed her.

When they reached the sloping green lawns, Allie stopped along the tree line where Naeemah and Liam fought against a man twice their combined size. Greyson battled three men with Gregg at his side.

The fires burned out of control here. Churning black smoke filled the sky as the clang of weapons crashed like thunder. Allie took a step away from Aidan's side, long enough to grasp Naeemah's wrist, wrenching her away from the blow that would have brought Gregg in to defend her—which would have been a grievous mistake for both Naeemah and Greyson. Now Allie had to convince her to leave. Emma needed her.

Naeemah turned, her eyes widening in fear when she saw Allie and her youngest son in the thick of it. Darius flew to Liam's side, helping him fell the huge Immortal giant.

"What are you doing here?" Naeemah raged at them.

"Emma needs you. They have Quinn. Go now, please." Allie sobbed, shoving her toward the path.

"Come with me, both of you." Her gift commanded them to obey.

"No!" Allie broke the spell. "We are needed here."

With a nod, she turned and fled along the path. Allie knew it took everything Naeemah had to leave her son.

The Immortal giant let out a loud roar and turned to dash through the open gates, trailing a nearly severed arm behind him.

"Allie?" Liam panted as he checked her over for injuries.

"I'm fine, but stay close, please?" She turned, grateful to have her brother near.

"What do you need us to do?" Gregg asked. He had full confidence in her and she was grateful for it.

"I, I don't know. I need a minute." She turned around, searching for clues. She was missing something.

"Where's Aidan? Graham, where's Aidan?" But only static sounded in response. She flung the useless thing aside.

"He was just here," Darius said.

"No ... It's still happening." Allie trembled, unsure of how to react. She was on her own now. She'd seen just enough of this to know it was bad, but the flickering visions of the last hours never gave her enough to truly understand it.

The blood moon broke through the clouds to flood the sloping lawn with light. "Gonna need that distraction we talked about, Dare!" she called over her shoulder as she frantically searched for Aidan. "I'll need you to get me out of here in a minute, Liam. And Gregg, you need to make sure there aren't any witnesses. I'm not sure what state I will be in. Liam, don't let Gregg interfere. Aidan will be fine. We just need to find him

... *now*," she roared, feeling the desperation of her rage fighting for release.

An ear-splitting shriek sounded behind them along the path back to the orchard. Darius's distraction. As she surveyed her surroundings, there were few witnesses, and even fewer who would realize....

She saw him then. The veil of smoke lifted and a tall, muscular man grappled with Aidan at the edge of the forest near the gates. When had he left her side?

This was it. Her rage boiled over as the man overwhelmed him, drawing Aidan's blood with a dagger to his side.

It was the sight of his blood that made her snap.

Aidan was somewhere else. He wasn't in the zone. If that was the case, he would be winning. With a peaceful smile on his face, Aidan slumped to the ground, blood oozing from his side. The man held his head in a vise grip. She was too far away to stop it—they all were.

Aidan! She tried to reach him through their connection, but he was blocking her.

"Aidan!" Gregg cried, but Liam held him back. The world grew quiet and everything slowed. Allie saw it all again, only this time she understood. She experienced what Aidan's life would be like without his gift of healing. The man was strong and he would overpower Aidan, but he wouldn't drain him. Still, it would be enough to ruin him. He would never recover, never forgive himself when he couldn't save someone who needed him. He would still love her, but he would never be the same. He would be forever scarred by this event. If she let it happen. He would be a healer no more. If she let it happen, things might go better for them all; she might keep her power in check and no one would ever know. They were winning—despite the horrifying loss of Ming Lao's life. If she let it happen, other lives could be spared.

If she let it happen....

But she couldn't. She'd known all along she'd never be able to hold it in—the rage. It nearly overwhelmed her now, her power, churning like a tempest inside her. She'd thought it would be a decision, but the decision was made; she had no choice. This man was guilty and deserved her judgment.

Her fists clenched at her sides, an otherworldly screech ripped from her throat as the rage consumed her, flooding her body, feeding her anger like oxygen feeds fire—chasing sadness and grief away, leaving her firm resolve in control. Blood oozed from her nose and eyes. Her clenched fists opened the crescent-shaped scars along her palms and her blood stained the grass at her feet. She knew she looked like a freak show straight out of a horror movie, but she didn't care.

Gregg, Liam, and Darius watched her in absolute shock.

When the man dared to touch Aidan's gift, she judged him, weighed his character, and found him lacking. She knew without a doubt that he deserved her punishment. Blood bubbled from Aidan's mouth as Gregg fought to reach his son, but Liam did as she asked and kept him from interfering.

Allie's gaze zeroed in on the man who threatened Aidan and blood filled her sight, painting her world red as an eerie silence muffled everything around her. She roared in outrage and gave in to the urge to unleash her fury. She didn't know what she was doing; she only knew it had to be done. The man would pay for ever thinking of touching Aidan, but also for all the others he'd killed and maimed over his long lifetime. Hundreds of Immortals deserved retribution and she would be the one to deliver it. Releasing the anger, like a shockwave, was a high unlike any she'd ever experienced. She soared, drawing on her power, letting it run free and wild in a way she'd never dared before.

Golden-green light filled the clearing and dead silence

echoed in her mind as her anger wilted. A strange calm swept through her after the rage. She collapsed to the ground, just as her victim did. He fell, weak and disoriented, giving Gregg the opportunity to help Aidan scramble away.

She caught Aidan's gaze for a moment and it was filled with awe—and so much love. She didn't deserve it. Gregg stumbled back from Allie. She couldn't bear to see the fear and accusation in his eyes, so she looked at Aidan and Darius instead. She saw only love there. Different kinds of love, but neither of them would ever look at her with fear or disgust. Their unwavering confidence bolstered her. She fought to rein in the power that consumed her. She didn't want to hurt them.

The storm withered within her, replaced with a wave of regret so overwhelming she wasn't sure if she could come back from this. She curled up on the ground in a heap. Her tears mixed with blood as a sorrowful wail escaped her. Her raw screams tore at her throat like hot lava.

"Little one," Liam called softly, "come with me, now. We must go."

She knew it had to be this way; she couldn't be near anyone right now. She scrambled away from her brother, terrified she might hurt him too. There was a chance Liam would be immune to whatever this rage-gift-nightmare was, but she couldn't risk it. Her bloodshot eyes filled with tears as she saw the look of fear on her brother's face. Her cheeks were streaked with blood and soot and her bloody hands clawed at the grass around her.

"Allie, deep breaths. Rein in it, sweetheart. You did well," Gregg said softly, like he was talking to a volatile monster that might strike at any moment. "But you must go. *Now*. Liam will keep you safe and I will be right behind you. I'll see to Aidan. Thank you for saving him—I'll never be able to thank you enough for sparing him such a terrible fate. It's so much harder at this age, to lose a gift."

"Gregg ... you know we cannot let that woman escape again. She's—"

"I know, brother. I will bring Livia to you. Now take your sister and go. She can't be seen. She will never have another moment's peace if even a single witness leaves this place tonight knowing what she is capable of."

CHAPTER 32

Allie refused to let anyone touch her. She managed to get to her feet and followed Liam uncertainly, her legs shaking beneath her. She'd never felt so weak, but it wasn't safe to let her guard down now.

"Wait," Darius called. "I'm coming with you."

Allie turned to see him charging along the path through the woods, back toward the orchard.

"No," Liam said.

"He's coming or I'm not going," Allie choked. She felt better just having him near. "Keep your distance—both of you. Don't touch me ... it's not safe."

"This way. We're taking a detour through the woods. It seems we have someone waiting to *help* us." Liam stepped off the trail and led them through the dense forest of evergreens. He seemed angry, but not at her. His eyes glimmered with the use of his gift that would lead them to whomever waited.

Allie stumbled over the uneven ground when the forest floor beneath her suddenly became gravel. She looked up through her glazed eyes to see a familiar car waiting beside a dilapidated shed.

"Vince?" she whispered, too stunned to fathom why he and Kayla were there. "It's too dangerous," she mumbled. They had broken up to keep him out of her dangerous life and yet here he was, caught up in the middle of it again.

"We'll follow you back. Make sure no one is tailing you," Vince said.

"Liam, no." Darius reached out to grab his uncle.

"He has the Coalition stink. Both of them do," Liam snarled. "It's the only explanation."

"We can trust them." Allie sighed, sinking to the ground again. She didn't have the strength to stand.

"That's good enough for me," Darius said. "I don't care why they're here. She trusts them and we have to get her out of here. Now."

"We know nothing. We don't want to know anything. We just want to help," Kayla said, her voice trembling. "Are you okay, Allie? Is she all right?" Kayla stepped toward her and Allie curled into a tight ball, gravel scraping at her skin.

"She'll be fine," Darius said.

"Don't touch me!" Allie screamed as Kayla knelt beside her. "It's not safe."

"I won't. I'll just sit here and when you're ready to get up, we can go."

"Leave now, while you still have the chance to walk away," Liam insisted. Allie could hear the venom in his voice, but everything felt so far away. Like she was underwater and she couldn't reach the surface.

"No," Vince said. "Like it or not, we are helping. We're not here to interfere, but there are too many Coalition swarming around here and I'm getting you all out of this in one piece, right now. Get Allie in the car and get her home. Get home to your daughter."

"What do you know about my daughter?" Liam said, taking a menacing step toward Vince.

"It's your job to take care of her and if you get caught,

Kahlynn will be alone." Vince took a step toward Liam so they were nearly nose to nose.

"What's it to you?"

"That little girl ... means *everything* to us." Vince gestured at Kayla.

Vince's voice sounded strange and distant to Allie's ears. She closed her eyes and curled into a tighter ball. "No, Vin. He won't understand," Allie murmured. She wanted to keep sinking into herself, but too much was happening around her. She had to snap out of it.

"Liam? Look at Kayla," Allie whispered. "Imagine Kahlynn at this age." She sat up and looked at her brother. "If they aren't asking questions, we shouldn't either. You know this isn't safe for them. We can trust them to watch our backs. They have a vested interest."

Liam took a step back, his eyes wide in disbelief as he looked from Kayla to Vince. "Right. Get in your car; you can follow at a distance. Text Darius if you see anything." He headed for the shed where an old, unremarkable sedan waited for them. One of several bug-out vehicles Lucien and Imogen had placed around the property.

Allie had done all she could to ensure those she loved survived. Now it was time for her to get as far away from this place as she could.

Liam came to crouch beside her. "I know what's going on in that head of yours, little one. Your gift is a frightening thing, I will not lie, but I, and everyone else who loves you, will never fear you. You are a powerful girl and I trust that you will not hurt me or Darius. I know what living with that constant fear is like and I won't let my sister live like that. It is difficult to maintain such rigid control. But I will teach you. We will have you back to school in no time. I'll be kicking Aidan out of your room again—possibly Darius now too, it seems."

"It's not like that," Allie and Darius said together.

Liam's chatter calmed her like nothing else would have. His unfailing trust in her pulled her out of the desperate spiral she was in. But she wasn't there yet. Her power still whirled inside her and if she lost complete control, she might never recover.

She carefully got to her feet. They needed to keep moving. Livia would come after her soon and Allie needed to know for certain that she wouldn't hurt Liam and Darius if she went with them now.

Allie leaned against the car. She just needed one more minute, and then she'd pull it together.

Sobs wracked her body and she beat the car with her fist until her knuckles were bloody. Who was she to decide who lived and died? She understood now, what she'd done to the man who'd attacked Aidan. She could feel his immortality wrapped around her like an invisible cloak. She'd taken it from him—in essence, killed him. How was it possible that Allie, a seventeen-year-old girl, had broken a powerful Immortal man—left him mortal? He would die someday, and his Complement, a woman he'd yet to meet, would never know the completion they all desperately needed to survive the crush of so many years. Who was Allie to ruin two lives? But she knew she'd do it all again if it meant saving Aidan from the life of torment she'd seen for him in the space of a heartbeat.

"Little one."

Liam's touch filled her with fear and she whirled on him.

"I'm fine, sweetheart. You won't hurt me. I cannot leave you to sob your heart out like this." He pulled her into his arms and held her tightly. A deep chasm of grief filled her as she bawled on his shoulder. How could she ever live with herself? But she had to pull it together now. She drew a shaky breath.

"We have to go," she whispered, her voice hoarse and

brittle to her own ears. "I cannot be trusted yet. Not till we know for sure what this is."

"Gregg will meet us soon and we will regroup and sort this all out." Liam held his hand out to her. She took it carefully as he helped her into the backseat.

"Darius, if you're coming, get in the car. We have to leave now." Liam slid in the front seat and cranked the car, checking for Vince and Kayla in the rearview mirror.

Allie still wrestled with the anger bubbling within. But her anger was directed at herself now. Exhaustion swept through her as soon as her head rested on the seat. She curled into a fetal position and hugged her knees to her chest. She was too tired to think and too scared to sleep. What if she lost control? What if she hurt two of the most important people in her life?

Darius. She didn't know what this was, but without thinking, she reached between the seats for his hand. His fingers laced through hers, resting on the console between the front seats. He didn't even hesitate to touch her.

"What is this, Liam?" Darius asked, his voice low and distant.

She could hear them, but they felt so far away, like she was underwater again.

Maybe this was all a dream and I'll wake up soon. But Allie stared at the back of the seat in front of her, her eyes like glass.

"Tell me what happened?" Liam said.

"Before the fighting—we bonded. But I don't understand it. It's not like any bond I've ever heard of."

Liam swore softly under his breath. "I can sense it. It's strong."

"What does it mean?"

"I don't know much about it. Gregg will be able to help you."

"It's my job to protect her," Darius said. "I can feel it."

"She can protect herself." Liam chuckled. "Clearly she can fight her own battles. She just needs you to be the voice of reason."

"Reason? Have you met me?"

"Fate has a sense of humor, nephew."

"So I'm supposed to advise her or something?"

"Just be the friend she can trust unfailingly. You'll figure out the rest."

Liam's phone chirped with a message from Vince.

"We're supposed to take the next right for four miles and then we'll hit the back roads till we cross back into Ohio." Darius responded to Vince's text and set the phone on the console to watch for updates from their tail.

"So what's our next step?" Allie asked. Her voice like gravel in her throat.

"We get back to the underground as soon as possible," Liam said. "But we have to make sure we aren't followed. You doing okay, little one?"

"I have control now."

"That's not what I mean."

"I'm okay." But even she didn't believe her.

Hours later Allie finally sat up. Inside, she was still a mess. She wanted to curl up and wallow in her misery. *I'll do that later. Later, when I'm home, I can fall apart.*

"We're almost there." Darius answered her unspoken question.

"Vince spotted a tail. They showed up as soon as we hit the Cleveland area," Liam said. "He helped us lose them in Strongsville. We're almost to Rocky River now to get another car before we head into the city."

"And by 'get another car' you mean what exactly?" Darius asked.

"Borrow it."

"Liam. I'm a cop. I can't be stealing cars."

"That's why I said borrow. We're not going to keep it."

"You can't tell me you McBriens don't have an extra car around here somewhere," Allie said. She felt a fierce urge to protect Darius from even the possibility of getting caught in a stolen car.

"Can't you just use your badge to seize one?" Liam sounded irritated.

"No." Darius glared at him.

"Fine. I have a car stashed at one of my bars on the other side of the Metroparks. We'll ditch this one at the marina."

Allie waved as Vince and Kayla drove past them, signaling that it was safe for them to head home. As she watched them leave, she saw her future with them in it. This wouldn't be the only time they would risk their lives to help her. This was just the beginning of their involvement in her world. Breaking up with Vince hadn't spared him anything.

"Time to take a walk. You up for this, Allie?" Liam slowed to a halt in the marina parking lot.

"I'll follow you," she said absently.

As they marched through the woods along the well-tended trails of the park, Allie somehow managed to keep up with her brother's long strides.

"You think she's okay?" Liam asked Darius, casting a glance back at her.

"She's holding it together," Darius said. "She's a tough cookie."

"Don't talk about me like I'm not here," Allie muttered.

"From the look on your face, little one, you're a million miles away."

"I'll be fine."

"Just let her be, Liam. She just needs some time to herself. The more you ask her how she's doing, the more irritated she'll get. She'll snap out of it when she's good and ready."

Allie moved woodenly, her arms crossed protectively over her chest as if she were trying to physically hold her power back. She concentrated on putting one foot in front of the other. She was exhausted, but it felt good to stretch her legs and empty her mind. It was almost morning now. Still dark, but the birds were just beginning to stir. It was over. They'd made it through the worst of it and as far as she knew, they'd come out of this not completely unscathed, but better than any of them had a right to hope for. She'd just never realized the magnitude of what she would do to that man. It was inhuman, what she did. Even more of an abomination than what Livia did to Ming and Jin.

"Wait here," Liam said. "I'll go get the car."

Allie and Darius crouched in the shadows along the tree line behind Liam's bar. It was a crap dive bar, but it suited him.

Allie climbed in the front seat beside Liam and pulled Darius in beside her. She felt better having them close now that she was more in control. She pulled her feet up on the seat and wrapped her arms around her legs.

"What now?" she asked.

"We go home." Liam headed along Cliffton Boulevard toward downtown.

"Aren't we taking the ferry?" Allie asked.

"Nope."

A few minutes later they pulled into the garage at Terminal Tower in the heart of downtown. For a second, she thought they were going to park and take the RAPID to some other location before heading home. But the trains didn't run this early. Before she could ask what they were doing, Liam pulled onto the tracks and they drove through the tunnel where the trains turned around. Terminal Tower was where the trains converged. The tracks ran from the east side to the west side, passing through the station at Tower City.

Darius hopped out of the car and crept along the dark tunnel, running his hands along the wall. She wasn't overly surprised when the wall opened up to reveal another tunnel, just big enough for the car.

"Please don't tell me we're about to drive to the island through this tunnel."

"Okay. I won't," Liam said.

"No freaking out, Allie," Darius said when he slid back in beside her. "We'll be there before you know it."

"How do I not know about this?"

"We have dozens of ways on and off the island. This one is a last resort," Liam said.

"And why is that?"

"It fl—"

"The entrance is too public, right, Liam?" Darius shot him a sharp look.

"Right. Way too public."

Allie stared ahead as Liam drove through the dark tunnel. The drive was smooth for a while and then the path turned into little more than a dirt road, dotted with puddles and potholes. The way was bumpy and slow going.

"Is that ... lake water gushing down the walls?" Allie's voice shook and she closed her eyes.

"Yep." Darius made a loud popping sound on the "P."

"I'm just going to shut my eyes and you tell me when we're there, or when I should start swimming."

"Will do." Darius gripped her hand tightly. He didn't like this any better than she did.

"It's freezing down here," Allie whispered.

"That's probably for the best," Liam said. "The mud's frozen so we shouldn't get stuck."

It took far longer than the ferryboat would have, but they finally drove out of the long tunnel that she was pretty sure flooded quite frequently. They arrived in the underground, but it was part of the underground she'd never seen before. The vaulted ceilings were just like the main hall she passed through every day, but this was a different hall, much smaller ... and deeper. It was cold when she stepped out of the car. She could see her breath.

"What is this place?" Allie asked.

"The crypt," Darius said.

"Fitting name," she murmured as she followed him across the intricate stone floor, covered in tile mosaics. Huge archways led to different rooms and a stone staircase rose above them. Allie headed for it, assuming it led to the common room above.

"Not yet, little one. We have business to attend to first." Liam guided her toward an arched opening in the wall.

"Do you want me to come with you?" Darius asked.

She wanted to tell him no, that she could handle this on her own. That she didn't want to drag him into her mess, but she nodded and took his offered hand. There would be few secrets between them after tonight.

CHAPTER 33

"Seriously, what is this place?" Allie asked as Liam led her into a dark room. It was cold and damp, which meant they were probably at the deepest part of the lake.

"It's, uh—"

"It's our totally illegal prison," Darius said.

"Prison?"

"Not exactly," Gregg said.

Allie turned to see him standing in front of a door with bars in the window.

"Looks like a prison," she muttered.

"How are you, Allie?"

"Glad to see you." She rushed across the room but stopped herself. She remembered the fear she'd seen on his face when she did what she did.

"I'm so proud of you, Allie." Gregg pulled her into his arms without hesitation. "You saved us."

"Is ... is everyone okay? Aidan?"

"Aidan is fine, thanks to you. And you were right—they all needed to be there. I should have listened to you."

"Ming?" Her lip trembled at the thought of what she had caused.

"Aye, we lost Ming and her parents too. They tried to

avenge her death and were no match against Livia's people. The family is a wreck. Imogen and Lucien were taken. We don't know yet if they were executed. She has such a rare gift, I believe they will be safe. At least for the time being, and we may be able to work out a trade. Dean was also taken, along with three of my lieutenants." Gregg's voice was weary and full of sorrow for the family they lost.

"Gen?" Allie's eyes filled with tears.

"You saved her life. You did good, sweetheart. We've managed to come through this well enough."

"And Erin?" Darius asked.

"She is still with us. Thanks to Allie."

"Greyson? George? Naomi?" Allie asked.

"All fine.

"How is Jin? Chloe?"

"In shock. This won't be easy for them. We've never dealt with this before. It will take time."

"How did you beat us back?" Darius asked.

"Helicopter. We had to move quickly," Gregg said.

"Why are we here?" Allie asked, gazing around.

"We have a few ... guests. We have no other choice but to keep them here until we decide what to do with them."

"Allie?" The voice sent a shock right through her. She turned to find a familiar face on the other side of a prison cell.

"Quinn?" She rushed over to him, reaching for the bars. "Why is he in a cell?"

"It's not safe for us to be with the family yet," Quinn said miserably. "I won't trust myself until I'm in full control of my power again."

"He asked us to put them here," Gregg explained.

"It's a long story, Allie. But I'm glad to see you." Quinn reached through the bars to clasp her hands.

"I'm so sorry, Quinn. It should have been me." For the last

eight months, she'd wanted to apologize for what happened. His face was haggard and drawn. He looked so much older now.

"I'm so glad it wasn't you. It was better this way." He gestured over his shoulder to a petite girl sitting quietly on the bed in the corner of the cell. She sat with her knees against her chest, a look of shock and relief on her face.

Allie wanted to hug Quinn, to ask him about his friend, but there was something in his eyes. He wasn't quite himself yet and might not be for a long time.

"Just ... don't judge her too harshly, Allie. She's a heinous bitch, but she's had a hard life. She's never really had a choice."

"Who?"

"Livia," Gregg said. "She's here. We couldn't risk letting her escape this time."

"Take me to her, please?"

"Are you sure?" Gregg asked her.

"Yes." It was time they had a talk.

"I suppose you want Liam with you?"

"Yes." She reached for Liam's hand, leaving Darius behind with Quinn.

"She's in a pissy mood, as you can probably imagine. And she's not thrilled with you."

"I bet not." Allie heaved a huge sigh as she followed Gregg into another room where the cell bars practically hummed with magnetic energy.

"Oh good, you brought the brat."

Allie cringed at the sight of the tall woman, pacing her cell like a caged panther. She looked the same as she had two summers ago, when Allie caught a glimpse of her leaving their house in New Zealand.

"Do you know why you're looking for me?" Allie asked. She was proud her voice didn't shake.

"Of course. But I won't be telling any of you that." Livia eyed Allie up and down, scouring her face like a woman starved for answers.

"Not the reason your boss wants me. Do you know why *you* are so intrigued by me? Why time and again you come looking for me?"

"What do you know?" Livia paced to stand as close to the bars as she dared.

"You're my sister." Through all of the thousands of visions she'd had in the last few days, Allie was only able to put the pieces together when she saw Livia again. Not until she stood face to face with her. But she got it now. Livia had their father's coloring and height, and she had their mother's eyes and temperament. But circumstances had made her the hard, jaded woman who stood before her now.

"Not possible."

"Of course ... *Alivia*," Gregg whispered. "I haven't thought of her in more than a century." He stared at Livia, putting the pieces together. "Do you remember when you were taken?" he asked. "You were so young. I can't imagine you could remember much of your natural mother and father."

"I was adopted. I'm no natural born."

Allie could see it in her sister's eyes—she wanted to know everything, to fill in the gaps in her memory. The part of her life that didn't make any sense. Allie knew what that was like.

"You remember a woman with hair like mine, don't you? You said it the moment you laid eyes on me in that warehouse last year when I was the one behind bars. I remember her too, just vaguely."

"The necklace? Let me see it," Livia demanded.

Allie tugged the chain from under her coat and held it in the light.

Livia did the same, pulling a long chain tucked under her

jacket. The pendants were nearly identical. The serpentine figure around Livia's necklace was more clearly an ouroboros with ruby red eyes.

"It makes no difference. I was raised by the man I call father. That is all that matters." Livia turned her back to them. She was a strong, proud woman. She wouldn't accept this easily.

"I don't know you. I don't know who you work for. I don't know anything about you, but you're my sister," Allie took a step forward.

"She isn't worth the effort, little one." Liam stood beside her.

"She's my sister." Allie looked up at her brother. His face was hard as stone.

"You saw what she did to Ming and Jin?" he said.

"She broke them somehow, but I don't understand. I can't fathom how Ming could really be dead."

"She broke their Complement bond. And to make it even more unnecessarily tragic, she murdered Ming Lao in front of their daughter."

"To be fair, I was aiming for the other one. It's usually easier for the woman to survive without her Complement, especially when she has natural children. I was trying to be nice," Livia said.

The rage surged within her again, itching to be released, but Allie kept a tight rein. She was more in control now. She wouldn't lose it again.

"Little *sister,*" Livia sneered. "What a joke. I'll get out of this hellhole of yours and, so help me, I will take you with me. I'll break you just like I did your buddy Quinn. I'll wear your gifts like a cloak and then I'll hand you over to my father. He's been looking for you for thousands of years."

"That's enough for tonight," Gregg said.

"What will you do with her?" Allie asked as she turned to leave, ignoring Livia's vitriol.

"She will be treated kindly, but we can't let her go. Not yet."

"I-I'll come see you again," Allie said.

Livia scared her to death, but Allie wanted to know her. If she could be redeemed ... if she could be the woman Allie only vaguely remembered from the visions she had during her Awakening, then she wanted to give her that chance. It was what their parents would want.

"Don't bother. Go live your little charmed life and forget about me."

Allie whirled back toward her sister, marching right up to the bars. "I don't know anything about what you've been through, Livia. But you don't know shit about me and what I've been through either. You and I can be enemies, or we can learn to work together, filling in the gaps for each other. There's a lot I could tell you about our parents. It's up to you which way this will go. You can bend or you can break, but something tells me you're too strong and too smart to break. I know I am."

Allie followed Gregg from the cell, leaving Liam behind to watch over Livia, Quinn and his friend ... and the other one. Allie could sense him in another cell, deep within the confines of the underground, even deeper than where they were now. She could feel the pulse of his Immortality all around her. The closer she was to him, the stronger she sensed it. *I wonder if I can give it back?* In her rage, her judgment led her to protect Aidan. But she wasn't sure anyone deserved what she'd done. Allie shuddered. She couldn't even fathom how she was capable of doing something so monstrous.

"It seems we need to have a chat before you can go rest," Gregg said as Darius joined them and they made their way up the steep stone staircase. "This bond you share has no doubt left you both completely baffled."

"You could say that. Da, what is this?" Darius asked.

"It is a very ancient bond. And Lord knows I never would have expected it from you two. Few will ever know what it means to have what you have. Fortunately, I spent nearly all my life sharing such a bond with a very important woman." Gregg led them into his office. Allie knew what he was getting at. That woman was her mother.

"Allie, if you want to truly understand this bond, there should be no secrets between you two. Do you have anything you need to tell Darius before we continue?" He gestured for them to take a seat on the sofa.

Allie turned to face Darius. "I think he means he shared this kind of bond with my mother," Allie whispered.

Gregg nodded.

"Lily?" Darius frowned.

"Carson and Lily are the only mother and father I have ever known, but my biological parents were Kassandre and Ashar. I just found out last year."

"So ... you're a natural born. And your parents were pretty ... impressive." Darius nodded as if that were the end of it.

"Livia is my natural-born sister," Allie added. "Kassandre—our mother—was the daughter of Alísun, the last Queen of Indriell." She felt it when his heart skipped a beat—hers mimicking his.

"The prophecy?" Darius managed not to choke on the word.

"It's about me."

"It's about all of you," Gregg added. "Remember, the prophecy says, 'He—or she as it turns out—will surround herself with her equals.' Not her equal, which is obviously Aidan, but her equals. Plural."

"Sorry I seem to have dragged you into this." Allie hung her head. She loved Darius and the last thing she ever wanted was to force him into a role he didn't want.

"Are you kidding? This is awesome." Darius flashed her a grin. "Pleased to meet you, Your Highness."

"Knock it off, Dare." She punched his shoulder with a quick jab.

"We're getting off-subject," Gregg said. "Kassandre was my Syntrophos."

"Syntrophos? I've never heard that term before," Darius said.

"It's not common knowledge. Those who have it tend to keep it to themselves."

"What does it mean?" Allie asked.

"In the Greek translation, Syntrophos means foster sibling, as in the old way when a child would foster with another family to learn a trade or become a warrior or knight. Kassandre was my Syntrophos and Ashar's Complement. She was the glue that held us all together. She was our anchor. Ashar and I were like brothers and she was ... everything. I was her left hand in battle and he was her right. She was my comrade-in-arms. She was my best friend and the love of Ashar's life. Together, the three of us were one. When they died ... a piece of me went with them."

"But it's nothing like a Complement bond, right?" Darius asked. "No weird ménage relationship that I really do *not* want to hear about happening between my parents and Allie's. Please tell me you all weren't, like, romantically involved?"

"Ew, Darius? Did you have to go there? My brain never went there. What's wrong with you?" Allie glared at him.

"What? I'm a little worried. I'm crazy about you, but at the same time, I don't really see you that way ... but I also wouldn't say a little somethin' somethin' might never happen between us once you're older."

"It's a complicated relationship, son." Gregg laughed. "It will not make much sense to anyone outside of your relationship. But I can assure you our Syntrophos bond was never anything weird or kinky or inappropriate. So let's let that be the end of such discussion, please."

"This sounds so complicated." Allie sighed. She couldn't deal with complicated.

"Aye, it is. But when Naeemah and I finally bonded, she gave us the balance we desperately needed. Before then, it was not always easy. Jealousy plagued us for years, but our bond kept us close and we dealt with it."

"Like walking a tightrope," Allie said.

"Your mother always said the same thing." Gregg chuckled.

"So this is something that has always been?" Darius asked.

"The Syntrophos bond began with the earliest Queens of Indriell. The queen's council was made up of the Syntrophos who were the heads of their noble houses. They acted as her council, but they were also her army, despite their small numbers. They were that powerful. Some say they were the direct descendants of the original Immortals. Some say they are mere legend—that when Zeus separated their souls, he broke these few into thirds and not halves. Some believe the Syntrophos only arise when the world is in need of them. The stories are just stories, but I am living proof the bond is real."

Allie squirmed in her seat. She loved Darius, but this was intense. And after everything that passed between her and Aidan before all of this began, she wasn't sure how she would be able to handle this—loving them both so fiercely. It seemed like a doomed situation and she refused to come between the brothers.

"After the Great War, the Syntrophos who survived the executions were precious few," Gregg continued. "Those who lived disappeared, but their bloodlines have carried on. Even mortals have legends about them. In the fourth century B.C.E., mortal historians called them the Sacred Band of Thebes, an army of one hundred and fifty 'lovers.'"

"Lovers?" Allie asked.

"Aye, but perhaps the more correct term would be an army of 'beloved.' The army fought in teams of three, the strongest at the center with the left and right fighting alongside them, but always with the purpose of protecting their center. There were many women who led as the anchor. Mortal historians like to make men responsible for all the great strides in history, but women have always been more capable than mortal men have ever wanted to admit. The Sacred Band of Thebes was invincible and they were successful because they each cared deeply for those who fought at their sides. That was the first time in mortal history where the Syntrophos was most plainly evident."

Allie wasn't sure if she was in the right mental state for a history lesson. But Gregg's voice was filled with such passion she clung to his every word, hoping he would say something that would help her understand the warring emotions she had for both Aidan and Darius.

"Plato even spoke of it at his symposium." Gregg cleared his throat as he continued.

"—If there were only some way of contriving that a state or an army should be made up of lovers and their beloved, they would be the very best governors of their own city, abstaining from all dishonor, and emulating one another in honor; and when fighting at each other's side, although a mere handful, they would overcome the world."

"He speaks of our bond. Although he doesn't know it, he has given the truest definition of what the Syntrophos means.

Kassandre was my beloved. Not in the same way as Naeemah, of course. It is a very different kind of love, but it is still love. The only love you will ever know that supersedes what you two have now will be with your Complements."

"So ... um ... what does that mean for our dating lives?" Darius asked.

"You can probably expect that Allie will passionately believe no woman will ever be good enough for you." Gregg gave him a sympathetic look. "Kassie rarely interfered in my love life, but she was never very friendly with my lady friends. She adored Naeemah, however. But at the same time she was insanely jealous of her."

Allie sighed. "This is going to get difficult."

"Yep." Darius ran his hands through his hair.

"You let me tell Aidan," Allie said. "He needs to hear this from me."

"He's not good en—"

"Nope," Allie raised her hand to stop him. "I'm shutting this down right now. Repeat after me." She glared at him. "I, Darius McBrien, will keep my nose out of Allie's relationship with Aidan."

"Fine, I'll stay out of it, Red. He just better—"

"Don't finish that sentence, son. It's going to be very difficult for you to keep your instincts under control. So you'd better start trying now."

"Do you know any Syntrophos we can, like ... take lessons from?" Allie asked.

"The bond is feared by so many, Allie. You'll likely not find any willing to help. Those who have it keep it hidden and don't speak of it. It is thought to be a rare occurrence, but there are more of us out there than Senate would like to believe. A fully bonded Syntrophos would be a fearful thing. Multiple Syntrophos, banding together ... the Senate wouldn't allow it.

They never knew your mother was an anchor. They never knew of her heritage either. The Senate fears what they cannot control, so very few ever knew of the bond I shared with your parents. We only spoke of it with those we trusted."

"But how could you hide it?" Darius asked. "We didn't even have to tell you or Liam. You could practically smell it on us."

"Aye, and you'll have to learn to hide it, son. And quickly. You are safe here at home, but before either of you goes back to school or work, you must learn to mask the bond you share. You are both so young, it will be difficult, but I will teach you."

"So how did it happen for you, Da? Was it just out of nowhere?"

"It was years after we met when our bond first began to form. When they became Complements, Ashar and I struggled to come to terms with our boundaries. It was difficult at first. She felt torn between us—like there wasn't enough of her for both of us. Ashar was jealous of our connection and how well we knew each other, but in time, he realized there was no longer a romantic love between us. There was a time when there was, but it paled in comparison to what they had. The relationship can take years to fully understand. We always categorize the people in our lives. Family, friend, lover, enemy. A Syntrophos doesn't fit in any of those boxes so it takes time to define what the relationship means to those involved. It can be intimate and touchy-feely, but without the complications of romance and chemistry. It's actually a very innocent kind of love that is often misunderstood by those on the outside of it."

Allie sat back with a weary sigh, trying to absorb everything. "When it happened ... it felt so ... intense. It scared me to death," she finally said.

"I'll second that," Darius agreed.

"It's more like a family bond in the way it comes upon us so suddenly," Gregg said. "This is not something either of you had any control over. So it's best to accept it and work together to learn what it means for you as individuals and as a couple, because that is what you are now."

"So what do we do?" Darius asked. "This is insignificant compared to everything else we've got going on."

"Right now, you rest. It's been a long couple of days for all of us. We've made it through a difficult time, not without some profound losses."

Allie dropped her head, as the tears finally came. She was overwhelmed with shame and guilt for the death of Ming Lao.

"Sweetheart, she died saving her husband and her grandson. She died knowing her daughter will always have her father —knowing Quinn would return to us. Ming Lao died in battle, the way she would have wanted. And she would never want you to blame yourself for any of it. You did well, Alexis Carmichael. You did this family proud. It won't be easy moving forward, but we'll do so as a family, as we always have."

"What does this mean for Jin? For his ... mortality."

"This is unprecedented. But he is still Immortal. We can only guess what his future will hold without his Complement at his side. It is highly probable that a severe wound could kill him, but otherwise, he will remain unchanged by this event—at least physically. Emotionally ... I can't imagine."

CHAPTER 34

Allie made her way down the long corridor to the common room. Gregg and Darius returned to the crypt to speak with Quinn, and Liam was still with Livia—probably interrogating her, which Allie didn't even want to think about. She was so weary. She just wanted to check on everyone, grab something to eat, and go to bed for a week—preferably for a nice, long, dreamless sleep, and for that she needed Aidan. But the only one lingering in the common room was Sasha. She paced the length of the room, still dressed in her gear and obviously still reeling.

"Sasha?" Allie whispered.

"I heard you coming. What do you know? I just got back." Her curly hair stood on end and she had a crazed look in her eye.

"I was going to ask you the same thing."

"Have you seen him?"

"Quinn? Yes. He's fine."

"Where is he?"

"He asked them to lock him up in the crypt. He's still not himself. Livia had some kind of hold on him. She was using his gifts."

"She took them?" Sasha looked horrified.

"No. It seems she can take control of a gift without actually stealing it. He was in bad shape, but you broke him out of it, Sash. You did it. You brought him home. I don't think we could have gotten through to him any other way."

"Then what is this?" She threw her hands up in frustration, her eyes bright with unshed tears. Sasha didn't cry so Allie knew she was on the verge of a total freak-out.

"Calm down. Let's sit." Allie gestured to one of the many sofas that filled the common room. "What are you talking about?"

"I can *feel* him, Allie. Like I can feel his heart beating in my chest. Something happened out there when we saw each other."

Allie did a double take. She was so exhausted and overwhelmed, she'd missed it. She'd missed the shroud wrapped around her friend like a cloud. The subtle aura around Sasha was new and it vibrated with Quinn's energy. She could sense the bond that linked them, but Sasha didn't understand.

"Have you talked to Naeemah?"

"No, I haven't seen anyone since I got back."

"Who did you ride home with?" Allie wondered why no one had talked to her about this yet.

"I drove home alone. I followed Mom."

"Where is everyone? Where's Aidan?"

"I think Aidan's with Emma trying to treat Daniel's severed hand. He's in so much pain, but he heals so slowly—and with Ming gone, he's just a mess. I can't believe she is *gone* gone. Jin and Chloe are with Mom and Graham in her garden. They needed a quiet place to mourn. The others aren't back yet. They're keeping watch." Sasha had barely taken a breath as she babbled.

Allie grabbed her trembling hands. "Deep breaths, Sash. You've been alone, for hours, not knowing what this is?" Allie pulled her in for a hug. She could feel Sasha was on the brink of losing control. She was so upset, she wasn't aware of Allie's new bond yet. Allie held her and whispered comforting words as Sasha cried. "Just breathe; it's all going to be okay. But I need you to calm down. Focus on me. Let everything else go." As Sasha finally relaxed, Allie waited patiently for her to make the connection.

Sasha suddenly pulled away, staring at her in disbelief. "What *is* this bullshit? You too? With *Darius*?"

Allie nodded. "Let's go find your dad. You need to see Quinn, and Gregg needs to explain this to you both." Allie pulled her up from the couch where she sat, completely bewildered.

"I always wondered if Quinn might be my Complement," Sasha whispered as they headed back down to the crypt. "But it never felt right. I love him. I'd be proud if he were. It's just never worked; but this feels very ... Complementy."

"Quinn is a huge part of who you are." Allie pushed on the door leading to Quinn's cell, but it was locked. She knocked and waited. The longer they stood there, the more agitated Sasha became.

"I'm going to break it down." Sasha moved to kick the door.

"Darius, please open the door," Allie said. She knew he would hear her. She could sense him standing just on the other side.

"Well, this is about to get messy," Darius said as he opened the door, but Sasha rushed past him.

"Open the cell," she demanded.

"Sasha?" Quinn leapt to his feet. "I missed you." He reached through the bars.

"Get him out of there!" Sasha's eyes blazed with fury.

"It's not safe, Sash," Quinn said. "I need a few days in here—"

"You will *not* hurt me. You don't have it in you. Now get him out of there." Sasha glared at Darius.

"Will do." Darius stepped to the door and unlocked the cell.

Before Quinn could take a step out, Sasha ran in and threw her arms around him, locking her legs around his waist.

"Can you believe this?" Darius whispered. "I picked up on their bond when I came back in here to talk with him. He's been like a caged lion ever since I explained what little I could. He wanted to see her but he's still afraid he's going to snap at any moment until he gets control of his power back from Livia."

"They'll be fine now." Allie smiled. For such a strange bond to occur twice in the same night was incredible, but she couldn't deny it—Sasha and Quinn were also Syntrophos. *I'm gathering my equals.* She could see their hazy future and wondered what her friends' lives might have been like if they'd never met her.

"Who is she?" Sasha finally asked.

Quinn turned toward the girl sitting on his bed, Sasha still clinging to him.

"This is my ... girlfriend, Santi," Quinn said carefully.

"Hi," Santi said softly. "He forgot to tell me you were beyond gorgeous."

Sasha slowly slipped out of Quinn's arms and stared up at him, her eyes practically sparking.

"This would be the messy part I mentioned earlier." Darius crossed his arms with a smile, like he was settling in for the entertainment.

"You have a *girlfriend*?" Sasha said coldly. "You've been off in some kind of prison camp, have obviously been through hell, and you come back with a girlfriend? While I've spent the last eight months *dying* inside, you've been hooking up?" She gave him a shove.

"Sasha, it's not going to change whatever this bond is we have now," Quinn said.

"Wow, she's pretty feisty. I like her," Santi said.

Allie thought she was very brave for daring to interrupt Sasha's tirade.

"I—"

"Can we argue later, Sash?" Quinn asked. "Right now, I'm just really happy to see you." He reached to cup her face.

Santi clearly didn't like it, but she was smart enough to keep it to herself.

"This is not going to be easy for them," Darius said. "At least you and I are single."

"About that." Allie sighed. She didn't know exactly what she and Aidan were, but they were far more than friends now. She could no longer resist putting a label on their relationship. "Aidan and I are kind of together."

"When the hell did that happen?" Darius scowled.

"It's been on a slow boil for months, and it kind of boiled over right before all of this."

"You can yell at me if you want, but he's not good enough for you, Allie."

"He's your brother. Be nice."

"I am. He's a putz."

"I'm pretty sure you'd say that about anyone I wanted to date." She elbowed him playfully.

"Probably." Darius yawned.

"Let's get these two off to Gregg for Syntrophos lessons, and then I'm going to go find Aidan and go to bed," Allie said.

"Do you have to do that?"

"I'd like to have a dream-free night, so you're going to have to deal."

"Come on, you two," Darius said. "Santi ... uh, you should probably stay here."

"Fine by me; I'm exhausted. It's been a really long ... year." She stretched out on the bed with a yawn.

Quinn had trouble maintaining his emotions as they walked through the hallways of the underground where he grew up. Sasha whispered to him the whole way to Gregg's office, but it was obvious he was in for a long struggle to put the past eight months behind him.

"Sorry, Da," Darius said after Gregg let them in. He was busy making phone calls and taking intel from everyone still out there taking stock of their situation.

"You've got to be kidding me," Gregg said in shock when he realized why they were there. "You too?" He asked Sasha.

"I sense lots of group Syntrophos classes in our near future," Darius said.

"We're going to go." Allie pulled Darius toward the door. "We'll talk tomorrow, Sash."

"I'm going to go crash in Daniel's office," Darius said after they left. "But if you need me, just call. I'm always here for you, Allie."

"Thanks, Dare. This is all ... so confusing and overwhelming. But I'm glad it's you."

"If you have to have a Syntrophos, at least you got a fun one." He winked. "Night, Allie."

"Night."

Now she just needed to go find Aidan.

He was in his office. Sitting in the dark, drinking.

Not a good sign.

I'm just exhausted ... and glad to see you found your way to me. I was afraid—

That I would stay with Darius? This bond doesn't work that way, Aidan.

"So what is this thing you have with my brother?" He pulled her down onto his lap and offered her the bottle he was drinking from. Gregg's extra-potent moonshine.

"It's called a Syntrophos. It means we are connected in a special, non-romantic way."

"Non-roman-tic." He laughed—but if he were anyone else, she would have called it a giggle.

"How much have you had to drink?" she asked. It took some skill and hard work to get sloshed liked this.

"A lot." He took a long gulp straight from the bottle. "Say more things like non-roman-tic." He gave her a goofy grin.

"Drunk Aidan is super cute." She smiled back. "I don't know much about it yet, but your father was bonded to my mother this way. She and Ashar and Gregg found a way to make it work, and so will we."

"Yeah? I'm pretty sure my dad did your mom for a few centuries before she met Ashar."

"Aidan, gross!"

"Just sayin' there's something there I don't like."

"Hey. Look at me." She turned his head to meet her gaze. "This isn't going to change anything between us. But I'm too tired to figure it out tonight. I just want to take a hot shower and go to bed and feel you beside me. I want to forget about the awful things that happened. Every horrific thing I've seen and the awful things I've done. I just want to sleep and not dream."

"I can at least do that for you, Lex. Come on."

She followed him to the bedroom behind his studio, feeling a sense of dread about their future. She was suddenly unsure of Aidan's ability to cope with her new relationship with Darius. To choose between them would be impossible.

Aidan didn't speak as they changed out of their gear. He

didn't speak as he led her to the bathroom. His eyes were broody and sad as they stepped into the hot shower together. His kiss was slow and sweet, but he didn't push further. His hands on her body were methodical as he helped her wash the blood and grime away.

When he wrapped a towel around her, he pressed a kiss to her forehead. For once, she couldn't fathom what he was thinking. He had her blocked; whatever he was feeling, he hid it from her in a way he never had before. He had his own box now and suddenly the tables were turned and she was getting a taste of her own medicine.

Aidan? She stared up at him uncertainly.

I'm fine, baby. Just tired and trying not to think about ... anything. "Let's just go to bed. I'm happy to keep your dreams away."

She grabbed his hand and pulled him back. "You know that's not the only reason I'm here, right?"

The look he gave her said he wasn't so sure. It cut her to the quick. She backed away from him, taking a moment to change into shorts and a t-shirt from the drawer she'd stocked weeks ago. She threw some clothes at Aidan, not trusting herself to speak.

You know that's not what I meant.

"Aidan ... I'm here because I love you. I'm here because there is no one else I want to be with after the night we've had. What happened before ... back in my bedroom. That wasn't something I took lightly."

"I know, Allie. That's not what I meant. I don't know what I meant. I'm drunk. I'm still feeling Daniel's pain. I just ... I don't like this. I don't like feeling like a jealous fool. I need time—to get used to this thing you have with my brother. I'm not sure how to act and I'm messing this up, which is the last thing I want right now."

"Then trust me when I say your ability to give me a peaceful sleep is the cherry on top of all the other reasons I'm here."

"Say more things like that." Aidan smiled, pulling her close.

"Sleep. Pillows. Blankets. Please." She yawned into his bare chest. "And I wouldn't say no to chocolate chip pancakes either."

"How about pancakes tomorrow and sleep tonight?" His chest vibrated against her cheek with his laughter.

"M'kay." She lay back on the bed and curled up against him.

The last thing Allie ever wanted was to further complicate their relationship. Just when she was finally brave enough to test the waters with him, hoping they might find happiness together, the world reared back and punched them in the gut.

Chapter 35

Allie brushed her hair, trying to tame her wild curls. Chloe was so good at styling it for her, but she didn't want to bother her. Not on the morning of her grandparents' and her mother's funeral. She hadn't spoken to Chloe or Jin since Ming's death. She wouldn't blame them if they never wanted to see her again.

"I don't think I should go," Allie said for the hundredth time.

"Ming would want you there," Aidan assured her. "No one is blaming you except you. You've got to stop taking so much responsibility for things that are completely out of your control."

"I would blame me," she muttered as she twisted her thick hair back into some semblance of an elegant bun. "Have you ever been to an Immortal funeral before?"

"No. I think it's a new experience for most of us." Aidan paced to his closet for another tie, discarding a perfectly good one with the others piled on his bed. "We'll each have an opportunity to make a mark on her final resting place with our gifts, so be thinking about what you want to do for her."

Ming was to be buried in the crypt in a special tomb Hélène had turned into a garden. Allie wasn't sure what she could possibly do for Ming with her gifts, and she wasn't sure if the family would even want her to.

"Let's go, Lex." Aidan held his hand out for her.

The walk to the underground was long and somber as everyone converged in the main hall where Ming's casket rested between her parents' under the high vaulted ceilings of the place they all called home. Her parents had died trying to protect her. Poor Jin and Chloe had lost half of their family in one day.

Allie lingered toward the back of the line, not wanting to draw attention to herself. Quinn, Graham, Darius, and Aidan carried Ming's coffin at the front of the procession. A distraught Chloe and Jin followed behind the other two caskets.

Sasha and Santi drifted closer to Allie, falling in step beside her. The two girls were having a rough time with the new bond, but they seemed to have a mutual, albeit guarded, respect for each other. It helped that Santi was a complete stranger to Sasha before all of this happened. Darius and Aidan weren't handling it nearly as well. And Allie tended to disappear whenever they were all in the same room together.

The girls linked arms and followed the silent funeral procession to the final resting place for Ming Lao and her parents, Ju Long and Lu Li.

"Wow," Santi whispered as they stepped into the lovely garden deep within the recesses of the crypt. The three coffins occupied the center of the room. Trees swayed in a soft breeze. Emma had obviously done her part since the room blazed bright with sunshine, and Gregg's puffy white clouds drifted high above them. Everyone circled around the coffins and one by one, each person took a moment to say their final goodbyes and offer a gift for the departed. Allie watched as Aidan placed his hands on Ming's coffin and used his gift to bring a warm, balmy breeze to this oasis, deep within the cold crypt. Sasha stepped forward and called a host of birds to join the quiet garden. Allie heard them winging their way here through the halls until they burst into the room in a chorus of song.

Even Santi offered her gift. As she placed her hands on Chloe and Jin, something wondrous came over them. Their smiles and laughter chased away their sorrow, if only for a moment. It seemed to give them the strength to get through this terrible day. Allie watched as Santi took her place at Quinn's side, placing her small hand in his. Something about the way she selflessly offered her gift to a woman she'd never met solidified Santi's future among them. The small act of kindness may have changed the course of her life.

Allie had come to realize her clairvoyance would always be a challenge. She could only see so much, and she could only understand a portion of what she saw. The decisions she'd made that changed the future she'd seen in her dreams was done on instinct. That was the best she would ever be able to do. The future wasn't set in stone. The future was like a river, changing its course over time. But as small things were set into motion, the effects they had on the future could be monumental. All she could do was watch and see what she saw. Sometimes she would be able to act in ways that might alter the things she witnessed in her visions. And sometimes she would have to let nature take its course. Neither she nor her gift were infallible. She had to come to terms with that and accept the outcome of the choices she made.

When it was Allie's turn, she still wasn't sure what she could do for Ming Lao. She had very little talent for anything peaceful or serene.

Do whatever moves you in the moment, Lex. There is no wrong way to offer a gift.

As she stepped up to the coffins, she let out a sigh of relief. Graham had placed his gift here already. Dozens of mechanical butterflies with intricate stained glass wings, perched all over the coffins. Their wings fluttered as the moving parts of his creations brought them to life.

Allie took one of the dainty butterflies, cupping it in the palm of her hand and let her solar energy pour into each of them. Graham had linked them together like a hive, in preparation for Allie's addition. She gave them the energy they needed to power their solar batteries. Once charged, they would continue to draw from Emma's sunshine, so they would always fly.

The crowd gasped when the butterflies took to the air and Allie smiled through her tears, knowing Ming Lao would have loved it. As she turned, Chloe and Jin waited for her. Their grief was palpable and she couldn't fathom the enormity of their loss.

When Chloe took her hands and squeezed them gently, Allie lost it. "I'm so sorry," she whispered. "I'm so sorry. I should have—"

Chloe and Jin wrapped their arms around her. "She would be proud of you, Allie," Jin said. "She would never want you to blame yourself for what happened. You did everything in your power to keep this family safe and you helped bring Quinn home. She would have gladly sacrificed herself to see that happen."

Allie nodded. She would never forgive herself for Ming's death, but this day was about Chloe and Jin and honoring their grief.

As she stood, holding Jin's hand, she could feel how drained he was. He could barely stand on his own. Without a thought, Allie called on her own strength and gave it all to him, bolstering him for the difficult days ahead.

With a grateful nod, Jin stepped up to offer his final gift to his Complement. He reached into his pocket and brought out an ancient-looking fur slipper, crumbling with age.

Sasha let out a strangled sob as he placed it at the base of her obsidian coffin. "That's the shoe he lost the day they met."

As Jin knelt, he touched the ground, bringing forth a spring that circled the three coffins, creating a little island for them.

It was Chloe's turn last and Allie had no idea what she might offer her mother and grandparents. Silent tears streamed down Chloe's face as she knelt beside the new spring her father had created for her mother. She placed her palms against the surface of the water and began to sing in Chinese. Her voice was melodic and sounded so much like her mother's Allie closed her eyes and smiled. She could almost hear Ming Lao's laughter, like bells.

Sasha nudged her so she wouldn't miss what Chloe did next. As she sat, singing and trailing her fingers through the water, a figure emerged from the surface. As it mingled with her tears, it took shape and began to whirl around the coffins.

"A Chinese dragon," Santi whispered.

Chloe made three of them, each distinct. Although made of water, they each had an ornate design representing the fallen of her family.

Allie's mind whirled with images. Random snatches of things to come, and things that might never be. In every instance, she saw Chloe, sometimes at her side, but at others she stood in opposition. Regardless, she was an equal in every possible way. Chloe was a sweet-tempered girl now, but she would grow into a formidable, powerful, and respected woman. The death of her mother would have an extreme impact on Chloe's life. It would make her stronger, but if she didn't allow herself to fully mourn her loss and deal with her grief, it would send her down the wrong path.

“We should never, ever, ever, ever underestimate that girl,” Allie said softly.

Chapter 36

THREE WEEKS LATER

Allie heard Aidan's light step on her balcony below. She put the finishing touches on the new mural she was painting in her studio at the top of her tower. She didn't spend as much time there as she originally thought she would when they first moved to Kelleys Island, but it was still one of her favorite places to brood.

"I'm up here," she called.

"Are you hiding up here doing homework, Lex?" His boots a familiar echo on the stairs. "We're still on winter break for another week." Aidan flopped down on a chair and thumbed through the portfolio she'd been working on all afternoon. Things were finally starting to calm down in the weeks since Ming's death and Quinn's return. Life was taking on a new normal, as it always did whenever things changed.

"We only have a few months until high school is over. I've been accepted to most of my top-pick schools, but I still have to apply to the art programs. Portfolio reviews will be due in a few weeks and I have to be ready."

"Have you decided where you want to go?"

"I'd like to go to Kent State, but it's an hour away and I'm not sure I want to deal with the constant driving back and forth for training. It will probably be easiest if Sasha and I go to the same school so we can just train there."

"Um ... I have some news. I'm pretty excited about it. Can we go sit downstairs?"

"Uh-oh, this sounds ominous." Allie wiped her hands and followed him down the narrow steps to her room below.

"Come here, babe." He pulled her down on his lap as they sat in her armchair near the tall windows by the balcony.

"Aidan you're scaring me. I can't tell what you're thinking." Ever since she'd bonded with Darius, Aidan had kept his feelings about it carefully guarded. She didn't like being shut out. It made her feel ten times worse about all the months she'd locked him out. She vowed never to do it again.

"I'm leaving, Lex."

"What? When?" Panic rose in her chest. This had always been her deepest fear. Since the moment they met, she'd resisted loving him because she *knew* she would just lose him.

"It's just for a few months."

"Okay." She nodded, feeling the tightness in her chest relax enough so she could breathe.

"Where are you going?"

"Germany." He smiled. "Mom and Dad never wanted to let me go to the Music Conservatory there. At least not before I finished high school. But they've recently agreed to a compromise. I was accepted into their introductory program for musically gifted teens. I'll finish high school there while I get an amazing start to my college education. Then I'll come back here at the end of the summer and continue at Oberlin in the fall so we can be close."

"That's eight months," Allie whispered. So much could happen in eight months.

"It will fly by. I'll be back before you know it."

Allie nodded, trying to smile for his sake. She knew he wanted this more than anything and she wasn't going to stand in his way.

"I'll come see you this summer," she managed through a tight smile.

"Yes, I want you to spend the whole summer with me, Lex. This won't be so bad if we have that to look forward to."

"I'll miss you." She clasped his hands. "But I'm really excited for you too."

"I knew you would understand." He hugged her close and Allie sank into him, laying her head on his shoulder. The late afternoon sun streamed through the window as he absently ran his fingers through her hair.

"How long until you leave?" she finally said.

"Tomorrow." His voice faltered. "I just found out I was accepted for next semester."

Allie curled her arms around him tightly as if she could hold him here by sheer physical will. There was something he wasn't telling her. Like he was trying to spare her feelings. She wiped furiously at the tears that slipped down her cheeks. She would not be selfish. This was his dream.

"I'm proud of you, Aidan. I want you to go there and soak it all in. Don't worry about me." Her words weren't quite as believable, considering the way her chin trembled and her voice warbled and she wasn't even sure he could discern her words as English.

"I love you, Allie. That will never change. No matter where I go, no matter what I do. I will always come back to you. *Nothing* will ever part us for long."

Allie nodded, trying not to choke on the tears burning her eyes and throat.

"Take this time to be with Darius."

She gave him a baffled look.

"Not like that, Lex." He rolled his eyes. "Take this time to focus on the amazing connection you two have. I know how confused you are right now." He laced his fingers through hers. "And don't think I haven't noticed how you pull a disappearing act whenever we're all in the same room together."

"I'm sorry. It's just awkward. My mortal brain can't deal."

"Well, with me gone, it will be easier for you to come to terms with this relationship, to let it develop naturally. I understand it better now. I know how much you mean to each other and I know it's all very innocent. Dad let me see some of his memories of your mom so I could really feel how difficult it was for them in the beginning."

"You saw her?" Gregg had never shown Allie any of his memories of her mother and she'd never asked. She wasn't ready for that yet.

"Yes. She was incredible. You look a lot like her, but you're very different. You're more like your father. I saw how important it was for my dad and your mom to spend some time exploring what the Syntrophos bond really meant for them. As much as I hate to admit it, you and Darius need that too. A few months is probably not nearly enough time, but it's a start. And it's the longest I can fathom being away from you."

It was a good plan. It meant so much to Allie that he was trying so hard to understand and accept her connection with Darius.

"I just wish you weren't leaving so soon." Allie sighed. "We still have tonight, don't we?"

"Yes, Lex. We still have tonight." Aidan's lips brushed hers and she pulled him close. Saying goodbye was going to break her heart.

Did you forget we still have this?

Allie burst out laughing. *Yeah, I kinda forgot this still works with an ocean between us.*

As long as we have this, I will never be more than a thought away. "We're just going to have to figure out the time difference," Aidan said.

"Well, we've gotten better at blocking each other, so it shouldn't be too bad. I'll just miss this." Allie sighed, running her palms along his shoulders.

"That is the really crappy part. But let's not think about that tonight. I'd like to commit to memory every single inch of you." Aidan dragged her up from the armchair.

Allie smiled as he swept her up in his arms. They could survive this short separation. But as she gazed up at him, tracing the lines of his face with her fingertips, Allie saw what they faced and there was nothing she could do about it. He didn't know it yet, but Aidan was going to cut her out of his life and permanently block her from his mind. This wouldn't be months. This would be years.

Allie's heart shattered into a million pieces as they said their goodbyes.

EPILOGUE

FOUR MONTHS LATER

Allie left the crypt in disgust, marching down the hall to the stone stairs leading up to the common room.

"She is the most stubborn woman I've ever met! It's like arguing with a pile of bricks!"

"Allie, your sister *is* making progress," Liam called from behind.

Allie whirled around irritably. "You call that progress? Did you hear what she just said to me?"

"Slow progress." Liam smiled. "You do seem to bring out the worst in her."

"How can you stand spending so much time down here with that awful woman?"

"Have you asked Quinn about his experiences with Livia?"

Her real name was Alivia, the name their parents gave her, but she did not care for it ... at all. They'd all learned really quickly not to use it in her presence.

"No. He's doing so much better now. He's hashed everything out with his teachers so many times, I think he's needed us to just ... let him be. I haven't wanted to push him."

"You should ask him. He can give you a lot of insight into

how she's become the woman she is. She isn't all bad. There is a spark of goodness in her."

"I doubt it."

"Tiny spark." Liam gestured with his thumb and forefinger.

"She just makes me so crazy, and she's so *mean.* I know you guys think she can be rehabilitated or whatever, but I don't think it's working. And I don't know how long we can just keep her locked up like this. Eventually her father is going to come looking for her."

"Sisters fight, little one. It's only natural that you two would butt heads."

"You're my brother; you're supposed to be on *my* side."

"About that...." He rubbed at the blond stubble on his face. He'd been down here for days this time.

"What?" Allie eyed him curiously as he led her far away from Livia's rather posh cell. Liam had transformed the cell to a full apartment with every convenience Livia could possible need.

"There's a reason I'm the one working with her, little one," he said softly.

"What is it?"

"She's ... my Complement."

"What?" Allie's mouth hung open in surprise. "Seriously?"

"Yeah." He smiled.

"I'm ... sorry she's such a bitch."

"I think we can help her with that. She's our family, Allie. We have to show her she doesn't have to be the person her father made. She has a chance to become the woman she would have been if your family hadn't been torn apart. It's our duty to give her that chance."

"She doesn't know, does she?"

"She isn't ready to see me yet. But she will be ready one

day and I intend to give her the opportunity to learn who she really is before then."

"You two ... you just don't match." Allie shuddered. "I don't see it."

"Me neither, to be honest." He laughed. "But I've been working with her enough to know that carefully placed facade she wears is not the real Livia. She just needs time. And a few more cracks in the armor."

"So we really were meant to be brother and sister, huh?" Allie said. "Brother-in-law." She elbowed him playfully.

"It seems that way. That's probably why you are immune to me. Livia is too; she just doesn't know it yet. Only the blood sister of my Complement would be strong enough to be immune to my poison."

"So it looks like we really are stuck with her now." Allie saw the worry in Liam's eyes. For all his talk of giving her a chance, she knew he wasn't convinced Livia was worth it.

"I had a vision of her. During my Awakening. I didn't understand it then, but I saw this delightful version of her." She gestured back at the prison behind her. "And I saw another version of her too. With you and Kahlynn. At the time I hadn't met you so I didn't know who the tall blond guy was with the beautiful daughter."

"What was that Livia like?"

"Happy. Smiling. Not threatening to 'rip every strand of my ridiculous hair from my head and hang me with it.'"

"See, there's hope for even the meanest of mean girls."

"It was the distant future, Liam."

"I can handle it." He pulled her into a headlock and dropped a kiss on top of her head.

"Liam," Allie growled. He really was obnoxious sometimes.

"Thanks for giving me that promise to hang on to."

"Love you, big bro."

"Love you too, little one. Now I believe Gregg is waiting for you in the yard. You still have some training to get through before you're done for the day."

"Some things never change." She heaved a big sigh and headed up to the common room to grab a snack before she had to meet Gregg for her daily torture.

The yard was a little different now. When Ming Lao died, some of her contributions to the underground began to whither and fade. Her gift of manipulating earth meant she'd done an extensive amount of work to the underground, but after the first few days, something changed. The balance was restored and new life was breathed into everything Ming Lao ever touched. It was her daughter. Ming's blood flowed through Chloe and as long as she lived, a piece of Ming Lao remained with them. Through Chloe's connection with her mother, she was able to stop the underground from completely crumbling. But part of the yard flooded. Jin was able to control the extent of the flooding through his gift, and Chloe was able to seal off the breach that caused the flooding. But it resulted in a new lake along the border of the yard. They'd set up a small pavilion there with tables and an outdoor kitchen.

Allie headed there now. It was her new favorite spot and she was sure Gregg would be waiting there for her. But he wasn't alone.

"Navid?" She halted. It was him. She started to run, happy to finally see him in the real world. She hadn't heard from him in all the months since he'd left her to help Quinn and she'd started to fear something had happened to him.

"You're really here?" She ran into his open arms. They still had issues and so much to learn about each other, but for now she was thrilled to see him.

"You knew?" Gregg gasped as the father and daughter reunited.

"*You* knew?" Allie gasped right back at him.

"I was told you couldn't know." Gregg folded his arms across his chest, turning to glare at his long-time friend.

"And I was told *you* couldn't know," Allie said. "I've known him as Navid all my life."

"It seems your father has been up to your mother's old tricks." Gregg shook his head.

"It had to be that way," Navid said. "We needed you both to act carefully these last months. It wasn't the right time to tell you. I'm so sorry for the deception."

"Why are you here?" Allie asked. Surely Navid wouldn't risk showing up in person unless it was important.

"We must talk about your new gift, Allie."

No one had mentioned it after that night. She hadn't wanted to talk about it and everyone in the know followed her lead. The irrational anger vanished the moment she released it, using it and her "gift" to save Aidan.

"Seems more like a curse." She hung her head, staring at her nails.

"Let's sit." Navid gestured at the picnic tables under the shade of the pavilion.

Allie settled down opposite her father, picking at a knot in the wood. Sometimes she thought she'd imagined the whole thing, or that it was a one-time phenomenon she'd managed to do, but would probably never be able to repeat. She had no idea how she'd done what she did and she never wanted to try it again.

"You have a very powerful and very dangerous gift, my daughter." Navid took her hands in his, urging her to look at him. "It is a gift you've inherited from me. Those closest to me once called me the Judge, Jury and Executioner. Not many know I can sense a criminal's character, weigh that character against his crimes, and determine if he or she should be punished. My brand of punishment sends the guilty Immortal into a comatose state for a length of time fitting the crimes committed."

Allie's ability allowed her to do the same thing. Except her brand of punishment was a mortal death. Her victims would live out their lives with the constant fear of death looming over them.

"I don't want this." Allie felt hot tears welling in her eyes. "It's too dangerous. If I lost it like that again ... if I hurt someone I love...."

"It doesn't work that way, Allie. The innocent do not deserve your judgment. You will never be able to turn your rage on those you love. It isn't in your power or your nature to judge the innocent. You will only be able to call on this power when you have the truest need for it. When the recipient has been given every possible chance to redeem themselves and yet they still choose the wrong path. It is beyond your ability to accidentally hurt anyone with this gift."

"Are you sure?" She wanted to believe him, but she was so scared she would lose control and lash out at those around her.

"Positive." Navid squeezed her hand. "This gift is dangerous for you, Allie. It doesn't make you dangerous to others. But others will not see it that way. No one must know what you are capable of. No one outside of your most trusted circle can ever know. There is a possible future scenario your mother saw for you. Someone close to you may betray you to the Coalition. We cannot let that happen."

"We will continue to protect her," Gregg said. "Liam, Darius, and I are the only ones who know. She may want to confide in Aidan at some point–I think he was too out of it to really understand what happened. But other than that, no one else will be told. At least not until she is Proven."

"Once she is Proven, she will be better equipped to protect herself," Navid agreed.

"I don't want to live in a bubble until then," Allie said. "I want to go to college and train with my friends."

"You can still do those things, sweetheart. But you will always need to be guarded," Navid said. "We cannot assume that no one saw what you did to save Aidan. If one of Livia's people witnessed the event, you are not safe. Those who do not know you will believe you should be controlled. We cannot allow that. Under any circumstances."

"Your life can continue on as usual," Gregg added, "but we must move forward with extreme caution."

"Wouldn't it be easier if someone just took this gift from me?" She wanted nothing more than to be rid of it.

"This gift is who you are, Allie. It's not something you can just give away. What you can do will be vital to your survival. Your mother and I have done all we can to prepare you for this. You have the strength and character you need to wield this powerful gift. No one else has that right."

"So I'm just supposed to go on with life as usual?"

"Yes, but it will be important for you to forgive yourself," Navid said.

Allie nodded, but she knew she could never forget what she'd done to that man.

"There is another reason for my visit," Navid said. "I've spoken with your grandfather, Allie. He is in hiding in South America, but he sought me out recently."

"The Scholar?" Gregg asked in awe.

"You've met him several times, Gregg, you just don't

remember. Alexander prefers to be forgotten. It's how he's survived for as long as he has."

"The Scholar is my grandfather?" Allie asked. She'd read about the mysterious man who seemed to be more of a legend than an actual person.

"Your grandmother, the queen, has escaped her prison. For thousands of years, your mother and I believed she was a Coalition captive, stuck in some remote corner of an ancient cell and long forgotten."

"Where is she now? Who is with her?" Gregg asked. "The last time she was a free woman, the most technologically advanced invention on the planet was bronze."

"We do not know. She is on her own, most likely completely overwhelmed in this modern world. It is paramount that we find her as soon as possible. And for that, we will need your help, Gregg."

"You needn't ask." Gregg nodded. "My resources are at your disposal."

"Who imprisoned her if not the Coalition?" Allie asked.

"A man we believed to be dead since the Great War. But he survived and has kept the queen under his control for well over two thousand years."

"Who is he?"

"His name is Teigan. He was betrothed to your great-grandmother, Eiselynn, before she met Ían and became the first royal to bond with her commoner Complement."

"Teigan was the one Ían defeated in the Book of the Indriell Queens?" Allie asked. "Ían took his gift."

"And he wants it back," Navid said.

"Ían was executed by the Enlightened." Gregg shook his head, looking as perplexed as Allie.

"But Teigan has been searching the bloodlines of Indriell

for thousands of years, seeking the one whose gift most closely resembles the one he lost," Navid explained.

A bolt of fear coursed through Allie. "It's mine, isn't it? He wants my gift?"

"He doesn't know yet." Navid reached for her hands again. "That is why we must keep your gift a secret. As long as he doesn't know about you, you're safe. Teigan's mind is twisted. He is over seven thousand years old, extremely powerful, and he is dangerous. He is also the man who raised your sister."

How are Allie and Livia sisters? What has Teigan planned for the Immortal world? Discover what's next in **Captive (Immortals of Indriell Book 3)** and find out how Livia became the woman she is. Available on Amazon, and free for Kindle Unlimited readers.

DON'T FORGET YOUR FREE BOOK!

In Judgment, find out what happens when Allie finally shares her secrets with Aidan. And then download your FREE copy of SCHOLAR and discover everything there is to know about the Immortals of Indriell.

Visit **bit.ly/ScholarOffer** to download now

About Melissa A. Craven

Melissa A. Craven (the "A" stands for Ann—in case you were wondering) writes Young Adult Fantasy with crossover appeal to other genres and audiences of all ages. She believes in stories that make you think and she loves twisty plots, and playing with foreshadowing, leaving clues and hints for the careful reader. She draws inspiration from her background in architecture and interior design to help her with the small details in world building and scene settings. Melissa is also the indie manager and a staff reviewer at YABooksCentral.com. You can follow her reviews and her contributions to the YABC blog at the link below. And if you love Sweet Romance and Contemporary Fiction, you can find Melissa's books in those genres under her pen name, Ann Maree Craven.

Instagram, Twitter & BookBub: @Melissaacraven
Facebook: Melissa A. Craven Author
Join Melissa's Underground on Facebook
Website: Melissaacraven.com

ACKNOWLEDGMENTS

The journey to create this book has been a difficult one. I struggled to find a balance between the way I wrote the first book (aka the wrong way lol), with everything I've learned about writing since the concept of Emerge was just a story in my mind.

My biggest thank you is for all of my readers who have waited patiently for Judgment after the massive cliffhanger of Emerge.

To my family and friends, I could never do this without you. A special thanks to my mother, Debby, who never tires of talking about Allie. And to my awesome dad, David, for giving me his very special gift of sarcasm. To Jenny, thank you for the fantastic family tree and saving me when I tried to update it myself.

A huge thanks to all my beta readers: Kayla Howarth, Michelle Lynn, Stacy Randolph, Kimberly Readnour and Jenny. Your feedback has been priceless. To Chase Night and Robin, my new editing team, Thank you! I was very nervous about switching editors but you both brought some much needed expertise to the table. And to Zoe Shtorm and Daqri Combs for the amazing cover art. These designers never cease to blow my mind.

A big thank you to the city of Cleveland and to Kelleys Island especially. The island as it is portrayed in the book is purely fictional, but is based on the real Kelleys Island near Sandusky, Ohio.

The last eighteen months since I published my first book has been the biggest learning experience of my life. To all of my author friends across the world, thank you for your constant support, encouragement and sense of community. The indie community is an amazing place and it is such a comfort knowing I am not doing this alone.

To C.J. Redwine, Author of The Shadow Queen and my YABC mentor. Thank you for bringing me on as the site indie manager and for providing ALL the books. The experience has been invaluable and I look forward to the future of YABooks-Central.com

Finally, I thank God for the constant reminder that I am doing what I'm supposed to be doing. Over the past years, circumstances *always* bring me back to writing—my favorite thing to do in the whole world.

www.ingramcontent.com/pod-product-compliance
Lightning Source LLC
Chambersburg PA
CBHW030525310726
48979CB00010B/1802/J
9781970052084